Life in the
Petunia Patch

Life in the Petunia Patch

SEVENTH IN THE PRAIRIE PREACHER SERIES

P J HOGE

iUniverse, Inc.
Bloomington

LIFE IN THE PETUNIA PATCH
Seventh in the Prairie Preacher series

iUniverse books may be ordered through booksellers or by contacting:

iUniverse
1663 Liberty Drive
Bloomington, IN 47403
www.iuniverse.com
1-800-Authors (1-800-288-4677)

ISBN: 978-1-4620-6887-6 (sc)
ISBN: 978-1-4620-6888-3 (ebk)

Library of Congress Control Number: 2011961231

Printed in the United States of America

iUniverse rev. date: 11/29/2011

**Books in the
Prairie Preacher Series:**

Prairie Preacher
Victoria's Nest
Rainbows and Rattlesnakes
Z
Kartoffel Noggin
Coot and the Gophers

For more information:

www.PJHoge.com

1

CARL KINCAID HEARD THE ALARM go off and groaned his six foot three body out of bed. Carl shaved and scrutinized his reflection in the mirror. He frowned as he ran his comb through his thinning, gray hair. No doubt, he was beginning to show his sixty-three years. He thought catching the bullet in his upper chest earlier that spring certainly aggravated the process. He knew he had more hair before all those surgeries to repair his blood vessels.

Then he studied his physique. Yah, the month in the wheelchair had accelerated the 'muscle-to-flab' exchange. He had actually lost weight, but was by no means thin. He was glad that Maureen Harrington had said she would marry him. A couple more years down the road, she might have decided against hooking up with such an old geezer.

He smiled, 'Don't know who I'm kidding. Mo calls me the Old Coot all the time as it is!'

Sixty-one year old Maureen was an energetic spitfire. She had a crazy sense of humor, a big heart and best of all, she made him feel like he was worth something. She had been widowed fourteen years before and left to raise her eight children alone. Mo did, and did it well. She was straight forward and didn't mess around with the small stuff. Mo had a big dimpled smile, dark auburn hair (Clairol 163 she said) and a nice round figure. She could run circles around women a lot younger.

He dressed and headed to the kitchen where the Schroeder household gathered every morning to pay homage to their coffee pot. Today, the Schroeders would be home from the Hawaii. Carl had volunteered to oversee things on their farm while Elton and Nora were gone. It was easy enough.

Carl had lived with them since he got out of the hospital. The Schroeders had opened their home to him since he had nowhere else to go.

He had been a loner since his Cecelia died thirty five years before. It worked out well with his career with the FBI. He devoted his entire life to it. However after being shot, he could no longer work and had no one to take care of him. That is until these crazy people came along.

Carl was working on a case involving an evangelist psychopath and his unstable wife. Two of the wife's siblings helped Carl and a young Boston detective, Ian Harrington with the case. When law enforcement finally had a showdown with the psychopath, the psychopath attempted to shoot his own little girl to keep her quiet. Carl saw it. He flung himself over the girl and managed to take the bullet himself. The little one was injured after the bullet passed through him and lodged in her hip, but at least she was alive.

Ian Harrington was shot by the wife, Naomi. So all three, Ian, Carl and the girl ended up in a Shreveport hospital. The psychopath was killed by law enforcement and his wife committed suicide, so the little girl was orphaned.

Zach and Ruthie, Naomi's siblings came to Shreveport to care for little Miriam and be with her while she was in the hospital. While working on the case, Ruthie and Ian had become quite interested in each other, so she wanted to be with him too.

At first, Carl figured they were just being polite, would stop in, thank him for saving the girl and be on their way. He couldn't have been more wrong. Those kids, their friends and the Harrington family brought him into their lives as one of their own.

At the time of his release from the hospital, he still needed care and could not be on his own. The doctors said if he had no one to care of him, he'd have to go to a rehab facility. Zach was a physician and had served as his power of attorney while he was in the hospital. He insisted that Carl allow himself to be taken to North Dakota for his recuperation. He would stay at the Schroeders farm.

He hated being a burden and a victim, and couldn't wait to get back to his apartment and his solitary life. At least, that is what he thought. He grew to like being part of this crazy conglomeration of friends and family that called themselves the Engelmann Clan. Even more attractive was the chance to see Maureen again.

She lived in Boston. After Ian was released from the hospital, she took him back there. However, Ian and Zach had become close friends, and Ian was going to be Zach's best man when he got married later this summer. That meant Ian and Mo would be out to North Dakota to visit. Carl wasn't about to pass up the chance to see her again.

Ian and Mo came to the central North Dakota early to visit, since Ian couldn't wait to see Ruthie again. They also stayed at Schroeder's large two story farmhouse. Carl was delighted.

Carl had begun to set down roots. He hadn't had a real home in decades and now thought he wanted one. When he heard one of the young clanners named Darrell needed an investor for his dairy farm, Coot stepped forward. He became Darrell's very silent partner. Now he owned land! And as part of the deal, both Darrell and Carl were building homes.

Carl had always scoffed at 'petunias', his name for well meaning, good hearted folks. He figured them to be weak and sappy. But while he was recovering, he came to realize that being a petunia took a lot more inner strength and work than he had ever imagined. He came to respect them and then wanted to be like them.

Carl Kincaid had never been someone content with second place, so once he made the decision to be a petunia, he was going to be the best petunia around. His home would be the ultimate Petunia Patch.

Andy, the Schroeder's youngest son, got word that he would be on R&R in Hawaii. He was in the Army in Vietnam. He and Darrell had best friends forever and they were both going to get married. So, the guys decided to have a double wedding in Hawaii. When they announced it, Carl volunteered to keep an eye on things for both the Schroeders and Darrell. He was there anyway and he wanted to pay them back for all they had done for him. They had been gone about ten days.

Tonight the wedding party would be home. He had to make certain that everything was shipshape. He checked on both farms and the Schroeder family mechanic shops. He wasn't doing the work himself, but he was overseeing it. Everyone assured him everything was fine, but he wouldn't be slipshod about it.

At breakfast, he was worrying about everything. "I'm responsible for all this and I have to make sure it's done. I don't know what possessed me to volunteer to oversee things while Nora and Elton were gone! I know nothing about this stuff."

"Leaping Leprechauns! Take it easy, you old Coot," Maureen patted his head. "It'll be just fine. Everyone did their part and things are in good. Just relax."

"Relax? How can I relax? If Elton, that jabbering Magpie, finds one thing out of place, I'll never hear the end of it."

Matt Harrington, Maureen's youngest son, listened to the whole thing and had to laugh. "You're goofy. Elton wouldn't get that bent out of shape and besides, everything is fine. Once they hear about the deal with Miriam, I doubt they'll pay any attention to any of the rest of it."

"Suppose you're right, huh?" Coot grumbled.

Grandma Katherine, Elton's tiny surrogate mother, smiled, "However you might catch hell for driving everyone crazy."

"Amen," Keith grinned. Keith Schroeder and his wife lived at the old farmhouse too. They had moved back from Wisconsin earlier that spring and were staying with his folks until they bought a home. In fact, at this time, Coot, Mo, Ian and Matt were there too. "Now, what are you going to do today besides have a fit?"

Carl looked at Elton's oldest son and then shook his head, "I don't know. I might start with my two whiskeys early today."

"No," Grandma Katherine stated, "You're going to get to work and help us get dinner ready for tonight. You can get out to the garden and get us some leaf lettuce, new potatoes and fresh tomatoes. Oh, some green onions too. You just buzz your little wheelchair out to the garden."

Carl made a face and gave her a salute, "Yes, Commandant."

"Hey Matt, how's Orientation at the high school this week?" Darlene, Elton's daughter-in-law, asked.

"It's been helpful and interesting."

"What subjects are you teaching again?" Carl asked his soon-to-be stepson.

"Algebra, Calculus, Advanced Math, Geometry and Physics. Then, in late afternoon, I go to St. John's and teach Calculus and Advanced Algebra."

"Sounds like you'll be running all over."

"The schools are only a short walk away from each other. It'll be just a nice break."

"Did you see that widow girl, ah, Debbie?" his Mom asked. "She teaches, right?"

"You mean Diane? Not yet. I think she'll be there tomorrow and Friday. Those are the days she missed when she had dental surgery."

Mo looked at her son seriously, "Does Diane know you're a priest?"

Twenty nine year old Matt looked at his plate and without raising his eyes, answered, "Don't know."

"Did you tell her?" his Mom probed.

"Well, gee Mom. What do you think? I'd just walk up to her and say, 'oh by the way, I'm a priest?' I mean, we've met several times and it'd be kind of stupid to say anything now. I really don't know what she knows."

Everyone at the table was watching him, even Grandpa Lloyd. The confused octogenarian leaned back in his chair. "Heading for the pickle jar to my notion."

"It's no big deal. I mean, what does she care?" Matt was trying to justify it in his own mind.

Ian knew this conversation was hitting a nerve with his brother. "Whatever. I'm heading out in about twenty minutes. Are you dropping me at the gas station before you go to Orientation?"

"Yes, sir. I just have to grab my notebook. Thanks for breakfast. It was great," Matt gave Grandma Katherine and his Mom a hug. "See you about four and I promise to help you then."

That late summer evening in 1970, everything was ready. All the chores were finished and dinner was ready. Pastor Ellison's family had arrived. Pastor Byron Ellison was Elton Schroeder's best friend and the family minister. The station wagon pulled up to the door and everyone went out to meet the family.

The travelers were all very tired but happy, except Annie. She had to tell her new husband Andy, goodbye so he could return to his unit in Vietnam. The dinner was filled with stories of the Hawaiian Islands and the weddings. It was a lot of fun. Annie assured the group the Super 8 film of the wedding would be ready after Sunday dinner.

Then Elton asked how things were back on the home front while they were vacationing. Marly, Pastor Byron's wife, picked up little Miriam and called all the little kids to go play in the guest room. No one said anything

5

until after they were all gone. Miriam was a tiny abused three year old girl. She was the girl Carl had saved when he became wounded.

Pastor Byron began to explain what had happened with Miriam. "Carl was babysitting for Clark Olson who had chicken pox. He was sleeping in the guest room here and Mo had closed the curtains so he could sleep. Later when Miriam arrived, Mo was carrying her and went to check on Clark. When Mo opened the door, Miriam took one look, screamed and went into the fetal position."

Kevin, Elton's middle son, continued, "She was barely breathing; the worst we've ever seen her. We're lucky to have a paramedic living nearby. We took her to the hospital. Zach met us there. She was nearly catatonic. Dr. Samuels heavily sedated her. It was awful."

Nora, Elton's wife, had a worried frown, "What happened?"

"No one could figure it out, but finally Kevin and Coot decided they're going to Texas," Keith explained. "They had to see what they could find out about what all those crazy parents really did to that little girl. Ian, Matt, Marty, Kevin and Coot went down there."

"Well, I'll be." Elton's face was a study, "Why did they all go?"

"Ian went because he had been the detective on the case, Carl went because he was the FBI agent on the case and Marty came along because he's a paramedic and wanted to keep Coot from bursting a blood vessel. You know, he isn't totally healed up from his injuries. I went because she is my little godchild and she my special buddy," Kevin explained. "Matt came along to keep us from losing our minds."

Carl leaned back, "Remember Agent Diaz from the Texas office where I worked? I called in a few favors. He got us lined up to talk to some of Ezekiel's gang that were in the slammer. He also got us a list of the addresses of some of hookers that were hanging with the gang to see what they knew."

"What did you find out? Those two parents were a real piece of work."

"Amen. This is what we pieced together," Ian said, "Josiah was about five then and Miriam just two. The kids had chicken pox. Ezekiel was in Houston setting up a job and wanted his men to all meet at back their house. He told Naomi take the kids and get out of there. He didn't want them around. She left, but not the kids. Some of the gang members arrived before Ezekiel and found a horrible mess. The kids were in the crib. Miriam had a bottle and they both had crayons. Apparently, Josiah had colored on the inside of the crib. All we know is that Naomi 'disciplined' him. Then she took off, leaving them there."

"It had been a couple days when the gang members arrived. Josiah was dead in the crib. His head had been smashed in. Miriam was whimpering in the corner of the crib suffering from chicken pox and malnutrition." Ian explained. "One of the gang members took Miriam to his drug addict sister who nursed her back to health. Two other guys buried Josiah in the backyard."

"Good grief. That explains so much," Elton ran his hand through his salt and pepper hair. "No wonder the poor kid freaks whenever she sees crayons."

Nora had tears rolling down her cheeks by now, "I can't imagine being stuck in a crib with my dead brother, for how long?"

"As best we can figure, about two days. Miriam had half a bottle of sour milk in her bottle. That was it," Ian said.

Annie was furious, "I can't imagine people being like that. No wonder the poor kid is so messed up." Annie started to cry and Matt put his arm around her. "How's Miriam doing?"

Zach answered. "Miriam's still too young for the information to make any difference as far as counseling right now, but at least we know. Dr. Samuels is a good psychiatrist. He got her settled again and she got out of the hospital a couple days ago. She's still a little fragile, but she's coming back."

"I thought she seemed a little quiet tonight," Elton shook his head, "How's her walking coming?"

"She was going to show you she could walk when you guys got home," Coot explained, "Even though her hip is better, she needs to regain her strength after this go-round. The bullet wound has almost healed. But this has set it back quite a bit. It might take her a while again."

Zach nodded, "Every time, she comes back faster than before though. Dr. Samuels said we should keep working with the crayon thing like we were doing before and maybe we can get her past it."

"I guess it's a good thing that we found out," Grandma Katherine said. "Every little bit we find out about Miriam, makes it easier to help her. She'll be fine if we don't give up. She is finally developing a vocabulary besides 'if you want to'. I love it when she tries to carry on a conversation."

"I doubt she'll be over the crayon thing by the time Sunday school starts," Kevin said aloud, thinking about how he was going to help with her Sunday school class this year.

Jeannie, Darrell's new bride, nodded, "Or by the time she starts kindergarten! Good grief. That's about all they do is color!"

"Let's not borrow trouble," Matt suggested. "Look how far she has come in this little time. Abuse is a difficult thing to get over,"

"Speaking of which, how is your orientation coming?" Jeannie asked. "Good so far."

Darrell nodded and asked, "Have you seen Diane?"

Matt shook his head no and changed the subject. "That's really a nice school you have there in Merton. All the grades on one campus is nice. I bet it saves money on gymnasiums and things like that, huh?"

Jeannie agreed, "Yes it does. How is St. John's?"

"It's pretty nice too. I had a good meeting with Mr. Morley. He still thinks he'll be back at school second semester. He seems to be recovering very well. So he'll be back to his class and I'll only work at St. Johns."

"That's good. He's a nice man. I've been expecting him to retire for the last while, but he says he loves his students."

"That's nice to hear," Nora nodded. "And how are the houses coming?"

Carl cleared his throat with his rehearsed report. "The dirt crew broke ground on Zach's garage. Our house is enclosed, Darrell's has the studding up and Ian's basement is poured. Everything is on schedule."

"Yup," Keith added, "And Darlene's baby is still scheduled for the end of October and Carrie's morning sickness is over and their baby is still scheduled for Christmas."

Ruthie had been very quiet all through dinner, and then she giggled, "And Ian and I have set a date! We were going to tell everyone on Sunday, but I can't stand it. Okay, Honey?" she asked Ian.

The dark haired young man's blue eyes sparkled as he grinned with his big dimples and said, "Tell them. I know it's killing you!"

"We're getting married Saturday, October 3! We need to pray that we have good weather for the outside wedding! Otherwise, I don't know what we'll do."

Kevin teased, "Oh Ruthie, I'm sure that you'll have at least eighteen contingency plans by then!"

"Ian," Ruth took her fiancé's hand, "Tell him to be nice."

Pepper, Schroeder's only daughter, commiserated, "Ruthie, I hate to tell you, but there's no hope for Kevin. So, might as well save your breath. Oh, and you guys, don't make any plans for Saturday night! We have a big bash all planned at Heinrich's barn for a dance to celebrate the weddings! Annie, do you think your family can come too?"

Annie smiled and got tears in her eyes, "I'll ask them. That sounds like fun." She paused and said quietly, "Everyone will be there but Andy."

"Hey, we'll have another one when he gets home and besides, you'll have so many fellas dancing with you that you'll hardly notice," Keith offered.

"Oh, I'll notice, but thanks you guys. It's a real good idea," Annie nodded. "I'd feel more comfortable if it was just Jeannie and Darrell's wedding dance. Okay? I'd feel very awkward if it was for us and I'd be alone."

"Okay, Annie," Pepper said. "We can do that."

"Mrs. Schroeder, I'd be honored to escort you to the dance," Matt grinned.

Annie looked at him and giggled, "Well, thank you Father Matthew. I have to check with my in-laws. Mom and Dad? Do you think he's trustworthy?"

They shook their heads no.

Then she giggled, "In that case, I'd be pleased to accept."

"Well, if that don't beat all!" Elton laughed. "I get to dance with you though."

"No, I do," Grandpa Lloyd who suffered from Alzheimer's, said. "She's my girl. Isn't she, Elton?"

"Why I believe she is, Lloyd." Elton answered, "I believe she is."

2

ABOUT HALF THE TEACHERS FROM the Merton Public School system met at the gymnasium of the Merton Charging Bison. The other teachers had attended the orientation for the upcoming school year two weeks earlier. Merton School district always ran it twice, so no one had an excuse to miss.

Matt came to North Dakota with no intentions of teaching anywhere. He was taking the six months of leave of absence to think. Actually, it was more like a suspension. He had been outspoken about a pedophile priest and received a serious reprimand from the Bishop. The church hierarchy 'suggested' he took the time to rethink his calling and decide if he would submit to their authority on this matter. Matt wanted to be a priest, but didn't know if he could keep quiet.

The nice looking slim man met with Father Vicaro at St. John's rectory shortly after he arrived in North Dakota and the elderly priest couldn't bear the thought of him not doing anything. He asked Matt into help with the CCD class at the church until Christmas at least. Vicaro promised to help him with the Bishop back in Boston but he made no bones about wanting to get some help from him.

Vicaro reluctantly agreed that Matt need not announce publicly that he was a priest at least until Christmas. Priests on suspension weren't encouraged to wear the clerical collar anyway, which was understandable. However Father Vicaro warned him that he was playing with fire. Matt thought he could handle it. The older priest was doubtful but gave him the nod anyway. "I guess you can't compare how life would be serving the Lord outside of the priesthood, if everyone thinks you are a priest."

The day after Matt had promised to teach CCD, Catholic catechism, Jeannie had some news. She had been at orientation and heard that one of the teachers at the school where she taught, Mr. Morley, was hospitalized and would be off until at least second semester. Morley was the math and science teacher at Merton High. She mentioned Matt to her principal because she knew he had taught those subjects, and wanted them to meet. The high school was in a real jam.

At first Matt balked, but she convinced him that it might be a good idea for him to teach in a public school while he decided about the priesthood. Matt was reluctant but he really liked Jeannie and Darrell and thought that they had a good point. Just imaging another lifestyle isn't the same as living it.

He met with the principal and agreed to teach until Morley could return. Then he told Father Vicaro. Father Vicaro grinned, "Okay, then you can teach at St. John's too. I need an Advanced Algebra and Calculus teacher, but I need one for all year!"

The old priest got on the phone to Boston. He managed to get Matt's leave of absence extended until the end of the school year. Matt wasn't very happy about that, but could find no serious reason to not do it.

"I'll have enough to live on while I'm teaching at Merton High, but what am I going to do for the last six months? Teaching two classes a day doesn't pay rent."

Father Vicaro grinned, "Well by then Matt, you can help me with more things. Then we can get you a modest salary."

Matt shrugged but was uneasy about it. When he discussed it with Darrell, he pointed out. "The first time you give a sermon or hear a confession, you'll be back to being a priest. Then you won't have any choice anymore."

Matt agreed but felt trapped. Father Vicaro was more or less his sponsor and was in charge. Besides he really liked the man. He was straight-forward and down to earth. Mostly, because the man was sympathetic to Matt's situation with the church and willing to cut him a lot of slack.

Matt asked Carl's advice. Carl told him honestly, "I don't think anyone should be a priest, but you know how I feel about all churches. I worked too long with the church scandals that crossed the FBI's desk and I could hardly stomach most of it. I'll support you if that's your decision. You know what? You should probably go talk to Byron."

When he talked to Pastor Byron, he was told to be patient with himself. "Give this a little time. You have four months and maybe by then you'll already know your answer. Relax a little. You may be glad to get back to the priesthood."

He had made the agreement only a week before Schroeders left for Hawaii and then Miriam had her problems. Things were moving fast and he felt were out of control,

Matt was only home from Texas a couple days before the weeklong Orientation started. Now it was Thursday. Like he had told his family, it had been interesting and he was pleased with most of it. He thought he might like teaching in a public school. Maybe those guys were right; just take your time and not try to hurry anything. Now if he could just make it work.

3

THURSDAY MORNING, AFTER THE FIRST hour and a half orientation meeting, there was a coffee break. Matt had just filled his cup and was heading out to the playground when there was a tap on his arm. "Hello, Tuck," a slender, brunette smiled sweetly.

He turned and smiled back. "Hi Diane, do you have your coffee?"

"No, just headed that way. I didn't know you for sure if you were filling in for Mr. Morley. Jeannie said she was going to mention it to you, but then I had my bad tooth," the young lady got an odd look on her face and shrugged.

"How did the turn out? Did they save the tooth?" Matt asked.

She looked away, "Fine. It's fine. Well, I must go get some coffee. Welcome to the team."

"Diane?" Matt asked, "After you get a cup, would you like to visit with me? I'll find a spot at a table if you'd like?"

She looked surprised and thought a minute, "I guess it wouldn't hurt. I'd like that."

Matt found a nice spot at the end of a picnic table for them and she joined him in a few minutes. "Have you been bowling lately?"

"Oh no," Diane answered. "That wasn't a very good idea. I shouldn't have gone. Have you been?"

"Tinker, the only bad thing about our bowling was how we did it! How can I say it nicely? Ah, we're awful bowlers," Matt chuckled. "They should give points for gutter balls!"

Diane giggled, "Yah, we're pretty bad! What else have you been up to?"

13

"Oh, been to Texas for a couple days and getting ready to go to Boston to move Mom's things here. She and Carl Kincaid will be getting married soon."

"Really? How exciting," the gracious lady smiled, "And your brother and his fiancée will be marrying soon?"

"Yes. Speaking of weddings, are you going to the dance for Darrell and Jeannie Saturday night at Heinrich's barn?"

Diane started to shake her head no before he even finished asking. "No, that wouldn't be proper. You know, Dean parents wouldn't approve."

Matt looked at her to try to read her thoughts, "How long do you have to wait, Diane? How long do they think your mourning should be?"

"I really have to go, Matt. It was great seeing you again. Bye," she said softly and dashed back into the building.

Matt sat holding his cup of coffee. 'Yes, there's something terribly wrong. I have to tell Darrell. She is almost as scared as Miriam. What the heck's going on?"

That afternoon, he saw Diane once and she took a detour to avoid encountering him. He couldn't help but think to himself that it was probably the best thing for him, too. But he was still worried about her. Someone needed to get close enough to her to find out what was going on. She was definitely hiding something.

That evening after chores, he went over to visit with Darrell and Jeannie. They made small talk for a little bit and then he got to it. He told them what had happened with Diane.

"Doggone it, Tuck," Jeannie said, "She has acted so funny ever since Dean got real sick. I just know that Waggoners have something to do with it. Why would she act like that? I have half a mind to go over there and start pulling some hair! She always has some bruise, some excuse . . . I just know there's something wrong. I just know it!"

"Down girl," Darrell warned, "You could get yourself into a lot of hot water, and her too."

"I know, Honey, but this is stupid. Tuck, can't you find something out?"

"I suppose I could ask Father Vicaro if he knows anything, but whatever he heard in the confessional, he can't tell me anyway. So, I don't know what I could find out. I didn't handle it very well today. I asked her too much. I should've just kept it light. I pushed too hard and scared her off." Matt was discouraged.

"Well, I've been trying to be gentle about stuff and gotten no where," Jeannie offered. "I think hair pulling would be more effective. I'll try to talk to her tomorrow. She told me to take lots of pictures of the wedding, so that's my excuse. Maybe I'll take the photos over to Waggoners. I might find out a lot more by just going over there."

Darrell frowned, "I don't know about that Jeannie. I don't want you getting hurt!"

"What should I do? Sit here and let her get hurt? I wouldn't like me very well. I'm pretty sure that her 'bad tooth' was really a punch in the jaw! I'm not that stupid."

They all thought a minute, and then Darrell said, "How about you and I both go over there? We think that she got in trouble for going bowling with us. Maybe if they see we are a married couple, they won't be upset. Want to come along, Matt?"

"No. She might think we're ganging up on her or something. Besides, she's avoiding me like the plague now," Matt pointed out. "Now if I was a priest, she might talk to me. In fact, she might even be allowed to go bowling with me."

Darrell shook his head, "You went to college, right? Earned degrees and all that? Amazing, all without brain cell one! You just keep that darn collar in your dresser drawer, will you? Besides, you have a date Saturday night anyway. You're a bride's date to her own wedding dance! Pretty fancy maneuvering! How do you plan to explain that to Father Vicaro?"

"Well," Matt stammered. "It seemed like a good idea at the time."

"Of course it is. I think it's sweet," Jeannie gave him a hug as she got up to get the coffeepot. "And I'm sure that Tinker will think so too. In fact, I might tell her. She'll understand how thoughtful you are."

"Why does that matter?" Matt asked.

"Oh, give me a break," Jeannie giggled. "If she thinks you're thoughtful and understanding, she'd be more apt to talk to you."

"That's right, uh?" Matt stammered. "It is hard out here in the real world."

"Tell me about it," Darrell grinned. "So, when are you taking off for Boston?"

"Tuesday. We're flying out and then driving back. Ian has his car and Mom has hers. It was nice of Coot to let us boys use his old beater, but he and Mom do need a better car."

15

"Didn't you have a car?" Darrell asked.

"Yah, I did, but it belonged to St. Thomas' Parish. It wasn't really mine. I can move my stuff in a suitcase, pretty much," Matt said.

"I thought Coot traveled light. We even forgot he had that old car until we went to get his stuff out of storage," Darrell added. "Of course, he wasn't well enough to drive anyway. Now he is crabbing he'll have to get a new driver's license."

Matt laughed, "That man can find something to grump about, no matter what!"

"He has a good heart," Jeannie said, "He's really a sweetheart."

"You say that about everyone," Darrell pointed out.

"No. I don't say that about Waggoners and I haven't even met them," Jeannie got up from the table and went to the phone book. She put her fingers to her lips in a hushing motion to the guys and dialed the phone.

"Hello, is Diane there?" She asked. "This is Jeannie Jessup. I'm her coworker. Well, thank you Mrs. Waggoner."

There was silence for some time.

"Hi Diane, this is Jeannie. Hey, I got the wedding photos back today and I was wondering if Darrell and I could stop by tomorrow before chores, to show them to you. Would that be okay?"

Jeannie made a face at the guys while she waited impatiently for at least five minutes and then turned her attention back to the phone. "Five? Okay, that'll be great. Yes, Darrell's coming too. Not necessary, we'll only be there a minute. Bye Diane."

She came over to the table and sat down smugly. She didn't say a word but took a drink of her coffee. Finally Darrell said, "Tell us! What did she say?"

"It was weird. Mrs. Waggoner gave me the third degree about who I was. When I asked Tinker, she had to explain the whole thing to them. I heard both of them quizzing her on who we were and what we wanted. Then a man said, 'is that husband going to be here too, the one you went bowling with?' He sounded really ugly."

"Oh great, I'm going to get killed!" Darrell groaned. "What does he think we did anyway? We just went bowling together. There was a bunch of us. Good grief. Now I want to pull hair."

"Darrell, once he meets you, he'll like you. Everyone does," Jeannie kissed his cheek.

"Not everyone. And besides, I don't like him at all. Gee, Matt, you better be on your prayer bones while we're having tea." Darrell chuckled.

"Sounds like it. Do you guys think I should try to talk to her tomorrow at orientation, or just let her ignore me?" Matt asked Jeannie.

Jeannie thought, "I think you should make it a point to have coffee with her. Don't let her just walk away from you. You didn't do anything to her and she needs some friends. I mean, don't chase her down the hall or anything!"

Darrell laughed, "I can see it all now! Old Tuck tackling the Tinker on the fifty yard line!"

"You are insane, Jessup. Truly insane," Matt glared. "Well, guys. I'd better get home. Thanks for the coffee."

"If you come over to help with chores tomorrow, we'll tell you what happened at Waggoners," Darrell said. Then he added, "And if we don't survive, do the milking for us, okay?"

Matt stood up and gave Jeannie a hug, "You got it."

4

MATT WAS A NERVOUS WRECK. He felt he was getting himself in deeper and deeper, but he wasn't certain that he wanted out. He was worried about Diane. That was true. However, he was attracted to her. That was also true. Other than Darrell, he didn't know if anyone else knew how he really felt. Probably Ian. Ian and he were close enough so they could read each other pretty well.

It'd be a mistake to let his feelings for her get in the way of his decision. He should keep his distance from her, but Jeannie was right. She needed friends. Maybe he could handle it. He knew he should talk to Father Vicaro about it, but didn't want to. He knew why he didn't. Vicaro would put the kibosh on it immediately. Something like that shouldn't be considered while he was making his decision about the priesthood.

He tried to sleep but couldn't. He didn't know what to do with himself. He tried reading and praying. Neither of them helped. Now it was two in the morning and not exactly the time to wake up Ian. He tossed and turned.

When he heard Grandpa Lloyd downstairs rummaging in the kitchen, he was almost grateful. He got up, pulled his jeans on and went downstairs. When he entered the kitchen, Lloyd had just started to take things out of the pantry. Matt turned on the light and poor Lloyd jumped about two feet.

"You came for supper?" Lloyd asked. "My Katherine is over at the church so I'll cook it."

"No, Lloyd," Matt went over to the tall, thin man, "I just came for a drink of water. You don't need to fix me anything."

"I'll cook. I haven't had a thing to eat for two days!"

"Hey, I'll fix you a sandwich," Matt offered, escorting Lloyd to the table.

"Do you know how to cook? I don't think you know how to cook," Lloyd grumbled. "I'll do it."

"He cooks just fine," Elton said. He had been watching from the doorway. "Matt's a good cook, but I can make it for you. He might be pretty tired and needs to go to school tomorrow."

"You go to school? What grade are you in? You must have flunked huh?" the Alzheimer's patient asked seriously.

"No. I teach school," Matt smiled.

"Oh. That's a fine job. You know if kids don't know anything, it'll be a mess," Lloyd nodded. "Man, am I hungry. What have you got to eat?"

"Want some toast or a sandwich?" Elton asked.

"Okay," Lloyd answered. "And fix some for this kid."

"Really Elton," Matt answered, "Water is fine."

"No," Lloyd said, "You need some meat on your bones. Fix him a steak. I think I want some chicken."

Elton opened the fridge, took out some sliced ham and made three sandwiches, while Matt poured juice for Lloyd. Then they all sat down and picked up their sandwiches. Elton had just taken a bite, when Lloyd frowned. "When do you plan on saying grace? You have to say grace. Don't you know anything?"

"Oh," Elton said as he and Matt put their sandwiches down. "I guess we're too hungry."

As the three men took each other's hand, Lloyd mumbled, "God. Please forgive these jug heads. They don't know that the hungrier a guy gets, the more he should thank You for food. Amen."

The other two said Amen and looked at each other sheepishly. Matt told Lloyd, "That's so true, Lloyd. So true."

"Well of course," Lloyd shrugged. "If I'm going to lie to somebody, it ain't going to the Big Guy. Don't want Him to get His dander up!"

"Good point, Lloyd," Elton agreed. "How's your sandwich?"

"You could have put more tuna in it, but it'll do. I'm pretty tired so I'm going back to bed. You young guys can sit up all night if you want."

"Okay," Elton agreed.

Then Lloyd looked at Matt, "Why did you wake me up? Did you want help with something?"

"No, I just couldn't sleep," Matt replied.

"Of course not. You should go to bed. I can't sleep in the kitchen either, can I? Am I right, Elton?"

"You surely are, Lloyd."

"This is my house, you know. I can sit wherever I want," Lloyd told Matt. "But you can sit here too. Okay?"

"I appreciate that. Thank you Lloyd."

"You're welcome," Lloyd answered nonchalantly and gobbled up his sandwich. When he was finished, he said, "Good night. Don't sit here too late. Katherine will iron your shirt in the morning."

"Want me to walk you back to your room, Lloyd?" Elton asked as he got up to help the man.

"Do you know the way?" Lloyd took Elton's arm.

While Elton was taking Lloyd back to bed, Matt cleaned the table and put things in the sink. "Is he settled in now?"

Elton nodded, "Yah. It's getting worse and worse. It breaks my heart. Thank you for getting up with him."

"I was awake anyway."

"Supper didn't set well?"

"No, I was thinking. Elton, I just don't know what to do!" Tears sprang into Matt's blue eyes and he just started to babble. He was rarely tearful or babbled, but he was doing it like a pro tonight. "I think I should just move on, you know? I can't do this. I thought I could. I'd just think about everything and then get a clear answer, make my decision and go about my life. It just gets murkier and murkier."

Elton refilled their Tropical Fruit punch glasses. "Mind going outside to the patio? We don't want Lloyd to get up again."

5

MATT NODDED AND FOLLOWED ELTON out to the patio. The August night was beautiful, warm and with just enough breeze to keep the mosquitoes at bay. In the distance, they could hear the calls of a hoot owl. They sat at the picnic table. Elton lit his cigarette and said, "Matt, I don't know what's bugging you except the leaving the church business, but I do know that moving on won't solve your problem. You might as well make your decision in one place as the other. God has a tendency to throw the same problems in front of us wherever we hide."

"You're right. I know that. I've even told other people that. But—,"

Elton grinned, "I know. It's so much easier to tell someone else as it is to tell yourself. Besides, if you're like me, I know me so well that I don't listen to me!"

"You're a goof ball," Matt smiled. "Lloyd told me I was heading for a pickle jar!"

"Well, he should know!" Elton chuckled. "What is it? If you want, I can try to help or I can call Byron. I don't know much about the Catholic church but maybe you can explain it to me."

"I just don't think I can turn a blind eye and a tight lip to what Butterton is doing. He has been reported and the higher ups know it and they won't do a darned thing about it."

"I wouldn't be able to keep quiet about that myself," Elton concurred.

"I know I can't either. I don't understand our Bishop. I think that's why I definitely made up my mind to leave Boston. I know I can't work there, but leaving the church; that's more difficult."

21

"Matt, I didn't think you were talking about leaving the church, I thought you were talking about leaving the priesthood. You can still be a Catholic, right?"

"Yes. And I would be."

"Maybe you should try to separate the two. I know Byron has talked to me some days when he has been ready to throw in his pastoral robe for a pair of coveralls, but he's never talked about leaving the church," Elton shared.

"Good point. What am I so afraid of? I don't get it?" Matt eyes reddened again.

'Probably change. You had made up your mind this would be your life. Now you have to rethink it all. That's a big job. You know, Matt, maybe you should break it down into a bunch of little decisions. Then in the end, you can look at your list and decide what the big decision is."

"What do you mean?"

"Like you decided to leave Boston. That's done. You don't need to make your ulcers bleed over that anymore. If I hear you right, you don't want to leave the Catholic Church. Am I right?"

"Yah. I couldn't imagine not being Catholic."

"So, that's solved. See, you already made two decisions. From what I heard, you're going to be in North Dakota until spring, right? So, that's solved too. No need to get out on the highway with your thumb out! So, you are making progress, my Man!"

Matt studied the man in his mid-sixties. He felt comfortable with him. "There's something else, too. I don't think I can make this decision right away and it's really eating at me."

"What is it?"

"Well, I talked to Carl about this mess and he told me straight out that he'd never be a priest, so there was no contest there. He did say he would support me though. You know, he is becoming a pretty good stepdad."

"Yah, after you chip away all the bull, he's the decent sort." Elton agreed.

"But since he feels that way, I can't really mention this to him. I haven't talked to Father Vicaro because I know what he'd say. No question about that either. But Elton, I don't know what to do!"

Elton gave the dark haired man a smile, "Let's dump this all out here, grab a stick and sort through it. Okay? Just between you and me."

Matt studied him a minute, and then nodded. "I'd like that. Well, I've never had a problem with celibacy. I mean, I've never felt like I was missing anything without someone to love before. Here lately, it's giving me a lot of trouble."

"Why do you think that is?"

"It might be because Ian and Ruthie are so close and all that. It is more than just them. I mean, almost everyone has someone special. Elton, between you and me, it is more than that."

"Okay."

"I finally realized that I don't like being totally humanly alone. I mean, I have great friends and all that, but-,"

"I understand. It took me many years, but I finally figured that out myself. And you know, so did Carl. Well, Matt, is that a decision you've already made too, huh?"

"No. I could still deal with it, except for one thing. I met this gal at Zach's wedding dance. We keep running into each other."

Elton looked at him, "Diane Waggoner?"

"Oh! You know? Does everyone know?"

Elton patted his hand. "Matt, I usually pick up on that kind of things. It's just that you mentioned her and you mostly don't mention anyone specifically. Yah, I guess I picked up on it when you told us that you saw her in church and then on the road."

"Well, like I said, I can usually talk myself out of it; stay away from the person and I get over it. This time I can't. First of all, I keep bumping her everywhere! We changed her tire on the road, she's a friend of Jeannie's so when we went bowling, she was there. Not like together, but with a bunch. You know."

Elton nodded.

"And she teaches, too. I saw her yesterday. It isn't that I just think that she is so naturally beautiful and graceful, but there's something about her, I can't shake. I know what part of it is, but not the rest."

"Sounds to me like you got bit good, Mister. Can I guess? You don't know if you want to shake it this time?"

"You're right. I don't know. See, the other thing is, there's something wrong. Jeannie, Darrell and I all picked up on it. She seems to be in a bad relationship with her in-laws. They're very domineering and we all wonder if they aren't batting her around."

"Really?" Elton frowned, "That's not good business."

"Yah, so we decided to help her out. I mean, she's almost as skittish as Miriam. I talked to her yesterday and mentioned the dance for Darrell and Jeannie. She immediately panicked and said she wouldn't be going. She said that she shouldn't have gone to Zach's wedding dance because it was improper. Like an idiot, I asked her how long she needed to mourn. She made an excuse and ran off like a deer."

Elton frowned, "I don't know anything about the Waggoners, but I do know some people have some strong ideas about how a person should behave when their spouse dies. Are they really hitting Diane?"

"We aren't sure. She missed part of the first orientation because her jaw was all swelled up. Jeannie said it looked like she had got hit, but then Diane said it was a bad tooth. When I asked her about her tooth yesterday, she was very evasive. Her jaw got swollen the night after we went bowling!"

"Hm. But you guys aren't sure," Elton was thoughtful. "And she won't say?"

"No, not a word. Jeannie and Darrell are going over to Waggoners to show Diane their wedding pictures tomorrow to try to find out what they can. Jeannie told me to make it a point to keep talking to Diane, because she needs to know she has friends. Jeannie says she needs to have someone she can open up to. I agree with all that, but Elton, I should avoid her for my own sake. Darrell says that she needs help, and that should be the important thing. He's right about that, too."

"I think you have our table full now. Let's start sorting through this. First thing I want to say, and I hope you don't get mad at me, but sympathy and love can easily be confused."

"I thought of that. I'm not in love with her. I don't even know her that well, but I'm attracted to her. I'm afraid that I could get very attached. You know?"

"Yah, I do know. Hell, I knew Nora about ten minutes before my goose was cooked! Of course, a lot of stuff could have changed it all between that time and when we finally knew for sure. So, just so you are aware of that. It sounds to me that you are. Why else are you attracted to her?"

"Oh," Matt seemed surprised, "I don't know. I guess her soft voice and gentle manner. She is very kind, treats kids like people and has a silly sense of humor." The young man started to beam, "She is intelligent and loves literature. She listens to people when they talk and makes you feel like you're the only person in the room."

Elton watched him, "She sounds wonderful. I'm glad you didn't just say that she was pretty."

"She's that too." Matt eagerly added, "But she doesn't get all made up. Know what I mean?"

"Yah, I do." Elton thought before he said, "So, you think if you talked to Carl, he would tell you to chuck the church and Vicaro would tell you to chuck Diane. Huh?"

"Pretty much, they would," Matt nodded.

"How about you do neither? I agree that she probably needs help. Sounds like it and Darrell is a real good judge of character. I think you should keep being her friend as much as possible; at least until you guys are sure she's okay."

"What about my vows?"

"What about them? You aren't planning on having an affair with her, are you?"

"Heavens no! She's in a predicament. Her situation isn't one that'd be good for that kind of involvement and mine certainly isn't. No, but I'm afraid if I don't stay away, I'll get more involved. I don't know what to do."

"It might not work for you, but this is what I'd do, if you want to hear it."

"Yes, I do."

"I'd make up my mind that I'm in a time of rethinking everything. My life is upside down, so I'm not ready for any commitment: to either a woman or to the church."

"My commitment is to God, not the church."

"Oh Matthew, God didn't ask you to give up being a human."

"Huh?"

"You heard me. There are a million ways to serve God and a lot of us do it married. I kind of figure we have enough trouble just getting by, we don't need to nail ourselves with a bunch of other rules to make things more difficult. But that's just me. I also think He put us here to help each other." Elton continued. "Sometimes we have to put ourselves in jeopardy to help. If that's the case, so be it. If you have to deal with some struggles to help Diane, too bad. She's here, you're here; the good Lord put her situation in front of you, more than once. I'd figure that since I keep running into her all over, that I was supposed to help her. Not fall in love with her, but be her friend. A guy can never have too many friends, you know. So if it was me, I'd be as good a friend to her as I could. I'd hope that along the way, I'd either get over my attraction to her or decide that it's more than that. Until then, I'd have to help her."

"Matt, if you have even vague plans about being out in the world as a regular person; you might as well realize that situations of a similar nature come up all the time. We can't give in to them, but we can't hide either. Life is risk, all kinds of risk. You know, Matt, our Big Boss doesn't give us a list of very many black and white rules. They are mostly written in a fuzzy gray on beige paper. You have no idea how much I hate the color!

"But the only person that really can decide some of this stuff is you, my friend. Try to start checking the little things off and then the big decision will be easier. As far as Diane, once things get sorted out; you may find that it you didn't like her as much as you thought. Something else I'd like you to consider, you said you don't want to have your feelings for her matter in your decision. I think that is a mistake. A big mistake. I think it matters a whole lot."

"Why?"

"What if God wants you to leave the priesthood? Maybe He wants you to marry someone, not necessarily her, or just be out in the world with us regular folks. You know the Bible is full of loving one another. You're a good guy Matt. I don't know if I did anymore than mess you up worse, but I wish the best for you. I know I'd feel real secure knowing you were in my corner and I think Diane will be too. Don't be so hard on yourself. I don't think this is a decision God wants you to make in a hurry. It's one of those 'sit and stew' things. I really hate those! It usually means God wants to make a big impression with those."

Matt nodded, "Thanks Elton. You really helped a lot. And if my stew pot gets too hot, I'll let you know."

"Matt, tell me to grab the potholders before you are well done, will yah? Ready to go to bed?"

"Yah."

6

MATT TOOK ONE OF THE last empty folding chairs in the meeting that morning. He sat in one of the only three open seats at the end of the row just a couple minutes to starting time. Matt had been in such a hurry that he didn't even look for Diane.

A flustered man rushed in, nodded and took the seat at the end of the row. "Started yet?"

"Not yet," Matt nodded as a lady brushed into the seat between them. It was Diane.

She glanced at him and looked around. Matt knew she wanted a different seat but there was none. She put her purse under her chair and took out her notebook, ignoring him totally. Matt was a bit dumbfounded.

He thought about what Elton had said about God throwing her in front of him for a reason. Matt stared straight ahead. Maybe it was test. Maybe that was the reason. He knew he felt terribly uncomfortable and found himself more than half-annoyed.

If she was going to ignore him, she should have sat somewhere else! Why did she think she should ignore him anyway? After all, what he had said was so bad!

The voice of the speaker turned into background noise and he was lost in thought. He couldn't remember the last time he felt like that. In fact, he wasn't certain exactly what he was feeling. He tried to pay attention but the man seemed quite boring. Maybe it was just because he was tired or because he hadn't listened to more than every other word the poor man said. He considered just getting up and walking out of the place. He would have if he hadn't signed the agreement to teach.

Without realizing what he was saying, he muttered, "Oh the hell with it!"

Diane turned and gave him a surprised look. Softly she whispered, "What did you say?"

Matt felt stupid and mumbled, "Sorry. Nothing."

Diane looked at him with worry and then patted the back of his hand.

Matt couldn't believe that. He was trying to absorb it all in his befuddled mind, when the man told a joke. Everyone laughed and applauded and so did they, even though Matt had no idea what it was about. When they applauded, Diane's pen rolled off her notebook and under the chair of the woman ahead of her.

Matt reached down to try to retrieve it but it had gone too far. He grimaced to her and shrugged. She smiled and mouthed, "Don't worry."

Matt handed his pen to her and then leaned back in his chair. As soon as he did, he realized that he had no other pen. Good grief! He was about ready to throw in the towel and run over to Father Vicaro begging to be reinstated. 'This is for the birds,' he thought.

Matt watched her from the corner of his eye. She really was pretty. She had huge, soft brown eyes that seemed filled with wonder at the world. She always reminded him of spring; a gentle rain, warm sunshine, white fluffy clouds, crocuses, daffodils, baby birds and bunnies. Yah, she reminded him alot of bunnies.

She was wearing a long sleeved high-necked soft chiffon dress of a peach color. There were soft ruffles at the neck and the wrists. The color was very flattering and gave her skin a soft glow. The skirt fell in gentle folds that did not mask her wonderful figure. He thought she was the most beautiful woman he'd ever seen.

He must've been staring because she turned and looked at him. She'd been furiously taking notes while he wrote nothing. Then she realized that he apparently had no pen. She reached down, brought her purse up to her lap and began rummaging through it. She found another pen and handed it to him. He looked at her in surprise and smiled. He took it and then sat forward as she put her purse back under the chair.

When she straightened up, the sleeve of her blouse had ridden up past her wrist. There was a huge black and blue mark, like someone had twisted her arm. He stared at it and noticed the finger marks. She noticed him in horror and pulled her sleeve down. She turned and began furiously taking notes.

Matt was fighting the urge to drag her out of there and plummet her with questions. He knew better, but it was killing him. He decided he'd better take some notes and at least pretend like he was vaguely interested in what was going on.

By the time coffee break was announced, enough time had transpired so they were both taking notes and paying attention. Things seemed more relaxed between them. Without giving her a chance to say no, Matt declared, "I'm getting us coffee, you find us a place to sit."

She looked at him ready to say no, but he just walked away. He decided that if Tuck had to tackle Tinker; so be it! He wasn't going to let her avoid him again.

As he was standing in line for the coffee pot, he noticed her go into the ladies' room. He became quite irritated. 'The one place I can't follow her. That's just ducky!'

He took their cups, stood by the ladies' room door and waited. It was quite a bit later when she came out. She looked around and then noticed he was still standing there. She was embarrassed.

"When I said find us a place to sit, I didn't mean in the rest room!" Matt gave her a serious look.

"I know. I'm sorry, but—," she started to make an excuse.

"Next time I'll specify," Matt smiled. "Not in the restroom. Let's go see if we can find a spot outside. Okay?"

Diane nodded numbly, "Okay."

He thought she might run off, but she didn't. She came over to the end of a bench he found and sat down. She took the coffee, without looking at him, and said, "It looks good."

"It's cold. Elton would have a fit. He considers himself a coffee expert. I have to agree, he knows his stuff." Matt smiled. "He was raving about the coffee his son got him in Vietnam. It was Caphe Cut something or Weasel Poop Coffee."

Diane's eyes twinkled, "I think you mean Caphe Cut Chon. Did you taste it?"

"No, but Darrell did. He said it was great."

29

"To each his own," Diane shrugged. "Weasel Poop Coffee doesn't sound very appetizing. Thanks for giving me your pen. I didn't realize you didn't have one. Were you planning to memorize the lecture?"

"Yah," Matt chuckled, his faint dimple almost appearing, "That was it. I hope it wasn't very important. I really didn't pay much attention to any of it."

"Don't ask me. I didn't pay any attention either," she admitted. "I guess if it is, we'll both be in trouble."

Matt looked straight at her, "Diane, I saw the bruise. I'm not going to pretend that I didn't."

"It's okay, really. I just fell," she murmured.

"You aren't a good liar. Look, I don't want to make you run off again, so I'm just telling you. Please, if you need someone to talk to or need any help, promise you'll let me know. Okay?"

"I'm fine, Matt. Please. It's no big deal."

"I'm not convinced. Like I said, I'll back off this time. However, if you get hurt again, I won't. I don't like my friends getting hurt."

"Matt, I don't think that we should be friends. It isn't a good idea," she looked off across the football field.

"Why? Is there something wrong with me?"

"That has nothing to do with it. It'd just be easier all the way around."

"Diane, I don't have many friends here. I'm new to this area."

She turned to him, "I think you're great, but I really can't have you for a friend. I hope you just accept that."

Matt looked at his cup, "You are probably right about that in more ways than you know. Can we at least be pleasant acquaintances?

She giggled, "Well, I've never had a pleasant acquaintance before. Okay, as long as we don't have to bowl."

"The world will rejoice if we don't bowl," Matt was surprisingly relieved, although he didn't know why. "Do you have big plans for the weekend?"

"No. Church on Sunday. Oh, guess what?" Diane asked, beginning to relax.

"What?"

"Jeannie called. She and Darrell are going to stop by and show me their wedding pictures from Hawaii tonight after school. I'm anxious to see them. I suppose you already saw them."

"I've seen a few. Jeannie and Annie were beautiful brides. They both wore Hawaiian dresses like Princess Kaiulani. You know, Victorian style."

"That sounds beautiful. How is Annie doing? That must have been hard to leave her new husband."

"Yah. Annie is very resilient. Did you know that her first husband was killed over there a couple years ago?"

"Oh my! No I didn't. Isn't she getting married again awfully soon?"

"I don't think so. He died over two years ago. That isn't exactly like she is dancing on his grave," then he noticed her expression. "Oh Diane. I'm so sorry. That was a thoughtless thing to say."

"No. It's just different from what many folks think," she said emphatically.

"Yes, my father died fourteen years ago and his folks are upset with my Mom because she is going to marry Carl. Fourteen years! I can't believe it," Matt said.

She watched his face, "Matt, you know some people say that you're married forever."

"It doesn't say that in our church, you know. It's until death do you part. While it is logical to wait some time for a person to work through their own feelings of mourning, the church has no time limit," Matt said. "In fact, in Bible times, people often remarried soon."

"Hm. I guess so, huh? But doesn't that show disrespect for the deceased?"

"Statistics have proven that happily married folks are much more apt to remarry when their mate dies than unhappily married people. I guess they aren't as willing to take a chance again."

"Interesting. Maybe people shouldn't get married at all," Diane observed.

"Diane, that's a basic human desire; to have some to love you and to love someone. We all need that." After he said it, he stared into his cup. The thought rang in his head, 'Who the hell am I to be spouting that?'

She sat quietly a minute and then said, "Matt? Did I lose you for a minute?"

"I'm sorry. I didn't get a lot of sleep last night," Matt excused himself.

The bell rang and they went back in. Even though she could've sat somewhere else, she didn't. She took her place beside him. The next speaker was either more interesting or they both felt better. They both took a lot of notes and exchanged glances while the woman spoke.

Matt was deciding if he should ask her to have lunch with him, when the speaker announced the Principal had a few words. Mr. Palmer thanked them all for attending, said he was looking forward to working with them and that they were excused for the rest of the day.

Matt and Diane walked out of the gym together and then Matt said, "It was great seeing you today. I'm glad you'll be my pleasant acquaintance. I hope to see you again soon."

She smiled sweetly, "Matt, have a great trip to Boston and drive carefully. See you when the school is in full motion." She waved and started to walk away. Then she returned and grabbed his hand, "Thank you." Then she ran off.

7

HE STOOD THERE A MINUTE lost in thought. He didn't know what to think about much of anything. Finally, he walked toward Elton's gas station and garage. Once there, he went in to his brother who was working on some invoices. "Hi big Brother."

"What brings you by? Got fired already?"

"No. They just sprung us lose early. Got something for me to do or should I go on home?" Matt asked.

Elton stuck his head in the door, "Or take us to lunch? Kevin should be back in about five minutes. Nora is cooking for the dance tomorrow, so she suggested that I grab something to eat in town."

"What do you say, Mattie? Can we buy this man some soup?" Ian asked.

"Oh, why not?"

Lunch at the Little Hen House was good. They all had burgers, fries and milkshakes. "I can feel my waistband expanding!" Elton grinned.

"You should weigh a ton for all you eat," Ian chuckled. "You're lucky you don't gain weight like most folks."

"I guess so. Hey, how is the arm, Harrington? It seems like it's getting stronger."

"I think it is, Elton," Ian agreed, with a chuckle. "Thanks to Pepper. Your daughter is sure a little slave driver when it comes to physical therapy. I know Carl sure thinks the world and all of her. I think he might be a bit afraid of her, and that's a blasted fact!"

"I guess all her years fending off her three big brothers have paid off. Are you going to see your neurologist while you're out in Boston?" Elton asked.

"I have an appointment. He needs to fill out some more papers. But look, I can bend my arm from straight down to the table all by itself!" Ian answered.

With pride, the young man displayed the movement it had taken him a month of practice to execute. He did do it, but it was painstakingly slow. It was a lot of progress however, considering his arm had been virtually useless after the shooting. However, he'd never have the quick reaction times that he needed to be a cop. That was over forever.

Hanging around the shop and grain elevator, Ian discovered that he had a knack for business. Pepper encouraged him with it and before long, he was helping Elton with the books for both shops and Doug's books with the grain elevator. Pep got him to sign up at Capital Commercial College and he was now taking courses in office management, business law and accounting. He liked it and did well with it. Then Doug and Elton decided to share him as an employee. He was their business manager.

After the trip to Texas where he and Coot both used their detective skills, he realized that he didn't want law enforcement anymore. When he returned from there, he asked Ruthie to marry him. They had just set the date. He was happy about that commitment.

Since a construction company was building homes for each Zach, Coot and Darrell, Ian got a significant discount by having their house built at the same time. They bought some land just north of Carl's new house and across the road from Elton's nephew and his wife.

Things were falling into place for the young couple. Harrington would be traveling to Boston to help move his Mom out to the Dakotas, but also to move his things. He would tell the rest of his family and his co-workers good bye and put that life behind him. When he returned he and Ruthie would start their own lives.

After attending Zach's wedding, Ruthie's mind was so filled with wedding plans that they set the date, October third. She was so excited and Ian loved that. He loved to see her enjoy life.

"Earth to Harrington," Elton was saying. "Could you pass me the catsup?"

"Sure, I'm sorry," Ian smiled. "I don't know where my mind was."

"Probably trying to figure out how to get out of this wedding?" Elton chuckled. "So where outside will the wedding be?"

"Ruthie and Suzy went over to the park in Merton. I guess they found a perfect spot by the picnic area. There's a shelter and some tables and stuff. I don't know. I just let her talk. Have you ever seen anyone so excited about anything in your life?" Ian's eyes just danced. "She's so happy."

"No, I have to say I've seen women excited about their weddings, but she takes the cake!" Elton laughed. "I sure hope it doesn't rain or something."

"Oh no," Matt agreed, "That'd be horrible."

Harrington's dimpled grin spread, "She has that all worked out. She rented this huge tent. So now, we're going to have the wedding dance there, instead of at Heinrich's barn. She wanted it there, but since she has to rent the tent, decided to have it there."

"Sounds sensible," Elton agreed.

"Bill and his Boys are still going to play for it though," Harrington went on. "If it rains, we'll just get married on the dance floor instead of in the shelter, or something. I just let her figure it out."

"Probably a good idea," Elton chuckled, "The way that girl gets her ideas flying, a guy could get hurt."

"And that's a blasted fact!" Ian chuckled. "Oh, you know, it makes me so happy to see her so excited about life. Remember how she used to be?"

Both men nodded and Elton said, "Now if we can just get Miriam straightened out. She is doing a lot better though."

"She is. That poor little kid is beginning to come out of her shell. She really does well with Kevin and Carrie," Matt pointed out.

"I know, I feel bad about that," Ian messed with his French fries, "You know, Ruthie is her aunt. We should be the ones she relies on."

"Hmm. Which book did you read that rule in?" Elton asked.

"I didn't, it's just—," Ian started.

Elton said seriously, "There's no rule. You know what Dr. Samuels said. It's very difficult for either Ruthie or Zach to deal with Miriam. They are only months away from coming out of all that themselves. When Miriam gets so terrified, it brings back the terror to them. Really, I'm just happy that we can make it through an entire conversation about the situation without one or both of them upchucking."

"That's a blasted fact!" Harrington agreed, "I guess I forgot that! Man, that's about all those two did when I first met them. Suzy and I handed out more barf bags than you can believe."

Matt nodded, "I was amazed that Ruthie made it all the way through dinner the other night when we told about what we had discovered in Texas without throwing up. She was very quiet but she controlled it."

Harrington grinned, "She was gripping my hand so tight that I thought I might lose feeling in that arm too! But you're right, she did make it through the whole thing. I was so proud of her."

8

AS PROMISED, MATT WENT OVER to start Darrell's chores that evening. He was about half way through milking when Darrell joined him in the barn. "Jeannie called Nora to say we were late, so we'll feed you tonight."

Matt nodded, "Thanks. I told her I might be late. I think that sliding door is stuck. I hope I didn't wreck it."

"No," Darrell said, "It's been sticking."

The men didn't talk about that afternoon while they finished the chores and repaired the door. When they headed to the house, Matt asked, "How did it go?"

Darrell raised his eyebrows, "Weird, man. Really weird."

They washed up and then both men gave Jeannie a kiss on the cheek before they sat down to eat. "Wow! That could turn a girl's head," Jeannie giggled as she put the hot dish on the table and sat down.

They said grace and began to fill their plates. "Tuck asked me how it went and all I could say was weird," Darrell admitted. "Can you explain it?"

"Nope," Jeannie said, "It was weird. We got there right at five and rang the bell. Mr. Waggoner opened the door and let us in. He ushered us into the living room, but never said a word. We just stood there like a pair of dopes until he motioned for us to sit down.

"Matt, that living room must have had three hundred pictures in it! One was Waggoner's wedding picture and another was them with Dean when he was little. The rest were all of Dean! No one else, just him alone! I've never seen anything like it in my life. It was creepy. It took a few minutes, but finally Mrs. Waggoner came in. She's a lot easier to talk to than him. She said that Diane would be right down and asked to see the photos. I handed them to her and she handed them to him. He looked over every one of them one at a time and then set them on the table. He nodded and told her they'd be okay!

"She handed them back to us. Then Diane came in the room and smiled, but hardly said a word. Mrs. Waggoner said I could show them to her, so I handed them to her. Neither lady ever sat down. She looked at them and said 'Wow! They're beautiful. You were a beautiful bride, Jeannie.'

"That is the first time that he said anything, 'Your name is Jean?' I told him it was Jeannie and then he asked Darrell his name. Darrell told him and he said something like oh, the goat guy. Darrell nodded and then he said, 'Why did you guys come here? What do you want?' I could see that Darrell was getting steamed so I said I wanted to show our wedding pictures to Diane because she was my coworker and friend. He said, 'she doesn't have time for friends.' I said that's too bad because we wanted to invite her to our dance at Heinrich's barn."

Darrell interrupted, "You should have seen the look on Diane's face when Jeannie said that! It was pure panic."

"Yes, it was, Matt," Jeannie said. "I was sorry the minute that I said it. He glowered at her and said 'The girl has work to do. She shouldn't be running around and I don't trust her out at night.' Diane blushed and I knew she wanted to just die. Then shock of shock, he looked at his wife and said, 'Okay. We'll all be there! What time is this thing? I want to check out who she's been hanging around anyway. It might be a good place to do it.' Then he stood up and said, 'Well you got to show her the pictures and we'll come on Saturday. Now we have work to do so you can go.' That was it. He walked us to the door and closed it behind us."

Matt just sat there, unable to put a sentence together. Finally he said, "I think they're nuts."

"That's my thought. Crazier than raccoons in heat!" Darrell stated.

Matt was killing himself laughing at Darrell, "You are insane, Jessup. Raccoons in heat? Really?"

"Well, they would be crazy I think," Darrell tried to justify himself.

"Whatever. I don't know what to make of it. I think we should go talk to Carl, and Ian. Okay? We can tell them what you saw and stuff. If anybody would know what to do, they should. What do you think?" Matt asked.

"I think that's a good idea," Jeannie said. "Right after dishes."

An hour later, they sat down on Schroeder's patio. Carl Kincaid was enjoying his evening whiskey and the others were having a beer or iced tea. When everyone was all settled, Darrell explained the situation.

Darrell had no more than started to talk when Elton caught Matt's glance and nodded. Matt knew he approved and it gave him the courage to tell what he had discovered at Orientation. He left out most of the conversation, but just shared with a few pertinent comments; like her big bruise and how she asked to leave it alone.

Carl leaned back and took a long draw off his cigarette. "Bastards. I don't know what those people are up to, but it smells rotten."

"Me, too," Elton agreed. "What do you think should be done, Coot?"

"What do I think? My guess is it has as much to do with money as anything. Most stuff boils down to that. It'd make more sense for him to just keep them at home and under his control."

"That's what I thought right away," Harrington agreed. "However, I can't see what they have to gain. Diane doesn't have money, does she?"

"I know that Diane had to borrow money from Dean's folks when Dean was dying. Since neither was working, they lost the house and had to move in with Waggoners. I guess they loaned her money for some of his treatments and medication," Jeannie said.

"Well for goodness sakes, why wouldn't they? He's their son! I'd think they would've just paid it," Nora replied. "That wasn't her bill. It was for their son!"

"Nora, not every one thinks like you do," Elton pointed out. "Some people have way different ideas."

Maureen had been listening quietly, "Well, I'd like to give them a piece of my mind. I can tell you that. What did you say, Mattie? Some folks think marriage is forever? Good grief, I thought only Mormons married for Time and Eternity. I didn't think Catholics believe there was marriage in heaven. They're Catholic, so what're they talking about?"

"Tinker, I mean Diane, didn't say that she thought that or that they did, just that some folks do. I don't know what she believes, but I get the feeling that she feels trapped or something," Matt said. "Did you guys think that?"

Darrell said. "It was like he controlled everything. He had to look over our wedding pictures before she was allowed to see them. What did he think? They were porno or something?"

"Who knows?" Coot shrugged. "He's probably nuts. So, what do you kids want us to do? I know it's something."

Matt smiled broadly, "Ah gee Dad, you got us figured out already!"

"Pretty obvious to my mind," Carl chuckled. "You're sitting here acting like you like us! You don't do that for nothing!"

"Well, we're wondering if you, Elton and Ian could maybe, like—talk to them at the dance and see what you can find out. I mean, you guys are investigators and Elton is almost psychic," Darrell explained.

"He's not psychic, he's just nosey. If you really want to find out something, I'd suggest you turn Ginger loose. That little girl would have the whole story in minutes and they'd never know what hit them." Carl laughed, but everyone agreed. "What do you say, guys? Shall we help these three?"

Harrington had been very quiet, "I will, but only to help Diane. I met her and she seems like a nice person. No one should have to put up with that."

"Count me in," Elton nodded."

"Okay, it's a deal." Carl decreed, "We'll check it out for you."

"We'll probably figure out more from how they react to a normal situation, than if these guys interrogate them." Nora suggested.

Matt cleared his throat, "But what if Diane gets into trouble again. What if like someone talks to her and she gets beaten or something?"

"We can't control that, Bro," Harrington pointed out. "She hasn't told you guys enough to know what she gets in trouble about, so we don't know how to prevent it."

"That's right, Matt," Carl agreed. "Until she feels she can talk to one of you guys, we have no way of knowing that."

"We'll have to trust the good Lord to keep an eye on her," Elton offered. "Okay? Maybe things aren't as bad as you guys think. It sounds like it, but we don't even know that for certain. I'm glad they're coming and we'll try to find out what we can. Okay?"

Everyone nodded thoughtfully, but no one was very confident.

9

MATT FELT LIKE HE HAD lived a million years from their talk that night at the picnic table until the next evening's dance. Annie was disappointed that neither her father nor brother would be able to make it. She had so hoped they'd come. Then of course, Andy wasn't going to be there; so she knew she'd be bummed about that. She really wanted to go to the dance for Darrell and Jeannie. However, she was having a hard time feeling like things were right without Andy.

When Matt brought the car up to the house, everyone except the Grandparents had already left for the dance. Matt came in and helped her with her coat.

"You look great tonight, Annie," he said, and she started to cry. He looked to Grandma in panic. "I'm sorry. Annie."

Grandma came right over and put her arm around her, "Look here Annie, I know that this isn't the way you'd like it to be; but it's better than it could be. You're married to Andy now! You had a wonderful wedding and a fantastic honeymoon! You're very fortunate. I know Andy would want you to go to Darrell's dance. Darrell is his best friend in the world! You have a wonderful guy to take you to the dance; good looking too! You just get out there and think you are the luckiest gal in the whole wide world! You hear me?"

Annie stood a minute and then nodded, "You're right. I love you, Grandma. I'm lucky and Andy would want me to go, I know that. And Matt is the best looking guy I know, right?"

"Thank you, Annie," Matt mumbled rather embarrassed. "Let's go have a nice time tonight."

"Now go. Johnsons will be here soon to visit and I know you young folks don't want to listen to us gab about the olden days. Have fun. Hear me?" Grandma booted them out the door.

"Yes Grandma," Matt kissed her cheek. Then they went down the steps and Matt opened the car door for Annie.

On the way to the dance, Annie said, "You don't have to hang around me if you don't want, Matt. I don't expect you to do that. I know you're just being nice when you offered to be my escort."

"Annie, this is probably your last chance to go out on a hot date! Now don't tell me I can't even talk to you!" he laughed. "You're as whacko as everyone else around here!"

Annie giggled. "Okay Hotshot! Let's go tear up the night!"

10

AT THE TOP OF THE hayloft stairs, Alfred and Myrtle Frandsen met them. Jeannie's parents told them to get ready for the wedding march. Annie explained that she wasn't going to participate because Andy wasn't there, but Myrtle said, "Jeannie told us that. You know, you were her maid-of-honor, so you're in her wedding party. Matt can be Andy's stand-in as best man."

Annie looked at Matt and shrugged, "Well, since we got all spiffed up and everything, okay? How soon will it be?"

"Oh, we thought in about twenty minutes or so. Just come back to the coatroom. That is where we'll line up."

"Okay," Annie said. Matt took her arm and they walked over to the table where Elton and Nora sat. She explained it to them and Nora just smiled. "That'll be very nice!"

Annie sat down next to Nora and Matt went with Elton to get the ladies something to drink. When they were alone, Matt asked, "Have you seen Diane yet?"

"No, I haven't seen her. Maybe they won't even show, huh? Tonight is heartbreaking for Annie," Elton said. "I appreciate you bringing her."

"I enjoy her company. We'll have a good time; we always have fun together. I hadn't considered being in a wedding march though," Matt grimaced.

"Matt, all attendants are, you know. Gee, Pepper and Darrell have been up and down the aisle so many times together and been attendants in so many weddings marches, I think half the neighborhood figures they're married to each other!"

As the men were heading toward their table, Matt saw Diane. She and Waggoners were just sitting down at a smaller table about ten feet away. His face gave it away, because Elton turned to look. "I take it that is them. Please close your mouth."

Matt frowned at him. "What should I do?"

"What were you going to do?"

"Take this drink to Annie," he mumbled.

"Then I think that's what you should do."

Matt put Annie's drink down and then sat next to her. He noticed that Mr. Waggoner had gone to get the ladies something to drink. He felt like he should go greet them but decided it might be awkward.

His Mom had seen them and went over to the table. Matt watched as Mo greeted Diane and then shook Mrs. Waggoner's hand. She visited a bit and then Mr. Waggoner came to back to the table. He put down the drinks and she introduced herself. He nodded but didn't shake her hand and sat down. His Mom visited for another minute or so and then said goodbye. She returned to their table.

Matt wanted to ask her what they said when he saw Mrs. Frandsen motion for them to come over. He and Annie crossed to the coatroom by the door. They walked right by Waggoner's table. He knew Diane saw him. He wanted so badly to say something to her but didn't know what. So, he just went on by.

When he got to the coatroom, Darrell and Jeannie were there and Darrell's parents, George and Alma Jessup. Mrs. Frandsen said, "Now, here's the deal. Bill is going to announce the wedding couple, and so on. We'll dance according to what he announces, you know, Mother-Son dance, Father-Daughter dance and blah blah. In the end, he'll say, "Enjoy the dance everyone!" Then we can dance with whomever we want. But we should try not to dance with our partners because Bill wants us to get the whole crowd in to motion. Okay?"

The music started and the group marched out to the strains of *We've Only Just Begun,* the Carpenter's hit that Jeannie and Darrell really liked. Bill announced "Darrell and Jeannie Jessup, the bride and groom."

They came onto the dance floor. Jeannie wore her wedding dress and looked absolutely beautiful. Darrell was dressed in a tuxedo. They did make a great looking couple. Everyone applauded.

When they had proceeded about ten feet, Bill announced, "Annie Schroeder and Matthew Harrington, attendants."

The couple stepped out onto the dance floor. Annie wore a full-length summer dress that had a slightly Hawaiian style with her hair held back with some flowers on each side. Matt wore his suit. Then Bill announced the parents and they all came out and started to dance. Matt was thanking God that he had learned how to dance so he only stepped on Annie's feet a couple times. The second time she grinned at him and said, "Will you relax? I might have to wear logging boots!"

He smiled back, "I'm trying."

Then they both laughed.

By the time it came to asking others to dance, he had started to have fun. He spied Ruthie and brought her to the dance floor. The next time Bill told everyone to change partners; he took Suzy's hand and danced with her.

He and Annie returned to their table. Soon they were engulfed in a conversation with Eve and Chatterbox about who knew what. Conversations with Eve and Chatterbox were like that. The dancing resumed and he and Annie danced again. He soon discovered that as Keith had predicted, Annie had at least a hundred men who wanted to dance with her. He danced with Pepper, Eve and then asked his Mom.

While they were dancing, he asked her what he was dying to know about her visit with the Waggoners. "Don't worry Mattie," Mo grinned, "I've been rooting out every truffle of gossip long before Coot learned the first thing about interrogation! I just went over and said hi, remember me from church and asked how she was. Then I said hi to her in-laws. I think it is him, not her. That Gladys's brain hasn't been turned on for such a long time, I think her connections are rusted. I think he is mean and she is crazy. I really like Diane. You should go over and say hi. I paved the way for you."

Matt grimaced, "Mom, what did you say?"

"I just told them that I was so proud of my boy that he was stepping in for Andy because he was still in Vietnam. I told them to check out how nice you looked in your suit."

"Oh no," the young man groaned, "You didn't. How humiliating."

"No, it's not. I didn't give birth to the two best looking men here so I could keep it a secret. Now, after you take your old Mom back to the table, you go over and say hello to them. Hear me?"

"I don't want to get her into trouble."

"Nora and I have fixed that. They're going to be so deluged with folks being friendly; they won't know who is what. Why look, Elton and Coot are there now and Ian and Ruthie are lined up to zero in next!"

"Gee, Mom. Women are a dangerous group," Matt observed.

"And don't you forget it!" she giggled. "Oh look, Elton has asked Mrs. Waggoner to dance. Mr. Waggoner won't know who to beat tonight!"

"You're just plain awful, Mom."

Matt watched as a myriad of the Engelmann Clan went over to the table. His Mom even asked Mr. Waggoner to dance while Coot danced with Mrs. Waggoner. As she danced by him, Mo gave her son a look. He knew he'd better get over to talk to Diane.

He saw Katie and asked her to join him in telling Mrs. Waggoner hello. They sat down beside her teacher. "Hello, isn't this dance fun?" Katie said.

"Hello, Katie. It's good to see you too. Hello Matt." she smiled at him.

Katie told Mrs. Waggoner "I got a book of Emily Dickinson's poetry this summer."

"What did you think of it?"

"I liked some of it, but I don't think she is my favorite," Katie answered.

"Mine either," Diane answered, "And you?"

"Not my favorite either, but I do like some of her work," Matt agreed.

Rodney Oxenfelter, a clanner Katie's age, came by and asked Katie to dance and she said yes. Now, Matt felt awkward. Had it been anyone else, he would've just asked Diane to dance but he was unsure if her should.

He looked at her and was trying to think of something feeble to say, when Kevin came up and asked Matt to hold Miriam a minute while he went to get something from his car.

He put Miriam on his lap and she looked nervous. "It's okay, Miriam. This nice lady is Diane. We call her Tinker."

Miriam studied her and instantly turned to crawl into his arms. She buried her face in his neck like she did when she was frightened. He patted the little three year old's back, "It's okay, Miriam. You don't have to say hi unless you want. Tinker won't hurt you. I promise."

Miriam turned and studied his face, "Okay Fodder."

"Okay. Want to turn around and say hello?" he asked after he felt her begin to relax a little.

"If you want to," the little girl said.

He turned her around and she looked at Diane. Diane smiled and said "Hello Miriam. That's a pretty name."

Miriam watched her a minute, leaned back into Matt's lap pressing her body as close to him as possible and then patted her own chest. The tiny girl said quietly, "Gopher."

Matt chuckled, "She calls herself Gopher. She has some crazy names for folks. She calls Elton-Uncle, Grandma Katherine-Chocolate and Kevin-Son."

Diane's eyes were dancing, "She does, and she calls you Fodder."

Miriam patted Matt's arm and repeated "Fodder."

Matt thought it might be a perfect time to tell Diane the truth, but chickened out. It didn't seem the right place. Blushing, he stammered, "I'll explain it to you sometime. I promise. But be assured, I'm not her father."

Miriam nodded, "Fodder." Then she pointed to Diane and said, "Stinker."

They both giggled, "No, it is Tinker."

Miriam nodded, "Stinker."

Diane giggled, "I think that's close enough, Honey."

Miriam corrected her, "Gopher."

"I'm sorry, I forgot. You aren't honey, you're Gopher."

Miriam nodded. "Poke?"

Diane looked to Matt for translation, "She wants to know if you want to polka or dance?

Diane said, "I'd love to polka, but I'd better not."

Just then Elton came up beside them and asked, "May I dance with little one?"

Miriam giggled, "Gopher Uncle poke."

She held out her arms to Elton and he took her. They swirled off across the dance floor.

"Hm. What do you think, Diane? Should we join them," Matt asked.

"I shouldn't dance," Diane started.

"If you really don't think you should," Matt replied. "I understand. Maybe we can just visit then."

"Okay, but not too much, if you get my drift?"

"Like a winter blizzard, lady," Matt chuckled.

Diane giggled and they watched the dancers.

When Waggoners danced by, Wag as she called Mr. Waggoner, gave her a dirty look.

"I think we'd better say goodnight," Diane said.

"I'd like to bring you something to drink, unless you think you'll be in trouble."

Diane thought a minute, "I better take a rain check."

The Waggoners came over and sat down. Matt greeted them. "Hello, I'm Maureen's son. I think you met my mom."

"Yes, I did," Wag scowled. "Don't you have a date?"

"Yes I do," Matt tried not to die a million deaths. Just then Harrington and Coot came up.

"Hi Bro," Ian said as he patted Matt's arm.

Waggoner started to open his mouth, but Carl just pulled up a chair and sat down, "So, I hear you're in the roofing business. Tell me about it."

It was either the authority or the gruffness in his voice that made Wag pay attention to him. Then Mo sat down and started to talk to Mrs. Waggoner. Matt took that as his cue to move on. Ian sat down at the table and visited with them.

Waggoners stayed a couple hours. Matt noticed when they gathered their things. He and Annie went over to say good night.

"Thank you for coming tonight," Annie smiled.

"I hope you had a nice time," Matt said, trying not to look only at Diane.

"It was alright," Wag nodded. "Gotta go now."

Diane smiled at him sweetly, "It was very nice."

"Just get your coat on and let's go," Wag ordered, sharply.

Annie gave him a dirty look, "Good night."

12

PEPPER'S ALARM RIPPED THE SILENCE of the Schroeder household. Soon everyone except Grandpa Lloyd was clustered in the kitchen, cup in hand, awaiting their morning brew. Grandma Katherine was in a good mood. "I want something different for breakfast. Anyone have any exotic ideas?"

Everyone looked at her blankly. Kevin popped through the door, Mr. Morning Cheer himself. "Something exotic for breakfast? Sounds great! Watcha making? Carrie will help you. She shouldn't go the barn this morning. She decided not to sleep last night."

Carrie smiled, "I'd love to help you make something exotic."

"Me, too," Darlene giggled.

"I want to get some things done for dinner today, so I'll leave it to you gals," Nora smiled.

"What are we having for dinner today? That stuffed pork loin?" Mo asked. "I'll help you and so will Coot."

Carl grumped, "I'm getting well now, you know. I don't have to be in the house all the time."

Elton cracked up, "Good. This morning, you get to come to the barn with us!"

"Ah, I didn't say that," Carl groaned. "Okay, I'll walk down there, but I'm not milking no damned cow!"

Everyone laughed as the door opened and Chris came in. Pepper ran to his arms and gave her fiancé a big kiss.

Carl rolled his eyes, "I can't wait until our place is done! These people are all Petunias."

Carl Kincaid made his first journey to the barn during chores. He had been there before and had been over to Darrell's barn, but not to help. He didn't do much but watch, and of course, grump. There was Chris, Kevin, Keith, Pepper, Elton, Annie, Ian, Matt and him. Carl looked around and announced, "Hell, you got more workers than there are cows!"

Elton grinned, "I know. Isn't it grand?"

"What do you guys do down here anyway?"

In the next hour, he found out. Some of the group milked, some fed the horses, pigs or calves. Some of the calves had to be pail fed yet. The water tank needed to be checked and water carried to the pigs, turkeys and chickens. The milk was separated and skim milk was carried to the pigs and calves. The livestock had to have all their pens or stalls cleaned and new straw put in. Livestock was let out into the pastures, since it was summer. Even though the family had their coffee break and goofed around for about fifteen minutes, they worked. When they left the barn carrying the eggs and cream to the house, everything was done and the place was in order.

On the way back to the house, Carl walked beside Elton. Elton looked at him and asked, "What did you think?"

"Well, I have to say, it'd be a lot of work for one person, but with this crew, no one really broke a sweat, huh?"

"Yah, and that's the way I like it. If everybody has one small job to do, it all gets done alot faster. So, when are you buying your cow?"

"I already did. Remember I'm partner in Darrell's herd and all those goats!"

"That's right, huh?" Elton clapped him on the back. "You are turning into a real sod buster."

"Stifle it, Magpie," Carl grouched. "The clay in this Petunia Patch is beginning to stick to my shoes! I suppose Chris and Ian will be dragging their cows in here soon?"

"Yah, they are going to each buy a Jersey, I guess," Elton nodded. "They told Jerald to start looking for some on his next cattle buying trip."

"What are you going to do with all those stupid cows?"

"You know, there're a lot of mouths to feed around here. We use every ounce of the cream and eggs. We have to butcher half a herd just to give everyone a bone! I don't think I'm going to mess with turkeys again. They are dumber than rocks."

"Good eating, though," Carl said.

"Great, you can raise them at your place next year! Sounds to me like a fine idea!" Elton laughed.

The kitchen smelled great. The exotic breakfast turned out to be Eggs Florentine and toast triangles. "What is Eggs Florentine?" Carl asked.

"Poached eggs on a bed of spinach fried with bacon and scallions with a bit of lemon. There's a cheesy sauce baked over the top and it is all served with little toast triangles," Mo explained.

Kevin inspected one of the triangles, "Man, I'll have to eat a dozen of them to get full."

Carrie swatted her husband, "You don't have to stuff yourself every time you see a plate."

"I don't?" Kevin teased.

After the group said grace, everyone began to eat their 'exotic breakfast' and most agreed it was wonderful. They all rehashed the dance the night before. It wasn't long before the conversation turned to the Waggoners.

Harrington began, "What did you make of that Wag, Dad?"

Carl leaned back and thought before he said anything. "Nasty piece of work, but he's not very smart. He wants to be a crook but doesn't have the brains for it, so he bullies folks to get what he wants. His wife has probably been around him so much, she doesn't even notice that she's as crazy as he is."

"I might say it differently, but that's what I thought, too," Harrington nodded. "I think she's relieved to have his anger directed anywhere but at her."

Elton listened and then said, "I doubt she even thinks his controlling is wrong anymore. Do you?"

"No, I don't think she does," Carl agreed. "He has battered her down to where he wants her years ago, would be my guess. He was bragging about how he cheated folks with their roofing materials! He doesn't know me from a hole in the ground. He has no idea if I could get him in trouble! The moron sat there and laid out all the details!"

Harrington went to get the coffee pot and returned to the table, "What did you ladies think?"

Nora said, "I don't think that Gladys could defend herself, let alone anyone else. I doubt if she'd survive on her own anymore. She watches for his cue on everything."

"I noticed that," Mo agreed. "I wouldn't last two seconds alone with that miserable excuse for a man. He glares at Diane all the time. At least he smiles at Gladys once in a while."

"That because he has her where he wants her," Harrington pointed out. "He knows he doesn't have control over Diane. He's still afraid of her getting out and talking. I'm surprised he even lets her work."

"From what Jeannie said," Matt offered, "They feel that she owes them a lot of money from when her husband died. She won't be able to pay them back if she doesn't work."

"That must be it then. I wonder how much she owes?" Harrington asked. "Does anyone know?"

Everyone shook their heads. Then Carl observed, "I doubt it matters. That man will keep making up reasons for her to keep paying them forever. He isn't give up his meal ticket."

Pepper piped up, "She's smarter than that! She must have records or something!"

Carl disagreed, "No Pep. However he first conned her into the situation, he'll keep playing it."

Chris spoke up then, "Both this Gladys and Diane are exhibiting classic symptoms of domestic violence. These people begin to doubt their own value and start to think the abuser is doing them a favor. Intelligence has little to do with it."

"That's right, Chris," Harrington agreed. "And it's reinforced every time they step outside of that, they get clobbered. Being beaten can leave a definite impression."

Matt took it all in and then asked, "So none of you think that Darrell, Jeannie and I are imagining things."

They all said no.

"So, what can we do?" he finally asked the hard question.

"First of all," Nora said, "You guys are right. She needs friends, so keep the door open for her to talk to you."

"Yah, but Matt," Harrington raised his eyebrow, "She'll probably be safer talking to Jeannie than you or Darrell right now. We have to figure out exactly what's going on and then get her out of there. I think if that Wag thinks that you and Darrell are too friendly, he'll stomp that out right now."

"I agree," Mo nodded. "He has no respect for any woman. That's easy to see. He wouldn't consider a woman as much of a threat."

Nora agreed as did the other ladies.

Elton put down his cup, "Let's see. He lets her work and go to church. Is there anything else we know he allows?"

Matt shrugged, "Jeannie said she used to be involved in a lot of things. Not long ago, she was helping Mrs. Schulz with some committee for the church. I'll try to find out what that is."

"If we can find some ways that she can talk to people away from him that he won't suspect, we can get to the bottom it. Until then, our hands are tied. We can't go in and drag her out of there," Carl pointed out. "I did think I might want to wander by the police station tomorrow and become friendly with the cop. I'll have to butter him up a while, but then he might want to know about the shenanigans that slime is pulling on his billing his roofing customers."

"Does he still work?" Elton asked. "I got the impression that he doesn't."

"He still owns the outfit and does the billing. He has some young guy running his work crew," Carl answered.

Keith frowned, "I've never heard of a Waggoner Roofing. Have you, Kev?"

"No, I haven't."

"The only one I know of around here is D. Albert Roofing. I don't know who owns it though. I always thought it was a Mr. Albert."

Kevin agreed, "We know that guy that runs it. What's his name again, Carrie?"

"Les Everett, I went to high school with him. We ran into him one day this spring at the grocery store. He said he was working there. He didn't seem real happy with his boss; said he was sort of odd." Carrie giggled and then said, "I think that we might have a cookout next weekend, huh Kevin? And like, invite some of our old high school friends? What do you think?"

"Why, that's a wonderful idea, Carrie. Just to catch up you know, huh? What do you guys think?"

"It's fine," Coot agreed, "As long as you guys are careful not to become obvious. Just find out if it's the same guy."

"You got it," Kevin agreed. "At least we'll be making some headway, huh? Besides, we really enjoy Les and his wife."

"So, what's our plan?" Elton asked.

"I'll go talk to the cop shop. Kev and Carrie will invite this Les over, Matt will find out about the committee with the Schulz lady and we'll all keep our ears to the ground until we think of something else to do. Okay?" Carl reiterated.

Harrington nodded, "Okay. If any of us can think of any way we can find out without becoming obvious . . . If it's obvious, he'll just close ranks. So be careful."

"Too bad we're going to be gone all week," Matt mumbled.

"Maybe not. It will give things time to settle down, so that Wag doesn't associate stuff with last night. You know?" Keith suggested.

"I think that's a good point, Keith," Carl grinned. "For a bunch of Petunias, you are a rather devious bunch."

Elton chuckled, "We work at it!"

❧✦ 13 ✦❧

AFTER SUNDAY DINNER, PEPPER AND Ruthie told the Engelmann clan to move their chairs so they could watch the film of the Hawaiian weddings. They were great and everyone felt they shared the event. The church, flowers and scenery was awesome.

That night, Matt went over to help Darrell and Jeannie with chores. While they milked, they discussed the situation. Even though they felt things were still a mess, at least they felt better knowing they had help.

Then Jeannie asked, "Did you get to see her at Mass this morning? I was wondering all day. Could you tell if she was okay?"

Matt stopped what he was doing, "Mom talked to her. You know Mom. She saw them and went right over to say hello. She told me that she asked Diane if she slept well last night and Diane said very well. Mom thought it was true. So she thought that she was okay."

They all agreed that Mo would be able to ferret out anything, so they were comfortable that she was okay.

The next day, Carl went into town to have coffee with Merton's only policeman, Alex Bernard, just law enforcement to law enforcement talk. They never discussed anything even vaguely connected to Waggoners but Carl started to make a friend.

The Harringtons and Carl were getting packed to go to Boston. They had a list of things to complete while there. Everyone knew it would be emotional for Mo to tell everyone goodbye. All of her other six children and their families lived there and they had been her entire life for years.

That evening, just Coot and Elton sat on the patio. Elton looked around, "Gee, it seems downright lonely here tonight. Where is everyone?"

"I think all the kids are telling their sweethearts goodbye and Matt is over at Darrell's place. Annie and Marty are at work. I suppose we could go wake Lloyd up," Coot teased.

"Not necessary," Elton leaned back in the padded Redwood chair. "He is probably resting up for later anyway. I should tell you something and I really don't want to."

Carl frowned, "What?"

"Well, you've turned out to be a great friend. I really have enjoyed having you live here. I thought I should tell you that," Elton chuckled, "What's more, I'll really glad you're moving into your own place!"

Carl didn't even smile, but looked at Elton seriously. "That means a lot to me. You guys have never hesitated making me feel like I belong, even when I was acting like an ass."

"I wasn't aware you were acting," Elton grinned. Then he reached out and shook Carl's hand. "I know, Carl. It's been good for both of us."

Carl shook his hand and then said, "Let's just keep this between ourselves, okay?"

"Fine by me." Elton sat quietly for a bit and then said, "Ready to meet all Maureen's family?"

"Scared to death. You know if I didn't know Harrington and Matt so well, I don't think I'd have the guts to do this."

"Those boys think a lot of you and I'm sure you can count on their support. They're good people and care about you, Carl. You know, they both call you Dad." Elton smiled at his friend, "Feels pretty good, doesn't it? I remember when Nora's kids started calling me that. That was something else."

"I suppose Pepper did first, huh?" Carl guessed.

"No. She called me 'Ellong' until she started school. I think it was Keith that started and then the other two boys did. I was so damned proud and terrified at the same time. It's hard to explain," Elton admitted.

"I think I know. Do you think real fathers feel that way?"

"Probably. I know they feel scared, but I think they expect to be called Dad. We know that our step kids don't have to call us that. It's quite an honor. I know I felt like I'd never live up to it."

"You're a good father to them," Carl said. "I've watched you. Don't let this go to your head, but I have tried to follow your example."

"Bad plan, Coot. Really shaky," Elton gave Carl a serious look. "Now, you should be watching Byron. Ken is his stepson."

"I always forget that. I just think of him as his real son."

"Lloyd told me that's the way it should be. If you can tell the difference, you aren't doing it right."

"Good point," Carl nodded. "He must have been quite the guy before that Alzheimer's got the best of him, huh?"

"Nobody better, but he never let me get away with much. I tell you, he never hesitated to call me on something. Sometimes, even before I had formed the idea."

"You guys all do that," Carl pointed out. "Hardly gives a guy a chance to get a bad idea in motion."

"It's usually easier to quit before you build up momentum."

Both men sat watching the stars for a while. Carl broke the silence, "So what do you think? Have you wondered if Ian thinks he's in love only because he wants so much for Ruthie to have a happy life? I worry about that sometimes."

"I have to admit, I did at first. But I've watched how they interact and I think that she's as supportive of him as he is of her. You know, she really wants him to be happy too. That's good," Elton said. "That's what it's all about."

"Yah, I guess" Carl took another swig of his whiskey, "What about Mattie? I wish he would've dumped the priesthood before he met this Diane girl. I think he's alot more interested in her than he's letting on. I hope it doesn't mix him up."

"I know." Elton said quietly, "We all know that he considered leaving the priesthood before he met her. They hardly know each other, so it may not go anywhere. She might just take off and go back to Maine once she gets out of Waggoner's clutches. Maybe they really have something between them. Can't knock that either. He told me that Lloyd told him he was heading for the pickle jar."

"I've heard him say that. I think he's right. Poor bastard. Life can sure get confusing, huh?" Carl observed. "I thought that once kids were grown up, there were fewer problems."

"Ah, my man," Elton chuckled, "The bigger the kid, the bigger the problems. And then just for fun, they marry and reproduce; so you have that much more to worry about! There's a reason that old folks turn gray!"

"Is there still time for me to run?" Carl teased.

"Doubt it. I think you're sunk."

As they were talking, Matt drove in. After putting the car in the garage, he walked up to the picnic table. "Beautiful night, huh?"

Elton agreed, "Yah, want a soda or beer?"

"Yes, but I'll go get it. Ready for your second whiskey, Dad? How about another Coke for you, Elton?"

"Thanks, you can take my glass," Carl drank the last bit in his glass. "Could you add some water to my shot this time?"

"You got it."

A few minutes later, he returned with the drinks and a beer for himself. He sat down, "Ready to go tomorrow?"

Carl looked at him, "I don't know. I'm nervous about the whole thing. What if your father's family starts in about your Mom and I?"

"Not to worry!" Matt grinned, "They won't say a word to you to your face. Count on that! All us kids think it is great! Honestly Carl, it'll be fine. Mom is a strong person with good sense. We kids know that, even though we don't always appreciate it."

"What about you, Matt?" Elton asked. "You ready to go see the Bishop? Will that be a problem?"

Matt turned his bottle on the table, "No worse than before I left. Father Vicaro really paved things over for me. I'm anxious to see my friend, Father Jeff. He was about where I was at when I came out here. I'm really looking forward to sharing alot of this with him and getting his input. When I left, he was thinking about leaving the Catholic church altogether. His dad was Episcopalian, so Jeff was thinking about that."

"Talking to him might be helpful to you," Elton said. "What else do you have planned?"

"I'm going to see Mrs. Frisbee," Matt smiled. "She was my housekeeper at St. Thomas' rectory and a real friend. She's the lady that took Ruthie shopping out there before she came out here. I got some photos from Ruthie for her and some of Grandma's recipes. I plan on weaseling some blueberry cheese cake out of her. Other than that, just help pack up and visit with the family."

Nora and Mo came with their iced teas to join the men, "It'll be nice to see the kids and grandkids again. This is the longest I have ever been away from them. I feel like I had a cast removed or something!"

Everyone chuckled.

"I imagine it'll be difficult to tell them goodbye, huh?" Nora asked.

"Hm. Well, I'll have a couple of them here and the rest will probably break into the *Hallelujah Chorus* when I pull out."

"Oh Mom, they're going to miss you a lot," Matt encouraged her, "Besides, most of them can't sing."

"That's true. Only a couple can," Maureen giggled. "Those Harringtons can't carry a tune in a sealed envelope."

"I've heard both Matt and Ian sing. They both have great voices," Nora said.

"I know and Abby and Colleen. The rest? They make shamrocks wilt!" Mo laughed, "And we need to pray that Charlie and Turk never sing a duet!"

"Now which one is Turk?" Carl asked.

"Turk is my daughter Nancy's boy. He is the baby of the grandkids. His real name is John Jr. after his daddy, but Uncle Patrick saw him right after he was born and he said the boy looked like a Butterball turkey. Within minutes, the poor kid was tagged with Turk."

Matt laughed, "Mom, he looks like a Turk and he acts like a Turk! The name fits!"

"How does a Turk act?" Nora asked.

"Like him!" Matt chuckled. "He's the same age as Charlie Ellison, but his exact opposite. Where Charlie is fair, blond, blue-eyed and wiry; Turk is dark, black hair, brown eyes and built like a bulldog. No matter what they do with his hair, it's always sticking straight up."

Mo agreed, "He usually wears a crew cut. He is quite the guy! His mind goes a mile a minute, like Charlie's, and neither of them can carry a sing at all!"

Nora shook her head, "Little Charlie really loves getting those tapes from Andy's Army friend, Chicago. He can't sing either! Maybe they should form a trio!"

Maureen took a sip of her iced tea, "I wonder how come so often people that love to sing, can't? Hardly seems right?"

"So, does this kid dig like Charlie?" Coot asked.

"No, I don't think I've ever seen him dig, have you Mattie?" Mo thought.

"No. He loves fish and lizards!" Matt grinned. "And if he asks you to reach in his pocket, don't do it! I can guarantee you will retrieve something alive, creepy, crawly and slimy!"

"Leaping Leprechauns! I was going to throw a pair of his jeans in the washer one time and checked the pockets. A newt crawled out and ran out of the washer! I nearly joined the Saints that day! I walloped him a good one. Good thing I don't believe in the death penalty, because I'd have pulled Turk's switch in a heartbeat. He just giggled!" Maureen explained. "He picked up the newt and ran outside with him. He loves those things."

"On second thought," Carl put down his drink, "I might just have to stay here and make certain the house gets finished on time!"

"It'll be fine, Dad," Matt patted the man on the shoulder. "They're all cops or married to cops, except Abby. She is married to Allen who works in the shipyards. He's a welder. She works for an insurance company. In fact, they don't even live in Massachusetts like the rest of them. They live in Maryland."

Carl swallowed hard, "I'll never remember all this. How many grandkids are there?"

Mo grinned, "Now you know how I felt coming out here! I'll write you a cheat sheet like you did for me, okay? There are fifteen grandkids, ranging from six to eighteen. Couple sets of twins in the lot, so that boosts the numbers. Abby is expecting in November."

Carl rolled his eyes, "Can we change the subject? I think my blood pressure is so high, my vessels are bulging!"

The next morning, Elton knocked on Carl's door about four-thirty. He had called Harrington, Matt and Maureen. Their plane left Bismarck at 7:10, so that had to get moving. Carl didn't mind getting up because he had hardly slept a wink.

They're just having a cup of coffee when Ruthie drove in to tell her Ian goodbye. Matt and Elton carried the bags to the station wagon. As they headed back to the house, Elton said, "I hope everything goes well for you out there."

Matt stopped and gave Elton a big hug. "Thanks. I have to say, I really am more nervous than I let on about it but Carl has enough to worry about. I don't want that poor guy worrying about me, too."

"He'll do fine if your Mom can keep a lid on him. But you, young man, I'm worried about. If I were you, I'd make up my mind if they gave me too much grief, I'd just tell them to stick it! Please remember that you have another choice. You know you have a place to be, so don't let them bully you. You're right about your disagreements with them and you're taking a correct moral stand."

"Elton, they don't want a moral stand, they want me to be a good little soldier. They want me to accept their judgment and authority. It is a matter of insubordination," Matt explained.

"You know Matt, some of those young boys that priest molested are probably not any better off than little Miriam. We know how awful things are for her."

Matt studied Elton's face and then gave him another hug, "Thanks. Thanks for reminding me. I'll try to remember that."

14

AFTER THEY WERE IN THE air and settled, Maureen reached in her purse. She put a paper in Carl's hand. "Remembered when you gave me a list of the Engelmann Clan when I arrived here? I made a Harrington List for you, Carl. The kids won't be as confusing then."

Carl took the paper and gave her a hug. "Thanks, Mo. I'm going nuts."

Harrington looked over from where he and Matt were sitting across the aisle, smirking at them, "If you two are going to neck, we might have to break you up."

Carl gave him a dirty look, Harrington had self-satisfied grin and picked up a magazine from the seat pocket. Then Carl looked at the note.

> Aaron, 40 is the oldest, married to Terrie. Aaron is a Pct. Captain with the Boston PD and Terrie works at a psychiatric clinic. Liddy, 18, starts college this fall to be a med tech. Pete, 16, and Joey, 14, both play football.
>
> Patrick, 38 married to Margie: Pat is a forensic accountant for the fraud division of the Boston PD and Margie works at the phone company. They have twins who are 18. Lonnie is starting college and wants to be a structural engineer and then Lorraine. She goes by Rain. No one knows what she wants to do.
>
> James, 37, married to Vivian: James is a detective and Viv is a stay-at-home mom, very active in school, civic affairs and the

kids' activities. They have Jimmy, 17, Bobby, 16, Mack, 14, Bill, 13, Linda, 12

Colleen, 35, married to Frank O'Hara: Frank is Public Defender in Boston and she is a legal secretary for a private firm. They have two kids, Frankie, 13, Molly, 12

Nancy, 34, married to John Kelly a beat cop. Nancy works part-time at a Senior Citizen home and they have three. The 8 yr old twins; Tony and Tammy, and John Jr. (Turk), 6

Abby, 33 married to Allen Adams, lives in Maryland. Allen works in shipyards, Abby in insurance and they are expecting their first child.

Carl read the note over a couple times, and it only made him feel worse. "I'll never get this all straight!"

"Don't worry. You will. First of all, you probably won't meet them all at once and they won't expect you to know it all right away," Mo patted his head. The she looked at him, "Cold feet?"

"Ice," Carl said as he put his seat back and closed his eyes. He held her hand until he fell to sleep.

The plane landed at Logan Airport about three o'clock Boston time. Matt reached everyone's carry-on bags from the overheads as they started to deplane. Carl was the last one. As Matt handed him his carry-on, Carl glanced at him. Matt knew he was about to panic. He patted his arm, "It'll be cool, Dad."

Carl nodded and took the bag. Matt's heart went out to him, but he knew he'd be okay. His siblings were an odd lot, but they knew if they gave Mom's beau a bad time, she'd hang them out to dry.

At the end of the ramp, they were met by a young lady and three kids. Carl knew she was a Harrington just by looking at her. She looked like a pretty, feminine version of her brothers. As they came down the walkway, Matt whispered, "She is Nancy and the kids are Tony, Tammy and Turk."

Within seconds, Nancy and Tammy engulfed Mo and Tony was hugging Ian and Matt. Turk just stood there watching the whole scene, unmoving. Then came a flurry of introductions and all the while, Turk still stood there. Carl noticed and felt a kinship with the boy. As the group started to move toward baggage claim, Turk followed behind his Mom. Carl listened to the family chatter as they walked along and then fell back beside Turk.

"I'm Carl," he said to the little boy. "Who are you?"

"Turk," the lad said without looking up. "You gonna be my Gramps?"

Carl didn't look at the kid either, "Guess that's the plan."

They walked in silence behind the rest. After a bit, Turk asked, "You got grandkids?"

Carl shook his head, "No. You're the first."

Turk looked at him in surprise, "Really? Do you know how to do it?"

"Nope. I was hoping you could help me. Would that be okay?" Carl asked without looking at him.

"Might." Turk answered, barely glancing at him. "I'm not a real good teacher."

Carl grinned at him, "That's okay. I'm not a good learner."

Turk studied the tall, gray haired man a minute while they walked. After going down the escalator, he reached over, without a word or a look and took Carl's hand as they walked along. Carl felt like he had won the lottery.

As they stood waiting for their bags to come down the carousel, Carl asked Turk, "I hear you like to fish. Is that a fact?"

"Yah. Do you?"

"I haven't been fishing since I was about your age. Do you go fishing a lot?" Carl asked.

"When Dad isn't working maybe he could teach you how. Don't you have fish where you live?" Turk asked, unable to fathom someone not fishing every chance he got. "You don't seem to know how to do much."

"We don't have an ocean like you do, and not as many lakes. There are fish there though. I just haven't gone yet. Think I should?"

"Yah, because then when I come visit Granny Mo, we could go fishing. I think a Gramps should do that."

"Well then, we'll have to do it. Do you have another Grandpa?" Carl asked.

"Grandpa Kelly. He's blind so he doesn't like being in a boat," Turk explained with a shrug. "So you're the only one I can go fishing with"

"Then I guess it's even more important, huh?" Carl agreed. "When I get back home, I'll find out where all the fishing holes are, so we can go when you come to visit."

"Okay. Can Tony come too?" Turk asked. "He likes to fish."

"Of course. And Ian and Matt."

"No girls, okay? They're goofy," Turk stated.

Carl noticed that Matt was listening and then gave Carl a smile, which made him feel a lot better about things.

Nancy took them to their home that was about a block away from Mo's home. She had lunch in the oven for them. Nancy seemed to be a nice person and Tammy was like a miniature of her. She was helping with the table for her mom.

After Turk told Tony that Carl would take them fishing, Tony got a little more interested in him. Nancy announced it was time to eat.

Turk took Carl's hand, "We better wash up. Mom gets spazzed out if we don't. I'll show you the bathroom."

A few minutes later, they were seated at the table, saying grace. After the amen, Tony accused, "Mr. Kincaid didn't make a cross, Mom."

Nancy blushed a little, "Carl goes to a different church and they don't do that."

Tony looked Carl over like he had just discovered an enemy infiltrator.

Matt grinned, "He's a good guy, Tony. Not everyone has to be Catholic like we are. He's Lutheran."

"What's a Lutheran?" Tony asked, still suspicious.

"They believe the same things that we do, with just a few different details," Matt explained. "One of the differences is that they don't make the sign of the cross."

Tony pronounced, "That's crazy! We're all Catholics."

The decision was made in his mind that he was not to be trusted no matter what anyone else said.

"Mom says you're quite the cook," Nancy changed the subject. "What's that specialty you usually make for breakfast, Carl?"

"Oh, I guess I'd have to say biscuits and sausage gravy. We usually have big breakfasts on the farm," Carl replied. "The guys are hungry after they come up from the barn."

Tammy got a funny look, "What do they do in the barn?"

Ian could see that Carl was beginning to panic, so he answered for him, "Milk the cows and feed the pigs, horses and such."

"I've never seen a cow!" Tammy replied. "Are they big?"

Much to Carl's relief, the rest of the meal was spent describing the livestock.

After lunch, Nancy said, "What are your plans, Mom? Do you want to visit, go someplace or go to home?"

Mo sighed, "After eating this fabulous meal and being so tired, I think we should go home and rest up. What do you guys think?"

"I definitely agree," Ian nodded. "I'm beat."

Nancy smiled, "Tonight, Pat and Margie are having most everyone over to their place, except Abby. She and Allen can't be up until Friday night."

"What time should we be at Pat's?" Matt asked. "I hope we have time to nap. I feel like a zombie."

"About seven-thirty. You should have time for a short nap, baby brother," Nancy giggled.

"Nan, how old do I have to get before you stop that baby brother business?"

"A hundred and ten," she teased.

15

CARL'S EYES TRIED TO TAKE in every detail of Maureen's home. It was a modest, two-story home with a garage that wasn't attached. The yard was immaculate and had tons of flowers and greenery. It was a white Cape Cod design with black trim. The garage sat a little behind the house off a walk by the trellised gate which opened into the backyard. It was beautiful.

Nancy dropped them off and Turk waved goodbye to his new Gramps-in-training. As they stood in the driveway, Mo reached over and put her arm around her fiancé. "Welcome to our home," she smiled. "Come in and I'll show you around."

They each grabbed what they could carry, leaving another trip for the boys. Inside the house was a cozy kitchen with a large table. Outside the window to the back of the house was the yard. It looked like a picture. Carl was transfixed. He was moving her to the middle of a prairie with nothing but dirt for yard. Here she had roses, ferns, trees, flowers of every variety and ivy covering the side of the garage.

She went over to him and took his hand, "What?"

"It's so nice. We have nothing like this in North Dakota," Carl mumbled.

"Not yet. We will. We have a garden area and I'll be planting like Johnny Appleseed come spring. Rest assured. Now I can try different things but still keep my favorites. It'll be gorgeous. Count on it," she kissed his cheek.

"You'd do all that for me?"

"No, not just you. For us and all those little gophers! I was thinking I could start teaching those kids how to care for plants instead of just digging!"

Carl frowned, "Might work with the girls, but I don't know about Charlie. He's more of the demolition type!"

"We'll see," Mo giggled. "I see you and Turk hit it off. He usually doesn't talk much."

"He seems like my type of guy, but I think Tony gave up on me the minute he found out I wasn't Catholic."

"Oh Dad, I wouldn't worry about it. One fishing trip and he'll get over that. I didn't know you liked to fish," Harrington said.

"I haven't been fishing since I was five! Turk just said that a Gramps should do that, so I said I would. I don't even remember how to bait a hook!"

"Don't worry. Ian and I will plan a half-day fishing trip on the ocean. The men on the boat bait the hooks there, so Turk will never know. Then when we get back to North Dakota, we can refresh your memory," Matt clapped him on the shoulder. "Problem solved."

Carl eyes filled with dread, "What if I get sea sick?"

Harrington chuckled, "Turk would think it was really the coolest to watch his new Gramps upchuck!"

Carl turned to Mo, "I sure hope your other kids are nice?"

She looked the boys over, "Sad to say, these are about the best of the lot."

Within twenty minutes, everyone was stretched out on some bed, sleeping soundly, even Carl. When the alarm woke them at six, they were refreshed but still tired. They took showers and got dressed for the evening at Pat's house.

They lived only a few blocks from Mo's home. Now Carl knew what she meant when she said they lived in each other's pockets. No wonder the grandkids all came to her house after school. Everything was within walking distance.

That evening, Pat and Margie had all the family except Abby and her husband there. Carl was glad that they arrived early enough, so he could get acquainted with Pat's family a little before any more arrived. He had always hated this kind of stuff but he knew how much it meant to Maureen. After all, it was her flesh and blood; of course, she would want to see them all.

Patrick was between Matt and Harrington in height and looked like them. Other than his hair being almost black instead of the deep auburn like theirs, but no one would ever doubt that he was a Harrington. Margie was blond and about as tall at Pat. She had the bluest eyes Carl had ever seen.

After giving his Mom a big embrace, Pat introduced himself to Carl. "So you're the man who stole my mother's heart. You must be a fine person because she's pretty fussy."

Carl smiled. He instantly liked the guy and knew he was trying to make him feel comfortable. Pat opened at beer for each of them and motioned for the guys to go out to the backyard. There they sat on the patio. Pat lit a cigarette and Carl was relieved. He asked if he minded if he smoked and Pat grinned, "Not at all, just not in the house. Margie would go into the spin cycle about that."

"We don't smoke inside at home either," Carl mumbled, wondering to himself which home he thought he was referring to.

"Mom says you're retired FBI, huh? I started out with the Boston PD as a beat cop, but now I'm a forensic accountant in the fraud division. I guess I'm sort of a sissified cop."

Carl nodded, "Probably much healthier. Did Ian tell you he is going to a commercial college? Accounting must run in your blood, huh?"

The Harrington men all looked at each other, "I guess it could be," Matt said. "Mom's father worked in the bank here all his life."

"And you have always been a numbers guy," Pat said. "I could never figure how a guy could like math and become a priest."

"Very simple, God gave Noah measurements, didn't he? Otherwise the boat would've sunk."

They were all laughing as Lonnie came out. "Mom says to start the grill now, Dad."

Pat introduced his tall, gangly son to Carl. "Lonnie, I'd like you to meet Granny's fiancé, Carl Kincaid."

The fair-haired Lonnie shook his hand and gave him a big dimpled smile. So far, Carl had not met a Harrington that didn't have dimples, although Matt's were the faintest. His only peaked through when he was laughing. "I guess you're the one that's going into structural engineering?"

"Yes sir," Lonnie answered. "I guess I'm stepping out of the family business."

Harrington offered his nephew a chair, "We were just talking about that. Carl pointed out that there are alot of number folks in the family.

Uncle Matt teaches Math, I am going to college to do accounting and Papa Finn worked in a bank all his life."

Lonnie smiled, "Well, that makes me feel better. Structural engineering is almost all math. I guess it's a family trait, huh?"

The sliding door came open. Lonnie's twin, Lorraine came out and ran right to her Uncle Matt's arms. "I just couldn't wait for you to get home, Uncle Matt! I want to talk to you as soon as we can. Okay?"

Matt returned her hug and said, "Sure, Rain. Whenever."

Pat frowned at his daughter, "Settle down, Rain. You're being rude. We all want to meet Carl and there are a million things to do before you disrupt things."

She turned and hugged Uncle Ian and then held out her hand to Carl. Unlike her twin, she was dark like her father with hazel eyes. She was about five six and slim. One look revealed she was full of the devil. "Hello. So you're Granny's main squeeze. That's way cool."

Carl liked her immediately, and smiled, "Thanks. Rain, is it?"

She rolled her eyes, "Yah, they named me Lorraine Agatha. Can you imagine? It sounds like the name of a warden in a woman's prison! I like Rain better."

Carl laughed. She smiled, "Ah, what do you want me to call you?"

"Whatever you want," Carl answered.

Patrick raised his eyebrow and said sternly, "You can call him Mr. Kincaid."

Rain grimaced, "I guess I want to call you Mr. Kincaid."

"Sounds like it," Carl smiled. "Turk's going to call me Gramps."

"How's the old dangling digits, Uncle Ian? Did you and your girl set a date yet? I started saving my pennies to get to the wedding," Rain hugged her uncle.

"My arm's much better. Thanks for asking. We decided on October third, so I'm glad you're saving. Have you got a job?" Ian asked.

"Kind of. I work at a sandwich shop. Dad wants me to go to college but then I couldn't go to the wedding."

Ian grinned, "What do you want to be after school?"

"A merchant marine," the devil sparkled out of Rain's eyes.

Lonnie rolled his eyes, "You can't be a merchant marine, you bubble head. Why don't you go to school like a normal person?"

"I hate being normal."

"Okay," Pat said, "Let's change the subject. Mom said you have a partnership in a farm, Carl. Is that right?"

"Yes," Carl nodded. "Darrell and I have some cropland, a lot of pasture and a dairy."

"How many cows do you milk?" Pat asked.

"About fifty cows and goats," Carl answered. "The milk is sold to a cheese factory in Bismarck We'll be milking more in the spring."

Matt asserted, "I've helped Darrell milk often."

"Wow! I'd like that, I think," Rain said. "Goats aren't mean are they?"

"They have a similar temperament as a cow, but are a lot smaller," Matt chuckled. "You probably would like it. I go horseback riding a lot with Darrell and his wife, Jeannie, and our friend Annie."

Rain perked right up, "Annie, huh? So Uncle Matt, do you have something you want to share with us?"

He shook his head, "No. I don't. She is a married lady. Her husband is in Vietnam. She is very devoted to him."

"Darn. I was hoping you'd give up all this priestly goobledegook."

"Lorraine Agatha Harrington. Stifle it! Now," her Dad wasn't kidding. "It's none of your business. Now mind your manners and show some respect!"

Rain dropped her head, "I'm sorry Uncle Matt."

"Don't worry about it, Rain." Matt put his hand on her shoulder. "What do you say we have that talk after dinner? We could go for a walk. How about it?"

"Sure, if you have time," Rain said quietly and retreated into the house.

The rest of the family began showing up. There was Aaron and his family, James and all his family, Colleen and hers and then Nancy. He had met Nancy's before except for her husband, John Kelly. John seemed like a nice guy. He was Turk's dad and Turk did the introduction.

"Dad, this guy's gonna be my new Gramps. Can you show him how to fish because there are no oceans where he lives?"

Carl shook his hand and John said, "I think we can work something out."

Harrington told John they had discussed a half-day fishing trip and before salad was served, the men had a plan. They'd schedule a half-day fishing cruise for either Friday or Saturday when everyone was off. If they could get Saturday, they hoped that Allen could make it. It would all the guys.

Matt and Harrington were in charge of the plans and everyone thought it'd be a great thing to do. Carl was a bit dubious, but Matt had given him a nod and a wink, so he thought it might be okay. There'd be eighteen

Harrington men on this cruise. Carl figured if it got to be too much, he'd just accidentally fall overboard clutching an anchor.

Dinner was fun and Mo relished in telling her family about life at the Schroeder farm, the plans for their new house and about Carl's cooking abilities. Carl was extremely grateful for all the woman's stuff he had learned during his months being housebound with Grandma Katherine and Nora. He was surprised how much he had actually learned.

The only awkward part was right before grace when Tony thought he had to announce that Carl didn't know how to pray. Carl decided he really didn't like that kid. He happened to catch Matt's eye. He was grinning like a cat that just fell in a cream can. Carl gave him a dirty look.

After dinner, the men went back out to the patio, while the pile of teenaged boys took to the basement to play pool. The girls, Molly and Linda who were both twelve were drooling over the latest edition of *Tiger Beat*, the teen magazine. They were squealing over every photo of David Cassidy, while Tammy, 8, was more interested in Brandon Cruz.

Liddy had left with her boyfriend to go to a movie, which just left Rain. She helped with dishes and after a bit, came out to the patio.

"What's up?" Pat asked. "Why the long face?"

"Liddy went out with Greg and the boys won't let me play pool. The women are all talking sewing stuff. Can I just sit here?"

Carl smiled, "Well, of course. That'd be okay, right guys?"

The men except Harrington and Matt were surprised, but all nodded yes. He patted the seat next to him and said to her, "Take a load off."

She was surprised and giggled, "Okay. Don't mind if I do."

They all talked about the upcoming fishing trip. It was obvious that Rain wanted to come along but she never asked. Then the subject turned to law enforcement.

After a short time, Matt patted her shoulder. "Want to go for that walk now while these guys relive catching the Cookie Bandit?"

She nodded and then asked her dad, "May I?"

He nodded and she followed her uncle out through the kitchen, where they were accosted by the women. "Where are you two off to?" Margie asked. "Rain didn't drag you away, did she?"

"No," Matt grinned. "I dragged her. We going for a walk. Is that alright?"

"Why of course, Mattie," his Mom said ending the discussion. "Be back in about an hour. We'll have hot fudge sundaes. Okay?"

"Sure Mom," Matt kissed her cheek and the checked his watch.

16

OUTSIDE THEY WALKED ABOUT HALF a block before either said anything. The young girl then turned to her uncle, "Thank you for coming out of there with me. I was going bonkers."

"I could tell. What's bugging you, Rain? Want to talk about it?" Matt asked.

She shrugged and kept walking in silence. After a couple blocks, Matt said, "It seems muggy out here after being on the plains. It's a lot drier there."

"Like a desert?"

"Not that dry. At night, Rain, you can see the entire sky. There are very few trees and no city lights, so you can see a million stars. It's really something. I even saw the Northern Lights once."

"Wow. I'd love to get to see that. Maybe one day, huh?" Rain said quietly. Then she started to cry.

Matt stopped and put his arm around her, "What is it, honey?"

"I don't know, Uncle Matt. I know everyone loves me and wants the best for me, but I feel so trapped. Sometimes I can hardly breathe. I suppose you think I'm nuts, huh?"

Matt chuckled, "Not at all. I feel that way myself real often."

"You do? Why would you feel like that?"

"Rain, people have a lot of stuff going on in their heads. We all feel trapped sometimes, and by all sorts of things. Sometimes even by ourselves."

"How can someone trap themselves?" she twisted her face.

"Well, we get some idea we think should be and then try to make ourselves live up to it, long after we've honestly decided it isn't a good idea."

Rain giggled, "I wouldn't do that! I'd just change my mind. You know me. I'm the one that's unreliable, unstable and almost everything else that starts with a UN."

Matt laughed, "Yah, but just by saying that, you have put yourself in a box; saying you'll be unconventional. Did you realize that?"

Rain scrunched her face again, "Doggone it. Now you goofed up my whole thing!"

"Sorry," Matt smiled as he started to walk again.

After half a block, Rain said, "No, you aren't."

"What?"

"Sorry. Can I ask you something and I promise I won't tell my parents?"

"Sure," Matt nodded.

The young girl really surprised him when she said quietly, "You seem sad. You've seemed sad since before you went out to the prairies. Are you feeling trapped too?"

Matt hugged her again, "Yes. Actually, I do. You're really tuned in to notice. Thanks for caring."

"I do like you, you know; even if you are a priest. I don't want to get a lecture, but I wouldn't even be a Catholic if it wasn't for Mom and Dad."

"Why is that?"

"I just can't get how they can have all the gold, robes and all that stuff when people are starving. I think that's hypocritical," she said sincerely. "I know you believe in all that, but I just can't buy it."

"It doesn't make sense, does it?" Matt agreed. "It isn't just the Catholics that do that, you know. Most churches do. I think some of it because people wouldn't want to go to a dump of a church, but agree with you more that you know."

"Really?" now she was genuinely surprised.

"A lot of people feel that way. I don't think that's what you're feeling trapped about, though. Is it?"

"No. Uncle Matt, everyone's always telling me I should do this and I need to do that, or shouldn't do the other! My whole life's all planned out for me. Every darned thing. I don't mean sin stuff, like you shouldn't kill somebody or that stuff. I agree with that. It's just like since I'm a girl, I have to like sewing and cooking. Uncle Matt. I just hate it. If I had to sit there and listen to the women talk about sewing, I'd set my hair on fire! I want to go fishing or play pool, but no one will let me."

"You never said you wanted to go on the fishing trip with us."

She stopped walking and looked him square in the eye. "Now think about it. What would be the first thing Dad would say?"

He chuckled, "Yah, okay. But you know what? Carl, Ian and I'd like to have you come along. Some of the other guys probably would too, but they never thought about it."

"For real?"

"Sure. Let me see what I can do about it, okay? Just don't say anything right now. Rain, your Dad loves you very much. He just doesn't know what to do when you confront him so often. Is there some way you could see fit to be nicer to him and not fight him on every detail? I think things would go easier for both of you."

"I don't know how. I open my mouth and Mom, Dad and Lonnie all say no before they even know what I'm going to say."

"How's that different from how you act when they say something?" Matt asked.

She walked a ways and grudgingly answered, "I guess I do the same thing to them. I didn't know that I was doing that. How do I quit?"

"Well, slow down before you say something. Think to yourself that you don't want to box yourself in. If they say something that you think you might like, say so. It might be fun to just shock them once in a while. You know, keep them off guard! I bet they'd have a heart attack if you asked them to explain something they're interested in. Everyone likes that. Be careful to not tell them it's stupid right off. And you know what? Even if you don't get interested in it yourself, at least you'll understand them better. They'll appreciate it."

"Like just what's Dad interested in? All he talks about is his work, sports and that crazy old car he's working on in the garage," Rain pointed out.

"There you go. Have you ever asked him what he was doing and ask if you could help?"

"Heavens no! That's his thing. I doubt he'd want me around."

"Promise me you'll try it. You might find out that he'd like having you help him. Of course, you'd have to follow his instructions."

"You think? I could try it. I've wondered sometimes about what keeps him so busy with it. I know Mom'd love to have me help her with that pottery stuff. It looks ridiculous to me. Getting all slopped up in mud to make some old vase. Good night, Uncle Matt! We must have a thousand of those vases around here!"

"Would it hurt? I mean, I know you aren't afraid of a little mud and it'd make your Mom happy. What's the big deal?"

"Yah, I guess it wouldn't be so bad, would it? I know I have nothing to talk to Lonnie about. He's my twin, but we're so different. I just can't imagine why anyone could get excited about how much weight a piece of metal can hold! That just escapes me." She crossed her eyes.

"Maybe you could ask him how he knows how much weight something will hold. I know I could never figure that out. They must have a way they do it. Let him explain and ask him questions. Before you know it, he'll think you're smart even if you only asked him questions. People are funny that way."

"Okay, I'll give it a whirl. I guess I have nothing to lose, huh? I don't know what I'm going to do about college. They have me signed up at the local junior college to just take the basics or whatever. I could care less."

"Is there anything at all you're interested in? If there was something that you could take—one class that you liked. It'd be more fun."

"I have the catalogue at home."

"I didn't ask you that," Matt grinned. "You're a real slicker. Have you ever looked at it, honestly?"

"Honestly, like in truthfully?" she looked at him. "Well, honestly no. I'm pretty sure I'll hate it all."

"When we get back, can you and I go through the catalogue and actually see if there's something there?"

"I suppose, but now I feel like I'm doing all the changing. Why does it have to be me? Why can't everyone else change?"

"First, you have no control over anyone else and second, because you're the one going bonkers!" Matt chuckled. Then he stopped, "I want to thank you for our talk. I needed it."

She frowned at him, "It was for me, not for you. You didn't need it."

"Yah, I did. You made me realize that I've been trapping myself by things I thought were important, but aren't. I appreciate that."

"Well, that was easy. I always thought I should be a shrink!" she giggled.

"You have?" Matt raised his eyebrows.

"Not really. I just think the human brain is interesting. How can two people be so much the same and end up so different! Like Lonnie and me. He always listens and behaves, and I never do. We have the same Mom and Dad and we're even twins. How can that be?" Rain asked.

"What do you think?"

She laughed, "You don't really want to know what I think."

Matt turned and grinned, "Try me."

"I figured he got more yolk from our egg when we split. I'm left yolkless."

Matt laughed so hard he had tears. "Hey! I have a great idea. Have you ever thought about studying Sociology, Anthropology or Psychology?"

Her eyes got huge, "Uncle Matt! That's science stuff. I hate science! It sounds horrible!"

"It is science but it's the study of why people think and act like they do. You might find it interesting." Then he laughed, "And even if you did nothing else, maybe you could figure out how much yolk you got!"

"Okay, I'll think about it. Let's go back and I'll get the catalogue. I have until Friday to get my classes lined up. It's already late, but Friday is the deadline." Then she stopped, "Uncle Matt, if I do this, will you make me a promise?"

"If I can. What?"

"If I really try this semester and still hate it to no end, would you talk to Mom and Dad for me so they don't keep spending the money on something I hate?" She said sincerely.

"Okay, but you have to promise me that you'll really try. Scouts honor?"

"Scouts honor." Rain shook his hand. "I love you, Uncle Matt. You're the only one who doesn't just tell me to be quiet and go away."

"Uncle Ian wouldn't either and you know who else is pretty good to talk to?"

"Who?"

"Carl. Of course, you have to get to know him better first."

"They're both police people. You know how they always think they know everything. I think it's because they have a badge."

"You're wrong about that. Some of them are that way, but so are some gardeners or butchers. You're putting them all in boxes again, little girl!" Matt pointed out.

"I suppose so. Have you talked to those guys?"

"Yup. Both of them. Neither of them think they know everything. Give them a chance."

They walked a ways and Matt started to laugh.

Her mouth dropped open, "Have you lost your marbles?"

"No, I just wondered if you talked to me because you thought I didn't know anything!"

She looked at him and laughed, "I didn't think so, but maybe, huh?"

⚜ 17 ⚜

THE NEXT MORNING OVER BREAKFAST, the family got serious about making plans. The boys knew they had to make the reservation to go on the fishing trip right away, because the trips book up fast. Mom had a list to call the newspaper, post office, the telephone, all the utilities and post office. Carl was going to get a moving company and talk to a real estate agent. Ian had to call his landlord, shut off all his utilities and plan a day to move. He also needed to talk to his doctor's office. Matt had to call the Bishop and wanted to contact Mrs. Frisbee and Father Jeff. Then they would all get to work with their packing.

The boys were able to line up the fishing trip for Saturday morning. They had to buy a group ticket that was good for twenty people. Matt thought it was perfect. That would give Rain a good opportunity to come along and they'd still have an opening if anyone else wanted to join them.

They called and told Abby. Allen immediately said to count him in. When he told Aaron, Matt asked if Liddy wanted to come along. Aaron asked but she had other plans.

Matt could hardly wait to call over to Patrick's house. Margie answered the phone and immediately asked Matt what he had done with their girl.

"Why?" he said, crestfallen, "What happened?"

Margie said "This morning she asked me if I'd take her to the college so she could see if there's still room to get into the Sociology or Psychology class! I almost fell over! I said of course, so we'll be heading out in about half an hour."

"Good. She just didn't know what she was interested in, Margie. Hey, is she around? I have something to tell her."

"That's the other thing, Matt. Pat is off today. When she found out, she asked him if he could use some help working on his car. He almost choked on his coffee! So, they're out there now. I hope they don't end up killing each other."

"Have a little faith, Margie. They'll be fine. Have them call here okay and tell them the fishing—,"

"Oh my God!" Margie gasped.

"What is it, Margie?" Matt worried.

"They're outside. She has a welder's mask on and it looks like they're laughing! I must be in the wrong house! Let me call them to the phone," Margie put the receiver down.

Matt was thanking God when Pat took the phone. "Good morning. What's up?"

"We got the fishing trip lined up for Saturday. We had to get a group ticket, so there are two empty spots. I wondered if you thought Rain might like to come."

"I would bet she would. Let me ask her." Pat chuckled.

Matt heard him put the phone down and yell, "Rain, want to go fishing with us guys on Saturday?" Then he came back on the phone, "She said yes! She's so excited. Guess what we did this morning?"

"What?"

"She wanted to know if I wanted help on my car? Can you believe that? I was just showing her how to weld a bead. She's pretty good at it, if I do say so myself."

"I guess she didn't fall too far from the old tree, huh?" Matt chuckled.

"Matt, I don't know what you guys talked about, but thanks," Pat said seriously.

"I didn't do anything. We just visited."

"Hey, if you guys need any help moving heavy stuff today, Lonnie and I can help this afternoon."

"Gee, thanks. We wanted to empty Ian's apartment today. We'll call, okay?"

"Okay."

Matt hung up feeling really good. It was going to be a good day.

Everyone got the appointments and schedules lined up. Harrington and his Mom set off to the utility companies while Matt and Carl went to talk to the real estate agent. Then they headed over to Ian's apartment to start packing his stuff.

Pat, Lonnie, Ian and Mom joined them about noon with a bucket of chicken and sodas. By evening, the family returned to Mo's place with Ian's place emptied and his things in Mo's garage awaiting the movers. His apartment had been cleaned and he was finished with it accept to collect his deposit.

Mrs. Frisbee had the new phone number for Father Jeff that he had left for Matt. Matt was pretty certain he knew what that meant.

That evening, James and his family invited the four over for dinner. It was nice to be able to visit with each family individually. James was a detective with the Boston PD and Vivian didn't work but was active in all sorts of civic organization. Her schedule would choke a horse. She was running for election to the school board, was president of the Hockey Moms, on the Library Committee, and teaching CCD at their parish.

Besides, they had five children. Jim 17, Bobby 16, Mack 14, and Bill 13, were the boys. Their only girl was Linda, 12. All the kids were in hockey, even Linda, who was a goalie! They were a decent bunch, but all very involved in activities. Carl had never seen a family that spent so much time at meetings and sporting events. The calendar on their refrigerator was filled in from morning to night every day! To his mind, it would be a miserable life, but they all seemed to be flourishing.

On the way home, Carl commented, "Is that a city thing, or what?"

"Is what, Coot?" Mo asked.

"To be involved in everything under the sun? I couldn't take it. Do they ever just talk to each other?"

"No," Harrington said. "I agree it's good for them to be involved, but they're a bit over the edge. It's rare that you ever see them all together. You should be honored. Most of them had to change their schedules so they could see you last night, tonight and then on the Saturday morning fishing trip! It was really something that his boys offered to help out in their spare time."

"That's right," Mo agreed. "They're always doing something with some organization."

"So Vivian's teaching that CCD stuff that you're going to do, huh? Why didn't you mention that you were teaching it too?" Carl probed Matt.

Matt groaned. "No, I didn't mention it. She wouldn't be surprised. Priests do it all the time, so it's not news. Dad, none of them know about the leave of absence. They only know I took a sabbatical."

"Why didn't you tell them?"

"Because they'd all start telling me what they thought I should do," Matt answered. "I don't think I could take it. It isn't like talking to the clan in North Dakota. They just let a person make up their own mind. These guys all think you should do what they say."

"And some of them would be very upset," Mo added. "There are a few that would be insulted. There would be tears and carrying on. You haven't lived until you have seen this outfit in their full glory! None of them are the quiet sort."

"I'll keep that in mind. How is it going to be when you decide?" Carl asked the obvious question. "Then you'll have to tell them."

"If I stay, they need not know," Matt answered. "And if I don't, I'll be far away when I tell them."

Kincaid grinned, "You're a devout coward, aren't you?"

Matt chuckled, "You got that right. Ugh! Tomorrow is going to be an ugly one. I'm going to Mrs. Frisbee's in the morning, and that will be fun. Then I meet Father Jeff for lunch, but about four I have that meeting with the Bishop."

Carl watched the young man's face fill with dread while he talked. "You'll be fine."

"Matt," his brother said, "You just keep cool. There were sensible reasons why you took the stand you did. If he doesn't get that, it's his problem. Not yours."

Matt nodded as he turned in the driveway. "Thanks guys. Tomorrow you have the doctor's appointment, right Ian?"

"Yah. That'll be another thrill."

"I'm coming with you, Ian." Mo smiled.

"You don't need to come, Mom. You got a lot to do here," Ian argued.

"Nonsense, I'm coming. End of discussion."

Carl shrugged and looked at Harrington, "I think she is going with you."

Ian made a face, "Yah, looks like it."

18

AFTER A QUICK CUP OF coffee the next morning, the family dispersed. Harrington and Mo had to hurry to make it to the doctor's appointment at seven-thirty. The neurologist had been nice enough to get him in at the start of his day because he knew of his limited time in Boston.

The exam went as expected. The doctor was pleased with the results of his therapy and his progress, but he still stuck to his first opinion. "I'll sign the papers for the police department, and transfer treatment to your new physician in the Dakotas. I'll send off this paperwork to him today. My recommendation is still for complete restriction from police work."

Harrington nodded. "I figured, but I'm showing improvement, right?"

"You are. I'm very pleased with your progress. What are you doing with yourself these days?"

"I got engaged to the sweetest girl in the world, going back to school and I have a job working for some friends."

"Congratulations! That's great. What are you studying?"

"Accounting, business law and management, that kind of stuff. It isn't a formal college; it's a commercial college. I started working for some friends, just helping out in their offices and they got me interested in learning more about it," Ian explained.

"Good for you. What kind of businesses do they operate?"

"One guy has a couple gas stations with garages and he repairs farm machinery and heavy equipment. The other man runs a grain elevator with an adjoining store that sells farm supplies," Ian explained. "You know, I really rather like it."

"That's great. You aren't doing too much physical stuff, are you? How many hours do you work a day?"

"No. They all understand my situation. I only work a few hours and if I have therapy, class or am just not feeling good, they skip it that day. They're great. It isn't like police work, but it's more interesting than nothing. I was going bananas sitting at home. And that's a blasted fact!"

"Well, it sounds like you have a good plan there, Mr. Harrington. A good attitude is as important as anything else in your recovery. It looks like you have a lot of things to look forward too."

"I do. Ruthie, my fiancée, and I are building a house. Life is looking pretty good right now. Not perfect, but pretty darned good. I just need to be able to tell the Police Department if I'll be back or not."

"I can answer that for you, right now. You won't be. In fact, that'll be in my report. You can pick it up tomorrow, all signed and sealed for you to deliver. I know how much your career meant to you, but I'm glad that you're wise enough to find a back up plan that you enjoy. Lots of times, folks get stuck when they have to make an unexpected turn. It not only messes up their physical recovery, but their minds too. I feel really good about you."

Harrington smiled and shook his hand, "Thanks."

He and his mom returned to the house before ten, with more boxes they had picked up. Carl was packing books in the boxes the moving company had dropped off. "The movers will be here on Monday to pack the truck. We should be able to get on the road Tuesday morning. Where are we going to stay Monday night? Should I get a motel?"

"With all my kids, I'm sure we can bunk in somewhere," Mo said before she went to change into her jeans and sweat shirt.

Harrington sat down across from where Carl was packing until his Mom left the room. Carl noticed and after she was out of earshot, he asked, "What is it?"

"Dad, I feel like I just slammed the door on my life. I sat there and sounded so happy telling the doctor about all my plans; getting married, the house, school and my job. After he said he was glad because my police career was over, I felt like I was in a science fiction movie. Honestly, I had everything I could do to keep from crying like a baby! I felt like all my blood had been let out! What the hell am I doing? Do you really think I'll

83

be happy with what I've planned or am I just pretending to keep everyone else happy?"

Carl stopped what he was doing and gave Harrington his full attention. "I don't know."

Carl moved from the floor to sit by the young detective. "I wish I could give you an answer that'd make you feel better but I honestly can't. I don't think that anyone fulfills all their dreams like folks try to tell you. That's all hype. You never get them all, or if you even get some of them—they're usually so messed up you can hardly recognize them.

"I always wanted to be an FBI agent and married to Cecelia. Well, I got that for about a year. It was great. Then she got killed in that car wreck; the FBI became my hiding place, not my dream job. There were many times when I thought I might really hate it but I had nothing else to do. After I got shot, I thought I had lost everything; which I really did. I figured my career was over. I had absolutely nothing else.

"Now look! Do I get worried I don't know what I'm doing? Yah, every day. Do I wonder if I'll wake up one day and figure I really goofed up? All the time. How long I will be happy annoying Darrell and babysitting the Gophers is anyone's guess. Are there things that I do know? You bet. I love your Mom.

"However I'm sensible enough to know that I won't always like it and I won't always think I made the right choice. I'm certain of that, too. But now, I also know that I have the capacity to make corrections in my life if I need to. I never thought I could before.

"Look at Mattie. He thought he had fulfilled his dream. He was doing exactly what he wanted. Then he found out that what he wanted wasn't what he had imagined. Now, it isn't that he doesn't have his dream, but that his dream has holes in it he hadn't counted on. He's just as torn apart as you are.

"And your Mom. She had a nice home, a wonderful family and a loving husband. Then death knocked and it all went to hell. She hung on to her dream for a long time; but in the end, she realized that hanging on to the past doesn't keep it real. How hard do you think all this has to be for her? She is really throwing caution to the wind with very few guarantees.

"Sometimes I feel like we're all floating without a net and having no control; half an inch from pure joy or total disaster. We don't know. We have to just make up our heads to that. We have to realize that dreams are just that. Some turn out great until we wake up and find it's a nightmare.

We do not know which it'll be when we start out. And at the best, we can be certain we're never going to get it all forever. That won't happen. Elton and Byron would say we need to have faith. I guess that's about all we do have. Some of you are lucky to have more faith than I do, but I figure there just isn't anything else." Carl patted the young man's knee. "Kid, you love your Ruthie and she loves you. Nothing else is as important as that. You have your family and the clan. That's something you can count on. It'll be okay."

Harrington turned and gave him a big hug. "Thanks Dad. I'll just hang on to what I got and take a risk, huh?"

"Not perfect," Carl smiled. "But there's no other choice to my mind,"

"Guess it makes sense," Harrington nodded. "Well I better get to working, huh? How many more boxes do you need over here?"

His housekeeper, Mrs. Frisbee welcomed Matt into her home with a big hug. "How have you been, young man? I've thought of you so often. Come, let's have some coffee."

She'd made coffee and blueberry cheesecake. He grinned, "I didn't even have to beg for your cheesecake. I've been thinking about it since I left Bismarck."

"Thought you might. So, tell me everything?" the gray-haired lady smiled. Mrs. Frisbee always reminded Matt of a pancake commercial although he never knew why.

"Well, I went to the wedding and the barn dance. That was really something else. It was fantastic. I brought some photos."

Matt opened the box of photos he had brought and they went through them. She was so sweet and so interested in everything. "So how's my little Ruthie doing?"

"Very well, Mrs. Frisbee. She told me to be sure to thank you for all your help bringing her back into the world. She hardly throws up at all anymore!"

They both chuckled. "That little gal sure held some sort of record in that department, I must say! She and your brother, huh? I have to say, I'm not a bit surprised. He was very taken with her that day he stopped to pick her up here! So how is my Mattie doing?"

"Don't really know, Mrs. Frisbee. I've taken a job teaching this semester at the local public high school."

"You've always loved teaching. Is it the maths? That'll be good."

"Yes, right up my alley. I promised the local priest that I'll teach a CCD class for him."

Mrs. Frisbee raised her eyebrows. "I hope he's a good sort."

"He is. Real good. He knows all about the trouble I had here and he's sympathetic. He thinks I just need to regroup for a while."

The middle-aged lady nodded. Matt looked at her, "I was surprised you weren't working today. Are you on vacation?"

She took a cookie and broke it to pieces while she talked. "I quit."

"What! You've taken care of St. Thomas Rectory forever! Why did you quit? I'm shocked."

"Matt, you don't know, do you? You just guess who they moved in to take your place?" She looked directly in Matt's eyes. "Father Butterton."

Matt jumped up and yelled, "Butterton! They sent that pervert to St. Thomas! Are they crazy? What are they thinking? He abused at least fifteen boys where he was. He should've been defrocked! How is it going to help to send him to St. Thomas? I think they've lost their minds. He'll just have a fresh crop of kids to molest!"

"I know," she went to him where he was beginning to pace, "Calm down. Matt, I wondered if you knew. They said he'd been for intensive therapy some place for a couple weeks and he was much better. It just made me sick. You'd worked so hard to gain the trust of the youngsters at St. Thomas and I'm afraid he'll just take advantage of it. I couldn't stand to watch it, so I quit."

"Did they say anything to you when you resigned?"

"Not really. Something about my loyalty should be to the church not a certain priest. I never even answered. They can give that Butterton all the chances they want, but I don't have to be there to watch it. I might not have much, but I have my conscience."

Matt plunked back down at the table and held his head in his hands while tears rolled down his cheeks as he thought of all the young boys he knew who were Butterton's favorite age. "I should warn their parents."

"Matt, you can't very well do that. What are you going to say? Don't allow your kids to go to St. Thomas? I thought about all that too. I did tell one of my friends, a gossipy one. She thought I was being a disgruntled employee. Folks will think that of you also."

"Yah, I guess they would. Once they learned I was on leave of absence, especially because of insubordination. Why on earth don't they send that guy to a place where he isn't within a hundred miles of a kid? What are they thinking?"

"I don't know Matt. I just don't know." The lady looked at him, "Now look what I did! I ruined your cheesecake!"

"No, nothing could ruin that," Matt smiled. "Oh, I brought you some recipes from the farm and a jar of chokecherry jelly."

The little lady stepped into the laundry room and returned with a planting pot containing a few bedraggled brown leaves. "I got something for you! I went out and dug it up when I made up my mind I was quitting. I probably shouldn't have been digging in the rectory garden, but I did anyway. This is your begonia that you were babying all spring."

Matt was really pleased and kissed her check. He took the pot lovingly, "Thank you so much! That was so thoughtful. Did it ever bloom?"

Mrs. Frisbee shook her head, "Matt, I don't think there's a miracle around that could resurrect that poor thing! But I know how much you wanted to make it grow. I figured someone else would just throw it away!"

"I'm sure that my begonia is grateful," he grinned. "I'll get it to bloom. You just wait and see!"

"I expect a photo if you ever get it to even turn green," she giggled.

"Oh ye of little faith!" he chuckled, and he hugged the pot.

"So, what about you? Have you made a decision yet?"

Matt got serious, "A few. I have a friend that told me to make alot of little decisions instead of trying to make one big one. I've decided that I won't work in Boston, but I don't want to leave the Catholic Church. As far as the priesthood, I'm still swaying; but between you and me, I'm leaning toward leaving it. I'm more concerned about finding some other way to serve the Lord besides in the priesthood. I'll use this time to see how else I can do God's work. I'm very much in two minds about things."

"It'd be horrible for you to leave the priesthood. You were gifted and did alot of good. But you know Matt, God can use good people all over. He needs them everywhere, coal mines and cabbage fields."

"Someone else told me that not long ago. I want to see if I can work that way. Not many in North Dakota know I'm a priest. So the little I've been out in the 'real world,' I find that some things are a lot more difficult as an ordinary citizen. The collar gives a person certain advantages."

"Yes, but it can also present drawbacks. There're some people who wouldn't talk to a member of the clergy if their life depended on it. They feel threatened by it. So, don't use it as an excuse."

"You never were one to round off the edges, were you?"

"Not so much, as you well know."

"Mrs. Frisbee, you know me about as well as anyone. What do you think I should do?"

She studied his face for a full minute, weighing her answer. "Matt, I think after you think about it, you'll know. No matter what, you're the one that has to live it, not me. You could do very well either way. A good heart can't be buried in a wardrobe, a career or a title."

Matt gave her a hug. "I'm going to miss you so much. I promise to send you more photos. You've always been my girl Friday and my trusted friend."

She hugged him goodbye. "I love you, my boy. Maybe someday Mr. Frisbee and I will go out west. He has a sister in Idaho. We could maybe stop in see you."

"I'd love that! Please do. That'd be so fantastic!"

❦❧ **19** ❦❧

MATT WAS LIVID ALL THE way to meet his friend Jeff. He couldn't get over the hierarchy placing Butterton in St. Thomas! That was beyond his comprehension. He wondered if Jeff knew.

He got to the restaurant pub and Jeff was already there. Jeff stood up by the booth so Matt could see him easier and waved. He looked great, very suntanned and relaxed. He was dressed in khakis and a pullover.

"Look at you! So totally casual!" Matt grinned as they sat down. Matt had worn his black suit and clerical collar.

"The cowboy life seems to be treating you right, too. A little sun and a few muscles! Been wrangling some critters?" Jeff teased.

"A few, in fact. I help milk twice every day and ride horse. I've been helping do chores and even did some summer fallow!"

Jeff grinned, "What's summer fallow?"

"It is when a field is just plowed and left with nothing growing on it so the soil can rest for a year. My friend Darrell thought I might enjoy doing it," Matt chuckled.

"Did you?" Jeff said as he looked at the menu.

"Yah, actually I did. You know, you get a lot of thinking time out in the field like that. How about you? Do you spend your time surfing?"

The waitress stopped to get their orders and then Jeff answered, "I'm getting ready to leave Boston. I haven't been working at all. I was really glad that you called so I didn't miss you."

"Me too. So, tell me about it." Matt said, "I assume you resigned?"

"I'm finishing out this month in Boston before I move home to New Mexico. Yah, I quit. The whole shebang: the priesthood, the church, the whole shooting match! I almost quit believing in anything! That's when I decided to throw in the towel before I went totally over the edge."

"Probably a good idea. So, how has it been?" Matt asked with genuine curiosity.

"Well the first week, I almost lost grips with reality. I was so worried I had made a huge mistake and all that. Then my Dad came up to see me. He grabbed me by the nape of the neck and told me to grow up!" Jeff grinned, "I was mad as hell as him, but he was right. He told me to start making plans. Any plans, even if it was just something to get my mind thinking again and to have some kind of direction. He said I could change my mind down the road, but I needed to do something."

"So? What are your plans?"

"I'm going to go back to Gallup, New Mexico for now. I applied for a job at the Juvenile Detention center there and got the job! I'll start right after Labor Day. I don't know if I'll like it, but it's a starting point. I enjoy working with young people, so it should be good, huh?"

"Sounds like a good fit, Jeff. You've always had a good report with young people." Matt looked at him sincerely, "I'm very happy for you. When did you finally decide to leave? Was it a slow realization?"

"The week after you went to the Dakotas, I attended a funeral for a fifteen-year-old who hung himself! He'd been raised Catholic, but the church wouldn't allow a High Mass for his funeral because he'd taken his own life. I knew the family, so I went to visit with them. They were so distraught, and the church's decision on the funeral was the final blow. They were devastated. He ended up with a service at the funeral home. While we were visiting, the parents revealed what happened. He was one of Butteron's first victims. After the abuse, he was never okay again and he just kept getting worse. His father blamed the church because he felt they never tried to help his son after it happened. He went from a happy outgoing kid to being a sullen loner. They'd reported it to the diocese, but nothing was ever done. There was a lot of talk that maybe the boy misunderstood, had been unstable before or stuff like that. That made the boy feel even worse,—like it was his fault! I tried to console them as best I could, but I knew nothing could take back what had happened to their boy.

"When I got home that day, I heard that Butterton was transferred to St. Thomas! What got me the most, the church wouldn't give the boy a High Mass, but they moved that creep into your old parish! I about went nuts. I tromped over there and told these characters they could stick the whole program. I'm so done with it, Matt. I couldn't even think!"

Matt nodded, "I just heard today about Butterton being at St. Thomas. Did you know Mrs. Frisbee quit when she heard he was moving to the rectory? What an unbelievably stupid thing for them to do! How did your family take the news of your decision?"

"I'd been so worried about it, but when I told them the whole story, they wanted me out of there! Of course, you know Dad has always been Episcopalian, but Mom was a devout Catholic. My wacky brother is upset, now." Jeff smiled for the first time. "He told me he doesn't competition with the ladies. No, he was actually very cool about it."

Jeff toyed with his salad, "Matt, after that first week, I have to say, I haven't felt so relaxed in ages. I'm still really angry about this stuff that's going on, but I don't feel like I'm involved in it. It's such a relief."

"That's great. So, it has been about a month, huh?"

"Yes, I'm just getting my stuff sorted out here. I got a monthly room and I'm moving home next week. I still feel a lot at loose ends, but I think some of that will go away after I get home. I wish you had been here. I could've used a shoulder."

Matt looked at this guy who had been his friend since seminary, probably one of his best friends in the world. "I'm sorry. I wish I'd have been here too. You should've called me. Didn't I give you the number?"

"You did, but I was so bent out of shape, Matt. Honestly after the deal with the kid, I think I was drunk for three days straight! My Dad called to check on me and I could hardly think, let alone talk. He was on the next plane. Boy, did I catch hell!" Jeff shook his head. "Matt, I've never been so frustrated, disappointed or without hope in my entire life. It was horrible. Now I know what folks mean when they talk about total desperation. It ain't fun; and the last thing I wanted to hear was some dimwit telling me to keep my faith! If I had any faith at all; obviously I wouldn't have been in that shape!"

Matt thought, "I guess, huh? Well, I'm glad that you are doing so well now. It is encouraging."

"There're a lot of things that are different, but life is so much better. Matt, I really know that I made the right choice." Jeff took a drink of his tea, "So, how's your thinking coming?"

"Don't know, Jeff. I think I have thought myself into more confusion."

The men spent the next couple hours discussing all the things Matt had done since he left Boston. Matt talked to him about everything from Father Vicaro, the trip to Texas to find out about Miriam's abuse, the situation with Diane, going to the dances, everything. It felt so good for him to have someone to talk to that really knew how he felt and what he was going through. Jeff listened, asked questions, chuckled, got mad but he never judged. It was such a relief for Matt.

Jeff understood so much that his family, though loving, couldn't begin to understand. It was good for both of them. Jeff looked at his watch, "Gee Matt, we've been gabbing four hours! Eleven to three! Wow! And I could talk another six. Want to come over to my place?"

"Oh no! Is that the time? I have to go meet with the Bishop at four. I really don't want to go, especially after I found out about the deal with Butterton but I guess I had better. Can we get together again?" Matt asked, suddenly feeling very sad. "We have to have more time together."

"We'll plan on it. Hey, if you need another pair of hands with the packing and moving, count me in! I don't have anything pressing except seeing the dentist tomorrow afternoon. What's the address?"

Matt gave him his Mom's address and phone number. "That'll be wonderful, Jeff. I'd really like that. Then you could meet Mom and Carl. I think you have met Ian, right?"

"Yes, seems like a good guy. Did you two ever get it figured out about that comic book? Like who stole it, wrecked it or whatever?" Jeff asked.

Matt shook his head, "That's a dilemma I tell you. I still think I'm right. Hey, if you get up early, I think Carl is making his biscuits and gravy for breakfast tomorrow morning."

"What time?"

"On the farm, we got up at six, but because of the time change, we don't start moving until about seven. If you can come around eight, breakfast will be ready. Then we won't feel bad about putting you to work."

"You wouldn't have felt bad anyway! I know you! I'll see you at eight. This was a great visit, Matt. I'm so glad to talk to you again. Hey, is it okay to talk openly in front of your family?"

"Only Mom, Carl and Ian know about the leave of absence. I think they're all suspicious about my feelings for Diane, but I haven't told them. I'm afraid they'd think there is more to it than there is and probably don't understand that we have to nip things in the bud. You know, to not allow it to ever get out of hand. I hate to give voice to it. You know, it may be nothing."

"Okay, I'll watch what I say. Good luck with the Bishop. Matt, I know he's going to want you to open your heart about everything. I wouldn't advise it. From what you told me, you have too many balls in the air right now. He'd take advantage and run with it. He isn't too happy about anyone questioning his authority because he's feeling threatened now and wants all us rebel rousers out of his hair."

Matt gave him a quick embrace, "Thanks, Man. I appreciate that. See you tomorrow."

Matt was less than excited to meet with the Bishop. Thankfully, the Bishop seemed to feel the same way about him and was extremely dismissive. He asked a few questions, said he had been in touch with Father Vicaro and told him he'd expect a decision before the first of the year. He pointed out that they couldn't wait around for him to make up his mind while they had positions that needed to be filled.

Matt was relieved. He never had to say much of anything and he didn't ask anything either. It was never spoken; but it seemed to be understood that he didn't want to come back to Boston and Boston didn't want him back. He had no idea where the Bishop would send him, but he wouldn't have been surprised to learn it was either the North Pole or the Equator. He couldn't wait to get out of there.

Once back in his Mom's car, he started to shake. Matt mumbled, "I guess I was more worried about that than I thought I was."

He sat holding the key in his hand for a good five minutes. He had the strongest urge to go back in and tell them he'd thought it over and he was finished with the priesthood. He even reached down for the door handle. As he was about to open it, he saw the Bishop get into his car. Matt watched as he drove off. Maybe it was a sign he wasn't ready yet. Or maybe he was a devout coward. Regardless of the reason, he couldn't do any more right then and he really needed to help at home.

When he got home, his family all seemed to know that he was upset and no one said anything. He helped them pack for a couple hours without comment. They were all invited over to Aaron's that evening for dinner.

His Mom and Harrington had gone to shower and Carl was labeling some boxes. Matt took over moving them to the growing stack in the garage. When he came back for another load, Matt apologized, "I should've been here today. With your weak blood vessels and Ian's bum arm, there really isn't anyone to help."

"It was okay. Two of James' kids came over, Jim and Mack. They helped a lot. We know you had things to do today." Then Carl looked directly in his eye, "Want to talk about it?"

"I don't know. I'm just sick." Matt started, "But before I forget, my friend Jeff volunteered to come over and help us. I sort of invited him for your wonderful biscuits and gravy breakfast tomorrow morning at eight."

Carl chuckled, "Nice of you. So you want me to wake up at six tomorrow so you can help? Since my biscuits are so wonderful, you might want to learn how to make them!"

Matt grinned, "Okay Dad. Yah, wake me up. Do I have to be conscious?"

"Kid, you haven't been conscious since we met, so why start now?" Carl laughed. "Now, how did it go with the Bishop?"

Matt started from the beginning and told Carl about the highlights of the visit with Mrs. Frisbee, Jeff and then the Bishop. He even told him about sitting in the car wondering if he should go back in.

Carl listened without a word. Matt waited for him to say something, but he didn't. Finally, Matt said, "Well? What do you think?"

"You don't want me to tell you," Carl said while he continued to label boxes.

"That bad, huh? I must've really disappointed you."

"Now how could you do that, you idiot? You don't disappoint me. I was thinking of how I'd like to give some therapy to Butterton that'd really help. He'd never bother anyone again!"

Matt gasped, "Carl. That's so wrong! People shouldn't have to pay for their mistakes with their lives. That's not up to us."

"No, and they sure as hell shouldn't have to pay for someone else's mistakes either! Instead of thinking about yourself, or Butterton, think about that poor kid!" Carl shook his head. "I don't think I can help you. If it had been me, I'd have gone into that Bishop and beaten his few brains right out of his head. I don't care if he is trying to protect the church's reputation. He's just flat out wrong. Unforgivable in my book."

"I know that. I think it's doing the church more harm than good by trying to cover it all up," Matt pointed out.

"Oh for Christ's sake! You're as bad a jackass as the rest of them! God is bigger than all those gutless creeps. Don't even try to feed me that. The church has survived all sorts of crap." Carl made no attempt to conceal his anger. "And look at your friend, Jeff! Did they care about how he felt? I remember watching Ruthie and Zach throw up every time they heard that Psalm thing! That Ezra and Josiah, both dead, and Miriam almost. This young man dead. I think a person has to stand up once in a while and take the heat for something just because it's wrong!"

"You think I should've quit today?" Matt was pale and felt very sick. He didn't like disappointing Carl and he felt he had.

Carl looked at him, for the first time realizing the effect he had on him. He went over to him and sat down. "I'm not good at this stepdad stuff. I know that. I shouldn't have lost it. I don't understand what all you're thinking, so I shouldn't say a word. I really kind of like your Petunia attitude most of the time, especially when you're giving me a break because of it. Stuff like this just makes me so frustrated. I've worked with church scandals for years. I'd almost convinced myself it was all bull. So my tolerance level is really low. I apologize."

Matt reached out to him, "Carl, you don't need to apologize, at all. I think you are right. I just can't figure out what's holding me back. Why can't I just tell them I am done? Jeff did. Mrs. Frisbee did. Ruthie did. You're right. I'm a coward. But Dad, I love giving communion, marrying people, giving a homily-,"

"What's a homily?"

"A sermon, teaching in Catholic school, all that. If I leave the priesthood, I won't be allowed to do that anymore. Ever." Matt looked down at his feet, "Selfish, huh?"

"No, not selfish. Honest. It's probably the most honest you have been to me about the whole thing," Carl said. "Matt, Harrington and I can't arrest a bad guy anymore, interrogate him and all that. We lost that authority and with it, the respect it brings. Does that mean that we have no power? Maybe, but not really. Look at Elton. Hell, he has never arrested anyone in his life. But that old Magpie is respected, because of who he is. I'd be willing to bet that he's probably given as many sermons as Byron, just not from a pulpit but one on one. He has heard confessions, frequently. I know, because several have been mine. I'll grant you, he never married anyone but he probably calmed alot of folks down enough to get them to the altar in the first place! Look at that goofball, Kevin. Who does Miriam cling to for dear life? Not a priest, minister or a cop! He's someone that she knows she can trust. I wonder sometimes if you think that you'd matter if you weren't a priest? Well, I'm here to tell you, you would. You matter a lot Matthew." He patted Matt on the shoulder. "I'll shut up now. I've said way too much and have no damned idea what I'm talking about."

Matt hugged him, "No, I think you do know. I'm glad you're straight with me. I'll try to be more straight with you."

"Yah, Matthew," Carl winked, "That not telling it all; well, it should stop. You'll just frustrate me if you keep it up."

"Dad, I think you just took me to the woodshed!"

❦⤳ 20 ⤳❦

CARL WAS ENJOYING THE NICE quiet dinner with Aaron's family. Colleen and her husband Frank O'Hara and their two kids, Frankie Jr. and Molly joined them also. Frank was a Public Defender and Colleen worked in a law office as a legal secretary.

Carl was glad he was becoming more familiar with Maureen's family. They seemed like a friendly bunch. Frank and Colleen insisted that they stay at their house after they had packed to the point it was no longer livable at the house.

Then Colleen asked her Mom, "Have you talked to any of the older Harringtons? Did Nana come over to see you?"

Carl was shocked when he saw Maureen tear up. He'd been so busy thinking about the boys and the packing; he hadn't noticed how Maureen was doing. How could he do that?

She answered with her usual light-hearted banter, but her tears gave her away. She wasn't mid-sentence before she started to cry. "I really thought that after all these years, they'd at least come over and say hello. I saw Nana in the backyard and waved over the fence, but she ignored me. Then I said hello to Pappy when I put the final check out for the milkman, but he just looked right through me. I guess I never believed that they'd shut me out so totally." Then she got up and ran from the table.

Colleen started to get up, but Carl stood, "Let me."

When he found her in the back hall, he put his arms around her. "My dear Mo, why didn't you tell me about this? They have no right to treat you that way. Why I have half a mind to go over there—"

"And what?" Maureen looked up from their embrace. "It's their prerogative. There is no law saying they have to talk to me. I guess they feel I betrayed them."

"That's ridiculous, Maureen. They have no right to hurt you like this. Is there anything that I can do? Just name it." Carl asked.

"Not everything can be fixed. It's simply the way is. I knew how they felt; I guess I just thought that somehow they'd overlook it. Why I thought that, I have no idea. Carl, there's nothing you can do. It has to come from them. I should just learn not to cry at the drop of a hat. I just upset everyone for nothing."

"Maureen, you should've told me. I want to know these things! Like little Ginger would say, 'I need to know your stuff.' Promise me that you'll tell me everything. Then maybe we can both cry when the subject comes up next time, promise?"

She made a face and then nodded, "I promise. We can talk more tonight when we get home. Carl, I know I'm not making a mistake. I want to be with you."

"And I want to be with you." They shared a brief kiss and then Maureen went to the rest room to freshen up while Carl returned to the table.

"Is Mom okay?" Aaron asked, as he sat down.

"She is just washing the tears off. She's pretty hurt by those people. I think a lot more than she'll admit. But she doesn't want anyone to say anything to them. She says it is their prerogative."

"Like hell," Terrie proclaimed. "Just who do they think they are? I might just go over there and knock some sense into them."

"Terrie, calm down," Aaron took his wife's hand. "We don't need a big feud. We'll still be living here when Mom's gone and the kids have a right to see their great grandparents."

Eighteen-year-old Liddy turned to her Dad, "Dad, if they can treat Granny that way, I don't think I want to see them! They're being unreasonable. I have half a notion to go get Lonnie and Rain! We'll straighten them out!"

"What about me?" Pete asked. "I get a say too! I think they're just being mean. They never even met Mr. Kincaid. Who knows, they might like him if they did."

Matt watched them, "Maybe it'd be better not to make a fuss."

"Or maybe it would be!" Ian snapped. "I'm going to talk to them, no matter what anyone says. And that's a blasted fact! Don't tell me to calm down. Dammit Matt, there are some things a person needs to have a fit about. Everything isn't solved by putting you head in the sand."

Just like that Matt was furious, "What the hell are you trying to say? That I don't face reality? Hide my head in the sand?"

Colleen swash buckled her way into the fray, "We all know you do that. You always have."

Then Terrie was livid, "Not everything is solved by throwing a tantrum either, you know. Calmer heads need to prevail."

"Just because you work in a shrink's office, doesn't give you all the answers!" Frank blurted out. "Matt and Aaron are always ready to kiss someone's behind."

Maureen came out to the dining room and looked at her family, who were now all arguing. She started to cry again.

At first, Carl panicked and then for some crazy reason, he started to laugh. They all looked at him like he was daft.

"I cannot imagine what you find so amusing?" Colleen fired at him.

"Every single one of you is giving those folks exactly what they want!" Carl chortled.

"Huh?" Ian frowned.

"They're probably enjoying their dinner, while we are all involved in a free-for—all. This isn't about if Terrie works for a shrink, or Matt tries to calm things while Ian gets mad. It's about what they did, not us. So let's all sit down and eat our dinner. If we can think of something nice to say, fine. Otherwise, let's just keep quiet until after supper. Then we can go out in the backyard and raise such a ruckus we all get thrown in the slammer." He stated as he got up and moved Mo's chair out, "Now sit and finish your dinner."

They all sat in shock, even Maureen. They ate in total silence for at least ten minutes before twelve-year-old Molly said, "Grandpa Kincaid? Would they throw us little kids in the slammer?"

He looked at her and smiled, "No Honey. Just the big ones."

"Good," she smiled. "Because I was wondering if you could play jacks with me after supper?"

"You'd have to show me how, but I'll try," Carl answered. "Do any of you other guys want to play jacks?"

Joey, Frankie and Liddie all said they would. Carl looked around, "No one else?"

Mo said she'd love to and then Ian gave in. Before long, the whole family had said they would. Carl asked Molly, "How about after dishes are done we have a jacks tournament?"

"Gee, that would be fun," Molly giggled. "I even have two sets of jacks."

"That's great," Carl grinned. "I take it, everybody is in, right?"

They all looked at each other and then nodded reluctantly. Then Maureen said, "I have a penny that says I can go longer than anyone without a miss!"

"You're on," Terrie giggled. "I used to be pretty good."

No one had dessert, but they all hurried and got the dishes done. Then they started the tournament. It was fun and lasted about an hour and a half. There was a lot of joking and giggling, but they all had a good time. It was funny to see cops, lawyers and teenagers all sitting cross-legged on the floor, playing jacks. Molly was delighted to emerge the champion!

Then Maureen suggested they eat the pies that Terrie had made before they went home. The grownups lingered over their coffee while the kids went to watch television. It became very quiet. Finally, it was Frank that said, "I'm really sorry I mouthed off earlier. I apologize. I didn't mean it."

"That's okay," Terrie said, "Me either."

In a couple minutes, they had all apologized. Then Ian said, "Thanks Dad, for straightening us out."

"Yes, thanks Dad," Aaron said with a wink and a smile. The others all nodded in agreement.

Maureen reached over and took Carl's hand. He was trying to keep from getting sentimental. He cleared his throat and said, "Knock it off. I think we should calmly and sensibly think of how we can handle this deal with the Grandparents. I don't want to see my Mo upset anymore than any of you. If we can come up with something, without killing each other, let's talk about it."

Matt went to get the coffee pot and came back to the table. "Maybe we should have a get together Sunday after Mass at the park or some place. We can invite them."

Frank nodded in agreement, "But Matt, I don't think they'd come."

"Maybe if the kids invited them? Do you think they'd say no?" Colleen suggested.

Terrie shook her head, "I couldn't tell you. I think we shouldn't go a park. Let's have it at Mom's house. It's right next door to them, so what can they say? That'll be our last time we'll all be at our old house, you know."

"How are we going to cook and stuff with everything packed?" Maureen asked.

"I know," Colleen said, "Frank, what was the name of that caterer that did that party for your boss? They do small gatherings and bring the tables, silverware and everything."

"Good idea, Sis," Aaron said.

Frank thought, "It is Riley's Grill. We could call them right now because they are open 'til midnight. That'd be great. We all need to get to the old homestead again. For pictures and stuff. Great idea!"

Before long, Riley's had been called and the get-together was set for Sunday at two. Then came the hard part. Carl looked at them all, "Who's going to invite the Harringtons?"

"I'll call Uncle Egan, dad's brother. He and Mom have been good friends and done a lot of stuff together since Aunt Millie died. He'd be understanding, right Mom?" Colleen asked.

"He might at that," Maureen nodded. "He might just."

Harrington looked at Matt, "Little brother, I'd be pleased if you'd come with me and keep me calm. Will you, Matt? I'm sorry for being so nasty earlier."

"Sure, and you can keep me from not wimping out. You're all right about that, too. Okay Ian?"

The two shook hands. Carl sat a minute and then said, "We better get home Maureen. I need to celebrate with my whiskeys."

"Gee, you should've said something earlier! I think I could drum up a bottle or two! You're a man after my own heart!" Aaron laughed and he brought out some glasses.

Only a few of them had a couple shots and then they all decided to go home.

During the short drive, Maureen said, "I was proud of you tonight, Carl. I can't remember a time when anyone got that crew to settle down. They were fixin' for a good brawl."

"They just didn't now who they were dealing with, did they, Matt?" Harrington asked.

"No, but I think they do now," Matt was very thoughtful. "I don't want to start something, but I'm glad that everyone pointed that I stick my head in the sand."

"I didn't mean that, Matt," Harrington said.

"Yes, you did and you guys are right. I know I do, but no one ever told me before. I think it's important. I have to quit that," Matt acknowledged. "Right, Dad?"

"If you think you should," Carl said. Then he added, "Matt, I was thinking about our talk earlier and I want to straighten something out with you. I remembered you got into all this trouble with the church because you *didn't* keep your mouth shut. You didn't let things get swept under the carpet. You reported it more than once. You did take a stand. So don't get too deep into the self-incrimination."

Ian's mouth fell open and he looked at Matt with new insight, "Dad's right! I never thought of that before. You did take a stand when you knew you would get into trouble. I never even thought about that."

21

ONCE BACK HOME, EVERYONE WAS a little restless. Mo and Kincaid decided to sit in the backyard while the boys went for a walk. It had been a long day for all of them. Carl was wondering if he had what it takes to live in a Petunia patch. He was trying his level best to be a good fiancé to Maureen and a stepdad for the boys. He had even convinced himself that he could handle the grandkids. Tonight, he was doubtful. He knew he had lucked out. Her family might have thought he knew what he was doing when he lost it at dinner, but he knew was losing grips on his last thread of sanity.

Major crime families didn't have many more problems and they don't have to pretend to be nice. A drunken barroom brawl is probably easier to overcome than a family dinner where everyone is trying to get their point across. Punching someone's lights out is much easier than trying to get someone to change their opinions and still like you.

He also worried because he knew that Egan and Mo had been close for years. Maybe she'd see that he was more what she needed. He had a history with all her children and was well-respected. And the old folks Harrington probably wouldn't object.

Maureen was down in the dumps, it was hard to believe she was the same bouncy person she'd always been. She felt guilty and humiliated by the way Sean's folks acted, and angry! Very angry! She was embarrassed that her kids got into a shouting match in front of Carl and the grandkids. And she was disappointed because Ian and Matt had both had such bad days. She knew that Carl was trying so hard and now he was in the dumps, too.

The older Harringtons behavior made her feel she had committed the ultimate betrayal. She felt like she was being an ungrateful daughter-in-law. She hated herself, and even more, was upset with them because she knew they were being unfair. She certainly didn't like it that her children and grandchildren all felt they had to defend her.

She brought Carl an ashtray and went to pour him a whiskey. She poured one for herself, too. When she came back and sat down, she raised her glass to his. She smiled, and they clinked their glasses and both took a sip.

"I wish we had our cuddling swing," she said softly. "I feel so bad about tonight. I bet you think we're uncivilized."

"Nonsense," Carl shook his head. "I feel bad because I should've paid more attention to you and what was going on here. The thing with Ian and Matt; well, they are really close. They both had very bad days, today. Ian is coming to grips with some major changes in his life. What he said to Matt tonight was just something that Matt has been beating himself up about today. I know a few words won't tear them apart."

"I don't want this to tear us apart. Carl, you're way too important to me," Mo took his hand.

"Maureen, if kids arguing tears us apart, we don't have much! I know we're way ahead of the game on that. Just don't you worry." Carl said. "I do want to talk to you about what each of the boys told me today. I don't know if they told me in confidence or not, but I want to tell you."

Carl told Maureen about Ian's doubts that he had expressed that morning and then about what Matt had said this afternoon.

"Now I see why that hit a nerve with Mattie when Ian said something about taking a stand. It must've been like a knife to him."

"Yah, but Harrington didn't know it. It wouldn't have been so bad if I hadn't given him hell about it too, earlier. He must've felt we were piling up on him. Mo, I just don't know if I can do a good job being a stepdad. Can't I just be a quiet one and let you do all the talking?"

Mo giggled slightly, "No. First, you'd never keep your mouth shut and second, the boys want to talk to you. They think a lot of you."

"I'm not sure I want it, Mo. I'm just an old loner; you know that. This is way out of my league."

She kissed his cheek, "No, it isn't. This is just a crazy time right now, for all four of us. In a few days, we'll be on the road back to our home. It'll be a relief."

They visited quietly in the warm evening. They were still talking when the boys came back from their walk.

"Want something from the kitchen?" Matt asked. "Mind if we join you?"

"I just got us new drinks," Mo said. "We'd like the company. Come and sit."

The two young men pulled their chairs to the table. Harrington took a swallow of his beer, "We want to apologize to you both. We shouldn't have acted like that tonight."

"Forget it. We were all wound up. It has been quite a day," Maureen said. "Carl was just telling me that he thinks he isn't doing a good job at trying to be a stepdad."

Both boys looked at him in surprise. Matt said, "You're doing a great job! We're just a handful. Ian and I alone have more problems than a dozen regular kids. I don't know about Ian, but I know that I depend on you, Dad. You've always taken time to listen."

Harrington sat quietly for a while, "I rely on the fact that you understand how I feel. I shouldn't have taken advantage of that. I wasn't thinking of how much Mom needed you or how much you needed us."

"Okay. It's over and let's not talk about it anymore. Only thing I want is a promise that you won't tell Magpie! He would gloat if he thought that I couldn't handle it a whole week!"

They all blurted out in unison, "No, he wouldn't"

"Wow! See how fast they turn!" Carl grinned. "So, we have to get serious about the rest of this packing tomorrow. We have tomorrow, Saturday and whatever time we can maneuver on Sunday. What have we got left?"

Mo ticked things off, "We have the basement, garage and attic completely done. All the books, good dishes, my sewing stuff are done. Everything is off the walls, windows and stuff. So, that only leaves the main floor bedrooms and some of the kitchen stuff. All that is left out here is this picnic table. The rest is the big stuff that the movers will take."

"Only? That sounds like a lot," Matt pointed out.

"Almost all the little fussy stuff is done and that takes the most time. Oh Mattie, you need to sleep on the sofa or in a sleeping bag tonight. We did your room today," Mom grinned.

"That sofa is very comfortable. I've slept there many a night. Where are we sleeping tomorrow night?"

"Abby and Allen are staying at Colleen's. We can bunk in with anyone, they have all offered," Mo said. "Just so I know where everyone is. When is your friend leaving Boston, Matt?"

"Matt and Ian, I hope you aren't upset but I told your Mom about today," Carl said. "I thought it was only fair that she knew."

"Thanks, I was going to tell her now. I talked to Ian tonight, too. It is better to have it out there. I should just find the courage of my convictions and tell them I won't be a priest anymore. I can't deal with that stuff, but somehow, Father Vicaro makes it seem like how I always thought it would be. It might be better working up there." Matt frowned. "Or is that hiding again? I don't want to be a quitter."

Carl stood up, "You aren't a quitter. Matt, take your time and decide what you need to do according to what you believe. We'll try to not go crazy on you. Regardless of all that, tomorrow morning we have to have breakfast on the table by eight! We had better be up by then."

"Good point."

❦❧ 22 ❦❧

THE NEXT MORNING, THEY ALL overslept so they were just starting to make breakfast when Jeff arrived. After everyone had a cup of coffee, it quickly turned into Cooking 101. Carl knew the biscuit recipe by heart. Matt and Jeff were in charge of mixing up the dough. Carl drafted Harrington to help him with the sausage gravy and eggs. Mo spent her time trying to find ingredients in her half-packed kitchen. That was a nightmare, because they had only bought a few fresh things when they arrived since they weren't going to be there long. But after a trip to the grocery store and lots of laughter, goofiness and improvisation, it all ended well.

By the time the buzzer on the stove rang, they were ready to eat. Maureen had set the table and she said Grace. Eating their culinary delights, they put modesty aside and proclaimed their breakfast the best in the world!

The remaining things in the kitchen looked pathetically lonely. Maureen needed to clean the refrigerator and stove before the movers came. They also decided that, other than the coffee pot, all the other cooking was over. The stove and oven would be cleaned and only the refrigerator was left for use.

Maureen did the dishes, while the men started the packing. By the time she came back from the local hamburger place with lunch, the house was beginning to look bare. They all enjoyed Jeff's company and he felt like family. Carl thought to himself that if he was Elton, he'd probably adopt him.

The bedrooms were all empty and cleaned. They'd put sleeping bags on the beds since they were still up, just not made. Then they hit the kitchen. It took them the rest of the day to pack all the kettles, spoons, serving bowls and oddball stuff that a kitchen accumulates.

Jeff was labeling a box he had just filled. He started to chuckle. When Carl asked him what was so funny, he pointed out it was the fourth box he had labeled as ODDBALL STUFF.

"Never you mind, young man!" Mo admonished him. "I know what's in them and it's all important."

Jeff smiled, "I see that!"

Carl chuckled, "I just labeled one JUNK DRAWER!"

Jeff left for his dentist appointment and Ian went to the doctor's office that morning and picked up the papers to take to the Police Department. While he was there, several of his detective friends, invited him to join them at their precinct's favorite hang-out Finnegan's Pub on Saturday. He was to meet them there about four or five for a farewell party.

While he was gone, Matt called his father's brother, Uncle Egan. He and his Mom had been good friends for years. When his wife Milly had passed away almost nine years ago, they attended most family events together.

"Sakes alive, Laddie!" Uncle Egan almost shouted, "I didn't know you were back in town. When did you get back and what are you doing?"

Matt explained their trip and all that had been going on. Uncle Egan listened and the blustered, "Those old people should be shaken out of their shoes! Lordie be! I'll be over as soon as I get my hat on. Tell your Mom, I want a brew ready!"

Matt hung up grinning. He, Abby and Ian had always counted on their Dad's only brother to help them through the tough parts of young lives after their father died. He was jovial, practical and rarely minced any words.

As he'd said, Egan Harrington was knocking at the door within twenty minutes. Matt answered the door and was immediately engulfed in a smothering embrace. "Looks like you got at little sun on the prairies. Good for you! Now where's that good looking Maurie? I need a fine embrace."

Maureen came to the door and instead of hugging her, he became stern. "Got my brew ready?"

"Yay, it's becoming rank from the wait, you sot!" Maureen giggled. "Faith and Begorrah! How've you been?"

They shared a hug and said, "Where's this big lug that stole the heart of my little Maurie?"

Carl came toward the door while Egan came in. He held out his hand, "Hello, I'm Carl Kincaid."

Egan shook his hand eagerly, "I'm proud to make your acquaintance! So you stepped forward to put the sparkle back in Maureen's eye, heh? Good for you. Now, where's that beer?"

Matt brought the beer to the patio and they all sat down. After a few preliminaries, Egan said seriously, "Well, little Maurie. I've a confession to make! I have a lady friend and actually, excuse me Father Matt, but we've been living together for some months now. I managed to not tell the old folks so they wouldn't get their wigs in a tangle. I tried bringing it up to them but you know how that travels! It was like trying to bulldoze a cliff with a noodle! I think that maybe it's time we go over there and flat out tell them. They're fortunate, not saintly, because their spouses didn't pass on. They've no idea what it's like. If they want to ostracize you, I guess they can ostracize their only remaining male child also! I want to get married and live like a real person. This is all blarney and they know it."

Carl was reticent, "We didn't come out here to cause trouble. Honestly. Mo and I meant no harm to anyone."

"I'm pretty secure of that, because I know Maurie. She'll cry in silence rather than cause a scene with them! But this is to be over as soon as my beer glass is empty! Matt, my boy, you and your old Uncle are trotting over to see the old ones. Carl and Maurie, you get braced to receive guests because I'll not take no for an answer. But be sure, I'm most upset that they never told me that you were in town. But of course, Maurie, you didn't jingle that bell either! Why not, I ask! Just why not?"

"I was embarrassed Egan. I felt like everyone thought I was an ungrateful daughter-in-law."

"Maurie, you ungrateful? Those people did a wonderful job of helping you when your kids were growing, but that doesn't mean that you have to spend the rest of your life devoted entirely to them! That is the fact of their problem you know! Not that either you and I met someone. They're afraid they'll have no one to depend on. None of the rest of the lot ever show their faces when they need help. They're just afraid that you and I won't be there for their every beck and call. It was always you and me that took care of them. When Pappy was sick, you cared for him. That was for months! When Nana had her surgery, you cared for both of them. Who painted their house? Me and the boys. Your boys took care of their lawn and yard for years! I mean, let's put the deeds out there. I have seen them swindle you and me both, after Millie went to meet her Maker. I know we loved our spouses, but they're in a better place; and damn it all, we're not! We're still facing life, every dad gum day!" The tall, blustery fellow with bushy gray hair and wild eyebrows to match stated emphatically. He gulped down the last of his beer and poked Matt. "Ready?"

"Ready, Uncle Egan. Do we know what to say? You're scaring me!" Matt told his uncle.

"Don't worry. Ain't been arrested in all my sixty-six years and I'm not about to start now."

"I hope you plan on being gentle," Maureen said.

"Maurie, we're going to just tell them the truth and it might rattle their cages, but I'm not about to keep my trap shut anymore. Why that'd be downright unHarrrington!"

With that, he and Matt went to the door. Just as they were about to open it, Ian came in. "Uncle Egan! It's so great to see you!"

"And perfect timing, Laddie. Your brother and I are on an excursion to talk to the oldsters. I'm thinking we need you to escort us. I'll fill you in on the way!"

Carl and Maureen stood at the door and watched Egan and his two nephews go down the sidewalk. "He's a ball of fire!"

"Yes, he always has been a crazy Irishman! He is much more boisterous than Sean, but they're very close." Then she turned and looked at Carl, "Think it'll kill the old folks?"

"Nah. If they've lived this long, they're survivors. Do you really think they'll come over?" Carl asked.

"I do. Egan won't take no for an answer. I'd better run a comb through my hair. Abby and Allen should be here soon anyway."

Egan rang the doorbell and after a couple minutes, Nana opened it. Her eyes became huge when she saw her grandsons. She greeted them with hugs and kisses and Pappy invited them in. They visited for a bit and then the subject came around to Maureen. Nana got up and left the table while Pappy went into a tirade.

Egan sat there and listened to him as if he was talking about the weather, until Nana came back and sat down. Then he let them both have it.

110

"Enough! You aren't kidding me. You really don't believe that she's doing anything wrong! You know better than that and don't even try to spoon feed that to the babies! You're being selfish. You're just mad because she's moving away and won't be here to coddle you every minute! She has taken care of you, done your laundry and taking you to the doctor—all that stuff. And what she didn't do, I did. So, here's the final word. I want you to know that I'm in love with Vanessa. The lady you met twice and won't even speak to. We're going to get married, and good thing too! We have been living together since June and I've been afraid of tell you people!"

Both grandparents almost fell off their chairs. Pappy was mad and Nana was crying! But, Egan didn't stop.

"You have a choice to be making. You can thank God that you still have each other and appreciate that maybe your family would like to have someone too! You can welcome Vanessa and Carl into the family and come to our weddings. You can stop acting like you've been slighted. We always have and always will take care of you. But you can be certain that neither Maurie nor I'll be blackmailed anymore. You either treat us right, or you can just sit here by your saintly selves. Maurie and I have families that have always included you, but they may not be so inclined if you carry on this way. I hope you understand, because this has stopped. Here and now! Either get off it or go on your own lonely road. We aren't hurting you, you are hurting us! Come Laddies, let's go visit people who have some reason. Let these two think about it. I'm hoping that they still have all the good sense that they raised us by. We'll be next door. You know the way. Clean up, come over and make it damned soon. Your time is up!"

With that, Egan got up and motioned to the boys. They all three got up and left the older people sitting at the table. Once out on the sidewalk, Ian said, "Do you think you were a little tough on them?"

Egan shook his head, "No. If you kids hadn't been there, I'd have been worse. I didn't want to teach you any bad lessons. Sometimes and some people, you just have to use a blast horn to get the wax out of their ears!"

The young men both looked at him and then he chuckled, "Now tell me Laddies, you weren't expecting any different, were you?"

Ian laughed first, "No. You're Uncle Egan."

"Do you think that they'll come over? They might not, you know." Matt observed.

"Their choice. I have to go call Van. I told her what I was going to do and she was worried. Think Maurie would mind if I invite her over?"

"Not at all. I think she'd like to meet her." Ian grinned. "I know I would."

Back at the house, Maureen and Carl were waiting to hear what happened. Maureen listened and then asked, "Do you think that's really it? That they are afraid they'll have no one to take care of them?"

"Sure as the rainbow points to the gold. They fussed and stewed when you were in Louisiana when Ian was in the hospital. You and I are their caretakers. You know that. Van tried to help, but they wouldn't speak to her. She did their laundry and cleaning while I worked on the yard. We were there the entire day, and they said not one word to her."

"Good thing I wasn't here, I would have given them the what for!" Maurie stated.

"I know you would have. Besides, they have four daughters. If the oldsters don't want to talk to us, they can depend on those gals!" Egan smirked.

"Egan Harrington! You know that none of those girls have ever lifted a finger to help! Ever, that I can remember!"

"I know and they know that too. So they better get their heads on straight. Lordie above, they never even said anything when Demi got divorced and remarried! I'll grant you her husband was shacking with somebody and had that kid. She should've divorced him but why was it okay for her to remarry? Because she was never at their beck and call! Whether she was married or not, didn't affect them."

"Guess you're right," Maureen said as the phone rang. "Oh hello, Abby. No, we are all here and Uncle Egan is here too. Okay, that'll be great. See you then."

"When is Abby coming?" Matt asked.

"They just got to Colleen's. They're going to be over after a bit. What are we going to feed everyone?" Mo asked.

"I'll call the Fishing Net. They deliver. It will be my treat, Maurie. There should be at least eight of us, huh? Fish, chips, coleslaw, what else?"

"That sounds good," Ian said. "I think Mattie and I'll pick up some more soda, beer and then a big bucket of those ribs and their buns from Jumpers! Sound good?"

Matt asked, "Mom, do we need paper plates and napkins?"

The boys returned about half an hour later, just as the Fishing Net was delivering. The feast was placed on the table and it looked grand.

Vanessa had arrived while they were gone. She was a friendly, outgoing person with a big smile. Unlike Uncle Egan, who had a lingo all his own, she spoke very much like the high school English teacher she was. She had platinum hair, bright blue eyes and alabaster skin. She was gorgeous and it was easy to tell that she and Egan adored each other.

Then the kitchen door opened and Abby and Allen came in. Abby was the next one older than the boys and always considered one of the babies. The boys were closest to her of all the siblings. She was much fairer than they and about the height of her mom. Allen was a tall, blond young man with a muscular build. He was quieter than most of the Harringtons, but when he was comfortable, he could talk up a storm.

They were enjoying their dinner and catching up on their lives. The phone rang. Mo answered and got a blank look on her face. "Of course, that would be wonderful." Then she hesitated, "Abby, Allen, Matt, Ian, Carl, Egan and Vanessa. Okay, in a minute."

She hung up and came back to the table without a word. Everyone looked at her, "Nana and Pappy."

Abby asked what was up and they explained it to her. Allen leaned back in his chair, "I hope they can get over it. Do you think Abs and I should leave?"

They all said, "No."

Then Mo continued, "You're family. You have every right to be here! I think the best thing to do is act like nothing happened."

Everyone thought a minute and then agreed. "Unless they start something," Abby said. "Then I'll let them have it."

Allen grinned, "I hope they don't get Abs riled, in her condition and all! Carl, I am warning you, these Harrington women are a fiery bunch!"

The doorbell rang and Maureen wanted to answer it. She told everyone else to stay behind so she could speak with them on her own at first. When she opened the door, she could see that Nana had been crying. Maureen just put her arms around her and gave her a big hug. Then she invited them in.

When Pappy came past her, he stopped. "Will you be forgiving a stupid, old man?"

"It's already done, Pappy. Come in. Abby and Allen just arrived. Egan and Vanessa are here and I'd like you to meet Carl." Then she looked him in the eye, "I think you might like him."

113

"Does he treat you good?"

"Very good, Pappy. Very good."

"It's as it should be then," the old man nodded as he came in.

Egan stood up and greeted his parents, while the boys brought them chairs. "Do you want fish or ribs?" Ian asked his grandfather.

"A piece of both? Could I do that?"

"That's what I did. How about you, Nana?"

"Just the fish, I think," the elderly lady answered and Vanessa passed them to her. The white-haired grandmother looked directly at her and smiled, "Thank you Vanessa. How have you been?"

Matt and Egan shared a wink. They all visited for a few minutes before Mo introduced Carl.

"Nana, Pappy. I'd like you to meet Carl Kincaid," Maureen said as she stood behind her fiancé.

Carl extended his hand to Pappy, "Mr. Harrington. Pleased to meet you."

Pappy just nodded and shook his hand. Then Carl reached toward Mrs. Harrington and when she took his hand, she said, "You can call me Nana. Everyone else does."

Carl grinned, "Nana is nice. I'd hate to tell you what they call me."

Pappy asked what that would be, and Mo, Ian and Matt all answered in unison, "Coot!"

Nana giggled, "I think I like Nana better. So you're getting married soon, Ian. Is the girl Carl's daughter?"

"No, Nana, but we're all very close friends. Her name is Ruth Jeffries," Ian smiled and took out his wallet to retrieve her photo. He handed it to them.

Nana looked at it and smiled, "She is a pretty girl. Is she Catholic?"

"Yes, Nana. She is," Ian answered with a grin, "However she works at a Lutheran Church and has a room at the Lutheran minister's home."

"Sounds peculiar," Pappy frowned.

Then the family started to explain how they knew everyone in North Dakota and how they met. When they explained the situation with Miriam, Nana's grandma's heart began to open. Carl reached in his wallet and proudly brought out the photo of Miriam he had taken after the Vacation Bible School program. When he pulled it out; the photo of him and all his 'gophers' fell out. So, he showed them that too. Then Maureen got the box of photos that she had brought from North Dakota. By the time everyone poured over the photos and ate their dinner, things were much more congenial.

Egan met Maureen in the kitchen when they were getting the table cleared, "Saints Above, Maurie! I think we won them over. It's still a bit on the shaky side, but I think it might just turn out okay."

Maureen hugged Egan, "Thank God. I was so worried. Thank you, Egan. You have always been a bulwark for me. I've been fortunate to have you for a brother-in-law. I think they have turned the corner with Vanessa also."

"Why I almost believe that. Oh, and I wanted to talk to you. My middle one, Melissa and her husband have been thinking about buying a bigger home. Melissa was so excited when she heard about your house being for sale. She and Kent are very interested. They're going to talk to your real estate man. I think they might be wanting to buy your place! That will make the old folks even happier!"

"That is fantastic! I'd like that myself. We can talk about it tomorrow morning."

"Melissa and Kent have always liked this place, so it would be perfect," Egan grinned.

"Yes, it would."

23

THE NEXT MORNING BUBBLED WITH expectancy and excitement. Rain and the Harrington men, including Pappy, arrived at the fishing boat by six in the morning. Even though he was a good swimmer, Carl had never been a big fan of water, preferring his to be in a shower or bathtub. But he'd promised Turk. He figured since he had learned to dig, he could learn to fish too. Yea gads. He had never considered how much work this Petunia stuff could all be. He had somehow imagined that grandchildren did what grandparents wanted them to do. He should have read those instructions more carefully.

Turk latched right on to him when they got out of the car and showed him everything explaining it all in great detail. He even explained what a fishhook was! Carl was beginning to wonder if Turk thought he was an imbecile but he seemed to be enjoying teaching him, so Carl didn't care.

Tony was a different matter. He avoided this non-Catholic like a case of leprosy! He not only stood physically away from him, he didn't speak to him. Carl did notice however, he watched him like a hawk. Tony was also distressed that Rain came along. Everyone knew that girls shouldn't go fishing with the guys. The little boy was even more upset that no one else seemed concerned about it!

The morning was almost still and the air was fresh. The sky was brilliant and the ocean reflected its blueness. It was one of the most beautiful sights imaginable. It was old hat to the New Englanders, but not to Carl. It reminded him of the prairie or the vast Texas desert being able to see from horizon to horizon with a huge sky in between. Carl could now really understand how someone could answer the call of the sea.

The men were all happy, jovial and relishing the drops of the salt water that splashed on their faces. It was a great day. Pappy's attendance made the day even more wonderful.

Turk watched Carl for the first sign of seasickness and after about half an hour was disappointed his Gramps-in-training didn't show any signs of motion sickness. Turk who had stayed within a few feet of him the whole time, sat next to him trying not to show his disappointment. "Guess you feel okay, huh Gramps?" the little boy asked.

"Pretty good, Turk," Carl grinned. "I'm sorry."

The little guy shrugged, "That's okay. I have two extra tissues in my pocket if you need them. Maybe you'll get sick later."

"Thanks for letting me know that. It is good to know that you got my back," Carl patted the boy on his shoulder. "Not everyone does that for you."

"I will," Turk affirmed with great seriousness. "How big was the biggest fish you ever caught?"

"Oh, I guess about a foot long."

"How long is a foot?"

Carl showed him and Turk wrinkled his nose. "You must have been fishing for bait, huh?"

"Yah, I guess," Carl answered.

"When you get one of the real fish, I'll help you pull it in until the gaffer gets here. The gaffer is the guy that brings the gaff and stabs the fish to pull it into the boat," Turk explained. The look on his face was very reminiscent of little Charlie when he was trying to explain something to the little girls. It was one of controlled patience.

Without thinking, Carl hugged the little guy. Turk pulled back and looked at him in surprise! "You can hug me, but don't kiss me! I don't want any germs. You know what is the worst? Girl germs! They're really bad. So, don't kiss girls!"

"I'll try to remember that. How about your Grandma Mo?"

Turk thought a minute and said, "That's not as bad. She has Grandma germs and they're different. Just wipe it off real quick when she isn't looking any more. That's what I do."

"Good advice," Carl chuckled.

John Kelly, Turk's dad, came over to rescue Carl. "I hope he isn't driving you crazy. He can do that."

"No. I really enjoy our talks. He reminds me of one of the kids I babysit. I call them my Gophers. Turk is just like little Charlie and about the same age."

"I thought you didn't have any kids," Turk asked.

"He isn't my grandkid, he is one of my Gophers," Carl explained.

"How did he get to be a Gopher?" Turk asked.

"Because all my Gophers dig. We dig trenches and make dams," Carl explained. "We dig all over."

"I'm not much of a digger. Can a kid be a Gopher and a grandkid?" Turk asked. "Maybe if I teach you to fish, you could teach me to dig. I think I could do that, huh Dad?"

"If Gramps wants to teach you," John said. "It'd be a fine idea."

"But can I get to his house before I'm old?" Turk worried.

"We're going to fly out there in October when Uncle Ian gets married and I think that Carl is going to marry Grandma Mo a couple days later."

"Is that like when I'm old?"

Carl chuckled, "No, it's not far away at all. It is like only six Sundays away. In fact, I bet you'll still be able to wear the same shoes!"

"Wow!" the he sat very quietly and never said anything. The men looked at him and wondered what was bothering him.

"Turk," his Dad said, "What is it?"

"Can I take a shovel on the plane?"

John started to answer but Carl interrupted, "Not necessary. There'll be a shovel for you in my tool shed with your name on it, just waiting for you to come! You can be a Gopher grandson"

"Did you hear that Daddy? My own Gopher shovel! Cool."

The fishing started after the boat got to the designated fishing grounds and it was very productive. Carl was impressed. The fish were huge by comparison to anything that Carl had ever seen, and the men who worked on the boat did most of the work. It was great.

Within an hour, the wind was beginning to come up and the sky became overcast. It started to sprinkle. The waves became much deeper, and sometimes it was impossible to see the horizon when the boat was at the bottom of the wave. Nothing was visible but a humongous wall of water. Carl was nervous, but everyone else seemed to be aware of it and not particularly concerned.

Then it started to rain in earnest. Being soaked was not the only problem that created. The deck became slippery and the captain told all the younger kids and Pappy to stay back from the railing. Ian rounded up the kids and Rain took Pappy to sit down. Ian wasn't very comfortable because he knew he had a lame arm, so he sat with the kids to keep them occupied. Carl came over to join them because he was still not in the best of health. Tony ended up with nowhere to sit but between Rain and Carl.

He threw a fit and wouldn't have any part of it. He decided to run over to the rail just as the boat lurched. He managed to slip between some netting and a piece of railing. It was only about sixteen inches wide, but just enough for Tony to start to slip through.

Carl saw it and yelled. Immediately he lunged after the kid and grabbed his foot just before he went over. Laying spread eagle, he held on for dear life, thankful that he had grabbed him with his good arm. Ian was right behind him, yelling like a madman.

The crew of the boat retrieved the child and got him back on deck in minutes. Tony was furious and frightened. He didn't mind being saved by the crew, or even receiving a couple major swats on the rear from his Dad, he was most upset that it was Carl who saved him.

His Dad knelt down in front of him, "Tony Harrington! What on earth possessed you to do that? You know that the rules. You never, never run on a slippery deck! You could've died. If you ever do that again, you won't be allowed to go fishing until you're grownup. Understand?"

"Yah," Tony whined. "But Dad, why did it have to be Granny's friend that saved me? I don't like him."

John looked at his offspring and for a brief moment considered throwing him overboard. "You ungrateful brat! He could've let you drown. You should thank him."

"Dad, he isn't even Catholic!" the boy explained.

John sat down and put his son on his lap, "No, he isn't. Did you ask him that when he grabbed your foot? Did it matter when you were dangling there?'

"No. It didn't." Tony looked down, suddenly ashamed, "I'm sorry Dad."

"You should be, but I'm not the one that you need to apologize to. You need to talk to Carl. Look Tony, there are many folks in this world and we don't all belong to the same church. That doesn't make one guy better than another! It's how people treat each other that matters. If you're only going to talk to Catholics in your whole life, you are going to miss out on some real nice folks."

"But Dad, I don't even know him," Tony pointed out.

"And you're never going if you keep acting like a jerk. I'd bet that if you'd talk to him, you might find out he's a pretty nice guy," John said sternly. "I know because I did. I really like him."

"You do?" Tony was amazed. "Even if he doesn't make the sign of the cross?"

"Yes. I don't care if he does. That's not my business, or yours either. Did he tell you that you can't make the sign of the cross or give you a bad time about it?"

"No sir."

"Then you're just being impossible!" his Dad studied his face. "Why do you think you should tell him what to do when he isn't trying to tell you what to do? Honestly, what's it to you?"

"Nothing I guess." Tony asked quietly, "I made a big mistake, huh?"

"Yah, I think you really did. You go fix it and do it now."

Tony climbed off his Dad's lap and sat down next to Carl. "Excuse me."

"What is it, Tony?" Carl leaned toward him. "Are you feeling okay?"

"I'm okay. Thank you for grabbing my foot. I'm sorry I have been so mean about you not being a Catholic. I was bad."

"It's okay. We all goof up once in a while. You don't know me from a hole in the ground, so it's wise to be cautious," Carl said. "Maybe we should start over. Would that work?"

"Probably."

"I think so," Carl smiled and reached out his hand. "Hello, my name is Carl. And what was your name again?"

"Tony Harrington," the boy grinned as he shook the older man's hand. "Pleased to meet you."

"You too," Carl chuckled, "So tell me, Tony Harrington, have you ever slipped overboard on a fishing vessel?"

"Yah. This morning."

"I was wondering, what did you think while you were hanging upside down off the side of the boat?"

Tony smiled shyly, "I was glad I had forgot my pocket knife this morning because it would've been lost forever!"

"Yes, it would have. Well, you're really a lucky guy then, I'd think."

"I really am." Then the boy looked at Carl and gave him a little hug.

Carl hugged him back. "Turk says we can't kiss because of girl germs. Have you heard about them?"

Tony giggled, "Yah. They're gross."

"So I hear."

The rest of the trip was uneventful. Everyone caught plenty of fish and had a great time. Rain had a ball and none of the guys gave her a bad time. Her Dad seemed very proud when she caught one of the biggest fish. No one else went overboard and the rain had stopped by the time they reached the dock at one o'clock. However, Carl figured he had landed the biggest catch of all. He couldn't wait to get home to tell Mo.

❧ 24 ❧

WHILE THE GANG WAS FISHING, Egan and Van came over with Melissa and Kent. After talking to the real estate agent, the deal was made. The kids would buy the place. That made everyone very pleased, especially Nana. Egan made it a point to warn her not to take advantage of their better natures.

He assured them that he and Van would watch out for them as would Melissa and Kent. Then Maureen told them that Carl had promised they'd come to Boston very often to visit and see them. She also let them know that her other kids'd do whatever they could for them. If they needed someone was ill or something, she'd come and care for them. Nana was very relieved and promised that Pappy would be too.

When the fishermen returned, they all had lunch at Nana's. By two o'clock, the four were back in their home, putting the finishing touches on the packing. At three thirty, they declared it finished!—and so were they. They were all tired out, but it felt good to have everything in order.

Maureen and Carl got ready to go for dinner with her card buddy friends and were looking forward to getting home at a fairly early time. They were beat.

Matt and Ian showered and took off for their evening plans. Ian would go meet up with his buddies at Finnegan's. Ian was looking forward to hanging with his old buddies and tipping more than a few. He'd have some of the guys drop him off at Jeff's place because he and Matt were going to bunk there for the night.

Matt helped Jeff finish the packing that he had left and then ordered some chicken. Jeff had almost a full case of beer that they decided it was not a good idea to take it back to New Mexico. It would take up so much room, and probably not travel well. They concluded that they should just drink it so that it wouldn't be wasted

The two men talked about everything for several hours. Matt was so relieved to tell Jeff about his crisis of conscience and his feelings for Diane in more detail than their visit before. Jeff was compassionate and very understanding. He was able to open up to Matt about his concerns about his decision. He was still very nervous about what he'd done, even more than he had let on before.

"It's not easy to walk away, you know. I know I had to, but there isn't a day go by that I don't wonder. I hope things go well in Gallup. I'm not sure how I'll handle it. It should get better but I wouldn't want to bet. Maybe I am being disobedient and strong-willed. Maybe I had no real reason to stomp out. I think you're better doing it more slowly like you are. Or, maybe there's no easy way to do it," Jeff confided.

"I feel so torn. And then this attraction to Diane, I've never felt like this before. I know I should just stay as far away as possible, but I don't want to. I've been very careful to not tell Father Vicaro about her and am scared to death she'll find out I'm a priest. What the hell's the matter with me? I don't even know her that well." Matt set his bottle on the table, "I'm not one bit certain how much of leaving has to do with her and how much it has to do with all other business."

"Matt, don't put that out there. You were fed up with the Butterton deal before you ever knew she existed. I think that you're probably less likely to stay away from her because you've already made up your mind, way down deep." Jeff looked him straight in the eye, "You know you can't keep condoning this. I think you're still trying to hold on to the ideal. I know I did. It's a great idea, being a good priest. You probably wouldn't even get to stay in North Dakota with that Vicaro. You'd be sent from this diocese and I can about tell you if the Bishop thinks you want to go there, you won't. Discipline you know.

"Maybe some guys can sidestep the arbitrary rules the church has! They were often made for less than noble reasons. Now millions are trying to keep these rules and getting all messed up in the process. We've talked about it many times, even before Butterton. I agree. It's just too bad that you didn't get this out of the way before you met her, but anyone who really knows you, knows better."

"That's what my friend Elton said when we talked. He also said that God must be putting her in front of me for a reason. Maybe to help me make my decision. Gee Jeff, I have messed my life up so royally, I can't believe it," Matt almost cried.

Jeff threw his arm over his pal's shoulder and broke into a big drunken grin, "You and me both! Here's to us!"

They had just clinked their bottles and were laughing when there was a pounding at the door. Jeff opened it and there was a detective and a uniformed policeman helping one very intoxicated Ian into the room. The cop asked, "Does this guy belong here?"

Jeff chuckled, "Sadly, he does. You guys want a drink?"

"No thanks," the detective hiccoughed. "I think we've had enough already. Well, now O'Malley here gets to take me home before my old lady kills me!"

O'Malley laughed, "That's what I need. A good case of domestic violence!"

The next morning was painful for the three boys. None of them felt very well when Jeff's alarm went off. They met Mo and Carl for breakfast at a local café and then went to church. Carl, Matt and Jeff went to the Lutheran church while Ian took his Mom to their home church. It was great for her to see many of her old friends there.

After church, they told Jeff goodbye and he left for New Mexico. He announced that he wasn't planning on traveling very far that first day at all. If he could, he'd try to make it to North Dakota for the weddings, but didn't know how his schedule would work out. Anyway, he planned on seeing them soon.

As Matt and Carl watched him drive away, Carl patted Matt's back. "You'll see him again. He's a great friend. I thought to myself that Elton would adopt him! You know, he'd make great clan material."

Matt looked at his soon to be stepdad and grinned, "I think that you'd adopt him too, huh?"

"Yup, I would. I hope he helped you bury some ghosts," Carl gave Matt a serious look. "Especially about Diane."

Matt squinted at him, "You old fox. Yes, he did."

"Did he point out to you that you are mixing up the two? Leaving the priesthood and your feelings for her?"

"Yes, he did. He helped me see that. He thought maybe it is because I've really made up my mind to leave and so am not as interested in trying to stay away from her," Matt said as they got into the car. "He might be right. It is crazy, because we haven't even dated or anything. I don't know what my problem is."

"It is something that happens to all us, you know. You can just talk to some gal and it's like there is more. Maybe it is a wavelength, or pure unadulterated lust," Carl chuckled.

"Nice. Real nice," Matt scowled. "Is that how you thought about Mom? Unadulterated lust?"

"Nope," Carl chuckled. "But when we first talked, I have to admit I felt some sort of a connection. At first, I thought it was some drug they gave me at the hospital, but then I realized I didn't feel that way about anyone else. Crazy thing. Don't understand it one bit."

"Me either. I should ask Ian if he felt that way about Ruthie," Matt said. "Oh, I don't need to ask. I know they both did. When he came to pick her up at the rectory that day, Mrs. Frisbee and I could both tell they had a connection and I don't think they even knew it."

"Yah. Well, let's go hit this picnic thing. I really like the family and your Mom's friends, but it was nice this morning to be with just us. Don't get me wrong, I think they are great, but I feel like a spectacle most of the time."

Matt cracked up, "I imagine you do. I would've thought you'd be used to being a spectacle after all these years! Well, tomorrow we'll be on our way home. I'll be glad to get back. I wonder what has all gone on there while we were away?"

"Hard to say," Carl mumbled. "I honestly used to think that living in a Petunia patch would be quiet and downright boring, you know—nothing ever going on! Boy was I wrong! Good grief, I can hardly keep up."

"You and your Petunias!" Matt laughed. "It's a treacherous patch you live in, Dad. You might as well get used to it."

"Good grief," Carl groaned. "Magpie's crew probably has that Waggoner guy all strung up by now, Lloyd has his car hotwired and Miriam will be walking. Oh, and the new cows should be there. How soon does your school start when we get back?"

"The day after Labor Day. Both of the schools. I'm a nervous wreck," Matt admitted.

"Ah, you'll do fine with the classes. It's the lollygagging that keeps you hopping. How soon do you plan on telling Father Vicaro that you're leaving?"

"I don't know yet if I am. Jeff pointed out that I probably wouldn't be sent to North Dakota, especially if this Bishop knew that's what I wanted. He wants me to learn discipline. If I had to leave North Dakota now, I don't think I'd even consider staying in the priesthood."

"You should tell Diane."

"Yes, I know. But you tell me, what can I say to her? Really? She has her hands full as it is and the last thing she needs is to hear my problems."

Carl looked straight at him, "Besides, you really don't want her to know, do you?"

Matt waited for the light to change before he answered. "No, I really don't."

"I understand, but Mattie," Carl added. "Don't let it go too long. You're creating a problem. It isn't fair for her not to know."

Matt nodded, "I know."

Then Carl laughed, "Don't worry, I'll keep on you!"

Everyone gathered for the picnic and it was a lot of fun. When Abby and Allen left at six to get home for work the next day, the rest of the folks took it as their cue to leave too. The four were sad to say goodbye but glad they left. They were all tired. They picked up the bits of trash and hit their sleeping bags. The movers would be there at seven.

❧ 25 ❧

THE NEXT MORNING, THE ALARM was too loud and very obnoxious. However, everyone was up and dressed before the movers arrived. Rain came over as did Aaron and Nancy. The more things that went into the van, the sadder Maureen became. By the time the van door closed and the movers drove off, Mo was in tears.

No matter what anyone said or did, seemed to make any difference. She was just sad. Putting many years of her life in the back of a truck was sad. She wouldn't change a bit of it, but her tears didn't understand that.

It was Rain who brought her out of it. "Granny, for goodness sakes, you have to go and get all ready for your big wedding. I want to be a bridesmaid, you know. I'm sure you just forgot to ask me, right? Then Mom and Dad will have to let me come along! And maybe I can even stay there with you! Wouldn't that be swell?"

Mo giggled, "Yah, it really would be. So, what would you do in North Dakota?"

"Uncle Matt says he helps milk goats and rides horse. I could do that, I think. Maybe I could get a job talking? I'm good at that. So, do I get to be a bridesmaid?"

"I hadn't even thought about it, at all. You really wouldn't want to be your old Granny's bridesmaid, would you?"

"Of course, as long as the dresses aren't all ruffles and pink! Then forget it," Rain was on a roll. "I was thinking something more plainer. You know. Like a Jackie Kennedy kind of look."

"That does sound nice," Mo said. "I don't know even who we're going to have. All I know it Mattie is giving away the bride."

"That isn't very much. I'm disappointed. I thought you'd have all sorts of stuff planned."

Carl overheard the conversation. "I think Rain would be a good bridesmaid!"

Mo thought, "I have to have Nora. She's like my best friend up there. Okay, Rain. You'll be one of my bridesmaids. I was thinking we would have a tiny, family ceremony, but it doesn't look like it. I'll talk to your Mom and we'll get your dress all worked out. You have to make me a promise though."

"What is that?" Rain asked reluctantly. "I never like it when someone says that."

"To really study at school and get good grades."

"Oh that's okay. I already promised Uncle Matt that." The young girl was excited, "I just can't wait, Granny. You promise you'll call or write me as soon as you know. Okay? I can't wait! It'll be the most fun ever."

Right after a quick lunch at Nana and Pappy's, the family waved goodbye. Turk and Tony were there to say goodbye and so Turk could remind Carl to get his shovel. Most of the family showed up and there were hugs and tears all around. It was a good thing that the weddings were only six weeks away because it gave everyone something to look forward to. Over lunch, Pappy even announced that he and Nana would be out for the weddings, with Egan and Van!

Matt and Ian drove Ian's car and Carl drove Maureen's. They drove a lot further than they originally planned, but seemed to want to get some distance put away. They finally stopped a little east of Cleveland, Ohio for the night.

That night they called Schroeders to let them know they were ahead of schedule. It was exciting to talk to everyone and know that they'd be waiting for them. No one got to talk very long, because once Ian and Ruthie got on the phone; it was over for everyone else. Carl, Mo and Matt walked over to the coffee shop and ordered their supper, while Ian continued to talk.

After they gave their order, Carl chuckled, "I don't know about Ian and Ruthie! Good grief, he talked to her yesterday. What could they have to talk about?"

Mo poked him, "Sweet nothings."

"Rain is quite the girl," Carl grinned. "I really like her. She seems to be having a hard time trying to figure out what to do with her life."

"She'll be fine," Mo giggled. "She just dislikes being stuck in the conventional roles. You know, in the sixties, high school counselors told girls their job choices were to be a nurse, teacher or a secretary. If you went to Catholic school, you could be a nun. That was it! Look at all the options a boy has! In the last couple years it's finally beginning to open up more choices for women. Can you imagine telling little Ginger that is all that she could be when she grew up?"

They all laughed. Ginger was one of Carl's Gophers. Pastor Ellison's little girl was a real tomboy and loved dirt. She was the original gopher. She was probably the only little girl in North America that had a dirt collection in her room. She had at least a hundred jars of dirt from all over the world. The seven-year-old studied it, drew it, read about it and thought about it! It was amazing.

Matt looked up from the menu, "I wonder what she'll be when she grows up? Wouldn't it be something if she became an old-fashioned housewife and her sister Katie became a daredevil?"

"Never happen," Mo giggled. "Katie isn't of that nature. She is such a little lady and definitely the most domestic of anyone in their household. Have you seen her needlework? For a fourteen-year-old girl, she's fantastic! It looks to me like Ken will be a mechanic like his Uncle Elton."

"I don't know about that," Matt suggested. "He is a good at that, but he likes a lot of things. I bet he becomes a minister."

"Really?" Carl leaned back. "I'd have never thought that! Hmm, I guess I could see it though. I could see Katie being a minister. Well, now Charlie. I know he won't be a preacher!"

Everyone was thinking about that when Ian joined them. "Why are you all grinning?"

"We're just talking about what Charlie would be when he grows up!" Mo giggled.

"I think," Ian said seriously, "We should be wondering if he'll grow up! Ruthie just told me his latest adventure. Seems he adjusted the outflow from the downspout from the house, and redirected it. It rained real hard and washed out his dam. It ran directly to Uncle Elton's garage and flooded it! I guess there was about two inches of water on the floor! He's in big time trouble!"

"Did Elton skin him?" Coot asked in horror.

"No. You know Elton. He huffed and puffed, but never really got too mad. He did make him help clean out the whole garage. That thing is huge. How many cars does it hold anyway?" Ian asked. "At least eight and then the area at the end where we put together the model planes! It's enormous. So, Charles is in charge of cleaning it out. He started working on it this morning. Ruthie said by noon, the little rat had decided that he was going to use concrete to build his next dams so they won't wash out! Keith and Darrell were trying to convince him that he should never, ever work with concrete! The pictures that flash through your mind when you think of Charlie with a bag of concrete make you hair fall out!"

"Amen," Matt said. "I love that little guy, but he's a ball of fire."

"So is Turk," Carl grinned. "I can't wait for Turk and Charlie to meet each other!"

Ian's eyes got huge, "Man, I can! That's something that doesn't need to happen in like forever! And that's a blasted fact!"

"I was thinking I'd like them to be my ring bearers!" Coot smirked.

"Oh dear God, no!" Matt and Ian both gasped. "Mom, say no!"

"Honey," Mo giggled. "Do you honestly think that'd be a good idea?"

"No," Carl laughed, "But it would keep everyone's eyes off me! Everyone almost died when Zach and Suzy had Charlie at their wedding. He did a good job!"

"I wouldn't want to press my luck!" Mo pointed out. "We'd probably come down the aisle and fall into so drainage ditch that Charlie had dug! Besides we don't need two ring bearers!"

"Maybe they could light the candles?" Carl suggested.

"Yah," Ian nodded, "I'm sure St. Johns wants to build a new sanctuary after a massive fire. Remember when Charlie brought that straw to church? He had enough straw stuffed under his shirt to feed fifty horses and it was spread all over the church before he was done. And don't kid me, Dad. You wanted to clobber him!"

"Yah," Carl nodded. "I have to admit, I really did. But you know, he was trying to do me a favor. He just wanted to weave me some gold like in that fairy tale."

Matt nodded to the waitress when she set down his soup, "I don't know Dad. I'd suggest you sincerely give this alot of thought! A real lot! And then if you have them in the wedding, what about the Gopher girls? Ginger is okay, but what about Miriam? She is getting so she wants to be a part of everything the other kids are in, so I don't think that she'd be happy to sit with Uncle Elton like she did at Zach's wedding. She'll want to be with Ginger."

"That's true. I don't know if she could handle being a flower girl, do you?" Carl asked. "Or could she?"

"I don't know if she'll even be able to walk well enough. However, Ruthie did say that she is walking on her own now. Kevin rigged up a little walker thing for her and she can really get around. They're all hoping she can walk without it on her own in a couple weeks. That mess with the chicken pox really set her back again. But I think that her hip is finally healed enough so she'll be able to walk again." Ian shook his head. "I can't wait until she can go a whole week without having one panic attack."

"She is getting there," Mo pointed out. "Remember how she was when we got her down in Louisiana? Gee, she was lucky if she weighed twenty pounds. She is still really tiny."

"Zach said she'll be small like Ruthie, but of course that malnutrition and neglect sure didn't help. She isn't very big now." Ian said. "Ruthie and I took her to Merton with us one day and we saw some kids her age. They were almost all twice as big as her!"

"I noticed that at the Bible School program," Carl nodded. "You know, I have to say something though and please don't think I'm awful. I love it when she cuddles into your arms like she does. If that doesn't jerk your heartstrings, you have to be stone."

"She never does that to a woman." Mo pointed out. "The closest she comes to doing that is to Carrie. Not even Marly, who is with her almost all the time. I guess the specter of her mother looms very large in the poor kid's mind. That woman must have been a piece of work."

"She was deranged, Mo," Carl explained. "I wonder what the hell all happened to her. I guarantee it wasn't good at all. It makes one grateful that Ruthie and Zach turned out like they did. Those two are wonderful people."

The next morning, the family got on the road early. By coffee break, Mo and Carl had finished up all their wedding plans. By the time they stopped for lunch in Indiana, they had been changed.

The two younger Harringtons had a great chance to visit while they were driving also. They talked more and in more detail, than they had in years. It was good and they both felt they had a true confidant in each other. However, with all their talk, they still never remembered what actually happened with the comic book, except that they both felt maligned.

By the time the family checked into their Des Moines motel that night, Mo and Carl had finalized their plans. It was going to be a surprise and the boys were actually afraid to hear what they had ended up with!

The next morning, they all overslept. It had been a couple days of heavy driving and they were beat. It wasn't until eleven that they had finished their breakfasts and were ready to get on the road. They decided to only drive to Fargo. They would stay there that night and then be fairly rested when they got home Friday afternoon. They would have Labor Day weekend before they had to get into the groove again.

25

FRIDAY AFTERNOON ABOUT FOUR, THE family drove into Merton, North Dakota. They were all delighted to be there for a variety of reasons. It'd been good to see the family out in Boston but it was even better to be home.

The next few months would bring tremendous changes to all of them, but some were eagerly anticipated. As with any change however, came uncertainty. They all had a large measure of that too.

When they drove down main street of the sleep little town of Merton, Ian looked over at the Farmer's Union Elevator and Schroeder's Garage. That's where his career would now be. He loved those guys; Doug who ran the elevator and Elton who ran the garage, but it was a total career change for him. The thing he was most certain of was his Ruthie. He knew their life wouldn't be perfect, but he also knew he didn't want to have a life without her.

Maureen was worried about getting settled in her new house and building a good life with Carl. She'd lived in Boston all her life and this would be so different. She was confident that she could count on Nora Schroeder, Marly Ellison and Grandma Katherine. They could help her through anything. She also knew that she'd miss her kids that were still out East and the life she had there. Some of those friends she had known for decades. She'd miss them terribly. However, she loved Carl and looked forward to their life together.

Matt could see the Merton School as they passed by. In a few days, he'd be a teacher in a public school. Few folks knew he was a priest and he wanted it that way. But right now, he had one foot in both worlds and

133

knew he couldn't do that for long. He'd have to make up his mind. In truth, he was so torn that he had seriously considered just running away from everyone and everything. He was alone. He could do it. But he also knew that he'd let way too many really wonderful folks down if he did that.

Carl was probably the most unsure and yet the most certain of the lot. He knew what he wanted. He wanted to be Mo's husband and stepdad to her kids. He wanted to be the head of the Gopher Brigade and Darrell's partner in the dairy. That he knew. What he didn't know was himself! He should be able to do all of it, if he could trust himself. And he didn't. This was all new territory for the old loner. If he could just keep himself in check, he could make it in the Petunia Patch. Keeping his old self in check, now that was the fly in the ointment.

Everyone breathed a sigh of relief when the gravel road passed Trinity Lutheran Church. It was only a mile until they were home. When they turned into the Schroeder yard and stopped in front of the house, folks started to appear.

Grandma and Nora came running out of the house, as did Annie. Ruthie was in Ian's arms before he was all the way out of the car. Just then, Elton showed up in his car. Little Charlie came whirling across the yard heading for them as fast as his little legs could carry him. He had his big floppy Chicken Man hat on tied on with a piece of purple yarn. Mo looked at Coot and they just laughed. There were hugs and kisses all around and one mid-air jump into Matt's arms from little Charlie and they knew they were home.

They all went into the house where Ginger and Miriam were waiting with Katie. When they came in, Ginger told them to all stop at the door. "You have to see this. Watch real good!"

Miriam came to the kitchen door from the living room with Katie behind her. Miriam was had such a big smile and was so proud. Slowly, the little sweetheart walked with her little walker that Kevin had made for her, toward the family. Everyone clapped and she giggled. "Gopher walk."

Coot couldn't stand it and picked her up before she crossed the whole room. He gave her a hug and with tears in his eyes, he said, "I'm so proud of you, Gopher. You can walk! Good work, Sweetheart."

Miriam patted his cheeks and nodded, "Coot proud."

"Very proud," he said and then the rest of them all praised her efforts.

"That's a really nice walker you have there," Ian said. "Where did you get it?"

The little girl got very serious and related, "Son bend, Owey! Son say no more."

"What is she telling us?" Mo asked.

Elton grinned, "Well when Kevin was making the walker for her, he bent the aluminum pipe and a piece snapped off, cutting his hand. He swore and Carrie bawled him out!"

Miriam listened and then shrugged, "No say no more Son."

Matt held out his arms to her and she went to him, "How is my little one?"

"Gopher walk Fodder?"

"Yes, I can walk with you if you'd like. Where do you want to go?" Matt asked.

"Ginger cars."

"She and I were racing cars in the hallway. Guess what, Tuck? My eyes are better so I can be a good racer now. Want to race with us?" The little tomboy Ginger asked.

"I think I'd like that. But only for a little bit, because I think I saw some of Grandma Katherine's kuchen," Matt said as he turned Miriam's walker to face the living room. Then he stood her up and gave Katie a hug. "Hi Kate. How goes it?"

"Good. Oh Matt, I got a new poetry book from the library. If you have time later, maybe you'd like to see it?" the blonde teenager asked.

"I'd like that, Kate."

Matt raced cars with the little girls until Grandma called them for coffee and kuchen. Before he sat down, his Mom asked if he would bring in her small bag from the car. Elton offered to help him bring in some of their things.

At the car, Elton turned to him. "How did the stuff with the Bishop go for you, Matt? I thought about you so much while you're gone. I hope it was okay."

"I have so much to talk to you about. Elton, I missed you, too."

"I know that!" he chuckled with his signature smile. "Darrell is just about dying to talk to you."

"I can't wait to see him, either." Then he looked at Elton, opened his mouth as if to ask something and then decided against it.

Elton nodded, "She's okay, Matt. Jeannie stopped by the shop this morning and said she had talked to her. Diane is fine."

Matt hugged him, "Thanks. I was so worried."

"We can talk about that later too, but just know she's well."

After coffee, Matt went into the sewing room where Katie was working. "Hi, I decided I'd better leave the table before I ate another piece of kuchen. It'd mess up my dinner."

Katie giggled and put down the beading she was working on.

"What're you doing there?" Matt asked.

She showed him her work and then explained that she was doing it just to practice working on Ruthie's wedding dress.

Matt admired it, "You know Katie, this is truly fantastic! You really have a talent for this. I can't imagine how you can do it."

"I could show you sometime if you want. It really isn't hard."

Matt grinned, "I don't know. It looks hard to me. Where is your book?"

Katie handed him the book of American poets. He paged through it and asked her whom she liked the best.

"I think Carl Sandburg is okay but not my favorite. I'm really not into TS Eliot although he seems to like cats a lot. My favorite is Frost, I think. How about you?"

"Yes, he is my favorite, too. Did you know that Frost is from the same part of the country that I am?" Matt asked.

"I read that. Someday I'd like to visit there. I can't imagine how big an ocean must be. It must really be something," Katie's eyes danced with anticipation.

"It is. Try to imagine the prairie being all water from one horizon to the other! And then the big blue sky above! It's great. Maybe sometime when I go back out East to visit, I'll take you along. Would you like that?"

"I really would. Mrs. Waggoner is from Maine, you know. Is that near where you grew up?"

"Not that far. It is more rugged in Maine, a beautiful state. Well, I suppose I had better get ready to help milk. I hear we have some new cows huh?" Matt grinned.

"Yes, two more. They are Jerseys. Pepper named one Pepper and Ruthie named the other one Sugar," she shook her head, "Honestly Matt, I don't want to sound mean but those girls have very little imagination!"

Matt laughed, "I'd have to agree with you there!"

After chores, the whole family, Ellisons, Zach and Suzy Jeffries and Darrell and Jeannie Jessup came for dinner. It was great to see everyone again. Miriam was doing well, Ginger's eyes were now much improved and she'd only have to wear glasses for reading and writing. She'd be able to rejoin her regular class after being out over half of last year since her chemical burns. Charlie was going into first grade and couldn't have been less interested. His major concern was getting the Uncle Elton's garage cleaned before the Labor Day picnic on Monday.

Kevin and Carrie were signed up to help Joan Sandvahl with the little kids Sunday School class at nine o'clock and it'd be started the following week. Kev was getting cold feet, but Carrie was prodding him along.

Darlene and Keith were looking forward to the arrival of their new baby in about six weeks and Darlene was ready to start her new job. They'd put off buying a place until at least Christmas. "We have too many irons in the fire right now," Keith stated.

Kincaid's house would be ready in a week, and Jessups the following week. Then it would be a couple more weeks before Ian and Ruthie's house would be completed.

"I see painting and moving furniture in our future," Elton grinned.

"And I see wedding dresses!" Nora giggled. "We have Carl and Mo, followed by Ian and Ruthie. Then Kevin and Carrie's baby. Then it's Christmas and Pepper's wedding. It makes me tired to think about it."

Elton made a face, "No it doesn't! You love it every minute of it."

She gave her husband a kiss, "Yes I do."

After the dishes were finished, most of the family gathered around the patio. It was Carl who finally asked what they had found out about Waggoners while they were gone.

Kev started, "Well, we had that cookout and Les Everett and his wife came over. Nice people. He said that D. Albert Roofing is Mr. Waggoner's company. It was named after his son, Dean Albert Waggoner. Les certainly has no respect for the man. He says his boss is a crook and as soon as he can, he's getting a different job."

"That doesn't surprise me from what Wag told me that night at the dance about how he cheated his clients. I still can't get over how he sat there and told me all about it! What an idiot." Carl shook his head. "He certainly isn't very smart."

"And I found out," Darlene interjected, "That Diane isn't working on that committee with Mrs. Schulz anymore. Mom and Mrs. Schulz are good friends and she said that Diane had to quit because she said she was too busy with family stuff. It was a committee that made quilts for missionaries. What anyone could find threatening about that is beyond me!"

"If you aren't hooked together right in the first place, I guess it isn't a big leap," Ian added. "So what's there to do at the school that she is involved in?"

Jeannie said, "She dropped everything last year. She and Dean used to help build floats for the homecoming parade. She was advisor to the theater group and the poetry club. I don't know if she'll be doing any of that this year. Although, she has to help chaperone at least a couple of times. School rules."

❧❧ 26 ❧❧

SATURDAY MORNING AFTER MATT GAVE Lloyd a ride in his old Ford, he and Annie took Ginger for a horseback ride. They went over to Darrell's place. He was too busy to go with them, but Ginger was all excited that she was able to ride over to her Uncle Darrell's.

That afternoon, Matt helped Elton grind feed. "I'm glad that Darrell showed you how to do this. I've never had anyone help me but my boys before. You're getting to be a real farmer there, Matthew."

"This is a pretty itchy job if I do say so. You know Elton, this is a lot of work for you. All these kids bring their cows home and you get to grind the feed. You didn't plan that very well," Matt winked.

"No. It's Lloyd's fault. He and Bert Ellison always gave the young men this speech about having to buy a cow before they got married. Now I have a barn full!" Elton chuckled. "But you know we use every bit of the milk, so I guess it works out."

After they got finished, they took a break in the shop. Charlie had actually done a pretty good job with the shop and managed to get it finished by Friday night. He was taking Saturday off.

"I felt bad for the poor kid," Elton explained. "It really was an accident that his dam broke. But I thought I better let him know that it's important to be careful. He got a lesson in back-up plans. Yea gads, now he thinks he needs concrete! No matter how fast you think you're thinking that guy is at least six pages ahead of you."

Matt chuckled, "Poor Byron and Marly. I don't know how they can keep from going off the deep end."

"Byron handles it pretty well but poor Marly about loses it. The kids all say that she goes to her wit's end."

Matt chuckled, "And gets red fire coming out of her eyes!"

"Yah," Elton raised his eyebrows, "I have to say, I've seen it myself! I don't know how she can do it. The first two are good kids and always have been, but these last two are something else! Marly's mom always says it's payback because Marly was such a devil when she was little. Of course, Byron's dad Bert always said that Charlie was the spit and image of his dad. So, I guess they come by it naturally."

"I would've thought that Ken would be more like Byron was when he was a kid."

"Ken is Byron's stepson. His real dad was killed in Korea before he was born. He was only about year and a half old when Marly met Preacher Man. Ken never knew any other Dad. He has always been a quiet thoughtful boy. He is a fine person."

"Really? I'd have never guessed that. He is so much like Byron."

"Byron has been my best friend forever. I say that, but actually it has only been fifteen years ago we met," Elton lit his cigarette and handed Matt a Coke.

"Hm. I thought he married you and Nora?"

"He did. Twice in fact!"

"Twice?" Matt shook his head. "Were you two divorced?"

"No. See, we met when she moved out here from Minnesota after her husband was killed in a mining accident. She had four kids and was alone. So her aunt, Gilda Heinrich and her husband Bill moved them out here. I met her at a barn dance that Preacher Man and I went to. Keith was fourteen, Kevin was thirteen, Andy was five and Pep was three. Nora was the most captivating person I'd ever met in my life. I was done for in about two seconds flat."

"She must have gotten married very young the first time," Matt observed.

"No, Keith and Kevin are her brothers. She took care of them after her parents died. Then before we got married, Nora and Pepper were mauled by a sow and in the hospital. It was nip and tuck if they'd even survive. So we got married right away and then I adopted the kids, so they wouldn't be split up. That way if the worst happened, at least we'd have each other. Then after every one was healed up, Nora and I got married in the church. Byron married us twice. Between you and me, I liked the first time the best, except Nora was so sick. I'm not much for the fancy foo-foo stuff.

She almost died, my Nora. Gee Matt, she hung on death's door for over a week. I was almost a mad man. Thank God she lived."

Matt watched Elton while he talked, "Is that why you have so much faith?"

Elton grinned, "Hell, Matthew! I have so little faith it scares me! I just hang on by my skinny skin-skin most of the time. Now Preacher Man, he has faith. Personally, I'm counting on that bit about the mustard seed!"

"Ah, I don't believe you. You seem to keep your head on pretty straight. I think you have more faith than I do," Matt pointed out.

"Nope, don't believe that either. I know that if things are going well, it is a lot easier than when everything is in turmoil. That's when you need faith and that is when it is the hardest."

Matt nodded and told Elton the story about Butterton taking over his parish and about the young boy who committed suicide. Elton listened without a word and then when Matt was finished, he just shook his head. "That's terrible. He's now in your parish? That's rotten! I bet you wanted to knock some heads together, huh?"

"Yah, but I just sat in the car." Then Matt explained how he debated and debated about telling the Bishop he was all done that day. "I guess I'm a moral coward."

"No, you aren't. You're just being careful. You said your friend, Jeff is it?—he is still struggling with the decision he made. It isn't going to be easy. You know Matt, my guess is that you've made your decision already, you're just working out the details. Am I right?"

Matt looked at him. This guy was really clairvoyant. He nodded, "Yah, I think I did. I had this delusionary hope that I'd maybe come to North Dakota and work with Father Vicaro. He is like I always thought it would be. But Jeff pointed out that our Bishop would never to let that happen, if he could help it."

"Well, Matt. Seriously, God has a way of working things around. You might be surprised how it works out. So you would stay in the priesthood if you had a place like Merton. Then you haven't really made a decision yet. But my question is what do you want to sort out before you make your final decision?"

Matt smiled, "You know, you're the first person who has asked me that. I think I just want to know if I can first handle things in the real world and then if I can feel I'm doing God's work out here."

"I can answer part of the last question for you. There is tons of the Lord's work to do out here. Now how you handle it or feel about it, that I can't tell you. It will take you some time to figure out. You know, it is like you really won't know how it feels to not be a priest until you aren't a priest. It is sort of like being married. Unless you are, you aren't."

Matt shook his head, "Good grief! I'm beginning to understand you!"

Elton had a good laugh, "What're going to tell Vicaro?"

"I think I'll just tell him straight out. He doesn't seem to be much for any other kind of conversation."

"I think he'll appreciate that," Elton agreed. "As long as he isn't throwing down the gauntlet, that'd be the best approach. He doesn't seem to be that type of guy."

"Elton, what about Diane?" Matt asked very quietly.

"Don't know. What do you think?"

"Well, I hardly know her at all really. It isn't fair to not tell her but I'm not certain what'd happen if she thought I was a priest. She might think I was a terrible person for even thinking about leaving it. She seems to be a devout Catholic."

"Matt, you think she is. I doubt anyone knows right now how much is her and how much is them. I'm sure Waggoners would think you're awful, but they think everyone is. She might have a whole other take on it. You can't not tell her for very long. If she finds out from someone else before you tell her, you'll be the Rat from Hell; no matter if she's sweet on you or not! That I can promise you! Women are really weird that way. On the other hand, she has enough on her plate right now for ten folks to handle. So, I agree. Now isn't probably the best time."

Then he thought a minute. "On the other hand Matt, it might be if she knew about your dilemma, it'd take her mind off her own mess for a while. That isn't all bad either. Just think about it and at least give her a hint and see what comes of it. If you confide in her, she might feel more like she can trust you. You know?"

"That's right, huh?" Matt grinned. "I'm even more confused now."

Elton slapped him on the back, "Good! My day was a success then! So are you a better batter, pitcher or catcher?"

"Huh?"

"In softball! They always have a softball game at the fairgrounds on Labor Day. The women have this big picnic dinner planned and there'll be potato sack races, three-legged races and horseshoes. All kinds of stuff.

I just need to know if you can pitch. I used to pitch for all the games, but I'm getting old."

Matt laughed, "You aren't old! I'd like to see you and Carl run the three-legged race!"

"You'll never live long enough to see that young man. Never. Yea Gads, he would grump about everything. I'd have to strangle him before the whistle blew."

27

MONDAY MORNING AFTER CHORES, THE family all gathered their picnic things together and headed over to the fairgrounds. They brought their own collapsible tables and put them together so they had a table big enough to sit at. Elton and Carl scouted out a big tree or two for shade and got into a debate about which place would be best. Then when they finally decided on one and the ladies put the table cloths on it, a bird perched above did its business right smack on the table cloth. That set off a new round of recriminations. Finally, Nora and Mo threatened their lives. Thankfully, Keith and Kevin challenged them to a horseshoe match and got them out of everyone's hair.

The picnic grounds started filling up and soon the place was packed. It seemed the entire county was in attendance.

Ginger wanted to play croquet, so Matt went with her to get their mallets. While they were waiting to play, Matt heard a familiar voice. It was Diane. "Hello, Matt."

Matt smiled hello and introduced Ginger to the Waggoners. Darrell and Jeannie came by and invited them all over to their table for some pie after their game.

"We haven't eaten yet, so I think Ginger will have to have her hot dog before pie," Matt pointed out.

"Tuck," Ginger frowned. "That is so mean! Why don't you have to eat your lunch before you eat your dessert?"

"Ah," he stammered.

"Yah, Tuck," Darrell agreed.

"You're such a trouble maker, Jessup!" Matt groaned.

Katie giggled, "You guys should run in the three-legged race together!"

"Good idea! I'll go sign us up. Of course, I'll probably have to drag you across the finish line!" Darrell said with bravado.

"Don't be bragging on yourself, there!" Matt boasted. "I'm very fast."

A half an hour later, the three-legged race was called. Tuck and Darrell were tied together. Keith and Kevin were a team as were Zach and Chris, Pepper's fiancé. Everyone was jumping and cheering for their favorites, but the gold ribbon was taken by the Owens brothers.

When the little kids all got in their sacks for the sack race, Miriam was shattered. Charlie, Clark, Ginger and even Maddie got to race, but she didn't. Then they announced a parent-child potato sack contest, Matt took one look at her little sad face and asked, "Would you like to be my partner in the sack race, Miriam?"

Her little tear face broke into a smile and she held up her arms to him, "Fodder tado sack."

The next thing he knew, he was lined up with other adults holding the toddlers inside their potato sacks. He had never hopped that far in his life, especially holding a child inside a potato sack! There was a first time for everything, but he was very certain that it would be the last time!

They came in third and Matt was worn out! "I don't ever want to hear anyone say that Miriam is tiny. That girl weighs two tons! Trust me."

Miriam grinned, "Gopher tons!"

Nora pinned the ribbon on her tee shirt and Miriam was beaming. "Gopher Fodder hop! Mighty fine indeed!"

Matt sat recuperating under the tree with a Coke. The older Waggoners and Diane came by. "That was really nice of you," Diane said. "Miriam really had fun."

"Tell that to my lungs!" Matt groaned. "How far was that anyway?"

"About a hundred feet! It isn't that far, really!" Annie giggled as she came up beside them.

Matt scowled at her, and then teased. "Watch it, Hot Shot. Next time you take her!"

"Hey Tuck," Nora yelled, "I have a couple hot dogs over here with your name on them."

"Okay," Matt said as he got up.

He filled his plate with potato salad and hot dogs. He visited with Alma and George Jessup while he ate. They were almost finished eating and soon excused themselves to watch the softball game.

Father Vicaro came by and sat down to visit with Matt. "Glad to see you made it back from out East in one piece. Ready to start school tomorrow?"

"Yes," Matt nodded, "I have to admit I'm a bit nervous. New classes, new schools and all, but I'm rather looking forward to it."

"Good," Father Vicaro nodded, "Could you stop by either tomorrow night or the next after school?"

"I was planning to," Matt offered. "I really wanted to talk to you about everything that went on out there."

"Okay, I just wanted to give you the stuff for CCD. That is Wednesday night you know."

Various folks wandered by, greeted Father Vicaro and he smiled back. They were all very friendly to him and it was obvious the whole community thought a lot of him. Matt remembered how that felt. It was heartwarming to have the church community all say hello. He also remembered that none of them were close friends, but he never felt left out. He really did miss that.

Then Waggoners came with their plates and sat down. Wag was very nice to Father Vicaro and was extremely friendly to him. Vicaro visited with them a couple minutes and then had to go referee the broad jump. Matt was worried that Father Vicaro might let something slip but he didn't. It still made Matt very nervous. The only good thing was that Diane sat across from him. Gladys sat next to him, while Wag glared at him from across the table.

Father Vicaro patted Matt on the shoulder and then said, "Well, be seeing you soon then. Glad you're back, Matt."

Matt said goodbye and Father Vicaro moved on into the crowd.

"He's a nice man," Diane said.

Matt nodded, "He certainly is."

"Well hell, he should be. He's a priest," Wag grouched.

Matt looked at him in surprise. He had been so nice around Father Vicaro in front of him and the minute he stepped away, the man returned to his ugly self. He wondered to himself how people could be so two-faced. He felt certain Father Vicaro thought that Waggoner was the most wonderful thing since chopped wood.

"Are you ready for school tomorrow?" Matt asked Diane.

"I thought you were married to that Indian!" Wag interrupted.

"What?" Matt shook his head. "Who?"

"That woman you took to the dance."

"Oh, you mean Annie? No, she isn't my wife. She is married to Andy Schroeder. We went to the dance together because he's in Vietnam. We're very good friends," Matt said.

"Women shouldn't be going out with anyone while their men are at war! And a decent man wouldn't take them out," Waggoner barked. "But what do you expect from a squ-"

"Don't say it," Matt interrupted sternly, shooting him a dirty look.

"So if you aren't married to her, who is the mother of your kid?" Matt knew that Waggoner was relishing having him under the microscope.

"Miriam isn't my child."

"Like hell. She calls you Father," the bald man accused him.

"I know. And she calls herself Gopher. She isn't a gopher either"

"Should give the brat a damned good beating until she gets it right," Wag grumbled. "Not right to let a kid talk that way."

"You just leave her be!" Matt was even surprised at the tone of his own voice! It certainly was forceful, because even Wag got quiet. Matt was relieved that Wag had shut up.

Matt gathered up his things and left the table. He didn't know where he was going but he knew he had to get away. He threw half a plate full of food into the garbage, walked past the outhouses and down a slope. He sure didn't like that guy.

He went through the row of lilac bushes and trees toward the creek. There he found a big rock and sat on it. He began tossing pebbles into the stream while he thought about the situation.

Ian was right. People do treat nuns and priests better than other folks. Obviously, Waggoner would've never said those things in front of Vicaro. Maybe that was another reason Matt had liked being a priest. He wondered if he had so little patience with Waggoner because of how obnoxious he was or because of Diane. He guessed it didn't really matter. He just didn't want to be around him.

He must have been there a while, when he heard someone approach. He turned to see Diane coming toward him. "May I join you for a little minute?"

He nodded and she sat down on a log.

"I'm sorry Wag upset you. He's just really gruff. He doesn't mean much by it. He doesn't know what that little girl went through, Tuck. I'm sure if he did, he wouldn't have said that."

Matt shrugged. He felt irritated at having to be so duplicitous. Suddenly he was very tired of trying to do the right thing. He didn't like living like he had been and he wanted to just blurt everything out. Instead he just shrugged again.

"Matt, what is it?" Diane seemed concerned.

"Oh, I haven't been up to my old self lately. I shouldn't have snapped at him. It wasn't fair. I'm sorry." Then he turned directly to her and said sincerely, "Diane, there's a reason she calls me Fodder."

"And I bet there's a reason she calls Mrs. Engelmann Chocolate too." Diane asked gently, "Do you want to talk about it?"

He looked at her and smiled. What he really wanted to do was grab her, give her a very passionate kiss and blab out everything he had been thinking for the past couple weeks. Instead he just shrugged again. "I guess I'll wait for a while, like you do."

"Ah," Diane winced, "I knew that was coming!"

"I'm sorry. That wasn't very nice of me to say, either. I'm being awful today. Guess it's different when the shoe is on the other foot, huh?"

"Usually it is," Diane caught his glance. "If you need a sounding board, I want you to know I'm a willing listener."

"You'd probably just get into trouble with Wag," Matt pointed out.

Now Diane shrugged, "I just don't want you to be upset."

"No big deal, really. It's just me."

"If you're sure," Diane said. "I'd better go."

Matt nodded. "Yah, I guess. I don't want you to get into trouble."

"I don't either. I better get back before Wag forms a search party."

"Diane, thanks for asking. I'd like to talk to you sometime when we have more time. Okay?" Matt was very sincere.

"Okay. I'd better run. Maybe we'll see each other at school. You have a good day, my pleasant acquaintance," Diane said softly. "Could I ask you to wait a bit before you come back? I don't think it'd look good if we both came out of the lilac bushes at the same time!"

"No," Matt smiled, "Probably not. Thanks Diane."

Matt sat there for quite a while. He was digesting everything that had transpired. Why did she come after him? She had also said she would be his willing sounding board. She must like him or she wouldn't have risked getting into trouble with Wag. That almost pleased him, but now he had no excuse to not tell her he was a priest. He decided he had better tell her soon. If she liked him, it was imperative for him to tell her.

He threw the rest of the handful of pebbles into the creek and headed back to the picnic grounds. He went over and watched the softball game. Then Annie and Pepper snagged him to play on their volleyball team. He saw Diane once while they were playing. When he got back to the table, Waggoners had gone home for the day.

Matt was very quiet all evening. He helped with chores and then went to bed almost immediately after dinner. He was tired and nervous about the next day. It didn't look like life was going to give him a break to figure things out. It looked to him like he was going to have to make a decision way before December. Coot was right. Life wasn't easy in the Petunia Patch.

❦❦❦ 28 ❦❦❦

IAN'S LABOR DAY DIDN'T START out much better than Matt's. He went to the picnic with Ruthie. She was happy and perky as usual and chatted with the ladies. While most of the guys were busy with games, either participating or organizing, like he'd have done had it not been for his arm; he just watched. He helped keep score for the baseball game but other than that, he mostly just wandered around.

He had always been very athletic and involved. Everyone was very friendly, but he felt left out. After the baseball game, he got a beer and went to sit on the bleachers to watch the volleyball game.

Before he knew it, Carl was sitting beside him. "Bored out of your mind?"

"Is it that obvious?"

"Not really. I just know that you're dying to be out there. Did you used to be good at volleyball?"

"Yah, actually I was on a team in high school." Then he turned to Carl almost in tears, "What the hell am I going to do with myself? I totally hate this!"

"Dunno," Carl shrugged. "Maybe we can find some sport that you're good at."

"Like what would that be? Even Miriam was in the sack race!"

Carl grinned, "Can't see Matt holding you in a sack race though. He darned near had a heart attack as it was! I bet that's hard to do."

Ian nodded. "Yah, I imagine it is."

"How about miniature golf? Want to play me a hot game? They have a course over there. I'll only use my good arm to make it even," Carl asked.

Ian shrugged, "Sounds pathetic."

"That sounds like a yes to me! Let's go!"

Ian followed along, without much interest. When they got there, they had to wait their turn to start. Then Darlene and Carrie came up behind them. "Hey, you guys want to play teams against us?" Darlene bubbled.

Of course, Carl had a soft spot in his heart for Darlene so he wanted to. Ian could tell he did and said okay. They ended up having a ball. Before they were finished with the eighteen holes, they had decided that Carl should build a miniature golf course in his backyard!

"Yah Dad," Ian chortled, "To go with the sandbox, slide and animal cages."

"Animal cages!" Carrie gasped. "What sort of animals are you going to put in cages."

Carl chuckled, "Gophers! The kids misunderstood and thought that I was going to build cages for animals! Then Charlie wanted to put chickens in the house so Mo wouldn't have to go outside to gather eggs and Miriam wants 'Splurches'. You know, ducks. This whole house idea got totally out of hand."

Darlene was very quiet and frowning.

"What?" Carl asked.

"Where is the slide? Are you going to have a swing set?"

"Might, but since Ian the Supermouth had to open his trap, I'll tell you. The slide will be inside the house. I was worried about if we had a pile of Gophers at the house and there was a tornado. I remember how much trouble we had getting everyone into the basement in a hurry at Magpies. So I thought, if we had a slide from the playroom to the basement, we could get the kids downstairs in a quick hurry!"

Darlene raised her eyebrows, "I imagine you could, but how're you going to keep them from sliding all the time?"

"We'll keep it locked way up high, so they can't." Carl explained.

"I just know my baby will love being at your place, Carl. But I am afraid you and Mo will have the child spoiled rotten."

"My baby, too," Carrie said. "Just think, this year you will have Maddie Olson, Miriam, Jenny and Danny's baby, Matthew, and then Darlene's in October and ours in December! Wow! A real nursery school!"

"Yah, but except for Maddie and Miriam, the others will be too little to be Gophers. But I did get a new one!" Carl boasted.

"Really? Where?"

"When I was out East. My grandson-to-be, Turk wants to be a Gopher! Harrington, be sure to remind me to get him a hard hat and shovel!" Carl grinned.

"I will Dad. And remember, you promised him that you'll find a good fishing hole before he gets here!"

"Oh yah. Do either of you girls know where to go fishing?"

"Sure do. Ask Danny Schroeder! He was born with bait in his mouth! And then don't forget Sammy, Darrell's brother. Those two go fishing a lot. I'm sure they'd love to take you," Darlene grinned. "Then you'll have to build a shed for all your fishing poles too! You're really nuts, you know that?"

Ian slapped Carl on the shoulder, "I tried to tell you, Dad."

By the time the group returned to the rest of the family, Ian felt a lot better about things and decided that he needed to find some athletic type things that he could do until his arm got better. He'd talk to Pepper. She was usually full of good ideas.

While he was eating his hot dogs, Eddie Schroeder sat across from him. Eddie was Elton's younger brother who ran a cheese factory in Bismarck. Eddie has lost one of his arms from the elbow down when he was a kid. He was also another of the Engelmann Clan and a very nice guy.

"Mind if I join you?" Eddie asked.

"Not at all. In fact, you might be just what the doctor ordered," Ian grinned.

"Why is that?"

"I just played a game of miniature golf and was sitting here trying to figure out what else I could do with one arm. Any ideas?"

"Restless, huh? I remember feeling that way. I practiced pitching and got pretty good at it. And you can run, can't you?"

"Oh yah, I guess," Ian shook his head. "I never even thought about that."

"Next picnic, you and me—the three-legged two-armed race!" Eddie laughed. "We will mop up the competition!" Then he got more serious, "It was different for me because I was a kid when I lost my arm, but since you're older, you've already learned to be dependent on two arms. I wasn't. I even learned how to play pool!"

"Really, I'd love to do that! I used to like that."

152

"Okay, you and Ruthie come in some evening and I'll show you how I do it. We can work something out. And darts! They're good too. I used to do some badminton, but I got too old. See if you can find someone to practice with you. I used to shoot hoops with the boys, but I'm not a very good shot. And hey, next Friday night, Lucy and I were going to go with Danny and Jenny to bowl. You and Ruthie should come along."

"I don't know if I could do that," Ian frowned.

"I know you can try! That's all we ask. If you can't, you can keep score and eat!" Eddie chuckled. "Hey, I heard you're doing the books for Elton and Doug, huh? I was wondering if you had time, if you could help me with some of my bookwork at the Cheese Factory. Doug said you really helped him out. I need to get some of that stuff sorted out before February tax time."

"I'd be glad to. Any special time, you'd like me to come by?"

"Whenever you have time in the next couple weeks. Just call me in the morning. Well, I had better go find Lucy. She wanted some help with the cooler. It was great talking to you, Harrington. Anytime you want to do something, give me a holler. I'm willing, but I don't do skinny dipping!" Eddie chuckled as he walked away.

Ian was grinning as he watched him walk away. 'You really have to love these guys,' he thought.

Ruth sat next to him and gave him a kiss on the cheek. "How's my guy? Can I have a bite of your hotdog?"

"I can get you a whole one, if you want."

"No. I just want a bite." She took a bite and then watched him while she ate it. "You okay, honey? This must be hard for you, with the bum arm."

"Well, I was getting all ready to feel sorry for myself, when Carl dragged me off for a game of miniature golf. We played with Darlene and Carrie. Then Eddie and I were just talking and he invited us to go bowling with them next Friday. He said if I can't do it, I can just eat!"

Ruthie kissed his dimpled cheek, "You're so sweet. That'd be fun."

"He also said we should come in and he would show me how he plays pool and we can throw darts!" Ian's eyes were dancing.

"I've never played pool. Is it fun?"

"If you win," Ian laughed. "Would you mind going out with a crippled guy?"

Her face got serious, "I won't go out with a crippled guy but I'll go out with you. Okay? Honey, do you think we could set the wedding date up? I want to be married now."

Harrington chuckled, "No way, woman. You have way too many plans already made! But to make you feel better, I have something for you that I forgot to give you when we got back from Boston."

"What is that?"

"A little box of your favorite things!"

She threw her arms around him, "Caramels! You remembered to bring me my favorite caramels! I love you."

"No, you love the caramels. But they're back at the house, so remind me tonight when we get house. Then do you want to go over and look at our house? I want to check something out."

"Sure. What do you want to check out?"

"If there'd be room for a pool table in the recreation room and dart board in the basement and maybe a basketball court next to the garage."

"I'm sure there is room for both. That'd be great Ian. Totally."

That night after the chores were done, Ian got the caramels and he and Ruthie went over to look at their house. The construction was coming along fine and they'd be moved in on schedule. It was now enclosed.

Ian checked out the dimensions and was comforted to know there would be plenty of room for the pool table. Then he gave Ruthie the caramels. Before long, they were involved in some serious necking.

"It's a good thing we're getting married soon," Ian said. "I don't think I could stand it much longer."

"Me either." Then Ruthie giggled. "Remember when we flew out here from Boston and posed as husband and wife? I was so panicked when the stewardess asked what kind of soda my husband drank! Now, we're going to be married. I have to tell you something, Ian. I really liked you from the first time we met. I thought you were such a nice guy and so good-looking. I even told Suzy that."

"What kind of a nun were you?" Ian teased. "To be honest, Ruthie, I was so taken with you the first time we met, I could hardly breathe."

"Ian, I was throwing up every other minute!"

Ian broke into laughter, "I know. But I was conditioned after hanging around that crazy brother of yours, Zach the Vomit Machine! You were a much more graceful upchucker than he could ever be!"

Ruthie swatted him, "Speaking of crazy brothers! What was with Matt tonight? He was unusually quiet."

"I know. He's going through his own private hell right now. You know how you struggled about leaving the convent."

"Yah, I do."

"And besides, he was sitting with Waggoners for a little bit before he got so quiet. I think that was the main problem tonight."

Ruthie leaned back in Ian's arms, "I think I should have that talk with Mattie. We never did get our visit. I think he is kind of sweet on that Diane, huh?"

Ian grinned, "Yah, he is. He's feeling guilty about it now. He doesn't want that to be the reason he leaves the priesthood."

"That's why I think I should talk to him. He is putting a lot of pressure on himself. I know a little of how he's feeling. I'm not much good helping people, but maybe I can tell him how I felt."

"Did you leave the convent because of me?" Ian asked. "I have wondered about that many times."

"Yes and no," Ruthie said. "It would've been a lot harder for me to leave without you, I know that. I was already half way out the door before we realized what we meant to each other. Ian, would you have ever told me that you loved me, if you thought that I was going to stay a nun?"

"I honestly don't know. I've wondered about it. But when I got shot, that sort of changed how I felt about a lot of things. After I was shot, I didn't care anymore. And that's a blasted fact."

"Yes, it makes sense. Let's just hope no one has to get shot before he makes up his mind. Heck, he hardly knows her and maybe they won't even care if they get to know each other better."

"It'll be hard for them to find out, with that Wag keeping Diane on such a short leash. I did point out to Matt though that he was already thinking about leaving before he even knew she existed. He wants so much to do everything right. I don't think that it really has anything to do with it."

"It does, though," Ruthie pointed out. "If he is going to stay, then he'd be more inclined to avoid her."

"That's what he said. Ruthie, I think you should talk to him. You guys know more about that stuff than we outsiders do."

"Anyway, Ian Harrington," Ruthie giggled, "Now we're going to be getting married in less than a month! I'm glad that we made the decisions that we did."

"I'm too. I love you so much." Ian kissed her. Then he pulled away, "Let's get out of here before we get into trouble."

29

THE NEXT MORNING WAS BRIGHT and sunny. Chores were done in short order and by seven-thirty, everyone was ready for their day. Ian and Elton left for the shop and Matt was going to ride to school with Jeannie. He was glad that she had offered to pick him up this morning, so she could show him around. A couple minutes after the guys left, Jeannie pulled in the yard.

Grandma Katherine gave him a hug, "Have a wonderful day, Matt. I'll be thinking of you."

He looked at her and grinned, "That's a good thought. Thank you."

He ran out and climbed into Jeannie's car. She was such a nice girl and had been a very good friend to him. Her brown hair was worn in a bouncy bob. She had brown eyes and glasses. She was pretty and very down to earth, fun and fresh.

"Ready for your first day?" she smiled her huge smile.

"As ready as I'll ever be," Matt nodded. "I'm nervous."

"Don't be. You've taught school before so you know how it'll be. I can show you the important things though, like the coffee break room, rest rooms and your mailbox. Other than that, it's like any other old school."

"What's Jessup up to today?"

"He's going to finish up that last field and then do some summer fallow. He said to tell you that if you got fired, you could come out and help him," she giggled.

"He is always thinking, huh?'

"That he is."

As they drove by the Ellisons place, they saw the kids out waiting by the bus stop. They all waved as they went by.

"Darrell said he saw you sitting with the Waggoners for a bit yesterday. How did that go?"

"Oh, that Wag is a creep. I had everything I could do to keep from hitting him. He sure has no love for me."

"Or anyone else. He's just plain hateful."

"Jeannie, can I tell you about what happened with Diane?" Matt asked quietly. "I am still trying to figure it out."

"Sure."

Matt explained about Diane coming down to see him when he got irritated with Wag and left the table.

She drove a little ways and then said, "She must like you alot to risk that."

"Do you think so?"

"Yes, Matt. I do. Don't you?"

"I want to, but now I really have to tell her I'm a priest. It wouldn't be fair for her not to know. Would it?"

"No, I guess it wouldn't. Do you think that she can handle it with all her problems?"

"Do you think that it would just mess everything up?" Matt was very serious.

Jeannie thought a minute and then said, "I don't know. What do you want Matt? How do you want things to work out?"

"Honestly, I have no idea. None. I wanted to wait until December and then make up my mind all simple and straightforward. You know? It doesn't look like I'll have that luxury."

"Look Matt, life rarely gives us time to think things through thoroughly. No one can ever make a perfect decision. We don't know everything and we're probably not meant to. We can only go by whatever we know at the time. The rest of the time, we have to just wing it."

"Yah, I guess you're right."

"If it was me, I'd take one thing at a time and do the best I think at that time. See how it goes. You told her that you wanted to talk to her. So, what would you talk to her about if you didn't tell her that?"

"Dunno."

"Well, then. I think you're just not used to how things work in the real world. We are all just mostly getting by."

"You don't seem to me that you are. You and Darrell seem to have it all together."

Jeannie laughed, "I'm glad you think so! Because we don't. You know, Darrell and I were together since forever, but he never asked me out until Kevin's wedding this February. We both always just ended up together. I wondered if he really liked me, or if I just imagined that he did. Not long ago, he told me that he wanted to ask me out a long time, but he was afraid I'd say no. So he decided he'd rather we'd just be friends and not ever know how I really felt rather than asking me and finding out for sure!"

"What?"

"Yah, so do you think we know what we're doing?" She giggled.

"He isn't much of an Ann Landers, is he?"

"No. So, you're in no worse shape than the rest of us!"

"Is that supposed to make me feel better?" he asked, shaking his head.

"At least you need to know that you aren't alone in your confusion." She laughed, then said very earnestly, "Matthew Harrington, make me a promise to not think so much! Give yourself some wiggle room. If things are supposed to work out a certain way, they will; even if you're busy messing it up as best you can. Well, we've arrived. Come. Let me show you the ropes."

"Would Darrell be mad if I said I loved you?" Matt grinned.

"Don't care, I like to hear it." She winked. "Come Professor. We have innocent minds to tamper with!"

The day was fun. When Matt did have time to think, he reminded himself of what Jeannie had said. She made sense and he realized it was about the same thing that everyone else had been trying to tell him. He decided to quit thinking about himself so much and get busy. He felt a lot better that way.

He saw Ginger when he had playground duty and waved to her. Between classes, he saw Ken for a second and they nodded. At two o'clock, he dashed over to St. Johns. His two classes there went very well. He was pleased as he walked back to Jeannie's car at the parking lot.

She was just coming to the car when he got there and they headed for home. "How did it go today?"

"Good. You know, I really had a nice time. I got my mail here before I left for St. Johns. I guess I'm a chaperone for the Homecoming Dance on September 19th."

"So am I! Darrell will be there too. Are you going to help with the floats?"

"Never thought about it. Do you?"

"Yes, Darrell and I always do. It'll be cool if you're there too. The banquet will be held on Friday night and then the next day we have the parade, football game and then the dance."

"Sounds like fun. I wonder when St. John's has theirs."

"I think it's the following week. Do you have to help with that too?"

"I didn't hear anything. Maybe not because I'm only part-time."

"They'll let you know. You'll probably be asked to help, part-time or not."

"I really had a good time today. The students all seemed to be pretty bright, in both schools. I'm actually rather jazzed about it."

"Good. I'm so glad, Matt. Did you see anyone you knew?"

"I was surprised how many kids I recognized. I saw Ginger and Ken. Did you see Diane?"

"Just in passing. She was dashing off to playground duty this afternoon."

"I was rather surprised that we all have playground and lunchroom duty, even the high school teachers. I thought it would be just the elementary teachers."

"They do it because we're all in one school and there are kids of all ages. It makes a lot less work for any one person, if we all do a little. Don't you like to do that?"

"Oh, I don't mind at all. Not a bit. I just thought it was different. I actually like seeing the little ones, too. Oh, I almost forgot, I have to meet with Father Vicaro after school. He wants to give me the stuff for CCD class. You know, I'm going to be busy," then he chuckled. "It feels good. I want to thank you for talking me into doing this, Jeannie."

"No problem. It is nice to have someone else in the trenches with me!"

"Tell Darrell I'll be over tonight to help with chores. Okay?"

"You got it."

Matt nearly bounced up the steps into the old farmhouse. The ladies were all in the kitchen and turned when he came in.

"You don't have to tell us, Mattie! You had a great day!" His Mom said. "I can tell by your smile. It's so good to see my boy happy again!"

"It was wonderful but I can't wait to get into my jeans," Matt chuckled as he ran up the stairs to change.

When he came down stairs, Charlie had just arrived off the bus to do his Chicken Man chores. Matt offered to go out and help him. "How was first grade, Charlie?"

"Okay, if you like that stuff," Charlie groaned. "I like digging better."

"I know, but it all isn't bad, is it?"

"How can you like it? It must be an old people's thing," Charlie observed.

"Old people? I'm not old."

"You aren't a little kid. Did you like school when you were my size?"

"I really did, Charlie. But then I didn't get to dig."

"Oh no! What fun is it to be a little kid if you can't dig?"

"I guess not much, huh?" Matt laughed.

After he helped Charlie, he went over to help Darrell with the chores. He got home in time for dinner. Over dinner, the talk was of the new school year. Everyone was very pleased with their day. Miriam was at first upset when all the kids left for school, but felt better when she got Coot and Annie to herself.

After supper, Katie called to talk to Grandma. She was excited that she had Mrs. Waggoner for American Literature. The family sat on the patio for a while and visited, but Matt went in early so he could prepare for his classes the next day.

"It's good to see him so happy again," Mo said. "I sure hope it keeps up."

"He'll do okay, Mo," Nora said. "He was just at loose ends for a while. It'll be okay for him, I'm sure."

30

THE NEXT MORNING, THE MILKERS came to the house after chores and found a very unhappy Lloyd. The elderly man was sitting waiting for his coffee and extremely grumpy. Usually he was a happy person, even when his Alzheimers left him very confused. Today, he wasn't happy at all.

Elton brought him his coffee and asked, "What is it Lloyd? What's the matter?"

"That guy isn't going to give me ride anymore. I waited and waited for long time, and he isn't doing it. I think we should fire him," the old man explained. "I might as well sell my car. I'll give it to that tall kid."

"Maybe someone else can give you a ride," Elton explained. "Matt has to hurry to get to school on time. He doesn't have time."

"I'd take the time for him. I think I always did that, right Elton? I always try to take time for my relatives. Don't I?" the elderly man worried. To him, taking care of his relatives, whether he was related to them or not, was the most important thing he could do.

Matt's heart fell. Lloyd was right. Matt came over and patted his hand, "Lloyd, I'm so sorry. Let's figure out how we can have our drive. You're right and I was wrong. Will you forgive me?"

Lloyd took the young man's hand, "I think I will. Right, Elton? A guy should do that, right? But you need to shape up. I'll never find you a wife if you don't."

"You don't need to find me a wife, Lloyd. But thanks anyway," Matt smiled.

"Why not? Every guy needs a wife to do the cooking and ironing. Right Elton?"

"Oh no you don't, Lloyd. As much as I love you, I won't go down that rocky path with you. Nora will deck me," Elton grinned. "So when are we going to organize the drive? You know Matt, you don't have to help with chores. I have enough milkers. You could just give him a drive in the morning."

"He doesn't like to get up that early, and I need to help around here," Matt pointed out.

"Help with the milking and then let the others do the rest. You can come up and get him for his drive and we can all still have time for breakfast," Nora suggested.

"Good idea!" Lloyd face brightened up, "He'll do that."

"But then he'd never help clean barn," Pepper whined. "Maybe he could clean the calf pen. That doesn't have to be done as often."

"Good idea!" Lloyd clapped his knee, "He'll do that."

"Yah, but the horses take even less time," Keith pointed out.

"Good idea!" Lloyd said, "He'll do that."

Everyone laughed. "How about we just play it by ear and see how it goes each day. We'll just make sure that Lloyd gets his ride," Elton decreed.

"Good idea!" Lloyd nodded. "I will get my coat."

Matt went down to get his old Ford and gave Lloyd a very short ride that morning. When he got back to the house, he didn't have time for breakfast, but grabbed a piece of toast on his way out the door.

When the kitchen door closed, Lloyd turned to Nora, "He's a good sort. I was so glad I could help him this morning. He loves driving my car."

"That was very thoughtful of you Lloyd," Nora smiled.

The young man got to school with just five minutes to spare. When he picked up his mail, he saw Diane. She was wearing a rust colored suit with a soft crepe blouse of the same color. She looked beautiful. "Good morning," he said.

She gave him a smile, but he could tell she had been crying. Without thinking, he took her hand, "You okay?"

Diane squeezed it gently, and then let go, "I'm really fine, a little melancholy this morning. Don't worry. How're your classes?"

"They look good," Matt was enthusiastic. "Only interested students are the ones sign up for advanced maths. How are your classes? Katie was so excited that she got you for American Literature."

"I was glad for that too. Well, I'd better get to my room," Diane turned to leave.

"Tinker, what's your schedule for lunch?"

"I have lunchroom duty. Maybe tomorrow we could share lunch, okay?"

"I'll plan on it."

The day buzzed by. Matt ate lunch with Jeannie and Denise Anderson who taught biology for junior high and high school. "My juniors are all jazzed about getting to dissect their frogs! I tell you, they're a bunch of little ghouls!"

Both lunch mates chuckled, and then Diane came by and teased. "Keep it down over here. I don't want to have to send you to the Principal's office for being disorderly."

"Yes teacher," Denise answered. "The kids seem pretty well behaved today, so I imagine you have to pick on us."

"That's right. They haven't eaten the same meals over and over, so they can still palate them. Give them a month or so."

"Hey, I hear you're assigned to chaperone the Homecoming Dance, too. I think it will be Swanson, Jeannie, Matt, me and you. But this year we have to do the whole thing, the banquet the night before, too!" Denise said. "Did you notice that?"

"No, I never paid that much attention," Jeannie said. "Wow! That'll keep us busy. We're helping with the floats too. Guess that takes care of that weekend. Are you helping with the floats again this year, Diane?"

"Ah, I don't think I can. I really have to shove off here. Nice to see you all," Diane brushed away in her usual flight pattern.

Jeannie and Matt looked at each other and both knew what the other was thinking. "Those damned people!" Denise said.

"Pardon me?" Jeannie asked with surprise.

"Those Waggoners. I have no use for that old buzzard! He did my dad's roof and boy did he overcharge him. The bill was almost double by the time he got done. Dad hasn't paid him yet and he's trying to figure out what to do," Denise explained.

"I'd be happy to volunteer my brother Ian and Carl to look the papers over. They could help him. They've been upset with his business dealings too," Matt offered.

"I'll tell him. Thank you Matt, I'm pretty certain Dad will take you up on that."

Jeannie was thoughtful, "Denise, what has that got to do with Diane? Surely she has nothing to do with his business."

"Oh Jeannie," Denise went on, "I shouldn't say anything out of school, but Wag beats both Gladys and Diane. Didn't you know that?"

Jeannie played dumb, "Why doesn't she just move out?"

"It's a rotten deal. I got this from Myrtle Gleanson and you know—she knows everything! She is the real Sherlock Holmes of the neighborhood. Last winter when Diane lost the baby, she had to miss a lot of work. Then Dean got sick and so she had to take leave from work. Dean's doctor expenses were horrid. He worked for Wag then and his Dad said that he didn't need insurance, because he'd pay for anything that ever happened. When the bills started racking up, Wag made them sell their house and move in with them. Then as things went on, he made Diane sign over Dean's share of the roofing company to him. By the time Dean passed away, Wag had all the roofing company in his name and Diane had about $25,000 of notes signed to the old folks. He won't let her leave until she pays him back. You watch, he makes her walk to work every day except every other Friday! On payday, he brings her and waits outside until she brings her check out. She has to endorse it to him and he gives her ten dollars for spending money. At that rate, she'll have to stay there for a hundred years, because he is charging her room and board too!"

Jeannie gasped, "Diane has to know better than that. She should just get out."

"Yah, well he's a mean bastard," Denise said. "Remember her 'bad tooth'? Mrs. Saphron, who lives next door, told Myrtle that Diane had raked the leaves after Orientation that day and then the wind came up. She saw him come out in the back yard and yell for her to come out there and explain why she hadn't raked. She said it wasn't her fault the wind blew so hard and he hauled off and decked her. That's what happened to her tooth."

"Why didn't Mrs. Saphron call the cops?" Matt asked, barely able to swallow anymore.

"Her husband had called the cops on him shortly after they moved in. Waggoner was throwing his dead garden things over the fence into Saphron's yard. When Mr. Saphron asked him to stop, he told him to go to hell. Then when he threw the tree trimmings over the fence, Saphron called the cops. The next day, Saphron's little Pekinese disappeared. When Mrs. Saphron asked Waggoners if they had seen the dog, Waggoner just grinned and asked if it was worth it to complain to the cops."

"My God," Jeannie said. "He is worse than imagined. I didn't like him, but I didn't think he was that bad! Dean was so nice."

"Yes, he was. But he never had much use for his Dad. He told Eddie once that that only reason he talked to him at all was because he worried after his Mom." Denise put down her fork. "I'm sorry. Now I have ruined everyone's lunch. I bet you think I'm nothing but a big gossip, Matt."

"No, I don't. I'm glad you said something. Don't feel bad about talking. Some things shouldn't be kept quiet. Jeannie and I were wondering what was going on at the Waggoners." Matt said. "Please have your Dad talk to Ian. I'll tell Ian to look for him. That guy has got to be stopped."

"Well, lunch is almost over. Anyway, welcome to Merton," Denise smiled. "Really Matt, I'm glad you decided to join us."

"Thanks Denise," Matt took the girls trays while they went to wash up. When he was dropping off the trays, he made it a point to walk by Diane. "Have a great afternoon. I'm looking forward to our lunch tomorrow. Do you want to eat here or somewhere else?"

She flashed him a panicked look, "I have to eat here at the school."

Matt smiled, "The Gourmet Room at Merton Public sounds great to me. See you then."

The clocks that afternoon seemed to be crawling. Matt had difficulty keeping his mind on what he was doing. At coffee break, he sat with Jeannie.

"Wow!" Matt said, "I can hardly keep my mind on anything this afternoon!"

"Me either," Jeannie admitted. "Even one of my kids asked me if I had a headache. I can't wait to tell Darrell. He'll be livid."

"I know. I have an overwhelming urge to go over there right now and throw a fit," Matt looked at his cup and made a face. "Well, I really have to run to get to St. Johns. I'll be late tonight so I can't come help with chores, Jeannie. I hope I can get to talk to Darrell."

Father Vicaro was sitting at his desk when Sister Abigail let Matt into his den. "Good day, young man. How's it going?"

"I'm enjoying the teaching," Matt chuckled, "But it has only been two days!"

"It always starts out nice, huh? Here's the stuff for the CCD. How did things go in Boston?"

Matt was as straight with him as he could be. He told him that he had almost decided that if he couldn't be a priest in a town like Merton;

he'd probably just quit. He didn't want to get into another big city mess. He explained about how Butterton got his old parish. "Honestly, my only thought was to hurt him! Physically! And I don't like feeling that way!"

"No, that isn't good. I can understand it though. I have to tell you what I did while you were gone. I asked my Bishop what he thought my chances would be of getting a specific priest from Boston assigned to help here. He was very discouraging. He said there'd be many hoops to jump through and that it wouldn't be fair to the guys in this diocese that are waiting for an assignment. But he also said he'd look into it. He'll be covert," Vicaro grinned.

"I think you'd relish being a spy!" Matt chuckled.

"Ah, grant an old man a little joy from time to time. So, what else? There is something else, I can tell."

"I just heard some distressing things this noon about one of the families in this parish. It has bothered me. I know I shouldn't spread rumors, but I also know enough first hand to know that it isn't just idle talk."

He went into a lengthy explanation about the Waggoners. He left out a lot because he was very conscious that he didn't want Vicaro to know everything. He could be a little undercover himself.

Vicaro listened to the whole thing and then nodded, "It isn't the first time that I have heard this. I'm sure it's true. I don't know what could be done for Gladys, but Diane needs to get out of there as soon as she can. Earl is a cruel man. I've tried to talk to him, but it goes nowhere. Gladys won't even listen to any of it. Diane just runs off as fast as she can. I tried my level best to get her involved with things through the church, but he even made her quit the Quilting Bee! I keep trying, but I don't want to make things worse for her. I'm thankful she has friends like you and this Jeannie and Denise. Let me think of a different approach. If I can somehow wrangle Earl into thinking her doing something at the church will benefit him, maybe I can get her away enough so she can see a way out. I'll try, but I have to tell you, I have prayed for that situation more than once. So far, nothing has come to me in a brilliant flash!"

"Yah, I think God's batteries must be wearing out," Matt mumbled.

"No Matt, they aren't. We just have our blinders on. Anyway, young man, let me check back with the Bishop here and see if he made any progress. I'll keep my thinking hat on about Waggoners. I want you to know, I'd love to have you join me here at St. John's, but if you're that close to leaving, maybe that is just your answer. It shouldn't be the place, but the calling."

"I know. It isn't just St. Johns. It's the difference between rural and big city politics."

"Don't kid yourself, we have our share of politics too. Sometimes we're the lucky recipients of derelicts who were shoved out of the big city diocese. That is always fun, but do not despair. Things are always darkest before the storm, or something like that."

"Do you mean right before the high flood waters and damaging winds?" Matt laughed.

"Get out of here. You're bad for my optimism." Father Vicaro laughed. "See you downstairs under the sanctuary for CCD. I'll meet you there. You will know where we are. Those twenty-four kids should make enough noise to hone you in."

That night, Jeannie and Darrell came over after dinner. Matt had gone to his room to get his classes ready for the next day, when Nora called him. "I hate to interrupt you but Jeannie and Darrell are here."

Matt looked up and smiled, "That's okay. I'm having trouble focusing anyway. I'll be right there."

Out on the patio, Jeannie and Matt shared what they had learned from Denise. Then Matt told what he had learned from Father Vicaro as far as Waggoners were concerned. Ian got mad right away! "I'm glad that you told her dad to bring his papers over. Maybe we can nail him on that! It'd leave the women out of it."

"That's what I was thinking," Carl said. "Remember though Harrington, when a guy like that gets pressured, he'll take it out on whoever he can."

"I know," Ian said. "I wish we could get her out of there."

"But to where?" Jeannie asked. "She needs to be someplace where there're a lot of folks around all the time until Wag is out of the picture. He'd come after her if he could. I don't know if she would leave readily anyway."

"I don't know if she would either," Matt cleared his throat. "She and I are having lunch together tomorrow in the cafeteria. Maybe we'll be able to talk."

"Oh Matt," Jeannie said, "You won't. That place is like a zoo, and anyone will come by and plunk down. You might be able to talk, but not about anything private."

"Yah, you're right," Matt shrugged, "But where else?"

"I know what some of us do. When we want to visit, we go to one of our empty classrooms and eat a bag lunch. At least we can talk in private," Jeannie said.

"Ahah! My wife the conniver!" Darrell raised his eyebrow in mock suspicion. "And how do you know about this?"

"Because of you, Knothead, That is how you and I used to have lunch. Remember?" Jeannie giggled.

"Oh yah, that's right. Big Oops on my part, huh?" Darrell grimaced.

"I guess we could do that, but she might feel funny about it," Matt pointed out. "I guess we can just have lunch tomorrow and then maybe later have lunch in my classroom."

"Or," Maureen giggled, "Nora and I can put together a fantastic lunch and you can tell her that she needs to try it. Leave it to us, Mattie."

"Oh brother," Elton said, "I can see the candles and violin now!"

Both Maureen and Nora swatted him, "We're more subtle than that."

"I know," Jeannie grinned, "You can invite me too. I can bug out to correct some papers. I have to do that anyway over lunch."

"Lord, and men think they should plan the wars." Carl shook his head. "If the women did it, battles would be over before anyone knew what hit them!"

IT WAS A MORE ORGANIZED morning. Lloyd was up and ready for his ride when Matt brought the car up. They went for their ride and were back home before the milkers came in.

After breakfast, the ladies had a basket filled with thermoses. One contained homemade egg noodles, another with Beef Stroganoff and a third with coffee. There was a plastic container of tossed salad and another with French Bread. It smelled so good that Matt wanted to eat it for breakfast! In the basket were three plates, cups, napkins and silverware. Another container had some Chocolate Torte cake. It looked fantastic.

Matt didn't see Diane before lunch and was hoping it'd work out for their lunch. At noon, he went down to the cafeteria. He was about to give up on her, when she came in. "Hi, I thought maybe I misunderstood and we supposed to meet in the rest room," Matt teased.

Diane didn't think it was funny. "I was hoping you would forget that, please."

"I'm sorry, Diane," Matt apologized. "But I have a surprise for lunch."

"What would that be? How surprising can Spaghetti and Tomato sauce be?" Diane read the menu.

"How about homemade Stroganoff?"

"I love Stroganoff, but Matt. I told you, I have to eat here."

"I know, but you said at the school, right? Mom and Nora were cooking up a storm like they always do and made a bunch of stroganoff with all the fixings. They insisted that I bring it to school in a picnic basket, for you, me and Jeannie. We're going to eat in my classroom. Please don't say no."

Diane studied his face for a minute and almost said no. Then she smiled, "Okay. As long as it's the three of us, it should be okay."

Matt worried that she might run off when Jeannie left, but decided it was worth a try. When they got to his classroom, Jeannie had the desk set with the paper plates.

"Oh, this is so nice!" Diane admired the food. "And Chocolate Torte!"

They all said grace and then ate. Jeannie looked at her watch and said, "May I take my cake back to my room? I really have to get some papers corrected before class."

"Sure," Matt grinned and then noticed Diane's panic. "It'll be okay, huh Diane?"

Jeannie patted her hand, "Of course it will be. You guys still have almost half an hour left. No reason for you to rush just because I didn't get my work done. Let me refresh your coffees."

Diane was uneasy, but Jeannie did her best to be casual and put her at ease. "Thank Nora and your Mom for me. He can bring us food anytime, huh Diane?"

"It was delicious, but I don't think I can do this too often."

Matt tried to keep from locking the door when Jeannie left so she wouldn't run away, "Trust me, the ladies won't send it very often."

"Let me clean up," Diane started to stand up.

"Sit down, please Diane. We haven't even had our dessert yet. Grandma Katherine made this. She would be disappointed if I brought it home untouched."

"You mean Chocolate?" Diane giggled.

Matt was so relieved that she seemed to relax. However, her comment was like a flag, telling him he had to come clean. "Besides Diane, you said you'd be my sounding board. I want to tell you something and I don't want you to be upset with me. Okay?"

"How can I promise that if I don't know what it is? I'd like to promise though."

"I guess that's good enough. Yes, Miriam calls Grandma Chocolate because she gave her chocolate chip cookies when she first met her. She calls Kevin Son because Elton always calls him that."

Diane studied Matt's face, and then got a funny look of realization, "Matt. I'm not sure I want to hear what you're going to tell me."

"Diane, I am a—"

"No Matt. Please don't say anymore. I'm so sorry. I wanted to be your sounding board, but I just can't. I really can't," she almost cried.

"Okay, I'll be quiet."

"I think that we shouldn't have lunch again. It was a bad idea. Please erase anything I've said before."

"Dammit Diane, don't say that."

"What?"

"I want to be your friend. You promised you'd listen to me and try not to be mad at me. I want to talk to you. I thought I could confide in you. I don't think that you really know what I was going to say. So, please, let me explain."

"This is a real bad idea. I just want to go to my room now."

Matt took her hand and held it, "Diane. No one but Jeannie even knows that we're having lunch here. I know Wag doesn't know. I know you're terrified of him and I don't blame you. Okay? I promise I won't do anything to put you in jeopardy. You have my word. But I want to straighten this out because I'm worried."

She frowned, "Worried? About what?"

"What you think of me," Matt blurted out. "Okay? It really matters to me."

"If you're going to say what I thought you were going to say, it shouldn't matter what I think of you."

"But it does. It really does. Will you just listen to me for a bit? Please?"

Diane was almost stone, but finally nodded. "Okay, but I just don't understand."

Matt looked at her, "I want you to. I'm taking a big risk in telling you so please, do me the honor of listening, okay?"

"I'll try."

Matt nodded. Then still holding her hand, he told her a brief synopsis of his life. "From the time I was a little kid, I wanted to be a priest."

Tear started to silently overflow and fall down her cheeks.

"I became a priest about six years ago."

"So, I'm just a lost parishioner. Thanks for your honesty. You should really be more straightforward you know! Now I know why Darrell called you Friar Tuck when we first met. Did everyone have a good laugh at my expense?"

"Not at all. Please let me finish."

171

"I don't know what else you can say," she said quietly. "I think this was enough."

"No. Listen. I still have a couple minutes," Matt gave her real short version of Butterton, Jeff and Ruthie. Then he said, "Diane, I'm about a month away from leaving the priesthood. I want you to be my friend. I want your understanding and advice. Please?"

Diane was reticent. "Matt, you might be very honest and I'd love to think that, but I don't trust many men. I thought I might be able to trust you. Now I don't know. Now I don't even know if I can trust Darrell or Jeannie. My life is such a mess, I don't need this. Why didn't you just tell me right away?"

"I don't know. Our introduction just sort of happened. Then truthfully, I didn't want you to know. I know you have some serious problems, so I didn't want to say anything: but I couldn't stand not being honest with you either."

She looked at him with total mistrust, "That sounds good and I appreciate your sincerity, if that's what it truly is. I don't know why you care what I think and I should've known better to think anything in the first place. This is ridiculous."

Matt let go of her hand and leaned back in his chair, totally dejected. "This is why I didn't want to tell you. You aren't the only one with a messed up life. Okay, I understand. I was just hoping beyond reason. I really wanted us to be friends. I was wrong. So wrong. I deserve for you not to talk to me anymore. I had no right to subject you to my troubles. Please, Jeannie and Darrell are good people. I know you don't believe anything I say, but you can trust them. I'm sorry I messed up our lunch and our relationship. I guess I'd be happy now if you wouldn't hate me."

Diane didn't move. The tears were still running slowly down her cheeks. She never said a word. Finally, Matt handed her a tissue. "I'm so sorry I made you cry."

"I need to say something too, Matt. Since we are laying it all out there . . . I made a big mistake. Wag told me that people were married forever; I should have listened. When I met you, I liked you more than a married woman should. I tried to convince myself that you're right and we were only married until death do you part. I know this sounds silly to say, considering we hardly know each other, but I was actually beginning to think that I could have another life. I think I'm glad you finally told me. It was a good lesson for me. Wag is right. I need to keep to myself and behave."

"He's not right, Diane. Whether you care about me or not; he isn't right. Way down deep, you know that. Please don't let what I did change that."

Diane seemed to look right through him, "No. I know what is expected of me and I'll do it. You don't need to worry. If you don't mind, I won't be coming to you for confession or communion."

"No, Diane," Matt shook his head, "I'm not doing that. I'm leaving the priesthood. I just was afraid I couldn't handle the real world and I guess I proved that. I also know that I can't be a priest and not know any more about real life than I do. I'll stay until Mr. Morley gets back and then just leave. I need to start all over someplace else."

"Me, too." Diane gave him a funny look, "Wouldn't it be something if we ran away and ended up at the same place?"

They both chuckled. "Diane, can I make a very indecent proposal to you?"

"Why not, everything else went to hell in the last few minutes!"

"Will you still be my friend, or pleasant acquaintance? I really think that we could be good for each other. I mean, we neither know what we're doing. And I give you my word, nothing hanky-panky."

Diane giggled for the first time, "What kind of an indecent proposal is that? You priests are a weird lot!"

"So are you widows!" Matt teased.

"Okay. You know, I don't have very many friends, so I guess a weird one is better than no one. And besides, if Wag gets on me, I can tell him you're a priest."

"I don't think that would go over very well."

"No, it wouldn't. Okay, what the hell! I can't stand my life right now and I was thinking I needed to do something different. This'll be different alright! Just make me one promise and if you break it, I'll never speak to you again."

"What is it?"

"That you will keep me apprised of where you stand on leaving the church."

"I'm not leaving the church, just the priesthood."

Diane shrugged, "I have a lot to learn, and I hope I can be a good listener for you. But I really love chocolate. Do we have time for our dessert yet?"

"Yes, we do. Thank you so much. I feel the weight of the world is off me. You have no idea how much I worried about telling you."

"Let's not talk about us like we are something. Okay? We're just friends. In a crazy way, we are both married. Sort of like you and Annie."

"Boy Wag sure got hot about that, didn't he?" Matt remembered the picnic.

"Yes, he has quite a list of dos and don'ts. I don't know if even he can keep them all straight. So, Father Vicaro knows your situation?"

Matt knew Diane was trying to get back on a more non-emotional subject. "Yes. He has been great. He knows I've been trying to find my sea legs in the non-clerical world and has cut me a lot of slack. He warned me about not wearing my collar. But I didn't listen."

Diane shook her head, "It might surprise you; but I don't think you should either."

"Really, after you almost quit talking to me?"

"That was different. I don't know why, but I think it's different."

"So do I. Do you want some more coffee? Mine is cold" Matt picked up the thermos.

"We do have to quit arguing and start talking while our coffee is still hot. Okay?"

"Good idea."

They had to hurry and eat their cake to put things away before the first bell rang. Lunch hadn't been fun, but it had been necessary. Diane thanked him for lunch and scurried off just as his students began to arrive.

Matt had no time to think until he was driving home. He wasn't certain at all about how things ended up at lunch, but at least the truth was out. Apparently, they had both felt there was something between them. That was obvious. What would ever happen was anyone's guess. Matt wasn't even sure they were really speaking anymore. Who ever said the truth would set you free?

❧ 32 ❧

MATT HURRIED WHEN HE GOT home to get ready to get back to St. Johns. But the ladies did meet him with a pile of questions about how lunch went. Matt explained that the girls loved the meal and that he and Diane had a chance to talk. He told her that he was a priest. The ladies were all instantly concerned about how she took it.

"I'm not real sure," Matt said honestly. "But we're still talking and decided to be friends. How it will work, I don't know. She was very upset with me and I doubt that she trusts me at all now."

"I can imagine, but wasn't she glad you told her?" Nora asked.

"Yah, but she doesn't know if she believes me. I can't say that I blame her. Sadly whether she knows or not, it doesn't change her situation one bit."

Mo hugged her son, "Well, Mattie, at least she didn't refuse to speak to you. You'll just have to work a little harder to rebuild her confidence."

"She suggested we could be friends like Annie and I. Both married in a way," Matt said.

"No," Grandma Katherine said, "You can try doing it, except you're sweet on each other, not just friends. I think that you both admitted it, unintentionally. In a crazy way, it might've been painful but a good thing. You two will have to take some time to work out all your feelings. You guys need to hack through the jungle to find a pathway."

Matt laughed, "Gee, I don't know if that's a good thing."

"Hey, life isn't easy. Haven't you ever heard that expression, 'it's a jungle out there'?" Grandma giggled.

"Yah, I just never heard it explained this way before."

175

"Well, Matt, welcome to the watering hole," Nora giggled. "You better get changed so you can make it into St. John's on time."

Matt arrived at the church with ten minutes to spare. He was actually looking forward to having some time to not think about the events of today. Grandma was right. They both needed to digest it and he was rather certain that things might change.

He was able to follow the noise down the hall to Room 113. There was Father Vicaro and a pile of youngsters. Matt grinned. He was really hoping that his co-teacher was a big bruiser wearing boxing mitts. A quick glance told him it was only Father Vicaro.

"Hello, Matt. Kids settle down. I'd like to introduce you to your teacher, Mr. Harrington. He has a lot of experience in teaching this class and I'm certain if you give him a chance, you can learn a lot."

Matt waved hi at the kids and then as he put his papers down asked under his breath, "Where's my partner?"

"Not here yet. Keep your fingers crossed."

"They are. Trust me."

"Well, you kids take a seat and I have to go off to my class. I'll leave you with Mr. Harrington. Behave for him," Father Vicaro said as he left the room.

Matt looked at the room full of preteens. Thinking to himself that Father Vicaro had swindled him, he turned to the matters at hand.

"Okay, you all know who I am, now. Can you introduce yourselves? Do you want to stand up to do it or just stay seated?"

A unison yell was unanimous, "Stay seated."

Matt gave his class a big grin, "You seem to be in agreement about that!"

He was a least twenty minutes into a two-hour class when there was a knock at the door. One of the kids in the back got up and answered it. In walked Diane.

Matt's mouth fell open and so did Diane's. There was an uncomfortable silence and then the boy who opened the door said, "Are you our other teacher?"

"Yes, I am. I'm sorry I'm late tonight. I slipped down my front steps when I left the house, so I was a little late."

Matt looked at her with concern, "Are you okay?"

"Fine really. So, let's get going. I am Mrs. Waggoner. I'll just listen for a bit and try to catch up with you. Is that okay?"

"What do you say kids? Shall we let her get away with that?" Matt smiled to the class.

They all thought it was a good idea. The class went well and even though Diane said very little, there was a great discussion before they broke for the evening. After the kids left, Diane helped Matt pick up the papers and straighten up the room. Father Vicaro came in as they were straightening up.

"I see you made it after all," Father Vicaro shook her hand. "I was worried Matthew would be after my hide!"

"I wasn't much help tonight, but I'll do better next week. Actually, Matt did a great job and I don't think I'm needed."

"Yes, you are. He won't do it alone. He already told me that," Father Vicaro was adamant. "Any more than you would. If you want me to talk to your family, I'll be happy to do that."

"I think it'll be okay. If not, I'll let you know," Diane was embarrassed and tried to cover it up quickly. "Wag was concerned about me walking home alone at night."

"I'm sure Mr. Harrington would give you a lift, right Matt?" Father Vicaro asked.

"Be glad to."

"I told him it isn't like walking in downtown Detroit for goodness sakes. It is just barely dark. I can walk. I'll be fine."

"If you won't accept a ride with Matt, I'll get my car out. I don't want to have anything happen to you."

"Yes Father. You don't need to take your car out. I'll ride with Matt."

"One inkling of trouble and I want to know, your word?"

"Yes Father. I hear you."

"Well then, good night you two. God bless."

They never said a word to each to each other all the way to Coot's car. Matt opened the door for her and she got in. When he got in the driver's side, he looked at her, "Slipped down the steps, huh?"

"Don't start, Matt. Please. It's okay, He just didn't understand. I'm so glad I didn't know you were teaching too, or I wouldn't have come tonight."

"Thanks alot. I wish I'd known it was you. I'd have picked you up." Matt started to drive.

Diane's voice became very adamant. "Don't ever do that! Oh God, no!"

"I won't," he answered quickly. "I promise. Diane, you need to get out of their place. You know that don't you?"

"I have no where to go and I owe them so much."

"Baloney! How bad did you get hurt?"

"Just scratched up a little and a couple bruises. Really, I'm okay. No big deal. I do owe them. You just don't understand."

Matt turned into the bank parking lot and turned off the car.

Diane panicked again, "What are you doing? Do you want me to get into trouble?"

"Not at all. What's going on and don't lie to me?" Matt wasn't in the mood for messing around.

"You're telling *me* not to lie to you?" Diane was furious. "That's rich."

"Let's try not to fight. I can find you a safe place to stay. I promise. There's no reason for you to live in fear."

"You just don't understand."

"Then tell me so I do."

"I need to get home. Unless you want me to get into more trouble, take me home. And Matt, drop me off a block away from the house. Okay?" She almost begged. "And please don't let it slip around either of them that we teach a class together. Promise me?"

Matt looked at the shaking woman, "Okay. I promise, but this isn't finished. You have to get out of there and I'm going to find you a place where you can be safe."

"I owe them so much. I can't afford any rent. I'll never get them paid as it is."

"I'll help you. Okay? You don't owe him your health. I'm telling Father Vicaro. You might as well know that right now."

Diane panicked again and then broke into an unconstrained weeping. Matt put his arms around her and let her cry for a bit. Then he said, "Let's put you back together so he doesn't know that you spilled the beans tonight. Okay? Can I take you back to Father Vicaro's tonight? Sister Abigail will watch over you."

"No. I'll be fine if I get home soon. Really Matt. I need to go home. Okay? If you won't take me, I'll walk."

"I'll take you home but it's against my better judgment. If you don't come to school tomorrow or if you have one more bruise, I'm calling the cops. I mean it. I won't have this going on anymore. You have to get out of there. By tomorrow, I want you to have an idea of how you're going to get out of there. Is that understood?"

"I'll think about it Matt, but I've thought about it. I just can't figure anything out. Please, can we go now?"

Matt kissed her forehead, "Okay. Get rid of those tears. You're going to ruin my reputation if the word gets around I always make you cry."

"I won't tell. Thanks Matt. You've been a brick."

"I'd rather just get you out of there."

"I promise to think some more, until then, leave it be."

Matt dropped her off by the fountain in the park so she could sprinkle some cold water on her face. Then he took her home and dropped her off a block away as she asked. "How am I going to be sure you are safe?"

"I imagine he's passed out by now. He was pretty well tanked when I left."

"Diane-,"

"No Matt. Good night."

Matt watched as she walked away. He waited for a time and then went around the corner and in front of her house. The lights were all off except in one upstairs room. He hoped it was her room and indeed, Wag had passed out. It all seemed quiet so he drove home.

When he turned in the yard, the men were still sitting around the picnic table, but the ladies had gone in. He rolled down the window and said, "I need to talk to you guys, so please don't go in yet."

He walked up from parking the car and sat down at the picnic table. Keith handed him a beer. "That bad?"

Matt almost cried when he told them what happened.

"That son of a bitch," Carl almost yelled. "This is the end gate for him. Now I'm really out for him."

"Dad, what can we do? I shouldn't have left Diane tonight, should I? I should've taken her someplace else. I just didn't know what to do."

Keith patted his shoulder, "I would've done the same thing. You need to think this out. You can't just go off half cocked and make things worse."

Ian shook his head, "That creep isn't going to quit until he kills someone or gets thrown in the slammer."

Matt almost fell off the bench, "Oh no!"

"Just a figure of speech, Matt," Elton calmed him. "You said he was probably passed out. Take it easy."

Ian quickly backtracked, "Sorry Matt. I went over Mr. Anderson's papers and this afternoon he and I went to his attorney. He has to look it over, but he thinks he can nail him. He's going to try to get a few more of his clients and if they agree to press charges, he could go to jail for along time."

"What about Diane and Gladys?" Matt asked. "You guys said he could get worse if he's under pressure."

"I'll talk to Father Vicaro, Byron and Jeannie. I want her to come and stay here. We have plenty of room and she'd always have someone around here. She'd be safe," Elton said. "I want to talk to them first and see if it makes sense."

"Will she be safe here?" Matt asked.

Ian put his arm around his brother, "Look Matt, we all thought Ruthie would be safe here. I know that we can watch out of Diane. Trust us."

Matt nodded. "I'm trying. I should've just brought her out here tonight. I never even thought of it."

Carl said, "Okay. In the morning, Matt, you call Father Vicaro before school and tell him about last night. Let him know that Elton and I will be in to see him. Okay, Elton? Any time better for you?"

"I'll make time. Just give me the word."

"What about Nora?" Matt asked.

"She'd have had her out here already. You know her that well, don't you?" Elton asked.

Matt nodded. "What a hell of a mess."

Carl said, "Matt, I want you to find out if Diane knows of any place that Gladys can go. I don't want them together. I don't trust Gladys to keep away from Wag and besides it would be too much of a temptation for Wag. We should look out for her. Let me know. I think I need to see my cop friend in town soon. However, we need to get our ducks in a row. I don't want to get things out of sync unless something unforeseen event makes us have to."

"Like what?" Matt asked nervously.

"Calm down," Keith advised. "You did the right thing Matt, and you'll know what to do when the time comes, but you need to be calm. We'll take care of it. Okay? Can you do that?"

Matt nodded. "Yah. I should've marched right in that house and beat the hell out of him. Or driven Diane to the cops. I hope she's okay."

"Knock it off. Hear me?" Carl snapped. "We can't be holding your hand. Diane needs to be able to depend on you. So be there."

"You're right." Matt nodded. "This is a hateful mess. Dad, I don't like your Petunia Patch very much."

"Hell, it certainly isn't as delightful as I thought it would be," Carl agreed. "It is not for the meek, for damn sure."

❧ 33 ❧

MATT CALLED FATHER VICARO AFTER Lloyd's drive. He wasn't surprised that she had lied about being late, but he was surprised about the gravity of the situation. "Tell Carl and Elton than anytime will be fine. I'll be in my office all day. I will wait to talk to Wag until I talk to them. Thanks for letting me know."

Ian called Mr. Anderson and they decided to go into see the attorney as soon as they could get in to see him. Carl called Alex Bernard, Merton's only cop, and said he would take him to lunch.

Matt was riding into the school with Jeannie that day. He was worn out by the time he got into her car. One look at him and she shook her head, "Lunch went badly?"

Matt spent the trip to town explaining what had happened. Jeannie was not happy about it but not surprised either. "Is someone going to tell Darrell? He'll be mad if no one tells him."

"Elton and Ian were going to go over there on their way to work."

"Good. He's very protective toward her. He sort of feels responsible for her."

"I know. Your husband is a hell of a guy, Jeannie."

"I know that. Why do you think I love him?"

"Good point."

"Matt, I'm glad that you got to tell her the truth before last night. I think that's a good thing, even though it adds to the mess right now. Don't you?"

"I don't know. I tell you I'm so worried about her."

"Don't be surprised if she avoids you today. You can about count on that. She'll try to pretend like it didn't happen. I know her."

181

"But she knows I know."

"Won't matter. Anyway, I'm sorry that you didn't get more time for your thinking. Somehow life set its own time table."

"That it did."

As Jeannie predicted, Matt only caught a glimpse of Diane in the morning. Jeannie told him over lunch that she had just nodded hello to her and she dashed on by. Matt was relieved because he didn't have classes over at St. Johns in the afternoon, so he was going to spend some time in his room, getting some work finished before Jeannie's last class. He didn't want to fall behind with all the stuff going on.

A little after four, there was a knock at his door. He thought it was Jeannie and said to come in before he looked up from his student's equations and he noticed who it was. He looked up and Diane standing there. She looked tired and frail but still beautiful. The dark green suit with the same colored satin blouse looked stunning on her.

"Hi," he could barely get out. "Sit down. Want some coffee?"

"No thank you," she looked at him with her large soft brown eyes, as she sat on the edge of the chair. "Matt, I've decided something. I thought it all over last night. I don't want to see you anymore, be your friend or have any relationship. I appreciate that you want to help me, but it isn't helpful. I know you were honest with me, I know that. This isn't a good situation. I wish you the very best in life, but please just stay away from me. It isn't fair to either of us. I'm not your problem, nor do I want to be. Please respect that."

Matt could have fallen over. He had honestly felt that he and Diane had reached some sort of an understanding, even though he didn't know what it was. He was totally unprepared for what she said. He sat dumbfounded and then she got up. "Thanks Matt. I wish you the very best."

He stood up and almost ran between her and the door. "Diane, please think it over. Please don't shut me out totally."

Her answer was very matter of fact, "Oh, not totally. We still work together and I'll work with you at CCD this coming week. I'm going to tell Father Vicaro that he needs to find someone else. I don't dislike you, at all. In fact, I do like you. That isn't it. Just leave it be."

Matt touched her arm and she winced, "Dammit woman! You got hurt again, didn't you?"

"No, honest Matt, it's from when I fell down the steps. It isn't new."

"I can't believe a thing you say. You didn't 'fall' down the steps. You were knocked down them! Don't try to paint this with butterflies." Then he got tears in his eyes, "Diane, you don't have to talk to me, but you have to get away from that man."

"Good bye, Matt." She firmly pushed him aside and went out the door.

Matt was still standing there motionless when Jeannie came in. One look and she said, "Diane?"

He could barely keep himself together as he said, "Let's get the hell out of here."

In the car, he told her everything. "I feel like I'm on a rollercoaster. She's right. I should just get away from her. This is the most cock-eyed stupid mess I can imagine. It would be different if we're in love or something. We hardly know each other. This is flat out ridiculous. I can't take anymore of it."

Jeannie gave him a funny little smile, "Oh yeah? I don't believe you. But I do agree about one thing. You should give her space. If she thinks she wants to go it alone, let her. She doesn't appreciate what she's losing and she won't until she has lost it. Just be ready to jump back in when she finds out. Promise?"

"Maybe I won't want to by then, if she ever does."

"Ah, I know better than that. Don't even try to pretend to me and Darrell. This is all coming down, you know. Those other guys and the cop aren't going to let this go. Right now, Diane wants to pretend she can get under the radar. It is out now. Once she realizes that, she'll want your friendship back. You need a little tough love right now."

"Okay, smarty pants, what about you?"

"She hasn't told me to butt out yet. But if she does, I'm afraid I'd have to take my own advice."

"It's different. You guys were friends for a long time. She hardly knows me. And I'm a priest."

"Good grief, how I wish you weren't! Just quit that damned business! You're making me crazy." Then Jeannie looked at him in horror, "Oh Matt. I'm so very sorry. I should have never said that. It's none of my business. You have no idea how I want to take that back."

Matt just shook his head. "I'm not mad at you. I am going to quit it. I'm talking to Father Vicaro as soon as I can. I'm not even a levelheaded human being, how can I be a priest. I am a royal idiot."

183

"Matt, you aren't an idiot. This is the flip side of being in love, and yes, you are; so don't start with the jabber. Nothing else can make a person feel better or worse in so little time flat. This is just a bad situation. I have to learn to keep my mouth shut."

Matt laughed. "You? I haven't met a woman in this state that keeps their mouth shut!"

"It isn't that funny! Hey, when I talked to Darrell at noon, he said there was a powwow planned for tonight at Schroeder's, right after school. Want to stop a minute and pull yourself together before we meet the masses?"

"Ah hell, not much point. Thanks Jeannie. You're the best."

"I sure wasn't a minute ago," she grinned.

There was a pile of folks gathered in the dining room at Schroeders. Mr. Anderson and his attorney, Sherriff Bernard, Father Vicaro, Byron, Ian and Elton were already there and Carl was pouring coffee for Darrell. Jeannie gave her husband a kiss and everyone sat down.

Coot put the coffee pot down and Sherriff Bernard summed up the conversation. "Is this everyone? Good. We have a plan of sorts. Mr. Wolf, Anderson's attorney has contacted at least five more of Waggoner's clients. We're going to get depositions and their paper work from them. Mr. Wolf thinks it'll take a couple weeks to make certain we have all the tees crossed. Then he's going to the State's Attorney. Father Vicaro has tried to talk Diane into teaching this class at the church longer, but today she seemed to want to get out of it. We're trying to contact Gladys' sister in Minnesota to see if we can set up a safe place for her there. Elton and Nora have offered a home to Diane, but she hasn't been told yet. We want to arrest Wag on some minor thing so we can hit him with the big charges while he is in custody. Mr. Saphron will provide us with a little charge. He said that at almost any time, he can give a legitimate complaint about the man. That'll give us time to move the ladies away. If they'll go. I'm hoping that we can at least convince Diane to get out. It'll be a few weeks, so try to keep a low profile until then. If anything happens between now and then, I want to be informed. Not later, but right away! I'm counting her co-workers to keep an eye on her and let me know if she even calls in sick for a sneeze! I've heard rumors before, but had no idea it was this bad. The trouble with these situations is the intimidation. He has bullied those women so much. They know they're in jeopardy, but are the ones least apt to report him."

Everyone agreed and decided to back off until the attorney got the depositions. After everyone left, Matt went to change clothes and joined the guys milking. After he milked Buttermilk, Elton called him aside. "Will you go for a walk with me?"

Matt nodded, but wasn't very eager to talk any more. He was worn out. He was surprised when they headed for the pasture. "Where we going?"

"Oh, I thought I needed to check the salt block. It's out here."

"Yah and what else?"

"What happened today?"

Just like that, Matt shrugged. Elton stopped and put his arms around him and gave him a hug.

"I thought so. Let it all out. Anything you say will be unheard except by me and my memory isn't very good—so it'll be lost forever."

Matt went into profane tirade. A lot of it made no sense, but enough of it did, so Elton got the gist of it. After Matt started to settle down, Elton patted him on the arm. "You clergymen! I tell you. I've never seen the beat. Most folks just throw a tantrum right off, but you and Byron seem to store it up until it's a volcano. Then all hell breaks loose. Feel better?"

Matt shook his head. "You should never have let me get out of control."

"You aren't going to heal up until you clear out the pipes. If you want to scream at me, have at it, okay? Now I'm going to say my piece. I agree with Jeannie. I'm glad you told Diane though. It's be the best in the long run. Now, my man, you did what you could and you did a good job. Is that registered in your head? Matt, answer me?"

"Yah, I guess."

"Now, get your mitts out of the way and let God do His business. Stay out of it for while. When it's time for you to step in, you'll know and you'll know what to do. Okay? If you miss anything, I'm sure one of us will be more than happy to tap you on the shoulder!"

"You must all think I'm crazy."

"No. You just don't appreciate that most of us have had a good crack at the bat already. We know how much fun it is." Elton started to walk again, "So, did you know the furniture from Boston will be here tomorrow some time? We got painting and moving to do. Then you get your school work in line. You can't let that get lost in the shuffle. I recommend you do as much of it ahead as you can. I think you'll want every spare minute before long."

"Very practical. You're right, as usual."

"It really doesn't happen all that often," Elton chuckled. "And guess what? Ian and Eddie are going bowling with Danny Saturday night. I think that is good, don't you? And I need a favor from you. Kevin could use a pep talk from you?"

"Kevin, from me?"

"Yah. He has the first Sunday School class on Sunday morning and he is a basket case. Not only is he worried about Miriam, he's worried about himself. I'd appreciate it if you could talk to him. Can I count on you?"

"Of course, Elton. I'll do that." Matt grinned and punched Elton in the shoulder. "I know you really don't need me to do that, but thanks for asking me. You want me to get back in the game, right?"

"Yup, I do at that." Elton grinned, "I think the kids should be done by now so it is safe for us to head back to the farm. If we timed it right, we won't miss supper."

They walked along in silence for quite a ways and then Elton said, "It isn't over yet, Matt. Even though Diane said that, I'm almost certain it isn't. I can't guarantee how it will work out, but I know this isn't the final word. She just needs some time. Love also requires giving the other person time when they need it and keeping the door open so they can change their minds. Okay?"

Matt nodded. "Okay."

$$\sim\!\!\mathcal{S}\,34\,\mathcal{C}\!\!\sim$$

FRIDAY MORNING, MATT WAS PUT to work helping lick the last of the wedding invitations while waiting for Jeannie. Ruthie and Mo had some cool invitations that included both weddings, which were a couple days apart. His tongue was very glad when Jeannie drove up.

"You seem more together this morning," Jeannie observed.

"Yah, it'd be hard to be less together. Good grief, I was licking stamps for the wedding invitations, so I've ingested enough glue to put anyone together!"

"You should've heard Darrell last night. Wow! He went into a frightful rant, but he felt better afterwards."

"So did I. Elton prodded me into it. He says it's good to get it out."

"Yah, I think that is why women talk things over so much. It doesn't really change much, but it makes you feel better."

"If you have a confidant to listen to you! Elton is good that way."

"He's a good guy. I know Darrell thinks the world of him. I'd talk to Nora. She isn't any slouch either."

"I can see that. Well, let's hit the classroom and I'll try to act like a teacher today instead of a lovesick teenager!"

She looked at him and giggled. "And to think, some of the lady teachers here are jealous that we ride to school together! If they only knew!"

"Promise you won't tell them."

"How much is it worth to you?" Jeannie taunted.

Matt saw Diane coming down the hall toward him and made it a point to talk to a student so he didn't have to look her way. He knew she saw it. He didn't feel right about it, but he decided to start listening to real people instead of his own stupid ideas.

At coffee break, she came into the room after he did and the only seat was at his table. He stood up, offered her his seat and left the room. It almost killed him, but he knew that she got the message he was giving her space.

At lunch, she sat at the other end of the same long teacher's table in the cafeteria. He gobbled down his lunch and went out to shoot hoops with the students. By the time he headed over to St. Johns, he was relieved that he wouldn't run into her. When he wanted to see her, he didn't. Now that he didn't, she was everywhere!

When he met Jeannie at the car to go home, he was proud of himself. He couldn't wait to tell her of his grand efforts. She listened and then said, "I found out something today. Diane asked to be changed from the Homecoming chaperone events. I guess the school said they'd try to change it. She told them that she was expecting family from out of town or something like that. Do you believe it?"

Matt thought, "Maybe she contacted her family. That'd be good huh?"

"Her Dad has passed on and her mother can't travel. So, unless it's her brother who was in the service, I don't know who it would be. I think she just made it up to try to get out of it."

"Are you going to ask her about it?"

"Only if she opens up the opportunity. I know you want to know what's going on, but I don't want her to close off from all of us. She looked okay today though but rather down in the dumps."

"Thanks for telling me, Jeannie. I appreciate it." Matt looked out the window. "I have to quit mulling this over myself or I'll end up a nutcase."

"Will be?" Jeannie giggled. "What have you got planned for the weekend?"

"Painting and moving! The movers are supposed to get here and we have a day to unload it."

"Darrell wants to talk to you about that," Jeannie said.

"Of course, we'll help you guys move too," Matt said. "We'd planned on it."

"No, he wants to talk to you about something else."

"Okay. I'll call him or see him. Thanks for the ride, Jeannie. I want to pay you for your gas."

"No, you won't. Darrell said no way. Now for my part, I think the occasional caramel roll would do me wonders."

"You got it. Bye."

That evening after chores, the crew went over to Carl and Mo's place to finish the last of the painting. There were only two bedrooms and the kitchen left to do. With the large crew, it didn't take long at all. Jeannie and Darrell came over with some sodas and beer for the workers when they were almost finished.

Darrell spoke to Matt alone. "Hey, can I ask you a favor?"

"Of course," Matt replied. "I only owe you a million or so."

"No, you don't, but I was wondering. Jeannie and I'll be moving into our house in a week or so. The old cabin will be empty. In this country, that isn't good. I mean, I have to keep the heat on anyway or the pipes will freeze. Once I'm out, the mice will think it is the Hilton or something. I don't want to tear it down. There's nothing wrong with it except it's small. Could I interest you in living in it? At least this winter?"

"Huh?" Matt was shocked. "I never even thought about that? How much would I owe you? Why me?"

"If you have other plans, that's okay," Darrell said.

"No other plans at all. I just never thought about it. I mean, I have no money for rent."

"I don't want rent. Just pay your own expenses. It'll keep the place from going to ruin. Besides, I have a selfish motive. I'll be working more at the Cheese Factory in town this winter and I'd feel better knowing you could help my Jeannie get her car out and stuff. You guys go to work in the same place, you help me with chores, it's close to your folks," Darrell explained. "I thought it would be a good fit. Maybe you'd like living on your own instead with your Mom and Dad. And you wouldn't have to mess with a lease or anything, because if your situation changes, I'd understand."

Matt sat on the step, "It's fantastic! Really Darrell. What would I ever do without you guys? You always keep an eye out for me. I will say yes. I have to make sure that I give Grandpa Lloyd a ride every day, but I was thinking that I might change that to after school instead of in the morning. This is just too rushed. Other than that, it'd be good for me to be really on my own. I have to learn that, huh?"

"Do you have any furniture? We will leave the appliances because there are new ones in the house, but we have to take the furniture. So, you'll need some stuff."

"I have some things from Mom's home. I'll take care of that. Man, this is wonderful. I can never thank you enough."

"You'll change your tune when you go into battle with the mice over your last piece of toast or are shoveling the snow off the roof. I'll show you how to clean out the snow from the yard. I'd love the help. Really. We're doing each other a favor!"

That night was the first night that Matt actually slept well in days. It was partially that he was exhausted, but he also realized that things weren't as grim as he had imagined. There was life going on, if he'd just open his eyes and look beyond the mirror. The thought of having his own place was exciting. Other than his dorm room, which hardly counted, he'd never lived alone. When he was in the rectory, Mrs. Frisbee took care of him. It was something he knew he'd to face eventually, and this would be a perfect place to do it: within forks reach of both his Mom and Nora!

The next morning over breakfast, Matt told the family. Carl was a bit taken back but then smiled. "Good. Then you and Ian will both be out of our hair so Mo and I can honeymoon."

Mo swatted him, "I'll miss my boys. I'll be lonely."

"No you won't," Elton piped up. "I'm sure they will descend on you at meal time! And besides, you'll have so many Gophers, you'll need a nanny!"

"I was thinking the other day," Nora began. "You will have three babies to watch. Little tiny ones! Bottles and diapers! You're a brave one, Mo."

"I'll have help. Right Coot?"

Carl cringed. "I can handle toddlers, but babies? I don't know!"

"I'll teach you. It really isn't a problem." Mo grinned. "So Matt, what are you going to need for furniture?"

"If I can still have my bedroom set from home, then I'll only have everything else to get," Matt chuckled.

"Well of course, your bedroom stuff is yours," his Mom said. "So, you need living room stuff and a table and chairs. Huh?"

"You can have my stuff," Coot offered. "It ain't much, but it'll keep your butt off the floor. I have a table and four chairs, a Lazy Boy chair, coffee table, black and white TV and two bookcases. That will work for a while. If you want it?"

"That'd be great, Dad." Matt beamed. "I don't need a lot. It'll be just me."

"We'll find more stuff when we unpack," Mo pointed out. "You can have that desk from the den. I have the new one that I want to keep."

Ian smiled, "Well, I have the sofa and chair from my apartment. We won't have room for it, because we are going to make the downstairs into a pool room. I get a pool table!"

"I heard about that!" Matt grinned. "Good for you! And a dart board?"

"My own grownup playroom. Ruthie even said I can decorate it, but she has the right to veto anything. Somehow, that didn't really seem like I'd get a lot of say, but it's close."

Elton laughed, "Close as a married man ever gets."

"Elton," Lloyd said, "You're going to be in the pickle jar with that kid that drives my car."

"Oh, Grandpa," Matt said, "I was thinking. We should go driving in the afternoon. Okay? We'd have more time and you could sleep in longer. Would that be okay?"

"I think it would be, right Elton? Would it be?" the old man asked.

Elton nodded, "Yes, I think it's a good idea. Mornings are a rush."

"Okay," Grandpa said. "What is your name again? I know you, but I don't know your name."

"I am Matt, Grandpa."

"No, Matthew is a baby," Lloyd thought.

Nora answered, "No, his name is Matt also. Danny and Jenny's baby is named Matthew and so is this guy's name."

"Well, I'll be damned. We ran out of names! I figured it might happen one day, but not while I was still kicking. I think I will call you something else."

"Darrell calls me Tuck," Matt offered.

"What the hell kind of name is that?" Lloyd frowned. "But I guess when you run out, that's what happens, huh? Okay, Truck."

"I have a granddaughter we call Rain," Maureen smiled.

Grandpa rolled his eyes. "I imagine someone will be named Tractor next. It's a fright, I tell you. A real fright."

"We'll get by, Lloyd. I promise you, we will," Elton patted the old man's hand. "Want some more coffee?"

Before the last plate was cleared, the moving van turned in the approach. Carl and Elton went out to meet them. Carl climbed in the cab and directed the movers to his house.

He never imagined the pride he would feel doing that! He was actually directing movers to his home! The yard was still a mess, but the house was bright and shiny new. He was a very happy man. Maybe life in the Petunia Patch wasn't too bad after all! It was when they turned into his yard that morning that Carl decided that the next spring he would plant a huge field of Petunias! And it would be a surprise to everyone! He couldn't keep a smile off his face.

Every free person in the Engelmann clan was there with their work gloves on. The unloading went very fast. Ian's things were stored in the garage and the things that Matt would take were put in the empty spare room. The moving van left before eleven and by the time the whole family went over to Schroeder's for lunch, most of the big stuff was put away. By the chore time, almost everything was done. Stuff was still in boxes, but the boxes were at least in the right room.

Kevin and Matt helped Darrell do his chores. On the way home, Matt had a great opportunity to talk to him.

"So, tomorrow is your big morning, huh?" Matt started while they were driving back to Schroeders after chores.

"Oh Matt, I'm just dying. I want to do a good job and I know that Miriam needs extra attention. It isn't fair to Joan, Mrs. Sandvahl, to have so many kids and Miriam too, but I want to do a good job. You know, I'm such a knucklehead most of the time. I can never imagine why anyone would trust me to be their kid's godparent! Now Carrie, she is a natural, but me?"

"Kevin. You're a natural too, and I can tell you something. Very, very few people take being a Godparent as seriously as you have. Most folks just treat it like it doesn't mean anything at all. If I had a kid, I'd feel very blessed to have a guy like you be my kids' sponsor." Matt studied Kevin, "You have a compassion for folks that most people can only read about and not even begin to understand. And you are crazy enough, so the little kids love you. You'll do great."

Kevin was pleased, "So would you. Too bad you aren't a Lutheran. Pastor Olson would have you in the Sunday School room so fast your head would spin."

"Ah, you should see the CCD class! Twenty-four prepubescent kids! They are either giggling or whining! That is not mankind's finest age!" Matt shook his head.

Kevin chuckled, "I know some teenagers that make you wonder if God shouldn't rework his mold. I tell you! You think that Diane will help you with the class after all?"

"I don't know. I rather doubt it. Kevin, she made it abundantly clear she wants nothing to do with me. So, maybe it'd be better all the way around if she didn't."

"She'll get over that. I can understand a bit of how she feels. I'm sure she's sweet on you, or she'd have never risked going to the creek to talk to you. Maybe she was beginning to see a light at the end of the tunnel. Your revelation sort of turned the light into an oncoming train!"

"Thanks, that makes me feel real good," Matt gave a sarcastic chuckle.

"Yah, but you gave her the facts and she needed that. Seldom does anyone appreciate the facts. They're usually crappy things. When things work out with this Wag mess, she'll think it over again. I think you're doing the right thing. I know I don't know much, but if I thought you were going off the track, I'd tell you!" Kevin stated.

"I appreciate that. Honestly, I feel like it is over between us, not that we ever had anything between us! I think, it's just done. I messed it up totally."

Kevin shook his head, "Man, you really don't know much, do you? It is just starting. Things are always rocky, maybe not boulders like you guys are doing, but rocky. Take your medicine like the rest of us. This is how you really get to know the other person. You know, when everything is in the toilet. Because life is long and whether we want to admit it or not, a good share of it is spent in the bathroom!"

Matt started to laugh. By the time they turned in the yard a Schroeders, they had tears rolling down their cheeks! All they had to do was look at each other and they would start again.

When they got in the house for a cup of coffee, they were silly. Elton grinned, "What did you guys drink? Did you bring some for us?"

"No. We were just talking about Sunday School tomorrow," Kevin grinned. "Matt thinks I will do alright."

"Well of course," Lloyd pointed out. "You're my relative. We might not amount to much, but we work hard at it!"

"Thanks, Grandpa," Kevin gave him a huge hug.

"I have to go to bed now. I can sleep late because that Tractor guy isn't going to practice driving until after lunch," Grandpa said.

"It's Tuck," Grandma Katherine corrected.

"That's what I said. Truck. You better get to bed so you don't drive in the ditch!"

"I will Grandpa. Good night."

Before Kevin and Carrie left, Matt went to the bathroom and got a piece of toilet tissue and folded it neatly. He came out and discreetly gave it to Kevin to keep in his pocket during Sunday school. Kevin's eyes sparkled. "I'll do that Man. Thanks."

35

THE NEXT MORNING WAS THE usual organized Sunday chaos. The only difference was today the Harringtons were taking Ian's car to Mass. They pulled in the yard at Ellison's to pick up Ruthie just as Carrie and Kevin were leaving Ellison's with Miriam to go over to the church.

"Break a leg," Matt grinned to Kev. "And you have a good morning at Sunday school, little Gopher?"

Miriam patted her chest, unsmiling, "Gopher no go. Gopher Fodder go."

Matt gave her a hug, "No Sweetie, you go with Son to your school. I'm going to my school. Fodder is going to school too! Did you know that?"

Miriam made a funny face, "Fodder craffs?"

The men looked at each other, "Sometimes we do crafts. You and I'll be big kids huh and do a good job. You're lucky; you have Son with you. I don't."

Miriam looked at him with concern, "Fodder no Son."

"But I'll see you later, okay?"

"If you want to," the little girl put her arms around Kevin's neck, resigned to her fate. She really didn't like their plans at all; but she'd do it, if Kevin wanted.

The three went downstairs to the classrooms and there met Joan Sandvahl. She smiled at them and then stood tall, "Ready Team?"

They all nodded.

"Good. Let's get this over with!"

Miriam patted Kevin's cheek, "Over with."

Kev chuckled, "You can keep that to yourself too, Little One."

Kev held Miriam through most of class and Carrie and Joan handled the actual teaching. It seemed to work well to have an adult in a student's midst. Most of the kids had come to know Kevin during Vacation Bible School and considered him one of them. They watched what he did and tried to imitate him. It worked out very well.

Carrie and Joan had planned on a sticker thing for the craft instead of facing a crayon fiasco, so it went well. There were no panic attacks on Miriam's part, just vague unease. They were all pleased when the parents came to collect their children.

After the last kid left, Miriam asked Joan, "Over with?"

The middle-aged lady giggled, "Yes Miriam! It is over with." Then she hugged Carrie, "Thanks so much. You're great! I think we'll have this under control. I am actually looking forward to this year!"

Miriam nodded, "Over with."

Kevin gave the little curly haired toddler a big hug.

Matt had made up his mind to not look for Diane at Mass. That was easier said than done. He sat down with his Mom, Ian and Ruthie. Two minutes later, the Waggoners came in and sat right in front of them. Matt wondered why God was antagonizing him this way and then decided it was to see how he could handle it in Kevin's toilet. When he thought of that, he grinned. Ruthie took his hand and whispered, "What?"

He whispered back, "Just something that Kevin said."

Wag turned and gave him a foul stare for whispering in church and Matt just shook his head. He was determined he wasn't going to lose his positive attitude. He gave the obnoxious man a smiling nod and then ignored him.

After Mass, when they were leaving the church, Matt asked Ian for the car keys. Ian gave him a quizzical glance, shrugged and handed him the keys. After they shook hands with Father Vicaro and went down the steps, Mr. Waggoner nodded to Mo. She turned to talk to them and everyone said hi. Matt smiled, and said, "I'll bring the car."

He had to consciously make his feet leave. He wanted so much to ask Diane how she was, but he didn't. When he got back with the car, they were gone. He was disappointed, but that is what he had expected.

In the car, his Mom announced, "She seemed okay, Mattie, but I thought she seemed disappointed that you took off so fast."

Ruthie agreed, "I think it's for the best. Matt, can you and I have lunch this week? Just you and me? I want to go on a date with you."

196

Matt chuckled, "Well of course. Are we going to tell Ian, or not?"

Ian brushed them off, "Knock yourselves out! I can easily find another woman."

Ruthie made a face, "Keep telling yourself that, Romeo."

Maureen giggled, "I don't know what happened to those wonderful little boys I raised."

"Ruthie, late lunch on Thursday would be perfect. I don't have classes at St. Johns so I'm finished by two, if you can wait that long for lunch."

"Sounds great. I'll be out front of the school right after two."

Sunday's clan dinner was fun as usual and in the afternoon, there were many things going on. Darrell and Jeannie's house would be finished the following week and Ian's two weeks later. As soon as Darrell's were moved in, Matt would move into to their place.

Homecoming would take up alot of time in between and then the wedding plans were looming. Zach and Suzy offered their home for some of the Harrington families to stay as did the other clanners. Coot was going to stay at Schroeder's until after the wedding, but Mo was going to move over to their new house with Ian. It'd be mass confusion. She and Coot were going shopping in the next couple days to pick up three cribs and baby things!

Darlene loved her new job, even though she had only worked three days. Mary College was a long drive, but the work was what she wanted. She was a little disappointed that she wouldn't have more time before their baby was born, but was very glad that she had Mo and Carl to babysit.

Jenny, Danny's wife, was going to start her job at the ASCS (Federal Farm Services) Merton branch office in six weeks. Then Baby Matthew would become the first Baby Gopher in the Petunia Patch. Miriam of course would be the old timer and Maddie Olson would be there three days a week.

"It'll give me some time to ease into it," Carl groaned. "I'm just afraid that by the time I figure out that I don't like it, it'll be too late for me to get out."

Byron laughed, "You may not know it, but it's already too late, Buddy! And then don't forget, you'll have Charlie over there too. He and Ginger are not about to relinquish their Gopher status. I think the kids will be over after school a couple days a week."

"Every night, Daddy," Charlie announced. "If Coot gets his chickens right away, I will have to be his Chicken Man too."

"And Miriam wants duck, right Miriam?' Ginger prodded the little girl. Ginger was her mentor and relished the job. "You want Splurches, right?"

Miriam repeated, "Splursch!"

"Yes kids, that's true, but not right away. It will be after our weddings and we get settled," Mo grinned. "But we have a lot to do before then. Okay?"

"Okay, but we really wanted to have our pets," Ginger pointed out.

"Yes, Ginger, but we need to make plans for the yard and all that. And Mo wants to plant some trees this fall. So we need to dig holes for them. It's very important that they be deep enough and in the right place," Coot pointed out.

The kids couldn't have heard anything better! Important holes! There is little a Gopher Brigade would rather hear! The kids clapped and cheered.

After Lloyd's nap, Matt took him for his drive. "Grandpa, would you like to go see where I'm going to live?"

Lloyd frowned, "You live with me. I know that."

"Now I do, but I need to get my own place. I'm a grownup."

"That doesn't matter. I don't live alone. Do I?"

"No, Grandpa. You have family that lives with you. I don't have a family."

"You're really a dumb one. Of course you do. We're your family," the thin, elderly man shook his head.

"I know that and I love you all. But you know, Kevin and Carrie have their own place and so do Danny and Jenny. Right?"

"Yah, I guess. If I was you, I'd get a wife. She can make you caramel rolls. Otherwise, you'll just eat eggs."

Matt chuckled, "Good advice, Grandpa Lloyd."

Matt drove into Darrell's yard and pointed to the cabin. "That's where I'm going to live."

Lloyd just shook his head. "You can't. Somebody's living there. You'll get in trouble. I tell you Tractor, you'll end up in the Pickle Jar. If I ever saw a guy headed for that, it's you. I can help you, but you have to start listening to me. Okay?"

"Okay, Grandpa, What do you think I should do?"

"Get a job. Do you have a job?"

"Yes, I do."

"Then get a cow."

"Then what?" Matt grinned.

"A wife. See a guy gets a house and then you have to get a wife to take care of the it. It's a fright. Maybe you should get a dog."

Matt laughed, "That is the best idea I have heard yet!"

"You just can't let it poop in the house. It will mess up the floor."

"You're right about that."

That evening when Matt helped Darrell with chores, he told Darrell about the conversation. "Grandpa is really full of advice," Darrell agreed. "You know, I used to have a dog. It was a good dog, but it got sick and had to be put down. That was right before I had my heart attack. I just never got another one. We should have one. Every good farm has one."

"You know, it might not be a bad idea. But would it interfere with the goats and cattle?" Matt asked.

"No, in fact they can be a lot of help with the livestock. If they aren't good livestock, we can't have them around. You know, unless they're a house dog."

"What kind of dog did you have?" Matt asked.

"A black Labrador cross. Darn good dog. In fact, Swenson's have one of his pups. I wonder if they still have that dog. It was a great dog."

That night, Matt got a lot of work finished for the following week. In his prayers, he thanked God that he had such a fantastic support system. He prayed that Diane would have one too. That night, he dreamt that he and Diane were walking in a garden filled with Petunias with a huge black dog.

❧❧ 36 ❧❧

THE FIRST PART OF THE week went by in a flash. Everyone was so busy with painting, moving and unpacking, that insanity reigned. School was settling into a routine and Matt was a lot more comfortable with his classes. He still ran into Diane everywhere he turned. In fact, they had a head-on collision on the playground Tuesday. Matt came around a corner one way and Diane came the other. They ended up almost knocking each other over. Matt helped her pick up her books that she had been carrying and without thinking, brushed some dirt off her sleeve. When he did, she winced. He stopped to look into her eyes. He opened his mouth, but never said anything. She shook her head no and he shrugged. He turned away and she reached out to touch his arm.

He looked back at her and wanted so very much to give her a hug. Instead, he squeezed her hand. "Please be careful," he said and walked away. He wondered if she would've talked to him, but didn't know what to do. He just left. It made his head want to blow up.

When he told Jeannie about it, she thought he had done the right thing. "Matt, I think she's realizing how much she wants you for a friend. But if you jump too soon, you might scare her off again."

"That's what I thought. I wonder if she's going to show up at St. Johns tomorrow night?"

"Denise told me she had coffee with Diane this morning. I guess the school told her the day before that they were sorry, but she had to either find someone to cover for her herself or just chaperone for Homecoming. She said that her family plans had canceled so she'd do it. Denise asked her straight out what Wag thought and she admitted he wasn't happy about it. I guess they had an argument, but he finally realized that her job depended on her doing things like that."

"Argument? Jeannie, her other arm was bruised today." Matt explained. "I have to call Sheriff Bernard and Father Vicaro as soon as I get home. He'll end up hurting her real bad. But, maybe it's just me."

"Not just you," Jeannie nodded. "I agree. Let me know what Bernard and Vicaro say. Have a good night, see you tomorrow morning."

Everyone agreed that things weren't getting better at the Waggoners, but since the statements had been taken, things on that end were moving on ahead of schedule. Maybe it'd all be over sooner than they had anticipated. However, rushing it could throw a monkey wrench into the plan.

The next day went by as usual, only Matt didn't see Diane at all. That evening when he walked into St. Johns, he was convinced he wouldn't see her. He was surprised when she came in right behind him. He smiled and said, "I have to admit, I'm surprised to see you."

"Father Vicaro came down on Wag this morning. I don't know what he said, but Wag wanted me to do this. So, here I am. I'm sorry to not be a reliable assistant."

"Let's not spend so much time apologizing, okay?" Matt raised his eyebrows. "That only works if the situation is going to change."

Diane stopped dead in her tracks, "Matt. Please don't lock me out."

He turned, "I'm only doing what you asked. I'm here for you whenever you want me to be, but don't confound me any more than you have to. I'm at a loss as to what you want."

Diane looked directly at him, "Would you believe me if I said I don't know."

Matt smiled. "Yes I would. Let's get into our classroom before the onslaught. Okay?"

While they were putting the papers on the desks to ready them for their students, Father Vicaro came in. "I got my car out front. I'll bring you home tonight and take you to the door. No back talk."

"It really isn't necessary. Wag was fine tonight," Diane said.

"Yes, it is. Matt, I'm instructing you to release class a little early tonight. I want you and Mrs. Waggoner to go out to the rectory garden and you tell her what Schroeder's offered. I'm not messing around anymore. I'll tell you the rest on our way to your house."

Matt was stunned, but nodded lamely. "Okay."

Diane did the same and then the old priest left. The two stood there motionless for a minute until the first students came giggling in.

Class went well and Matt was relieved that Diane took an active part in the class. She was a good teacher and he easily understood why Katie thought so much of her.

As directed, Matt let class out fifteen minutes early. The kids thought it was great and were even eager to help their teachers straighten up the room before they left. Then they gathered their things and went out into the hall.

"I don't know the way to the rectory garden, do you?" Matt asked.

Diane nodded and they went out the back way. When they went through the gate to the garden Diane said, "I'm not certain I appreciate you guys plotting against me."

"Not against you, it's for you," Matt clarified. "Look Diane. What Wag is doing is illegal and immoral. It is wrong, whether it's happening to you or someone else. Sane folks don't let that go on. I have to know something, even though I promised I would butt out. How often do you get beat a week?"

Diane gave him a furtive glance and made the choice to ignore his question, "What did Father want you tell me?"

"Okay, play it that way." Matt sat down on the lawn chair, "We have a safe place for you to live, rent free. Everything is all ready for you whenever you want it."

"What? I have a home, I don't need charity."

"Shh. I don't even want to hear it. Elton and Nora have offered you a home. They are wonderful people and you'll be safe. Whenever you want to move, they have a room for you. Okay? You don't need to be afraid. If you want to come without your things, the Sheriff will go pick them up for you."

Diane's mouth fell open, "I couldn't. I mean, I just couldn't. Don't you live there?"

"I'm moving in a week. So, you won't have to be in the same house with me. I'll be out of the way."

"Matt, you don't understand how I feel. I mean—, I don't—, didn't mean that."

"No, but don't worry about it. Regardless of how I feel or we feel, you're going to end up dead if you don't get out of there. You know it and so do I; and so does everyone else."

"I can't believe that Schroeders would offer to put me up. How could I repay them? They hardly know me."

"There're some really great folks in this world and they are some of them. They know that you couldn't pay them. They'd want something from you though."

"What?" Diane asked, cautiously.

"For you to be safe and happy. Really Tinker. That's all they want. I can promise you that. Please, I know you don't trust me, but trust them. For your own sake."

Diane was overcome with thoughts and feelings, "What do you all want from me?"

"To think about your own welfare for a change," Matt pointed out.

"What about Gladys? What would happen to her?"

"You have to talk to Father Vicaro about that. I know they're trying to figure something out for her. Okay?"

Matt took her hands in both of his. "I really want you to consider this. It doesn't have to be forever. Just until you can get back on your feet. Okay? You'll love it at Schroeder's if you give it a chance. You like Annie and she lives there. And Pepper. Elton will probably make you milk cows, though and they will feed you all sorts of good food. Please, I beg of you, give it a chance. Your life doesn't have to be hell."

"But I—" Diane stammered. "I just—. I don't think I can."

The gate opened and Father Vicaro came in. "Did you tell her?"

"Yes, I told her that Schroeder's offered her a home. She doesn't think she can."

"Thanks Matt. I think we only have a couple minutes before I have to get this young lady home, but I want to bring you up to date. We have contacted Gladys' sister in Minnesota. They'd be willing to take her in once Wag is out of the way. Until they know that he is in jail; they won't touch it. So, we'll put her in Bismarck with some nuns until it's over."

"Why would Wag go to jail?" Diane stammered. "I won't press any charges against him. He is Dean's father."

"Neither you nor Gladys have to do a thing. This is all his own doings. Okay? I will explain it more on the way home. What I want from you is a promise. You have to promise Matt and me that you'll keep your mouth shut about this to Wag."

Diane raised her eyebrows, "There's no way I would mention this to him. You can trust that. I'd get killed." As soon as she said it, "I mean—."

"You're probably more right than you think. Okay. You need to get a copy of those papers you signed that you owe money to Waggoners to us. Put it in Jeannie's mailbox at school, as soon as possible. Can you do that?"

Diane nodded, "No problem. I can do that tomorrow. Jeannie's mailbox. Okay."

"And then you let either Jeannie, Matt or I know when you want out of there. We'll do it as soon as you want."

She started to shake her head no, "You don't understand."

"You're the one that doesn't understand," the experienced priest stated. "This is out of your hands. In less than two weeks, you'll have no choice. I'd be really irritated if you didn't have the courage to leave and ended up dead before then."

Diane was shocked and filled with fear. "I think you guys are mistaken. You are imagining it to be far worse than it is."

"Roll up your sleeve," Vicaro demanded.

"I beg your pardon." Diane was angry.

"Roll up your sleeve, now," Vicaro demanded.

With tears rolling down her cheeks, she rolled up her sleeve on her right arm. Even Matt wasn't prepared for the bruises and gashes on her arm.

"Oh dear God," Matt mumbled. "Diane, don't go back there."

Father Vicaro was adamant, "Girl, you're all done. God gave you one body in order for you to do His work. You need to take care of it. This isn't your decision any more, it's mine! You have to get out. I have half a notion to take you to Sheriff Bernard's this minute, but you need to get the papers out first. You do as I say."

Diane scrambled through her purse for a tissue, but found none. Matt handed her one from his pocket. "Listen to him, Diane. If I'd known how your arm looked, I'd have never let you go home. Papers or not."

"Can't you people just mind your own business and leave me alone?" Diane cried.

Father Vicaro put his arm around her and let her cry. "Girl. This is our business. Now run in the rectory, the bath is to the right. Wash off your tears and I need to get you home."

She nodded and went to the house.

After she closed the sliding door, Matt looked at Father Vicaro. "Did you see her arm? It was horrible."

"I know. Worse than I thought. You go on home now and tell Schroeders that we talked to her tonight. I'm going to take her in to

Waggoners tonight and if there is anything amiss, I'm bringing her right out tonight. Okay?"

Matt gave the priest a quick hug, "God bless you for your help."

Matt explained it all to the family on the patio when he got home that night. Ian and Coot were ready to make heads roll when they heard about her arm. Then Carl leaned back, "No. We need to use our heads. We want him out of the way or we'll just make things worse."

"Do you think she'll leave on her own?" Elton asked.

"I'd be amazed if she did," Matt answered dejectedly.

"I would be too," Carl said and Ian agreed.

✦❧ 37 ❧✦

THURSDAY WAS A DAY OF nerves for Matt. He and Jeannie were both anxious to see if Diane would give her those papers or even talk to either of them. At lunch, neither of them had seen her and they were getting worried, but when Matt went out front to meet Ruthie, he saw her. She gave him a bright smile and said, "I got the papers and am on my way to Jeannie's mailbox. You leaving so early?"

"Got a date with Ruthie for lunch," Matt said lamely. There were so many things he wanted to say or ask, but they didn't have time as the bell rang. "You okay?"

"Yes. Have a good lunch," she said as she hurried off.

Lunch with Ruthie was more fun than Matt could have imagined. Maybe it was because Diane seemed well, but Matt felt good. They went to the Bowling Alley and sat in a booth. It made it more private.

Ruthie got right to it. She talked about how she had felt when she left the convent and fighting the desire to be with Ian. She was more frank than Matt had thought she would ever be. He had always imagined her being very reserved and shy. When he mentioned that, she giggled. "Apparently, you don't know Suzy very well! She slapped that out of me in a heartbeat. Gently, but definitely. This is important stuff, Matt. It's your life. Not about an institution or an ideal. It is really about you. You might think this is really silly, but can I tell you what finally made up my mind?"

"I'd like to hear it, Ruthie."

"Something came up about God giving us life. It dawned me. I had spent so much of my life trying to make things worthwhile for God, like

He couldn't do it without me. In the process, I forgot that I was ignoring His most precious gift to me. My own life."

Matt dropped his fork and looked at her. He sat and let it sink in. "You're so right, Ruthie. So very right. You're amazing. My brother is a lucky man. I hope he appreciates you."

Ruthie tilted her head, "Oh Mattie, he really does. He is so very good to me. He is the one that gave me the courage to give life a chance. I owe him so much."

When Ruthie dropped Matt at the Schroeder farm, he realized that he felt better than he had in months. And he had little Ruthie to thank for that. Maybe it made no sense to anyone else, but it did to them. He knew exactly what she meant and he was so glad she had told him.

He went over to Darrell's to help with chores. He was dying to find out if Tinker had dropped off those papers. They met him at the door of the house and invited him in for pre-chores coffee. Without him having to ask, Jeanne burst, "I got the papers and gave them to Coot. They're taking them to the attorney tomorrow morning. And, there was a note for me. I want you to read it."

Jeannie,

I ask that you let Father Vicaro and Matt know that I will be very careful and not take any risks. I want to wait until it is all in place. I hear it will be soon. I worry about Gladys and I know that everyone is still living with Schroeders. Let them know I am deeply moved by their offer and I will accept it when the time comes. While I will have to accept it as charity for now, I will pay them back. Until then, thank you for being such good friends. And don't worry.

Tinker

Matt read it over and laid it on the table. "I guess it's good, huh? But I really don't like her being there. I wish she would just get out of there now."

"We all do, but Coot talked to Bernard and Father Vicaro. They think it'd be done in a few days. They appreciate that Diane probably knows how bad things could be for Gladys. They'll keep an eye on things. We don't want him to hurt her worse either. Bernard also talked to Saphrons and they promised to report any disturbance immediately. He is patrolling by there often. He's planning to arrest him Sunday afternoon."

Matt's eye opened wide, "This Sunday? Wow! I guess that sounds sooner than when someone says soon, huh?"

Darrell laughed, "And you say I'm funny! Hey, we had our walk-thru today. We're moving in tomorrow morning. So, you're moving tomorrow afternoon? Right?"

"What a shuffle, huh?"

Jeannie hugged them, "I'm so anxious for things to get settled again! But it's exciting, huh?"

The next morning, Pepper's alarm sounded better than Matt thought possible. It was going to be a wonderful day and then the next day would be even better. By noon lunch at Zach and Suzy's house, Darrell and Jeannie were moved in. Then the group moved Mo, Ian and Matt.

That evening, everyone gathered at Schroeder's patio like usual. "It'll seem odd to have folks go home tonight, but not odd enough! I still have the old grump living here," Elton groaned.

"Your heart will be broken when I leave, Magpie. Plan it," Carl chuckled. "So you won't have a phone until Monday, huh Matt?"

"No. Jeannie and I talked to the phone company and that's the soonest. I'll get their calls until then. So, if you need me, call them. Okay? When is this taking place on Sunday? Does Diane know?"

"No, she doesn't. Bernard will call us before they head over to make take Wag into custody. Then we can pick her up right away, and Father Vicaro will be shuffling Gladys to town. The State Police will be on hand since Bernard can't do it alone," Coot filled them in. "We should have Diane here by evening."

"Will he be out of the way for good?" Mo asked.

"No, he'll be in the County Jail. The other charges will be made while he is in custody. It'll take him a bit to get bailed out. Then he'll be out; the next few weeks will be hairy," Ian stated.

Matt went home to his cabin. Sheepherder or not, he loved it. Nora, Grandma and Mo had filled his fridge and cupboards. He loved that even more. Matt rearranged the living room furniture and then finally put it back where had been. He went outside. Walking a little ways, he could see the lights in his Mom's home and Darrell's house.

He heard a yell, "Hey Neighbor, want a beer?"

Matt grinned, "Thanks Darrell, I'd love one."

He joined Jeannie and Darrell on their patio. "I'm going to have to get a place to sit outside too. These evenings are wonderful."

"Don't get too excited. The snowballs will be pelting you in no time. Then you'll want to be indoors," Jeannie giggled.

"Tomorrow is the big day, huh?" Darrell stated the obvious.

"Yah, scary. I was hoping that Wag would never get out again. Now I have to worry about him making bail," Matt frowned.

"Yah, I hate that. But once Tinker is safe, I'll worry less. I know she'll be okay at Uncle Elton's and we can all help out," Darrell said.

"I was thinking about Homecoming," Matt said.

"Me too. Wag knows that she'll be helping with that," Jeannie agreed.

"Yah, but he wouldn't be that stupid to try anything there, would he?"

"No one has accused him of being smart. Well, we'll handle whatever comes up. Okay?"

That night, Matt struggled to get to sleep. It wasn't the new surroundings, he was very uneasy. He was up at least twice before a car came in the yard at about three with the horn honking.

Matt flew out of bed and opened the door. It was Kevin. "Get your pants on and come quick. I'm going to get Darrell. Hurry!"

Within ten minutes everyone was piled into Kevin's car and heading over to Schroeders. "Can you give us a clue?" Jeannie asked.

"Bad news. Real bad news. I want you to hear it all at once. Carl picked up Mo and Ian. We are all meeting at the farm."

Grandma was handing out coffee cups to a beleaguered bunch of folks. Elton directed everyone to sit down. Most of the family was assembled. When everyone sat down, Elton started to explain. "Very bad news. Sheriff Bernard called minutes ago. There was a big disturbance at Waggoners tonight. Saphrons reported it and Alex went right over. Wag was drunk on his ass and is now in jail." Elton cleared his throat. "He apparently decided that it was time for Diane to extend her wifely duties to include him." The group gasped, but Elton kept talking. "Diane fought back and it ended with him throwing her down the full staircase. She's on her way to St. Anne's Hospital now. She may have a broken neck. Zach will meet us there. Who wants to go in with us? Waggoner's in jail and Gladys was only slightly injured in the fray. Father Vicaro is taking her to town now. Matt, we're so very sorry."

Matt just sat there like stone. His mind couldn't grasp it all, but he wasn't a bit surprised by the news. It was almost like way down deep he'd expected it. All he could think of was the looks of her arm that night. He just sat there.

Kevin came over and said, "Come on Matt. You can ride in with me. Okay? Want some coffee in a mug?"

Matt just nodded numbly and sat there. He was totally without sensation. Kevin took his arm, "Come on, Matt."

Matt stood up and stared at Elton. Finally he said, "Is she alive?"

"Yes, she is. Matt, don't borrow trouble."

He looked at Jeannie, "Maybe she doesn't want to see me?"

Jeannie got up and gave him a hug through her tears, "I know she does. Just go with Byron and Kevin. Darrell and I'll be right here waiting to hear. If you need us, call."

Matt plaintively looked at Byron, "She won't die, will she? I knew she shouldn't go back home."

"Get your coat on," Byron grabbed his jacket.

"I just don't want her to die," Matt mumbled.

Kevin put his arm around him, "Come on, my car's right out front. We'll find out what's going on. Okay?"

Maureen gave her son a big embrace and put her Rosary in his hands, "Be strong my little Mattie. It'll be fine. Call when you know anything. We'll be right in if you need us. We're going to wait to see what you need and if we can move Diane's things."

Matt prayed the Rosary constantly all the way to Bismarck. Kevin and Byron never said a word. When they got to the hospital, they went into the emergency room entrance.

"I'll find out what's going on," Kevin said. "I'll be right back. You wait here."

Byron pulled Matt to sit down in the waiting room. Once they sat down, Matt asked, "She'll be okay, right?"

"Matt, it's in God's hands now. We need to trust His judgment." Then he put his arms around his friend and patted his back. "We'll get through this."

It was a few minutes before Kevin and Zach came out. "I'm glad I'm a doctor so I can find out more what's going on. Here's the deal. She's unconscious right now and they're taking her to X-ray. They don't know if her neck is broken, but she has no paralysis. That's good news. Her body looks like she has been used as a punching bag. We'll know more in a little bit. Dr. Johnson promised to come right down and let us know. Okay?" he looked at Matt. "Matt, okay?"

"Yes, I just wish I hadn't let her go home. I shouldn't have, you know. I knew it."

"Look, we did what we all thought was best," Pastor Byron became very firm. "Could you get us some good coffee, guys?"

Zach and Kevin nodded, "Sure."

Byron took Matt by the shoulder, "Now toughen up! You didn't know that. You're thinking that now. Think of your training, Matt. Why do you pray, if you think you're the only one in charge?"

"What? That's not fair, Byron," Matt blustered. "I don't think I'm in charge. Why did you say that?"

"Because you are trying to take the blame for tonight. It isn't yours. So quit." Byron was sterner than Matt was prepared for. "It happened, but it wasn't your fault."

Then Matt's eyes reddened. "I was so worried. I just had a pit in my stomach. I should've acted on it."

"We all were worried. You can't change a damned thing now and we did what we all thought was best. Don't you think that we're all berating our bad judgment? God has His reasons. So, how about you and I let Him do His work? Okay? I know it's harder than hell, but you can lean on me. I really do understand, but I don't want you burdening yourself with a bunch of baloney. You have your hands full enough. You have to be there for her now."

Matt stared at him a minute and then nodded. "She might not want to even see me, you know."

"I think she will," Byron consoled Matt.

By the time Zach came back with the coffee, they were talking more reasonably. Within half an hour, Darrell brought Jeannie in. They relayed the message that Bernard had told them they could go get some of her things out of the house first thing in the morning. Pastor Marvin was going to handle the Sunday services and so Byron could stay.

Matt felt really bad about that, but Byron didn't flinch. "You're family. Of course I'd be here. What do you think?"

"I never can repay you all. You have all been so good to me," Matt said.

"You will. I'm keeping track. I'll begin collecting soon," Darrell chuckled.

"Jessup, you're weird."

"So you say! I know how Elton feels," Darrell stated. "We're unappreciated."

"Yah, that's what it is," Byron shook his head.

A few minutes later, Father Vicaro came in the waiting room. "How's Diane?"

They filled him in and then he told them that Gladys was settled at Mary College with the nuns there. She's an emotional mess. "She seemed to justify everything that Earl did, except trying to attack Diane. That was the end game for her."

"What possessed the man?" Darrell wondered aloud.

Father Vicaro shrugged, "That sort knows no boundaries. Well, I'd better get back to St. Johns. Keep me informed, okay?"

"Will do, Frank," Byron said. "Marv is watching my store. I'll keep a lid on Matt and Diane."

"Anyone need a ride to Merton or anything?" Vicaro asked.

"No, don't think so. I'll be heading out in a little bit. I'm going to leave these folks to watch over things until I get the chores done. Then I can bring back anything you guys need," Darrell said.

"Me, too. I'm heading out," Kevin said.

"Good enough then. God bless," Father Vicaro went out the door. He stopped, "Matt, may I speak freely in front of these folks?"

Matt nodded.

"If she needs Last Rites, can I count on you to do it for her?"

Matt nodded vacantly, "Of course, Father. I will."

"Good. Byron, if you think he can't, call the hospital chaplain. Okay?"

"Certainly," Byron nodded.

38

AFTER ABOUT ANOTHER HOUR, DARRELL decided to go home and he'd be back in later. Then they paced. About quarter to five, the nurse came in and motioned for Zach. He left the room and returned in a couple minutes.

"Her neck isn't broken. It is seriously injured but a neck brace should take care of it. She'll be sorer than the dickens for a while. She has a concussion and she's coming around now. She has a lot of bruises, sprains and injuries, old and new. She'll be in the hospital at least most of the day after she wakes up for us. Then she can go home. At least there are some very serious charges against Wag now and that coupled with the others, Bernard said he'll likely not get bail. She is waking up now. Matt, do you want to go see her first?"

"Yes. But Jeannie should be near if she doesn't want to talk to me."

"We're all going upstairs. You just go in alone at first," Byron said.

Matt entered the room. It was filled with all the paraphernalia that hospitals seemed to love. He walked over to the bed. There was his lovely Diane, battered and bruised with a neck brace. She looked very vulnerable. He pulled a stool over and took her hand. It was also black and blue. Matt wondered if there was a square inch of her that was not injured.

She did not respond to his touch and so he sat down. "Diane? This is Matt. Are you awake?"

She moaned a little and then slightly moved her head, but didn't wake up. He recited the Rosary beside her while she lay motionless. When he said the Our Father, her split lips began to move while she recited it along with him.

He finished and then said "Hello Diane. It's Matt. Can you hear me?"

She repeated his name.

He smiled and said, "How's my Tinker? You'll be okay. You know that, don't you?"

She didn't respond. He continued, "Gladys is safe and she'll be cared for. So you need not worry, Diane. Things will be okay now. The doctors said that you can come home soon if all goes well. Won't that be nice?"

Diane shook her head no. Matt corrected himself, "I meant to your new home. With Schroeders. They are getting everything ready for you right now. You can have Grandma Katherine's caramel rolls. They're really wonderful."

Diane opened her eyes for a second and she slightly frowned with questioning.

"Hi Tinker, you're in St. Anne's right now. They had to check you out to see if you're okay after the jumble down the stairs. You'll be good as new in a couple days."

She squeezed his hand, "Matt?"

"Yes, I'm here. I won't go any place. Jeannie is here to see you, too. Okay? Everyone is praying for you. You won't need to be afraid any more. I promise."

"Matt?" she asked again, "Gladys?"

"She's safe. Father Vicaro has her in a safe place. She wants you to get well, Diane."

She tried to nod and then winced in pain. He spoke softly, "Try not to move your head until it feels better. Okay? Your neck is pretty sore."

Her eyes filled with tears, "Matt, I'm so afraid."

Matt leaned over her to hold her as close as he could and said, "Honey, you're safe now. I'm so sorry we didn't protect you well enough. I'll never forgive myself."

He felt her kiss his cheek. He didn't move away, "Diane, I only want you to get well. Would you like some water?"

"Please," she looked at him.

He helped her take a drink and then he moved back. She squeezed his hand again. "Do you want me to call Jeannie now?"

She looked at him and said, "Not yet. Matt, can you just be with me for a bit?"

"Of course, I'll be here."

She smiled weakly at him and closed her eyes again. He sat there and watched her sleep for a while. After a few minutes, she opened her eyes again.

"I'm so tired. Matt, will it be okay?"

"Yes Tinker, it will be. Jeannie is here and Darrell is coming back in to see you. You can come to Schroeders tomorrow if everything goes okay."

"School?"

"We'll tell the school Monday morning. Things will be fine. Just think, you'll be able to heal up and not get bruised again. You don't have to be afraid. Won't that be wonderful?"

"Wag?"

"He is in jail, for a long time."

She got a flash of realization and started to cry. Matt looked at her, "What is it Diane? What can I do for you?"

She shook her head, "Wag. He tried to—. I mean, Matt. Can I see Jeannie?"

"Sure Tinker. I'll call her. Don't get upset or move your head. Diane, you're safe now." He wiped her tears and then kissed her cheek. "I'll get Jeannie now."

He came out and sent Jeannie in. Then he got a Coke and sat in the waiting room. "How is she?"

Matt explained that she was asleep and then became more awake. He told the guys, "We talked only a bit, and she asked after Gladys. Then she suddenly seemed to remember what happened and wanted to talk to Jeannie."

"That's good," Zach said. "She'll be a lot more comfortable talking to Jeannie about what Wag did than any of us guys. From what Dr. Johnson said, Wag never was able to rape her, but she was only partially clothed when Bernard got there. I'm sure she has to work through that in her mind. Jeannie can do that better than any one of us."

Zach looked at Matt, "She'll come out of this just fine, Matt. And she did want to talk to you, right?"

"Well, some. I'm so relieved she is awake. Do you really think she'll be safe now?"

"Yes, she should be," Zach said, "As safe as anyone. It'll take her awhile, but she will get past this."

"Good," Matt leaned back in the uncomfortable vinyl chair and was asleep in minutes.

Byron covered him with his jacket. "Now all we have to worry about is Matt," he said to Zach.

Zach shook his head, "Yea gads, What next?"

Byron raised his eyebrows, "Don't even ask."

When Darrell returned, he took Byron and Jeannie home for some rest. Matt felt a lot better. Diane had gone back to sleep again, but this time it was more restful. Matt spent most of the morning in the room with her, watching her sleep, while Zach caught up his charts and made rounds on his patients.

About eleven, Diane woke up again and asked for Matt. He was dozing in the chair. When he heard her say his name, he moved over to the bed. "Hi, I'm here."

She smiled weakly. "Could I get a drink?"

He helped her with some water and then she said, "Matt. I have to know. Do you know Wag did?"

"Yes, Diane. I know."

"I'm so sorry," her eyes started to redden.

"It's nothing for you to be sorry for."

"I don't want you to think-,"

"I don't Diane. I know it wasn't your fault, at all. Okay? I want you to know that. So don't worry about it."

Tears started to run down her cheeks and Matt wiped them away, "I know. I do understand. You know what I'd like the most?"

She looked at him, "What?"

"For us to spend a whole day talking without you crying. Sometime we'll do that, okay? Promise?"

"I promise. I'd like that." Diane slightly smiled and fell back to sleep.

Matt felt good about that when he went back to that old ratty chair. It gave him something to look forward to for a change. About noon, Carl and Mo came in with Elton and Nora. Elton knocked at the door and motioned for Matt. He came out and joined them.

"How's she doing?" Elton asked.

"Better. Thanks so much for everything, you guys," Matt said.

Nora hugged him, "The guys want to take you to lunch and we'll sit with Diane. Okay? You need to eat something."

Matt nodded, "Let me tell Diane I'm going to step out for a bit. I can tell her you are here."

"We'll wait out here," Mo agreed. "Call us if she wants us to come in."

Matt went to her bed and took her hand. "Diane, can you wake up a minute?"

She mumbled and then opened her eyes, "Huh?"

"I'm going to go get something to eat, but Mom and Nora will be here with you if you need anything. Is that alright?"

She smiled weakly, "Okay."

"Okay, I'll get them. You won't be alone."

She squeezed his hand. The ladies came in and she smiled at them and then Matt said he would be back in a bit.

In the cafeteria, the men met up with Zach to eat their lunch. They updated the situation. Wag was in the County Jail and Jeannie, Darlene and Pepper had gathered most of the Diane's things from the house. They knew that she'd want to go back there soon to get other things, but they thought they had enough stuff for her to get by until she felt up to it.

"How's she doing?" Carl asked.

"She'll be out of work this week, but should be back the next week. She is pretty banged up, but going down a whole flight of steps isn't easy," Zach said. "Emotionally, it'll take longer."

"Just once," Elton said, "It would be nice for things to be less stressful. But I guess we can be thankful for what we got, huh?"

Suddenly Matt looked up, "What happened with the Sunday dinner today?"

"The clan is at Ellison's for lunch. Everyone knows that there are more important things going on. It is okay, Matt," Elton explained. "Besides, we'll be together a lot in the next month will all the weddings and everything."

"I hope this doesn't mess up the wedding plans," Matt said.

"It won't. Rest assured. Our ladies are very flexible and those gals could plan a gala wedding in a row boat!" Elton chuckled.

They all had a good laugh. Then Zach got paged. "Catch you later. Are you going to hang around and ride home with me or go with them?"

Matt was bewildered, "I haven't even thought about it. I'd like to see when she can go home."

"I'll find out and let you know," Zach promised.

❧ 39 ❧

WHEN THE MEN RETURNED FROM lunch, they went in to see the girls. The ladies were all chatting and Diane seemed quite relaxed. The nurse came in to work with her, and shooed them all out into the waiting room.

Before the nurse came out, Sheriff Bernard arrived and needed to talk to her and her doctor. Zach came by and waited with them. When Dr. Johnson came out, Zach had a long talk with him and then came back into the waiting room.

"He's going to release her in a couple hours. He gave me her prescriptions and orders, so we can take her home. She'll have Mo's room, right?"

"Yes, it's on the main floor. We didn't want her to have to manage the stairs right away," Nora added.

"Good. That's what I told him. We can bring her home about six. Okay? Matt, are you staying with me?" Zach asked.

"I'd like to."

"Okay, then," Elton said. "We'll head on out now and get ready for our new resident. I think that the girls were making Swedish meatballs for dinner, right?"

"That's the plan," Nora giggled. "And you are all invited. Suzy will be there and then just us and Jessups. We want it to be quiet for her tonight."

"Sounds good," Zach said. "We'll be along shortly. I'll get the prescriptions filled here so we have them with us when we get home."

When Sheriff Bernard came out, he talked to them briefly. "I got her statement. I just needed to get some things done today. I may have to talk

218

to her again later. I'll see you tomorrow. I'm afraid I might have upset her though, but it had to be done."

Zach nodded, "We understand. I'd like to go talk to her now."

Zach went in and found Diane crying. "I don't know if you remember me, but I'm Zach Jeffries."

"I know."

"Diane, we're going to get to take you to Schroeders in about an hour or so. You rest up. I'll be sort of a stand-in doctor for you until you get back to see Dr. Johnson. Is that okay?"

"Yes, Dr. Johnson explained that to me. I probably need a pediatrician."

Zach chuckled "Well you'll be a much nicer patient that Carl, that's for sure."

She smiled. "The nurse had me get up but I'm still pretty wobbly."

"No doubt. You have enough pain meds in you to make anyone wobbly. They should be wearing off soon and then we can go to the farm. I want your word that you'll let me know if the pain gets too much. Tomorrow will be the most painful. Bruises are like that. You don't need to be suffering like some sort of martyr. Okay? I will just get mad if you try that."

"I won't. Will I miss much school?" Diane asked. "I really need to get back. I have to chaperone this weekend for Homecoming."

"No you won't be doing that. I'll talk to the Principal. They can manage without you. Maybe you can do two others to make up for it!"

"I hope not." She frowned, "Do I call you Zach or Dr. Jeffries?"

Zach gave her his big grin, "Most the family calls me Smitty. It's a Darrell thing."

"He calls me Tinker." Diane giggled.

"Okay Tinker, you call me Smitty. Did the ladies bring you something to wear home?"

"Yes. They're so thoughtful. I feel like such a bother."

"Don't. We're all a bother once in a while," he grinned, "From what I hear, you're worth it."

She gave him a funny look. "Did Matt go home?"

"No, he is going to wait and go home with us. Is that okay?"

She nodded. "Should I get dressed now? I need help. Can you call a nurse?"

"Or Nora and Mo would be glad to help you. Which would you prefer?"

"I don't care. Whichever you think is best."

"I'll call Nora and Mo because they're going to be helping you at home. Diane, you need to accept this help now. Don't buck it. Worry about repaying later, but I need you to give me your word you'll accept it now."

She nodded. "Okay, Smitty."

He left the room and then went to get the ladies.

When they came out, they said she wanted to rest a little. "She was all tuckered out. Mother Mary and all the Saints, that poor woman is covered in bruises. I can't imagine how it must hurt," Mo was appalled.

"Yah, she is really banged up," Nora said. "But she has some spunk."

They left and Zach went back to finish his charts. "I'll be back when Dr. Johnson calls to get you guys," he said to Matt. "Are you going in with her?"

"I think so. That chair isn't very comfortable but this is even worse."

"You got that right."

Matt went into the room and she was sound asleep. He quietly went to the chair and sat down. Within minutes, they were both asleep.

Around five thirty, Dr. Johnson came in and woke them "Wake up, Sleepy Heads. I'm going to need this bed for really sick people, so I'm kicking you out now."

Diane smiled. "Thank you."

Matt introduced himself and said he'd call Zach. Just as he said that, Zach came in and said, "Call me what?"

"Let's give the girl some space so the nurse can get her together. Then take her home."

In the hall, he repeated some medical things to Zach and then said, "I want to see her on Tuesday. Take care and call me if anything goes awry. Watch out if she develops a severe headache or a bad cough. I'm worried about clots. Make sure she keeps that neck brace on. Try to make her get fresh air, exercise and rest."

A few minutes later the nurse appeared with Diane in the wheel chair. She smiled, "Lookie here, you got two good looking guys waiting for you. I should be so lucky."

Diane smiled weakly, "I'm lucky."

Matt waited with her until Zach brought the car up. He knelt down by her chair and said. "These are great folks, Diane. You can just relax and be yourself around them. You don't need to pretend."

She just bit her lip and then took his hand. "Matt?"

"What is it?"

"Will it be okay, really?"

"Really Diane. And if you want to call your Mom, let me know. We can do that when we get to the farm."

"I don't want to worry her. She'll just worry. I might just wait until I have it together more." Then she looked at Matt, "Does she already know?"

"Yes. Sheriff Bernard had to call her because she is your next of kin."

"I guess I'd better call her then. What will I say?"

"Just that you're on the mend, out of the hospital and safe. She needs to know that and where she can reach you. I can help you tell her, if you'd like."

Diane's tears started to come again.

Matt looked at her and grinned as he handed her a tissue. "We made it almost ten minutes that time!"

"You aren't very nice."

"Yup, the drugs are wearing off," he teased.

She slept most of the way to the farm, but managed to walk with Matt's aid up the ramp and into the house. She was worn out when she sat in the kitchen. She looked around, "It's so nice here. And it smells so good, too."

"Thank you," Grandma Katherine said. "I think a good smelling kitchen makes the home, don't you?"

Grandma gave Matt a big hug and then gently hugged Diane. "Call me Grandma or Katherine. Whichever you prefer. Would you like Tinker or Diane?"

Diane smiled a little and then said, "I think Tinker."

"Tinker it is. Matt will you show Tinker to her room so she knows she's at home. Then we can eat as soon as you're ready."

"We need to call her mother, Elton. Is that okay?" Matt asked.

"Of course, use the phone in the sewing room. It's much more private there."

After she said a few words to her mom, Matt answered her questions and promised to keep her updated. Then he walked her slowly to her room. He opened the door. The girls had all her things put away and it looked comfortable. She started to cry again. This time he gave her a big hug. "You're safe now. Do you want to rest or come out and eat?"

"I might rest. Will Jeannie be here?"

"She is on her way over. Why?"

"I might like her to help me get freshened up a bit."

"How about Pepper? Can she help you?'

"I guess. I think I have met her."

"We went bowling together, remember?"

"Oh yes."

"I'll go get her."

A few minutes later, Pep and Diane joined the group in the dining room. Diane looked at the huge dining room. "Do all these people live here?"

Nora giggled, "No, it is just for when we have Sunday dinners. But we are using this table tonight so we have room."

Jessups arrived and they all sat down. Everyone said grace and then began to eat. Diane sat between Pepper and Matt through dinner but was very quiet. She ate very little, but said it was all very good. After pie, the family started to clear the table. Diane wanted to help, but no one would let her.

"You'll have plenty of time later," Grandma pointed out. "Let folks wait on you when they are willing, because usually they aren't."

"Hey Tinker, if you want to use Coot's wheel chair, maybe Matt would like to take you for a walk. It is a nice summer evening and you might want a little fresh air," Zach suggested. "You'll sleep better if you get out a bit."

"That does sound nice."

Pepper got the chair and helped her into it. "Kevin fixed this with a motor, so if you decide to go for a run, just turn this on. Matt could use the exercise!"

"You're such a trouble maker, Pepper," Matt retorted.

"Dad, make him stop!" Pepper teasingly whined.

Elton grinned, "He isn't my kid, Pepper. You have to whine to Coot."

Carl chuckled, "Keep up the good work, Matt!"

"Wow! You're in so much trouble now, Mr. Kincaid." Pepper snapped. "See if I'll be your buddy anymore!"

Outside the two went for quite a ways. They were clear down by the barn before Matt stopped and sat on a stack of wood by the gate to the pasture.

"Someday when you are up to it, we can go out to the pasture. There's a big rock out there that some of us go sit on sometimes. It's a nice place to think."

Diane smiled, "Are these people always so nice or are they just pretending."

"This outfit does a lot of stuff, but pretending isn't one of them. They are this nice, and it's for real. Just don't lie to them or you'll be in hot water. I know."

"Matt, priests don't lie."

"No," he chuckled, "But they equivocate to beat the band."

Diane giggled, "That's not good."

They sat without talking for a bit and then she said, "I'm beginning to hurt. I think we should head back. Okay?"

"Sure."

When they got to the patio, Zach asked, "You okay, Tinker?"

"Just beginning to hurt a little."

"I'll go get you a pain pill. Then you can have a cup to hot tea with us before you go in. I want you to stay up for awhile so you sleep tonight. I need you to stay up as late as you can."

"Yes," Elton said, "Grandpa Lloyd is our official nighttime wanderer. It is his Alzheimer's, you know. We try to keep it down to only one or two wanderers per night. Oh, and if a horrific alarm goes off in the middle of the night, don't panic. It is the Pa Bell. We put it in so we can wake up if Lloyd decides to go outside at night. So don't panic when you hear it."

"Is it as loud as a fire alarm?" Diane asked.

"Louder," the group answered in unison.

"In fact, we hardly hear the fire alarm," Keith observed.

"That isn't very comforting," Pepper said. "Dad, you need to fix that."

After a little bit of quiet visiting, everyone headed off for home. Zach told Diane to be sure to call him if anything was amiss and said he'd be by in the morning.

"I'm going to take you in and then catching a ride home with Darrell and Jeannie. Okay?" Matt said.

When he got her to her room and helped her to the sit on the edge of her bed, she took his hand. "Thank you so very much for being there for me. You'll never know how much it means to me."

He kissed her cheek, "And you won't know how much it meant to me. Good night, Diane. I'll see you tomorrow after school. Please get some rest."

"You too."

"I'll send Pepper in."

❧ 40 ❧

MATT'S ALARM WASN'T NEARLY AS loud as Pepper's but it was equally obnoxious. And he missed his coffee. He made a pact with himself. He'd always set his coffee pot before he went to bed, so he only had to push the on button in the morning.

He met Darrell at the barn and started to get the goats in the milking stations. They didn't talk but only exchanged a nod. It wasn't until they were almost finished, they were awake enough to carry on a conversation.

"How is the batching it?" Darrell grinned.

"Not good so far. I had no coffee to greet me this morning! It was dreadful!"

"Hey, I saw a coffee pot with a timer on it. You should get that. Then you could wake up to fresh coffee! It was at the Hardware Store in Merton."

"Good idea. I might stop and pick one up when I get paid."

"I was thinking about a dog after our talk the other day. So, guess what I did?" Darrell chuckled.

"I never have a clue what you might do," Matt groaned.

"Well, with that attitude, I have a mind not to tell you."

"Ah, Jessup. You know you want to tell me. What? You're going to start a kennel?"

"Don't be ridiculous. I called over to Swenson's and asked about that pup they got. And guess what? They said they had a couple of his grand puppies about to be weaned. It was bred with a cross, so they are a Canardly."

Matt frowned, "What's a Canardly?"

"It is so mixed up, you can hardly tell what it is."

Matt frowned, "You're really a lot to take at six in the morning."

"Watch it or I won't invite you for breakfast," Darrell taunted.

"Breakfast? You'd invite me for breakfast?" Matt gave a phony smile, "You're a good friend."

"Yah, yah, yah. Save it for people that don't know you. Anyway, want to hear about the dogs?"

"Sure. The Canardly-Lab mix."

"Yah. Well they had four pups in the litter. Two of them are spoken for, but they still have two: male and female. One is black and one is blonde. I am going to pick them up today and you pick first. One will be yours and the other will be mine. Deal?"

Matt was stunned. "Gee, Darrell. I thought we were just talking. I really don't know if I have time to train a dog or even know how. I-."

"Look, it will be put down if we don't take them. I'd keep both myself, but I don't want to be selfish. It would ruin my reputation."

"Oh save me! Okay, but I might not like it. You know?" Matt frowned, "Can we have a male and female? Won't we end up with a million pups?"

"Ever heard of a vet? We'll get them both fixed." Darrell grinned. "You are going to require a lot of training."

"Yah, Grandpa Lloyd always tells me I'm really dumb."

Darrell nodded, "He might be right."

"What's for breakfast? Maybe it isn't worth being nice," Matt grinned.

"Swedish pancakes and sausage. It's worth it."

After breakfast and before he got ready for school, Matt called over to Schroeders to see how Diane was. Nora said she had slept rather well and only woke up a few times. She was in a lot of pain, but did walk around on her own. Zach had just left and said she was on the mend. Her ribs are very tender and her one hip and knee. He called the school for her and explained the situation. They told her not to worry about anything. Matt was pleased and then asked Nora to tell her hello for him.

"I have a better idea. She is rocking in the living room with Grandpa. I'll give her the phone."

Before Matt could say no, Nora took the phone to Diane. "Hello," she said softly.

"Good morning. How has your morning been?"

"Very nice. I had a wonderful breakfast. What about you?"

"Jeannie invited me for Swedish Pancakes. They were great. What did you have?"

"Carl's famous Biscuits and Sausage gravy. Then Zach came by and said I'm okay. He said I'd really hurt today and I'm a true believer. My jaw is so sore and I think I might have jarred another tooth loose. My one wrist really is sore, but I don't know what I did to it. So I'm relaxing and Grandpa is telling me all about the Treaty of Versailles."

"He'll love you forever if you listen to him talk. I have learned a lot from him, but I don't know if any of it is correct," Matt chuckled. "Has he figured out who you are yet? I noticed last night he just stared at you."

"He thinks I'm Katherine's sister and his relation," Diane said, "He's so sweet. "He really seems like a nice man. He said he will take care of me because a guy has to take care of all his family."

"He really believes that, you know. So, he has adopted you too," Matt chuckled. "He adopted me, but he thinks I'm the really dumb one. He might be right about that."

"He told me about you," Diane giggled. "The Tractor guy that needs practice driving. He said you'll end up in a pickle jar!"

"Yah. He always says that is where I'm headed," Matt was trying to tie his tie with one hand while he talked on the phone, "I'm going to have to hang up before I have such a knot in my necktie I can never get it off. Have a great day and try to relax. I'll see you this afternoon. Okay?"

"You have a good day too. Thanks for calling."

The day went by quickly and Matt got a lot of work done. It was about four-thirty before he drove into the yard to give Lloyd his drive. He went down to the garage and brought up the old Ford. Matt headed for the steps to the kitchen, just as Little Charlie came across from the coop, Chicken Man hat on his head.

"I bet you're sorry you missed helping me with Chicken Man chores, huh?" the little guy asked.

"I think I am. How did they go? Gather a lot of eggs?"

"The same. I know about something from school. Wanna guess?"

"Can you just tell me? I'm not a good guesser today?" Matt opened the kitchen door and they went in.

"Mrs. Lester's cat had a pile of kittens. She is giving them away. I'm going to ask Daddy if I can have some. Do you think he'll say yes? If he says no, I am going to ask Coot. He'll need some for all his cages. Don't you think?" Charlie relayed his contorted logic.

"I don't think cats like cages very well," Matt explained as he gave Grandma a hug. "Charlie is thinking, Grandma. It could get scary."

Charlie frowned, "I don't think scary."

"I know, I was just teasing."

"Tuck, if you help me with my math homework, I'll let you pet my kitty if I get it. Won't that make you so happy?"

Matt laughed, "It really will. How much homework have you got to do?"

"Three problems. I'll get it," Charlie threw his hat on the floor and ran off.

When he came back in the kitchen, Nora had her hands on her hips, tapping her foot and staring at the bedraggled straw hat. "Charles Elton Ellison. What is this?"

He made a huge grimace of horror! "My Chicken Man hat, Aunt Nora. I'll pick it up. I'm sorry."

"Do it now before I think about it!"

"Please don't think about it. That's never good." Charlie ran to pick it up. He put it in the mudroom and then went to Nora. "You aren't thinking, are you?"

"No, I'm not," she smiled. "Try to remember to take care of your things."

"I love you, Aunt Nora. I bet you have a treat for Tuck and me, huh?"

"Yes, a quick one, you little Swindler."

Matt had sat at the table and Grandma brought him some coffee. "Let's have our treat while we do the homework. Lloyd and I want to go for a drive."

"And me," another voice said from the stool by the sink. Diane had been watching the whole thing from the stool where she was sitting. "He invited me along."

Grandma shook her head, "That old bird sees a young woman and forgets all about me."

"Tractor, can we take my Katherine along too? She's going to put up a fuss," Lloyd said. "I don't want to be in big trouble with her. Right, Nora?"

"That's so right, Lloyd," Nora giggled. "But you need to get moving. It is almost time for chores."

Charlie only needed help with the first subtraction problem and got the rest himself. "You're a whiz kid," Matt chuckled.

"I know, but I'm a better digger," Charlie said as he finished his cookie.

Matt, Grandpa, Grandma and Diane went out to the old Ford. Grandpa sat in front and the ladies sat in back. They went for a short drive. Lloyd bragged all the way about his car and how he was hoping that the Tractor guy could learn how to drive before he got too old. Matt just grinned and drove along.

"Are we going to your house?" Grandpa asked. "I want Katherine to see your house. Katie, he thinks he can keep house! Can you imagine? He'll end up in a pickle jar for sure."

"Okay, then we'd better get back. I have to help Darrell with chores," Matt agreed, secretly a little proud.

They turned into the yard and saw Darrell out front of the barn with a big cardboard box. The old Ford pulled up and stopped. Darrell helped them out of the car.

"Watcha got there?" Lloyd asked as he knelt by the box. "Dogs?"

"Yes, Grandpa Lloyd. Matt and I are going to each have a dog. What do you think?" Darrell smiled expectantly.

"I think he can't take care of himself. Don't know what he'd do with a dog! Maybe the dog would take care of him, huh?" the old man chuckled.

Grandma was already holding the black one and Darrell had handed Diane the golden one. "Do they have names?" Grandma asked.

"The gold one is Skipper and the black one is Ranger," Darrell answered.

"Are they both male?"

"No, the gold one is a female," Darrell said as he scratched its ears while it licked Diane's face.

"Skipper for a girl?" Diane asked.

Matt helped Grandpa stand up and then the old man said, "I heard they ran out of names, so I guess that's the way it is. I'd have named her Doris. That's what I'd have done. Suppose that name is used up already."

"Must be, Grandpa Lloyd." Darrell nodded. "So which one do you want, Matt?"

Matt looked at both of them, "They're both nice."

Darrell rolled his eyes, "Gee man, just pick one."

"Ah, what do you think?" Matt asked Diane.

"It isn't my decision, but this one's sure friendly." Diane closed her eyes while Skipper licked her face.

Matt smiled, "Okay, I'll take the gold one. Miss Skipper will be my puppy."

"Cool, because I'm partial to Ranger. He reminds me of my old dog," Darrell said.

"Oh, I remember him. Bosco was a good dog." Grandma Katherine smiled.

"These are his bloodline," Darrell said proudly. "I hope they inherited the good stuff."

Grandma giggled, "I'm sure they did, right along with the bad stuff."

"Well, I got to get these guys home and be back for chores. I'll take Skipper," Matt grinned.

Darrell put the puppies in the box and said, "No hurry. See yah later."

Matt dropped the grandparents off at the house, but Diane offered to ride down to the garage with him. "Zach said I need to practice walking. Would that be okay?"

"Sure. Hop in front."

After he parked the car, they walked the quarter mile back to the house.

"I enjoyed the ride today, Matt. You're really a nice guy, you know. Everyone thinks a lot of you," Diane smiled.

"Not Lloyd," the young man smiled.

"Oh, he does. He is just afraid you aren't—, ah, let's just say, very bright?" Her eyes twinkled when she teased him.

"You have a pretty smile," Matt said. "Even if you are giving me a hard time. How did today go?"

"Good. I'm still quite disoriented and sore, but I feel like the weight of the world has been lifted. Father Vicaro was out to visit and so was Sheriff Bernard. They both said that Gladys is doing fine. Pepper will take me to the house when I feel better to get the rest my stuff out of there. Matt, I can never thank you, Jeannie and Darrell enough for helping me."

"We just want things to be okay for you. Hey, what do you think of the puppy?"

"Skipper?" Diane smiled. "I like her. I hope you do. I felt like you picked her because I liked her."

"I did, kind of. It was more because she liked you," Matt winked. "I figure she must have good taste. Jeannie and I met with the Junior Class group this noon and we are going to oversee the work on their float. I think they have it under control. You're really sneaky, you know, Tinker,"

"Why?"

"Squirming out of Homecoming things! You're so busted, Lady," Matt teased as he opened the kitchen door. "Well, I really hate to cut out, but I have work to do. See you tomorrow."

"Don't let Doris pee on your floor, Tractor guy." Lloyd grinned. Then he turned to Nora, "Doris will have his floor wrecked by morning. Bet on it."

"Thanks for the word of confidence, Lloyd." Matt opened the door as Elton came in from work, "Will you straighten out Lloyd? He is on me, steady."

"I'm afraid you might as well get used to it. He hasn't listened to me in fifteen years," Elton grinned.

❦ 41 ❦

AFTER THE PUPPIES SPENT MILKING time in their big box, the men each carried their choice home. Matt prepared a nice bed area for Skipper near the kitchen door, but she seemed to prefer being underfoot. She spread out across his feet all the while he made his dinner. When he ate supper, the pup sat on his foot and looked up to him, watching his every move. When he swallowed, she swallowed. Then she would lick her lips and cock her head to the side.

"You're a real beggar, aren't you?" Matt said. "You had an entire bowl of fresh milk at the barn. You don't need to act like you're starving."

It didn't help. Skipper didn't move. Matt had the television on and listened to the evening news. Then he cleaned up his plate and gave Skipper a few of his leftovers. When he put the dish down, the wide-eyed puppy looked at him as if she had no idea what to do with it.

He spent the next twenty minutes, sitting cross-legged on the floor, holding the dog and putting little bits of food into her mouth. Finally, his foot was going numb so he put her down and stood up. The pup walked over and cleaned up the plate in two bites! Matt laughed. "You sneak! You were just conning me! Okay for you, Skipper!"

After he did the dishes and set his coffee pot for morning, he took her out for a walk. She ran everywhere, but didn't do her business. A half an hour later, she finally did so he could bring her in. He wondered how often they had to go out.

He turned on his radio to the classical station and then did his homework. Skipper was bored and went to lay on the rug by the kitchen sink, watching him like a hawk. After he had a lot of work done, he stood up and stretched. Skipper sat up and yawned.

Matt chuckled, "Copy cat. Come on, let's go for another walk. And can you make it quick this time?"

If you consider forty-five minutes quick, she did. Matt did enjoy the evening walk though, but wondered how much fun it would be when it got cold outside.

He got ready for bed and put Skipper in her bed box he had made. He told her good night and then went to bed. The instant the lights went out, she started to cry.

Matt frowned, "Dogs aren't afraid of the dark . . . I don't think."

He turned over and thought she would settle down in a few minutes. A half an hour later, her cry had turned into a mournful howl. Matt got out of bed and moved the box into his bedroom. Before the next hour had passed, the box was next to his bed.

When the alarm went off the next morning at five-thirty, Skipper licked her master's head from her spot on the pillow next to him. Matt looked up and petted her. "At least you settled down. Let's not tell Darrell and Jeannie, okay? I'll never hear the end of it. You're going to be trouble. I can see that."

His coffee plan worked out well, and by the time he had his clothes on, the coffee was ready. Skipper was anxious to get outside, but Matt made her wait until had his boots on. Apparently, she knew when she had to go and he had to dash her out at the last minute.

Darrell looked over from his path to the barn, "Dog trouble?"

"Where's your hound?" Matt retorted.

"Jeannie is taking him for walk. She'll bring him to the barn," Darrell grinned.

"That's not fair! You have an assistant!"

During milking the pups peered over the box edge, Matt asked, "What are we going to do with them all day?"

"I'm going to put some straw in the pen I had for some lambs. That and some fresh water and they'll have to spend the day in the barn. Did your pup cry last night?"

Matt looked at his friend, and cautiously asked, "Why?"

Darrell grinned, "Yours too? Good. Ranger must be part bloodhound the way he carried on. Maybe we should leave them out here all night too!"

"Then why did we get them?" Matt asked logically.

"Beats me," Darrell said. "I suppose they're lonesome for their litter mates. Maybe if they slept together. We could send Ranger down to your place."

"I don't think so. I could send her up to your place."

Jeannie came up to them, "Or you can both sleep in the barn with them! Mr. Jessup, I love you to death, but that dog is not sleeping with us again tonight!"

Matt just about tipped over, he laughed so hard. All he could do is point and laugh.

Darrell squinted at him, "Skipper slept with you too, didn't she? Admit it. I can tell by your laugh!"

"But I don't have wife!"

"And you never will! And you won't for long! You two need to get your dogs trained. I have spoken!" Jeannie grumped and went back to the house.

Darrell shrugged, "I think she is mad. She didn't say anything about breakfast. I bet she didn't make anything, huh?"

"Wanna eat at my place?" Matt chortled.

"You're such a hyena!"

Matt's little Skipper bounced along beside him when he walked back to the house, her long floppy ears jiggling as she ran. She looked a lot like a Cocker Spaniel/Golden Retriever, but Darrell said there was some Collie and Sheltie in them. She would be a medium sized dog, because she had big paws. Her hair was golden, long and slightly curly. Around her chest however, the blonde was a much lighter shade, so Matt thought that might be from the Collie. She was a pretty pup, and seemed of a happy nature when she had her way.

It was a glorious morning and Matt was in a great mood. He made some toast and took his shower. Skipper thought it was a game and decided she needed to take a shower with him. By the time the shower was over, there was water all over the bathroom floor and Skipper was soaked. Matt dried her off and then she walked into his bedroom and shook all over next to his bed.

"Skipper," Matt knelt down, "You and I have to come to an agreement. See, I have the opposable thumbs, so that means you're supposed to listen to me. Not the other way around. Got it?"

She put her head down between her paws and looked up at him with sad eyes. She made him feel guilty. Then while he was tying his necktie, she came out of his closet dragging one of his favorite tennis shoes in her mouth.

"Oh no, you don't." Matt grabbed the slipper. "That is mine. You never eat Daddy's shoes. Okay?"

He put the shoe in his closet and closed the door. He turned and she was squatting to piddle. He grabbed her and took her outside. When he set her on the ground, she stood there and wagged her tail, ready to play. Matt glared at her, "You should be named Doris."

Just like that, she dropped to the ground. Skipper put her head down and whimpered. Matt had to chuckle. "You crazy dog. Come on, I have time for a little walk before I go to work."

By the time Matt had Skipper in the box in the barn and got in Jeannie's car, he was worn out. Jeannie looked at him, "I'm not so sure that you and Darrell make a good team. It is more like a dangerous combo. I'm worn out, how about you?"

"You have no idea, Jeannie. Are babies that bad?" Matt asked.

"At least they don't howl like a bloodhound!" She pointed out. "Did you check on Diane this morning?"

"No, never even thought of it. That dumb dog even drug my shoes out of the closet. She was into everything!"

"Well, that's a pup for you. Maybe they'll play all day in the barn and be tired at night, huh?"

"We can only hope."

By the time Matt drove into Schroeder's yard to give Lloyd his ride, he could hardly keep his eyes open. He was so tired. Diane was napping when he and Lloyd took their ride. Lloyd was very confused and didn't seem to care if he was riding or not. They made it a short trip.

Matt came back up to the house, and Charlie came in with his bottom lip hanging down to his knees. "What's the problem, little man?"

"Dad said no kittens. Katie is allergic, no matter where they come from. So, I'm kiboshed."

"What did Coot say?" Matt asked.

"He's thinking about it. So are Suzy and Ruthie. Ruthie has to ask Harrington because the kitten has to sleep at Mo's house before the wedding stuff. So, if Coot says okay, we could keep three of them there!

But some won't have a home. Unless, you and Uncle Darrell took one, that'd be two more. See, I can add, Tuck."

"Good work, Charlie. You add good, but we just got puppies and they're driving us crazy. I couldn't take a cat now. I'm sorry." Matt told the boy.

"How is Skipper?" Diane asked as she came into the kitchen. She looked weak but was walking better.

"That little dog cried all night and was into everything. I tell you, she's a handful."

"Can I get to see her?" Charlie asked. "Can you take me to see her?"

"Not tonight, but soon. Remind me if I forget. I think she'd like you." Diane smiled, "She loves to lick."

"When did you see her?" Charlie asked, deciding if he should be offended.

"Yesterday. Maybe Matt could give us a ride over there together tomorrow," Diane suggested.

"Tomorrow is CCD. How about Thursday? Would that be good Charlie?" Matt asked.

"If you think about the cat. There're all colors. I wanted a calico one. They are good luck, did you know that Tuck?" Charlie asked.

"No, I didn't. Did you Diane?"

"No, I never knew that. A little luck would be a good thing," Diane smiled. "I always had a cat until I moved here."

"What color was your cat?" Charlie asked.

"My first one was gray tabby and the next was black and white." Diane remembered. "I love cats."

"Well, Charlie. How soon do you have to find a home for a cat?" Matt asked. "I don't suppose Uncle Elton would want another cat here."

"No, Aunt Nora said Twiggy is 'torial'."

"What did she say again?" Matt asked.

"She said Twiggy is torial and doesn't like to share her room."

"Did she say territorial?" Diane asked.

"Yah, that was it," Charlie said. "Mrs. Lester says she has two weeks before they have to go. They broke her house so we don't have to."

Matt looked at Diane, "Do cats get housebroken that young?"

"Certainly, the momma cat usually takes them to the litter box right away. They are much easier than a dog to train. But if the momma doesn't do it, you can have quite a time."

"Please Tuck. I'll weed your garden for you if you take a kitty," Charlie begged.

"Let me think about it, but Charlie," Matt took him on his lap, "I don't have a garden and the puppy is making me crazy."

Charlie smiled, "You won't be crazy very long, will you? Maybe for a day, huh?"

"I'll think about it. Promise." Then he put the little guy down, "I have to go home now and get my work done."

"I was hoping we could take a little walk?" Diane asked.

"I can take some time."

Charlie rolled his eyes, "Aunt Nora, why are men so dumb?"

"Charles! Hush."

"I'm sorry Charlie." Matt blushed, "Come on Tink, before I get into trouble."

They walked down to the shop and then sat on a bench in the sun. After they sat down, Diane asked, "How was school?"

Matt told her all about the float and the school gossip. Then they talked about CCD and the banquet on Friday night. "How late does that usually go?" Matt asked.

"Between eight and eight thirty, at the latest. Why?" Diane asked.

"I was wondering if you would mind if I stopped by to see you afterwards."

She smiled, "It'd be nice to hear about everything, but you don't have to."

"I want to. I miss seeing you around the school."

"Matt, I still think we need to be just friends."

Matt put his elbows on his knees and his head on his hands. "I thought maybe we were past that."

"We are, but I think we need to be careful. You're still a priest and I'm still a mess. I don't want to go from the frying pan to the fire." Diane said and put her hand on his shoulder.

Without a thought, he turned and gave her a kiss on the lips. It was gentle but very passionate. If she didn't have the neck brace on, it would have been more passionate. She cautiously returned the kiss. Then he stopped and held her face in his hands. "I'm afraid I am in the frying pan already, but I understand. I really do. I'll back off."

Diane put her hand over his, "I don't want to be impossible."

"Really, you aren't. I am overanxious. Besides, I have another woman in my life right now."

Diane giggled, "Skipper?"

"You got that right. What am I going to do with her?"

"Can you be patient with both of us?"

Matt looked at her, "I'll try. I know that we have a lot of things for both of us to get sorted out. I'll be good."

"Let's go back to the house. I shouldn't have asked you to walk with me."

"Yes, you should. I want to walk with you. Even if Charlie thinks I'm dumb now too! I'm beginning to get a complex."

"Marly and Miriam came by today. She is a sweet. She remembered my name and called me Stinker. She is really a bright little girl."

"Yes, she is. I wish you could realize how improved she is from what she was like when she first came to us. Poor little thing."

"Nora told me. I really like Nora. And Grandma is going to give me cooking lessons tomorrow. Oh, and Katie was wondering if I wanted to learn beadwork."

"Have you seen Katie's work? Diane, it's really something. I can't believe it. It is professional," Matt raved. "Ask her to show it to you. You'll be impressed."

They went in the house and then Matt said his goodbyes. Charlie looked up from his latest dam plans and said, "Promise you'll think about the kitty. Please Tuck?"

"You got my word, Charlie."

When he got home, he had to hurry down to the barn. Jeannie and Darrell were both there. "Hey, guess what? We got our phones fixed today! And guess who my first call was from?"

"Who?"

"Charlie. He is peddling kittens. I told him we'd take some. One for you and one for me," Darrell grinned. "You can thank me later."

Matt opened his mouth and then looked at Jeannie. "Don't blame me. It is *your* husband. I only told Charlie I'd think about it."

"You need a cat," Darrell announced. "It will keep the mice down."

"What about the dog?" Matt was exasperated.

"Nah, dogs aren't much for catching mice," Darrell said and wandered off to check the milk machine.

Matt looked at Jeannie, "Would you mind if I kill him?"

"Not at all. I'll have supper ready when you are finished. We need to get rid of him before he drags home a rhinoceros!"

"No, but I was thinking," Darrell grinned undaunted, "You really need your own horse, Matthew."

"I only have a job until December! What happens when I'm unemployed?"

"I'll think of something," he grinned. "You worry too much."

After dinner at Jessups, Matt and Skipper walked back to the cabin. Skipper was nice enough to do her business before they go to the house, which Matt appreciated. He checked out his phone and called everyone to tell them his number. Then he set the coffee pot for morning, did his paper work and went to bed. He didn't even bother with Skipper's box, but just went for a short walk before lights out. He put Skipper in his bed and she curled up right on the pillow next to him. He shook his head.

He wondered about what exactly Diane was trying to say, but at least she didn't hit him or cry when he kissed her. Oh, how he wanted her. He had never imagined that he could feel that passionate toward anyone. Yah, as these guys would say, his goose was cooked.

He thought he'd tell Father Vicaro his decision as soon as he could. He knew Diane was right. He was still a priest. He had better get his ducks in a row.

✦✦⌒⌒42⌒⌒✦✦

OTHER THAN ONE MIDNIGHT WALK with Skipper, the night was peaceful. Matt felt refreshed for the first time in a week. Skipper didn't get in the shower due to some quick construction on Matt's part. He remembered to keep his closet door shut and made the decision to not set his briefcase on the floor unless he really wanted it shredded. He was learning. Skipper's training was coming along great!

The day just roared by at a great speed. Nora called when he got home from work that Lloyd wasn't feeling well, so the ride would be put off. That was good, because Matt had to get to CCD.

By the time he got home and was heating some soup for himself, it was nine-thirty. He hadn't had time all day to even think for himself. After giving Skipper the rest of the soup, doing some homework, he washed up the dishes and took Skipper for their walk.

It was a pretty night even though a little cooler than usual. His bed was very comfortable that night and Skipper seemed anxious to curl up for sleep too.

The next morning, it was raining. Matt learned another doggie lesson. Mud is a magnet to pups and pups don't wipe their feet! Before he left for school, he had to wipe up the kitchen floor. This domestic life was becoming overwhelming.

Mr. Palmer, the Principal, asked him to stop by his office before he went to class at St. Johns. He asked him if he'd consider staying on the rest of the year. Mr. Morley had decided to retire. Reports on Matt's work, though still new, had been good. They weren't offering him a contract, just a job until spring. It would be after the holidays before they could consider offering a contract. He would like to know by the end of the next week.

Matt was surprised. Not that Mr. Morley was going to retire; he had suspected that he would after his last visit with him. But that they'd offer him the job. They thought he was doing a good job when he had been so unfocused on his job! He'd spent a lot of the time he had been there worrying about Diane. He felt they were just desperate.

On his walk over to St. John's, he realized that he'd have to make his decision. He'd wanted to put it off until after the weddings, but he was discovering that God had a totally different calendar than he did.

After school, he mentioned it to Jeannie but never said which way he was leaning. Another few miles down the road, she made a comment, "You seem almost sad about it, Matt. What do you really want out of your life?"

He looked at her in surprise, "No, not sad at all. I like most of it. I'm not real thrilled about midnight dog walks, but I'm really enjoying most things."

"What is bothering you then?"

"Oh, just me and my calendar! You know. I wanted to wait until after the family was gone home after the weddings before I talked to Father Vicaro. I just didn't want to get into it with them all over the weddings. They'll have their ten cents worth to put in."

"You could tell the school and Father Vicaro, but not mention it to your family until after the weddings. Would that work?"

Matt grinned, "I guess it would. My family won't check out the school."

"Matt, how do you plan on telling them anyway? That tells me you aren't certain of your decision if you can't explain it to your own family."

"You see through me like a lace curtain. I wish I knew."

"How are things with Diane?"

"Okay. She said she wants us to just be friends. She has all this stuff to get behind her and I'm still a priest. So, she wants to back away again. I don't blame her."

Jeannie looked at him, "I might make you mad, but I'm going to say something. I wonder if it isn't more than that. I think that maybe you're relieved. Maybe it was just a passing infatuation with her and this will be a nice way out for you to skate away. No crime, no foul. Just a short game in the real world. Diane is nice, but after you got to know her better, she lost her luster. Ever think of that?"

He was mad and defensive. "I'm not playing a game, Jeannie. Not at all. I know that. I'm more serious about her now than before. You must not think very much of me if you think I'd do that!"

"You might not be doing it on purpose, but it looks to me like that is what you're doing. It'll probably look like that to her before long. You can't have it both ways! Get that idea out of your head. You're only heading for trouble."

Matt dropped his head, "You do think that's what I'm doing. I must be an awful person in your mind."

Jeannie stopped in front of the cabin, "No you aren't. You're one of my closest friends and Darrell's. We both love you. I just want to tell you what it looks like." she took his hand as he reached for the door, "Matt, please listen. I don't want you to be mad at me. I'm sorry I said anything."

Matt squeezed her hand, "No. I'm glad you told me. Is everyone else thinking that? Does Darrell think that?"

"He'd skin me if he knew I said that. He thinks the world and all of you and I doubt he thinks that. No. It's probably just me. Will you forgive me?"

He leaned over and kissed her cheek, "You're one of my very best friends. You have the right to say whatever you think. No forgiveness necessary."

He went in the house and changed his clothes. It was still drizzling out and chilly in his empty cabin. He flopped on his bed and pulled his pillow over his head. "Maybe she's right. Maybe that is what I'm doing? I sure don't want to lose Diane. Oh hell, I just need to tramp in there and tell them I'll teach and tell Vicaro I'm done and get this out of the way. And if Diane will have me, I want her. I know that's what I want. I just need to do it."

He got up and drove Coot's car over to Schroeder's. He thought if he took the job for the year, he could buy the car from Coot instead of borrowing his Daddy's car like some teenager. He needed to be a grown up and quit carrying on about it. When he drove in the yard, there was a strange car by the front door. Matt hesitated, but knocked.

Nora grinned, "We were just talking about you. Mrs. Lester brought over the box of kittens. The momma went back into heat and left the house. So she decided to hand out the kittens sooner."

Matt had met Mrs. Lester at school and nodded, "So the momma is a loose woman, huh?" Matt chuckled.

"A real lady of the night," Mrs. Lester giggled. "Charlie has been my best salesman. So, I think he said that you're taking one or two. Is that right? I find that his numbers seem a bit on the high side."

Charlie was beaming. "Coot said I can keep my cat at Mo's. We decided we want a smart one, so I picked this one. Doesn't it look smart, Matt?"

Matt looked it over, "I think it does at that! What are you going to name him?"

"Coot said Einstein is a good name for a smart cat."

"Yes, a very good name." Matt scratched the golden tabby's ears.

"And Darrell told me that you'll pick out your cat and his. So, do it." Matt chuckled, "Can I look them over?"

"Not too much, because Suzy picked this one. She is named her Miss Kitty, like on that cowboy show. And then Ruthie wants this boy and she named it Sprite, like a water elf." He had to stop his dissertation to cross his eyes. Then he continued, "Jeannie said you should pick her a girl one, so she can name it Jasmine. There are three left. One is all black girl and one is a boy is black with a white necktie. The calico is a girl."

"Is Diane here?" Matt asked.

"Sure, she is taking a rest." Nora said. "She should be getting up soon."

"I want to talk to her for a minute, before I decide. Okay Charlie."

"I suppose," the little boy was crestfallen. "I don't know why he has to talk to her."

"Charles," Nora frowned, "What did I tell you?"

"Sorry," then he turned back to his kitten. "I'm so sad that one has to go away. I want them all to all have a house."

Matt knocked on Diane's door and she replied, "Come in. I'm up."

"It's me," Matt said, "May I come in for a minute?"

"I guess."

"I know you said you always had a kitten. If you want to pick one out, I'll keep it at my place until you get a place to keep it. Is that a good idea?"

"Matt, I don't know how long it will be. I can't really take on that responsibility right now."

"You don't have to. I'll be responsible for them."

"Them?"

"I'm taking the last one. There is a calico and a black one with a white chest. Whichever you take, I'll take the other," Matt explained.

"What about Skipper?"

"Darrell said dogs don't catch mice." he chuckled.

"You're both crazy, I hope you know that?"

"Jeannie thinks so. Well, will you look at them for me?" he asked boyishly.

"Okay, but I'm making no promises about taking one."

"No promises. I got it."

Diane came out into the kitchen. She was a bit taken back when she saw Mrs. Lester. "Hello Francis. Matt didn't tell me you were the cat lady."

"At least he didn't tell you that my momma cat is a lady of the night. How are you feeling? I heard you took a tremendous fall down a flight of stairs."

"I'm recuperating thanks to Nora and Katherine."

Charlie was getting impatient. "Matt, can you just tell me which one, so I can take the other one to play before it gets thrown out."

"Oh Charlie, we aren't going to throw it out," the teacher said. "I wouldn't do that."

"Oh good," he sighed, "That's better! I thought it was a goner."

"Well first of all, the black girl with the white on her forehead will be Jeannie's Jasmine," Matt decided. "I think Jeannie would like her."

Diane knelt down next to Matt and looked at Charlie. "What are the choices, Charlie?"

"This one. It is a good luck calico girl and this black and white boy."

"Okay, I'd like the good luck girl and I will name her Lady. Okay? And so Matt will take the boy. What are you going to name him?" She patted her kitty.

"I think I will name him Murphy. He looks like a good Irishman." Then he smiled at Charlie. "There, they all have a home!"

Charlie got up and ran over to Matt and gave him the biggest hug the little guy could. "You are the most bestest guy ever!"

"Thanks, Charlie." Matt hugged him back. "It was good of you to worry about the little kitties having a home."

Then they stood up, and Matt helped Diane up.

"Will you be back at school soon?" Mrs. Lester asked.

"Monday, doctor's orders."

"Take care of yourself. Okay? Well, I have to get home. I'll leave the box. They are all box trained, drink milk and eat a little canned food. Thank you, Charlie. "Charlie walked his teacher to her car, "Bye Mrs. Lester."

"I have to run to town and pick up some litter. I wonder if Jeannie needs some. May I borrow your phone, Nora?"

Matt called and Jeannie said that Darrell had brought litter home today and had some food. He had also dropped some off at Mo's, so they were all set. Ruthie said that Suzy had her kitty's box fixed up already.

Matt decided to have a cup of coffee before they went for their drive, but asked about Lloyd. "How is he doing? I expected him to be up and waiting."

"Zach is stopping by, but he just has a cold. He is sleeping now."

"I hope he'll be okay," Matt worried.

"Zach said it is going around. He will bring something home for him," Nora assured Matt. "Besides, it looks like you have cat deliveries to make!"

"Want to ride along, Charlie? You could come and see my puppy too."

"Do I have time, Aunt Nora, before chores?"

"Certainly. I can count on Matt to have you home in time, right?"

"You can count on it," Matt nodded.

"Matt, you said that Tinker could come along too. I think we should let her, even if she's a girl. She did take the last kitty," Charlie pointed out.

"Yes she did." Matt nodded. "Maybe you would like to ask her."

Before long, they were all in the car. First, they dropped off Suzy's Miss Kitty. She was very happy they brought her and invited them in, but they said that they had lots of cats to deliver. She giggled. "Thank you so much."

Then they went to Mo's. They took the Einstein and Sprite in to her. Ian had just got home from work and welcomed them in. "Time for a Coke?"

"We'd love to, but we have to get our deliveries done," Matt explained. "How did shooting the pool go?"

"Oh Matt, it was great. It took some doing, but I got it to work. Eddie showed me how he managed with one arm with the help of the bridge! Man, he is good. Eddie and Lucy are such fun and Ruthie took to it like a duck to water."

"Matt, I have some leftover lasagna if you're interested?" Mo asked.

"I am. Thanks Mom."

"How is my little Tinker tonight?" Mo gently hugged Diane. "It's good to see you're getting out? Oh, what did your doctor say?"

"He said I'll be good as new and I can probably take the neck brace off by Sunday, if I behave," Diane smiled.

"Make her behave, Mattie." Mo ordered. "She has to be able to do the jig at my wedding, you know!"

"Oh, I don't know about a jig," Diane said. "Maybe a very slow dance."

"That's okay, too."

Back in the car, Diane said, "I sure like your Mom, Tuck. She's a nice lady."

"We kind of like her," Matt grinned. "I know she really likes you."

"Well, I like her too," Charlie said "I know she likes me. She says I'm a lepper guy."

"A leprechaun. Yes, she does, Charlie," Matt agreed.

"Tuck," the little boy asked, "Will that other kid my size be here for her wedding?"

"Yes, he'll be. Are you anxious to meet Turk?"

"I don't know yet. I have to meet him first."

"Good idea," Matt smiled. "I think you two will hit it off."

"Daddy says I can't go hitting."

"Yah, I meant you'll like each other." Matt explained and Diane giggled softly.

They pulled up in front of the house and Darrell waved from the yard. "Jeannie and I will be right down. I'll bring Skipper up. She is lonesome for her master," Darrell grinned.

They came into the house with the box and set it on the floor.

"I hope the kittens and the dog get along," Diane worried.

"Jeannie said she thought they would," Matt took off his coat and helped Diane with hers. Charlie's was already thrown on a chair and he was on the floor by the box.

In a couple minutes, Darrell came to the door carrying Skipper. "I thought I'd carry her up so she didn't get all muddy."

Jeannie came in and gave Diane a hug. "You're looking better, Tinker. How are you feeling? What do you think of Tuck's digs?"

Diane looked around, "Very nice. It is very nice."

Matt and Darrell fixed up the litter box in the laundry room and dropped the cats into it. Then Skipper came over and sniffed them. She watched them for a bit and then sat down on her rug by the sink.

"She seems unimpressed," Matt said. "I thought she'd be more excited about them."

Jeannie smiled, "There were cats all over the barn where they lived, so I don't think she'll pay them any mind."

They all visited a bit and then Jeannie and Darrell took Jasmine to their house.

Before they left, Jeannie suggested Matt might want to close them in the laundry room for a day or so until they got used to it.

"Good idea," Matt suggested. "See you later. I have to take these guys home so Charlie can help with milking. Then I'll be back."

Charlie was playing with Skipper and she was licking his face. "She is just like a girl. She gives all kinds of kisses. Matt, do girl dogs have bad germs like people girls?"

Matt chuckled, "No. They don't Charlie. Want a Coke, Diane?"

"No, we had better get home."

"Yah, I guess."

"Matt, can we take Skipper in the car on the ride home. I think she really wants to go with us."

"I don't know, Charlie."

Diane looked at him, "I think it'd be okay, don't you?"

Charlie looked at Matt expectantly, "You always let Tinker be boss, so Skipper should come along, huh Matt?"

"Okay," Matt was wondering about the wisdom of the plan, but then the last few hours had tossed all sorts of wisdom out the window. "Why not?"

When they got to Schroeder's, Charlie and Diane went in and Matt waved goodbye. He and Skipper headed home. Skipper rode the whole way with her head on his lap.

"'What are you doing Matthew?" he asked himself. "Just what are you doing?"

❧❧❀~❀43❀~❀❧❧

EXCEPT FOR HAVING TO WIPE up the kitchen floor three times, the evening was wonderful. Matt put the lasagna in the oven while he helped with chores. Darrell was in a good mood, so Matt figured that Jeannie hadn't said anything about their argument. Matt decided to not say anything either. They talked about helping the Junior Class kids in the afternoon after the Pep Rally. School would be dismissed at noon in preparation for the Homecoming events. They planned it would only take about four hours to get the float in shape. One of the parents had offered their shop to do the work on the float.

After chores, Matt and Skipper went to the cabin. Matt ate his lasagna and corrected papers. Then he did his lesson plans for the following week. The cats mostly rolled around with each other and Skipper watched them, but there was little interaction.

He set his coffee pot, put the cats in their room, took Skipper for her walk, scrubbed the kitchen floor again with the promise of foot wiping lessons and then went to bed.

He was pleased that he had a bit of a schedule. He liked that. He hadn't heard that he'd have to help with St. John's Homecoming and he hoped it would stay that way. Matt thought having one quiet week before his family started to arrive was a welcome relief.

Jeannie's question bothered him. He was very certain that he wasn't playing a game with his feelings for Diane. He knew he wouldn't go back to Boston and he pretty sure that Jeff was right about not getting assigned to North Dakota. Vicaro was right, too. One didn't stay a priest because of the location. Besides, he could no way remain a priest with Diane in his parish. That would be impossible. He knew he'd never be able to handle that scenario.

Then he thought of what his Mom said about her doing the jig at her wedding dance. Diane was right; no jig, but she might be able to do a slow dance. He looked forward to it.

Suddenly he sat straight up in bed, "I'm such a moron! How can I be with her at two weddings with my family all around and expect them to believe I want to remain a priest? Besides, no one here calls me Father except Miriam."

Skipper got up and crawled into his arms, worried for her master. He put his arms around his dog. "I really messed everything up, Skip. I built the biggest mess in the world! What am I going to do now?"

Skipper licked his face and wagged her tail. He was so glad that she still loved him. "By the time this mess was done, you'll probably be the only one that loves me, but I got to do it. Right? I have to get it over with. I want to be with Diane at the weddings. That's all there is to it."

He started to wrestle with the dog and soon he was chuckling. Then they fell asleep.

The morning alarm went off and Matt looked out the window. The sun was trying to shine though the low clouds. "Well, Skipper, today is the day. Your Daddy is going to put his money where his mouth is. You with me?"

Skipper jumped off the bed and ran to the door, "Okay, let me pull my jeans on."

Matt and Skipper went for their morning walk together, except Matt walked on the high ground and Skip walked in the puddles. Matt decided Charlie and Skip must be related.

Matt stopped the dog and went through a ritual of making each of her feet wipe on the carpet. She looked at him like he was daft, but patiently let him do it. It seemed to make him feel better.

Then they went in. When he was just taking his first swallow of coffee, the phone rang. He almost jumped out of his skin! He answered it while he wiped up the coffee he had slopped on the counter.

"Hello."

"Good morning, Matt. Did I wake you?" Diane asked in her gentle voice. He almost passed out.

"Ah, no. I was just giving Skipper her lessons."

Diane giggled, "What sort of lessons?"

"Foot wiping," Matt explained. "You're up early. What can I do for you?"

"You are teaching Skipper to wipe her feet?" Matt could hear the rest of the Schroeders and Coot laughing in the background.

"Tell them to hush. She'll be the best foot wiper you ever did see," Matt insisted. "Did you call to harass me?"

"Not really," she said. "I was wondering how the kittens did last night."

Matt opened the laundry room door. "There are fine. Curled up in a ball in my dirty clothes, sound asleep. No problem at all."

While Matt was raving about the cat's good behavior, Skipper came out of his bedroom dragging his shirt by one sleeve. "Skipper!" he yelled. "Drop my shirt. I'll call you Doris!"

Just like that the dog dropped on her belly and put her head between her legs. Matt started to laugh. He picked up his shirt and Skip just stayed there.

"What is going on there?" Diane asked.

"You should see her, Tinker! When I call her Doris, she drops right to the floor like she has been insulted. I have no idea why!" he reached down to pet her, "That's okay, Skipper. Daddy loves you. You just can't steal my shirt."

Diane was now laughing, "I think I had better let you go. Sounds like you have your hands full. Have a great day, Matt."

"Diane," he got serious, "I'm planning on stopping by tonight after the banquet. I have to talk to you about some important stuff. Okay?"

"Matt, remember what I said.'"

"Yes, I do. Especially the part where you said that had to keep you apprised of my vocation or you would never speak to me."

"Oh, that."

"Yes, that." It was silent for a minute and then Matt asked, "How is Lloyd?"

"He is much better, but Zach said he can't go for a drive until Sunday at the earliest. He is grumping about that, but he's better."

"How is your neck?"

"Very good. I slept without the brace last night and it wasn't even very sore this morning."

"Good." There was a hesitation, "Skipper, is that my belt? Drop it! Thanks for calling Diane. I have to go."

"Sounds like it."

250

Matt was anxious to get this day over with and he had promised himself, he was going to do it on his own, like a grownup. Even though, he was repeating the Rosary in his mind almost all day. If he couldn't lean on God alone for help with this decision, he certainly didn't have what it takes to be a priest. Almost everyone in the clan faced life's decisions, for Goodness sakes. He thought about Elton's goofy philosophy and it made him smile. He loved that guy. He knew he could talk to any number of folks, but this time, he had to do it alone.

At coffee break, he stopped by the Mr. Palmer's office. He waved him in, "I only have a minute but I wanted to tell you to count me in for the rest of the year."

The man smiled broadly, "Great. Thanks for letting me know. From your résumé I assume you know Latin?"

"Yes. Why?"

"I might need you to help out later. I'll keep you informed. We'll talk next week. I want to know your time frame with Father Vicaro, also."

"I understand. I'll talk to you next week, whenever it is convenient for you."

"Great. Thanks, Matt."

Matt was congratulating himself for having the courage to do that. It wasn't all that difficult after all. It was really not a big deal, but it was to him. He even had time for a quick cup of coffee.

44

AT CLASS, HE WAS CONCERNED when he discovered one of his students, Clyde Adams, had copied the answers of a test the kid sitting next to him. At the end of class, Matt asked to speak to him for a minute.

When the other's left, Clyde was still sitting at his desk. Matt sat in the desk next to him.

"What happened, Clyde?"

The teen shrugged.

"I know that you know better than this. Is something wrong?"

"Just expel me and get it over with. I won't be able to play in the game tomorrow and my Dad will kill me. Just get it over with!"

Matt thought, "Clyde, I know you know most of this math. Why did you think you had to cheat?"

"I just don't get this last stuff. I'm stupid, okay? So just get it over with."

"You aren't stupid. We both know that, but you're acting like a knucklehead right now. What stuff don't you get?"

The teenager finally looked at his teacher, "The last two chapters. I just don't get any of it. I tried, but it's like Greek."

Matt leaned back, "We both have to go now, but I have an idea. Do you think that we could talk on Monday? Maybe I didn't explain it very well. Next time that you don't get something, let me know right away. Don't wait for two chapters and don't cheat! We will talk on Monday and I'll try to explain the math better. Okay? Don't worry. I don't want you to be expelled but I need your word that you don't blab this around, okay? Keep it to yourself and we'll see if we can work something out."

He reached out to shake the boy's hand. Clyde looked at him with his mouth open. Then he shook his hand, "I won't tell. For sure. When do you want to see me on Monday?"

"When is your free period?"

"About ten."

"That's good. Come to my classroom and we'll brainstorm then. Okay? Hey Clyde, do you know if any other kids are having trouble with the last two chapters?"

"Yah, a few of them said they're lost."

"Well, then I think we need to redo them, huh? Thanks for telling me. Keep me informed, okay?"

"Okay, Mr. Harrington. I really thought I was dead meat."

"Not yet, just don't make this a habit or you will be in the sausage grinder for a fact! And if you don't take this time seriously, you still could be," Matt's look penetrated the gravity of the situation.

"Thank you Mr. Harrington."

As the next class filed in the room, Matt decided to be a better teacher. He needed to really pay attention to his students and see what was going on from their point of view. That was his responsibility. It was not the student's responsibility to worry about his problems. He had been very selfish lately. That had to stop.

When he went into the Pep Rally, he quickly discerned that maroon and white were the school colors. He knew it before, but had to chuckle at the flood of colors. Denise motioned for him to come join them and then asked, "Where are your school colors? You look like a funeral director!"

Matt broke into a big laugh and Jeanne jumped in to save him, "He has them, he just didn't wear them this morning. Right?"

"Right." Matt chuckled, wondering if he owned anything that was maroon.

When school dismissed, he and Jeannie got into her car. They headed out to work on the float. He looked at her, "I have school colors, huh?"

"Well, Darrell does. We can make do until you get your own. You seem in a good mood today."

"I am. You'll be pleased to know that I told Palmer I'll teach until spring. I just needed one of my best friends to hit me where I lived. Thanks," Matt grinned.

"That is so super great! Now we just have to get you some school colors. When Darrell hears, he'll be on you to get a horse!"

"Jeannie, I have a lot of more pressing things than a horse."

"Don't tell me, tell Darrell. He wants you to go riding with us and so you can't use my horse all the time. You need your own."

"What about Annie's Crenshaw?"

"What is she going to ride? You are a true pickle brain!"

"Jeannie, I'm turning into Old McDonald! A dog, two cats and now a horse?"

"The two cats were your idea." Then she giggled, "And likely one with ulterior motives! Keeping it for Tinker, indeed! Not even Charlie bought that one!"

By quarter to five, the Junior Class float was completed. They all thought it looked fantastic. They closed up the shop and locked it until the parade the next afternoon. It had been a lot of fun.

Sammy and Joey, Darrell's brothers, were going do chores that night so they could make it to the banquet. Jeannie told him that Darrell had two maroon neckties and he could wear one to the banquet. He was grateful. He asked them to drop him off at his Mom's place on the way home.

He asked to borrow Coot's car for the night and then asked if they had anything that was maroon and white that he could wear to the parade. "I'll look around, but I don't know. Ian has a maroon sweatshirt, but he'll probably charge you an arm and a leg to wear it! You got hot plans for tonight? Is that why you need the car?"

"Yes. I'm going to stop and see Diane on the way home. I have to hurry now, but I'm going to have a lot of news to tell you very soon."

"Mattie Harrington, do not be toying with your Mom! You know how I hate that."

"I know, but this time, I need to make these moves on my very own. Okay? It is important for me to do that. Oh, could you ask Dad how much he would want for his car? I might be interested in buying it."

"Sure Matt. But don't make me wait too long. My heart is weak, you know."

He gave her a big kiss and grinned. "I know."

"It must be something good, because I even saw the hint of your dimple." She hugged him.

"Mom, I love you."

On the way to the banquet, Matt stopped by Father Vicaro's place. He found the priest in his study. Father Vicaro was surprised to see his visitor, but welcomed him in. "I was just thinking of you, Matt. I just hung up with our Bishop. Bad news."

Matt sat down, "What is it?"

"They agreed I need an assistant and so, they're sending Father Bartholomew within the month. Matt, he also is a high school math teacher. They want him to take over your position at St. John's. I'm so very sorry. He said they spoke to your Bishop out in Boston and heard you were undisciplined and disobedient. He didn't think you'd be a good fit here."

Matt swallowed hard, "Not surprised. May I ask, did you hear any complaints about my work from here?"

"None at all. They really liked you. Your work was fine."

"That is comforting. Did you get into trouble for helping me?"

Father Vicaro grinned, "There is little they can do or say that would ruffle my tunic. I could care what games they want to play. If it gets too bad, I'll plead dementia!"

"What about CCD?"

"That's up to you. Matt. I thought that after our last visit, that you had pretty well made up your mind to leave or I'd have fought harder. If you want me to, I will."

"No Frank, the reason I came by was to tell you my decision. I decided to leave the priesthood. I can't keep one foot in both worlds and it isn't fair to you, or anyone else. I had no right to expect that I'd get St. Johns. I really don't deserve it. You need a more devout, obedient assistant. I know that. Besides, I know I could never work here and keep my vows."

"Too bad. I'd have loved working with you. You'd have been a great asset and I have no doubt about your obedience. Matt, it is about Boston right? Not something else?"

"Yes, it is. I was getting that mixed up in my own mind. I should have left right away to keep it neat. I imagine you realize that I made a mistake and allowed myself to get interested in a lady."

"Diane Waggoner," the old man grinned.

"You knew? How long did you know?"

"Oh, probably before you did. It was about when you started teaching at Merton."

"And you still asked her to teach CCD with me?" Matt was very puzzled. "I'd have thought you would've kept us apart!"

"Hey, I'm old. I don't think so good anymore!" The old priest winked with a chuckle, "I told you I'd been asking God for an answer to the Waggoner situation. Right? Well, I lied. He did give me a flash. I just was being covert about it. I think He put you here and her here and then me here to do a little stirring. This might just be the answer I was looking for! It took me awhile to get over the thought of losing a good helper. I know it's hard to believe, but He usually knows best!"

Matt was just slowly shaking his head, trying to appreciate this old priest.

"I have to say, I was about ready to slap you around. I was hoping you'd talk to me about it. I've never seen a guy to take so long to get square with himself! Didn't you wonder why I had you tell her that she had a place to live at Schroeders? I could've done that."

Shaking his head, Matt grinned, "You old Conniver! You should be the head of the CIA."

"Can I tell you a secret? I hope the folks in India are right about reincarnation. Cause next go round, I want to be a spy!"

"Frank, if I'd have been honored to be half as good a priest as you are. I'd have considered having you as my mentor a privilege! I hope we can always be friends."

"We will be and I will still be your mentor if you can be mine! I think this new guy will be a pain. Probably the sort that has the rule book memorized in five languages! I'll need someone real to talk to!"

"I'd love that. I have to get going to chaperone the Banquet tonight. But I wanted to let you know right away. You really stuck your neck out for me and you deserved to know first. I feel really mixed about it yet."

"You'll be for a time, but we can talk. I think you're doing the right thing. Just keep that between us though. Monday, I'll get the paperwork started."

"I'd be pleased if you would join me for dinner at my cabin sometime soon."

"I look forward to it. Monday night would be good. I'll be there. What time? I like a Brandy after dinner," the man grinned.

"Make it about six thirty. I'm living at Darrell Jessup's place." Matt gave him a hug. "I can never repay you for all you have done."

"Not yet, but you will. Just live well, my son."

❦❧ 45 ❦❧

MATT PULLED INTO SCHROEDER'S YARD at eight-thirty. He had to admit that he had thought very little all day about what he would tell Diane. Of course, he would tell her about the banquet, which went well. The rest, he would have to play by ear.

He knocked on the door and Elton let him in. "Good grief, Nora. He smelled my hot fudge!"

"There is plenty, Elton." Nora gave Matt a hug. "You can share."

"I get to dish mine up first," Elton decreed. "How was the banquet? Must not have fed you much, huh?"

"It was okay; not as good as your cooking Nora," Matt flattered his hostess.

"Be careful Nora," Elton winked, "He's angling for leftovers."

"How is Lloyd?" Matt asked.

"He's doing well. I thought he'd have a fit when Zach grounded him until Sunday. He is so spoiled," Katherine observed. "I imagine it's too late to change him now."

"Is Diane around?" Matt asked.

Elton looked at him in mock shock, "I thought you came to see me? I'm shattered."

"I did. I just thought I'd see her too."

"Yah, yah. She is getting freshened up. I guess she figured you would be by," Katherine smiled. "You seem different tonight. What is it?"

"Lots of stuff. After I talk to her, I have some news for you guys."

Coot said, "You finally got some spunk, huh?"

"Dad, don't steal my thunder."

257

"I won't, much. Your Mom called and said you wanted to talk to me about buying my car. I figured."

"What do you think? Will you sell it to me?"

"Kid, you don't begin to have enough money for that classic!"

"Classic? It is a piece of junk, Kincaid," Elton groused.

"Now look what you did, Matt. They'll be squabbling for an hour," Katherine giggled

Matt grinned and winked, "Good."

Then Diane came in the kitchen. She looked very nice. She had curled her hair a bit and put a little make up on. Her lips were finally healed enough so that they weren't peeling. She smiled at Matt.

"Can I take you for a walk, Diane?" Matt asked formally.

"Yes, is it muddy?"

"My yard?" Elton asked. "Of course, after Coot's Gophers got loose on my yard, it's nothing but one big mud puddle."

"It was before, Magpie. So quit your squawking." Coot retorted.

"You kids go on. If you stay on the walk, you won't sink in to your knees. There is Coke in the shop fridge, if you're interested," Elton grinned. "Stay gone long enough so I get my hot fudge."

Matt helped Diane with her jacket and they went down the ramp. He took her hand as they followed the concrete walk.

"I have been dying to hear your news. How did it go tonight?"

Matt gave her a brief synopsis of the banquet and she nodded. "Sounds normal. Is the float all ready?"

"Yes. Do you think you can make it to the parade tomorrow?"

"I don't know. Pepper and Darlene are going with me to Waggoners to get the rest of my stuff." She stopped and looked at Matt. "I don't know about going back in there."

"Want me to be there with you?"

"No, the girls will help me and Keith is coming along too. These folks have been so great. Do you know who I just love?"

"I hope not Keith," Matt teased.

"No, silly. I love Nora. She and I can talk about anything. I have talked to her about being a widow. Did you know that she was a widow? And so was Marly and Annie? And you know what else? This is confidential so don't say anything, but both Ruthie and Pepper had experiences with rape. They know how I feel about it. I'm so happy. It seems my life is coming out from the pit I was in."

Matt put his arm around her waist, "That's great. I'm so happy for you. Can I tell you my news?"

"Will it make me cry? We have talked for almost fifteen minutes and I haven't cried yet. Aren't you pleased?" Diane smiled.

"A record huh?" Matt opened the shop door and turned on the light. They went in and he put two Cokes on the workbench. Then he put his arms around her and gently took her head in his two hands. He was about to kiss her, when he asked. "Where is your neck brace?"

"I can have it off for a while tonight, okay?"

Matt nodded, "Okay, but we have to be careful."

They kissed gently and then she put her arms around him. They shared an extremely passionate kiss. He held her tight to him and enjoyed the warmth of her body next to his. "I want you so much Diane."

"Matt, stop."

"I know." Matt backed away, and sat at the workbench. "Anyway, I have to tell you my news. Okay?"

He first told her about Mr. Palmer's offer and how he thought about it. He told her he had told Palmer that morning he'd do it. She was surprised. Then he told her about seeing Father Vicaro tonight. "I told him Diane. I made the decision. It is just a matter of paperwork now."

She studied his face and never said a word. He looked at her and then became nervous. "I thought you'd be happy."

She leaned ahead and kissed his cheek. "I really am. I'm just overwhelmed. You will be here and not a priest? How long will it take?"

"Not that long, why?"

"Do you think that I'll have this Wag business behind me before then?"

Matt took her in his arms again, "Diane, I have all the time in the world. I want you to know that I want to be with you. I know we have a lot on our plates, but we can do it. Okay?"

Diane pulled back, "But Matt, I don't know. I have so many things to work out. What if it doesn't work? What if we don't—, I mean I still don't know that I can trust anyone or myself. I just can't make a commitment."

"You don't have to. You can take your time. I just want you to know where I stand. I am telling you I care about you. That doesn't mean you owe me anything. Okay? However, I'd appreciate the consideration."

"You have all my consideration, but I still think we have to go slow. Okay?"

"I agree. But I mean, I don't know. Can we like go steady?" Matt asked sheepishly.

She giggled, "Of course. I'd love to go steady with you. Right? I mean, no more pretense. Is that what you are saying?"

"Yes. I told you that Father Vicaro had it all figured out a while ago. We aren't very subtle"

Diane laughed, "And you're right. Does your Mom know you news?"

"Not yet, but my guess is that Dad had his dial finger swirling before we were two steps out of the house," Matt chuckled.

Diane's face fell, "Matt, what are we going to do about your family? You said you needed to tell them."

"I'm going to call them tomorrow morning. I'll tell one and the rest will know within ten minutes. Then I'm taking the phone off the hook and going to the parade, a football game and a dance!"

"You're such a coward."

"I know." Then he frowned, "I'm going to leave it to you to tell our family, though."

"Our family?" she frowned.

"Murphy, Lady and Skipper. Although I sort of told Skip last night, so I think she has an idea."

"Okay, I'll do that. We better go up to the house before they eat all the hot fudge, huh?"

"One more kiss, okay?"

It was very erotic and they probably would neither have been able to control their desires had not Diane's neck started to hurt.

Matt stopped, "I'm sorry. I have to cool it. You okay?"

"We both need to cool it. This is silly! We're acting like teenagers."

Then Matt chuckled, "My goodness, I hear a car! I'll bet you a nickel it is Mom! She'll have my hide if I don't behave like a gentleman."

Diane giggled, "Do I look a mess?"

"Your hair is a little disheveled! That is all." Matt teased, "I think that is sexy."

"Stop it."

The couple walked hand and hand to the house. Sure enough, Mo's car was there and the whole darned outfit was staring out the living room window watching them walk toward the house. Matt and Diane both started to laugh.

When they came into the kitchen, the family had rushed to the table and tried to pretend they hadn't been voyeurs. The couple came in and Nora asked if they wanted their sundaes.

Matt shook his head, "No point in trying to cover it up, guys. We saw you all pasted to the window like kids outside a chocolate factory! We have some news. Okay? Tonight, I told Father Vicaro that I was leaving the priesthood. He'll start the paperwork on Monday. I took a full time job at Merton High through the end of this year. If I do a good job, Mr. Palmer said they might offer me a contract in the spring. I told Diane tonight that I want her to be a part of my life, and she agreed. We have to take our time though, so please don't get pushy. You know, there are alot of things that need worked out. Okay?"

Everyone sat at the table, unmoving. Matt and Diane looked at each other, beginning to worry they all disapproved. Then Elton stood up and said, "It's about time! We're thinking we would have to knock your heads together!"

He gave a cheer and hugged Matt and Diane. The whole crazy outfit was filled with good wishes and happiness. It was wonderful. When they finally settled down, Carl said, "I don't know about you Mattie. I was suspicious when you escorted a bride to her own wedding dance, but you're a pretty fast mover!"

Diane smiled, "That is why we are going to take our time. We have a lot of things to work through before we can even begin to figure us out."

"But we can do that together," Matt pointed out. "Do you think it is wise?"

Everyone agreed that it was an excellent idea.

46

THE MORNING BROUGHT BRIGHT SUNSHINE and it was cool and no wind. Matt took a deep breath of the autumn air when Skipper had her morning walk. She wasn't very happy that he got home late the night before and she had been left in the barn so late. She liked being with Ranger, but she definitely preferred being the queen of the house.

The foot wiping lessons went well, but Darrell happened to see them. That opened a flood of foot-wiping jokes. Matt had never heard one before in his life, but apparently Darrell had stored up a bunch for just this occasion.

Matt gratefully accepted a breakfast invitation and even offered to bring some bananas. Darrell rolled his eyes when Matt brought in the mostly black bananas. "Yea gad, man. Have you no shame? I'd have chucked them in the garbage!"

"No way," Jeannie giggled. "They're perfect for banana bread!"

"I don't know how you manage," Darrell groaned, "You always skate by, don't you?"

After grace, Matt said. "Last night I went over to Schroeder's."

"Big surprise!" Darrell grinned.

"Well, I had to tell Diane something. I finally told Father Vicaro that I was leaving the priesthood and he'll start the paperwork on Monday."

Jeannie and Darrell both broke into huge grins. "I imagine that Diane was totally uninterested in the news," Darrell chuckled.

Matt smiled, "No, strangely she seemed rather interested. We're going to take our time, but we're going steady."

Darrell put his hands on his head in horror, "No. You go steady when you're in high school! You're older than me for crying out loud. You say you're a couple! Do I have to teach you everything?"

Matt laughed, "I guess so. And I'll be working full time at Merton. I've been relieved of my duties at St. Johns by the end of the month. Vicaro's Bishop talked to the guy in Boston and got an earful. So, these guys decided I wouldn't be a good fit!"

Jeannie took his hand, "Are you okay with that?"

"I wouldn't have expected less. I'm glad that Father Vicaro is still a friend and he is getting an assistant. Father Bartholomew will be here this month and teach my classes at St. Johns."

"What about the CCD stuff? That too?" Jeannie asked.

"Vicaro said it is up to me. I want to talk to Diane about it and see what she thinks. If she wants to do it, I will. Otherwise, I don't mind quitting. It might be hard for her to do while the trial business is going on. That's going to be very hard on her and Gladys."

"Sensible," Darrell said. "I'm so glad, man. Do you feel better now that you made the choice? You know. Sometimes not to decide; is to decide."

Matt stared at his fiend. "You're so right. Jeannie told me something like that."

Darrell gave her a frown, "Yah, she came clean about that last night. If it set a fire under you, I'm glad. I told her it really wasn't our decision. It was just so painful to watch you torture yourself."

"Well, I'm done with that now. Sure, I'm not one hundred percent, but I don't think any decision is that. Right, Jeannie?"

"Right." She got more coffee and kissed his cheek. "I'm so happy for you and for Diane."

"Well heck," Darrell grinned. "Now we need two new horses. One for you and one for her! Suppose Coot and Mo will be getting theirs soon. Now I know how Elton feels."

"You love it," Jeannie giggled. "I think that Harrington and Ruthie will be getting horses before Mo and Coot."

"Me too," Matt said. "Ian is getting antsy to do more physical stuff, you know. This housebound business is getting to him. He played pool with Eddie. He said that Eddie showed him how to use the bridge so he can shoot with one arm."

"I've shot pool with Eddie. Uncle Eddie is good," Darrell agreed.

"And Harrington is all jazzed because Ruthie said he can use the basement room as his place. He gets a pool table and dart board. He is tickled pink," Matt chuckled. "And he is putting up a basketball hoop."

"Hm, we might have to pay the man a visit," Darrell grinned, "Just to be neighborly, of course."

"Of course," Jeannie shook her head. "You two are something else."

Matt drove over to his Mom's to take the car back. Coot was there and they had coffee. "So, you want to buy my car, huh?"

"Yes, if you want to sell." Matt said.

"I don't. I'll give it to you though, if you change it over to your name and stuff. It isn't worth $200. I want to get your Mom and me a new car after the wedding. Then you can license this and get insurance on it. You should have a paycheck or two by then."

"I'll pay you for it," Matt said.

Ian spoke up, "We're getting Ruthie a new car after the wedding also. It would make more sense for you to buy Ruthie's car that Kevin got for her. You could buy it for Diane. She'll need wheels. Ruthie has a big asking price. The same amount Kevin charged."

Coot gave him funny look, "I thought he gave it to her."

"Yah, he did. That is how much she wants. Can you afford it?"

"Really? You know, it would be better if she just gave it to Diane. It'd make her feel like people were thinking about her instead of through me. You know?" Matt suggested.

"Ruthie already offered it to her, but she refused it saying she could never pay her for it." Harrington said.

"Okay, I'll take it and then license it at the same time I do mine. Thanks you guys. Oh, and Darrell wants to know how many horses he needs to make room for in the barn?"

"What? Has he lost his mind?" Coot asked.

"Yah, but I think that happened years ago," Matt chuckled.

"Well, I don't want one," Mo stated. "So don't even think about that!"

"Me, either." Coot said.

"I'll ask Ruthie. I have to say, I rather enjoyed horseback riding." Ian thought. "Tell him I'll think about it."

"Oh Dad, can I borrow your car today? It is the homecoming parade and dance tonight?" Matt asked.

"Oh good grief, Mo! I do get to enjoy having a teenager!" Carl groaned.

"Well, either that or I'm going to need a ride home. I want to call my siblings and tell them I'm leaving the priesthood. Any suggestions who I should call first?" Matt asked his Mom.

She and Ian looked at each other and raised their eyebrows. "If it was me, I would tell Abby," Ian said. "She is the most likely not to stroke out."

"I'd suggest Patrick. He isn't as avid as some of the girls. And then John, Nancy's husband. After that, I'd let the news spread naturally. It should take all of five minutes." Mo grinned. "You might want to make your first call to Uncle Egan. He'd be the best one and he'd be very hurt if he doesn't hear it first hand."

"Okay Mom. That will be my morning. Then I'm leaving the house for the day. Hopefully, they'll all have calmed down before they get out here."

"Dream on. They won't. My brood has a fantastic capacity to have more than one fit going at a time!" Mo giggled. "Good luck Matt. And tell them the whole story about Butterton. Do not mention Diane. Hear me? That will just add fuel to the flame and you don't want them to mix it all up. Got it? Listen to me on this, Matthew. You other guys too. I am very extremely serious."

"Yes Mom. I will. But what about when they meet her?" Matt asked.

"Today you act like this is just the final move of the process that started months ago, because it is. Make no connection between leaving and Diane. You don't and they won't. I'm adamant."

"Yes, Ma'am," they all agreed.

Matt made some coffee. His kittens and his puppy were all settled when he made his first phone call. It rang twice before Vanessa answered. She called Uncle Egan to the phone.

Matt didn't mess around, but got right to it. Uncle Egan never made a sound. Matt was sure that he was really angry. When he got finished, he stopped talking. Still nothing. Finally he asked, "Uncle Egan, are you there?"

"Yah, I am. I had heard some rumors about a couple of these characters in town. I'm sorry it had anything to do with you, my boy. You did the right thing. I wouldn't have been able to shut up either. The oldsters will probably wet themselves, but I'll change their drawers. Don't blame you a bit. I wish you had told me about it before you left here. I'd have done a little vigilante work."

Matt laughed, "That's why I didn't tell you."

"Probably a wise move on your part. Want me to tell your brothers and sisters? Some of them will be fit to be tied."

"No. I have to do this. I'm only going to tell a couple. They'll tell each other."

"Holy Shamrocks in a Creek bed, Van and I are going to have to go out of town for the weekend!" He laughed. "Your Daddy would say you did the right thing. Just know that."

"Thanks Uncle Egan. You're the best."

"I know. Did you buy my favorite beer for while I am there? I can't be without you know."

"Yes, I will stock up."

Abby cried and gave the phone to Allen. He listened and said they would support him. Patrick swore, had a fit and then said he would've had to done the same thing if it was him. John Kelly listened carefully until he was all finished. "One of our neighbors had a son caught up in that kind of thing. The church sent that priest to Florida. I know the damage those types of men can cause. You have my support, although Tony will probably have a coronary."

"Tell him I'm still a Catholic."

"That's a relief. Then he'll be okay. I will have to figure out how to break it to Nancy. Especially before the rest hear about it. Did you tell everyone?"

"No, since I'm a coward, I only told Uncle Egan, Abby, and Patrick. I'm not telling anyone else."

"Probably wise. I'm glad I am working this weekend. It will make my hookers and junkies look downright friendly! I can about imagine Colleen! Saints above! It'll be a disaster of massive proportions. Thanks for letting me know, Matt. I got your back. I couldn't stomach it either. Truthfully, I wondered if you had ever heard about it and how you could tolerate it. Take care."

Matt had to get ready to leave the house and the phone rang twice before he left. He was glad Ian had let him use the sweatshirt, even if he had to endure half an hour of ranting about that old comic book. He would look better for the parade. The phone was ringing again as he left the house. "Well, Skippy, there is no turning back now. Is there?"

Skipper looked at him and wagged her tail. Matt reached down and hugged her. "I love you and both of your floppy years!"

❦❦❦ 47 ❦❦❦

MATT WALKED ON ONE SIDE of the street by the Junior Class float and Darrell walked on the other. Jeannie and Denise Anderson rode with the teenager who drove the pickup which towed it. The parade lasted about an hour and then they all took it back to the shop. They tore it down and were on their way home by four.

Matt had been worried about Diane all morning. He wondered how the trip to Waggoner's house had gone. When he drove into Schroeder's yard, most of the family was sitting on the patio. Only Diane and the grandparents were absent.

"How did it go?" Matt asked as he came up to the picnic table.

"Want a Coke?" Keith asked.

Matt shook his head no and sat down. "Thanks anyway, but I just had one. I'm dying. How did it go?"

Darlene answered, "Pretty much as expected. I didn't go this morning because I have this stupid cold and Pepper had to work. So Nora went with her."

Nora nodded, "Keith, Kevin and the two of us met Sheriff Bernard at nine-thirty. She was fine until she started up the steps to the porch. We could all see it was getting to her."

"She did well, though," Keith said. "It was traumatic but she really handled it pretty well. That living room is right out of Twilight Zone! There must have been a thousand photos for Dean. It was creepy."

"That's what Darrell said." Matt agreed.

267

"That is when she started to cry. Not a lot, but the tears were right there. She just looked around and shrugged. Then she said, 'I don't even know where to start. I don't know what's mine or where it is, or what Gladys wants.' Sheriff Bernard assured her that she could come back again when she felt better. Then we went upstairs. That's when I thought she was going to pass out."

Keith explained, "My god, those steps her pushed her down are steep and all hard wood with no carpet. It comes down and turns. There was blood on the wall where she apparently hit. I'm surprised she didn't get killed."

"We were going to move her dresser and stuff, but she just shook her head," Kevin said. "She wasn't sure if she wanted it. It wasn't hers, it had been Deans before he married. Waggoners had sold all their stuff. We took about six boxes of her stuff out of the upstairs. Then we came downstairs and that's when we almost lost her."

Matt's eyes widened, "Lost her?"

"She and I went into the kitchen," Nora continued and she picked up a porcelain teapot. She patted it and said, 'This was mine. Wag threw it against the wall one time and broke the handle off, but I used to love this old teapot. My Grandma gave it to me. Then she just broke down in tears."

Nora continued, "After a bit, I got her to start talking again. I told her that her Grandma would rather she be safe than have an old teapot. I asked her if she had anything else. She looked around and said that she and Dean had received a set of china for six as a wedding present from her family. She wanted that. We went into the dining room and the boys started packing the china. She looked around and picked up one photo of Dean. 'I used to love this photo, but I hate it now. Look how many they have in here! I makes my skin crawl. I don't even have a photo of him anymore."

Nora took a swallow of Coke, "I told her to take the one she was holding because someday she might want to have one. She could keep it packed away until all this is past. She handed it to Keith and when she did, she saw the piano. Then she really cried."

"She has never even mentioned a piano. I didn't know she played," Matt said.

"No wonder," Keith said. "I asked her if it was hers and she nodded yes. I told her we'd take it and she just shook her head no. Mom took her out to the porch to relax. After we got those dishes packed, Kev and I started to move the piano."

"Honestly, Matt! We opened the front and the strings were all cut! Every damned one of them! Some of the stuff inside looked like it had been hit with a sledge hammer. It was trashed. Then Keith opened the bench and it was filled with sheet music. We thought that we could save that for her, at least," Kevin explained.

"When I picked them up, they were all slashed to pieces. The whole works was destroyed." Keith was getting angry all over again. "That old man was nuts."

Matt shook his head. "I wonder what all went on there? So, you left the piano, huh?"

"Yah," Kevin said. "It would cost more to fix it than to buy a new one. And I doubt she wants the memories. Apparently, she used to play a lot. All the sheet music had her name on them."

"It was not easy stuff, either. Lots of Chopin and Bach. There was a book of classical Catholic music that had all the pages stripped from it. She must have taught music at some time, because she had lesson books for little kids in there too," Keith reported. "I bet she was a good musician."

"The boys and I are thinking that we need to get a piano for our house," Nora smiled. "I think one would fit on the wall behind the Grandpa's chairs. Don't you? It might be good for her to start playing again. What do you think?"

"I would think so, but I don't know how she feels about it. You don't need to go buying a piano for her. They are expensive," Matt said. "I could buy it."

"No. Kevin and I are going to Mandan to Eckert's Music sometime this week. They have used pianos for a real decent price. I called and we can get one for as low as $50. Of course, we want something that isn't junk."

Matt listened, "She's real funny about charity."

"Oh well, it won't be. None of these little ones have ever had piano lessons. I doubt that we could get Charlie to do it, but the girls would love it. I know Katie would give her eyeteeth to learn. Don't know if Ginger could do it with her missing finger, but maybe Miriam," Nora said. "And Becky Oxenfelter has wanted to take lessons before."

"Keith and I both have babies in the hopper. They need some lessons. So, if we go together and get her a piano, we'd want free lessons for like almost forever for all our kids," Kevin chuckled.

Matt watched these crazy people. "She'd probably really like that."

"We know," Keith grinned. "Darlene and I already talked about it and she thinks that it'd be great. I guess one afternoon, Diane told her that she used to teach little kids piano and she really loved it. That was back in Maine. When Darlene asked if she thought about doing it here, she said she didn't play anymore. It was a waste of time. Then she quickly changed the subject."

Kevin put his arm over Matt's shoulder, "So Tuck, we have an assignment for you. You need to find out how she feels about music. We don't want to get her all upset. Use your wily charms and report back before Wednesday. Keith and me, we are going to Mandan Thursday and we need to know if we have to take the pickup."

Matt nodded. "You guys, what can I say?"

"That you'll do it." Nora smiled. "I'm sure you want to talk to her. The others are all napping. Zach stopped by after we got home and gave me a tranquilizer for if she couldn't settle down. She was going to try to rest without it. That's why we came out here. Come with me, I'll take you in."

Inside, Nora and Matt were not prepared for what they encountered. The house was quiet until they turned in the hall. They could see Grandma Katherine sleeping on her bed with the door wide open. That was unusual because she nearly always closed the door.

However, even more out of the norm, were the sounds they heard from Diane's room. The door was partially open and they both had to stop and listen.

Grandpa Lloyd was consoling Diane, "Don't cry Girl. I'll fix it for you. Did someone hurt you? I won't stand for that. Nobody hurts my girl!"

"I'm okay Grandpa," Diane answered, "I'm just sad."

"Well, then don't cry. It makes me worry. Elton says I have too much to worry about. Did someone forget to give you a present?"

"No, nothing like that."

"Did that Tractor guy hurt you?"

Diane said, "No Grandpa, Matt would never hurt me."

"His name isn't Matt. Matt is a baby. He is Tractor cause they ran out."

"Ran out of what?"

"Names. Damned funny name to my notion."

"We call him Tuck."

"Truck is a funny name. That would make me cry, too. Is that why you are crying?" Lloyd patted her shoulder.

"No. I'll be fine," Diane tried to assure him.

"We'll have a party for you so you can be happy. Okay?"

"I don't need a party, Lloyd. Thank you. I just need a rest. I feel better already."

"Okay, we'll have a party. Is it your birthday?" Lloyd asked.

"Actually, my birthday is the 26th. But I don't need a party."

"Okay. Is that this year, Girl?" Lloyd was now determined.

"Yes, it's in a week."

"This year? Do you like chocolate cake? Some people like white cake. I hope you don't. I'll tell Katherine you like chocolate. Did you know that is my favorite?"

"Yes, I did," Diane giggled softly.

"Okay, we both like chocolate. Now you quit crying? I'll get you the cake."

"Thank you, Grandpa." Diane said.

Nora and Matt knocked and came in. Grandpa was sitting by Diane on the edge of her bed, with his arm around her. He had been consoling her. He looked at them, "Bout time you showed up. Nora Girl, you need to make a chocolate cake so this girl quits crying. I don't want my girl to cry. You fix it, Tractor guy. I'm going to find Katherine. I think she is typing for Byron."

"Come on Lloyd," Nora helped him up. "I will pour you some coffee. Katherine is taking a nap."

"She should finish her typing. Then she could make the cake. Do we have any chocolate cake? I want some," Lloyd said.

"I never would've guessed," Nora smiled.

As they left, Nora pulled the door closed. Matt sat down by Diane. "I see Lloyd was looking out for you. That was very kind of him."

"He is a real gentleman, isn't he?" Diane leaned her head on Matt's shoulder while he put his arm around her. "He was so kind."

"Did he steal your heart away?" Matt teased.

Diane nodded, "Pretty close."

"How did it go today? Keith and Kevin told me some of it. Pretty tough, huh?"

She shook her head, "I'm so mixed up, Matthew. I hate this. You know what Grandpa said? If I wasn't hurt, I shouldn't cry. He's right you know. I should be happy that things are so good now. Why do I still cry?"

Matt kissed her forehead, "Honey, it's still a lot of emotions and turmoil. Don't expect so much from yourself."

She hugged him, "How was the parade?"

Matt grinned, "Good. Fun. I have to get moving to help Darrell milk and then we have to get to the dance. I won't be able to get over after the dance tonight, unless you want me to come."

"No, Zach gave me a tranquilizer to take if I can't settle down. You'll be tired after the dance. Will I see you tomorrow?"

"Plan on it. We can pick you up for nine o'clock Mass. The entire clan always meets here for Sunday dinner. I'll be here for that."

"How many? Will all those tables be full?" Tinker's face filled with worry. "Matt, I don't know if I'm ready to meet all these people. What will they be thinking of me?"

"First, you know almost all of them. Second, they're part of the Engelmann clan. They are Lloyd's relation that he's so proud of. If anyone of them even began to think anything bad, the rest of them would have their hide. Trust me. It'll be okay. I promise."

"I don't know if I'm up to it. I can't even think about going to school on Monday."

"Mr. Palmer told everyone you tumbled down the steps. Only a few of us know the truth and we aren't going to tell. It's no one else's business. Okay? And you have to get back in the world or the bad guys will have won. You hear me?"

"You will be here?"

"Wouldn't miss it. I'll be right here for you. Okay?"

She nodded. "Matt, I have to tell someone. It's killing me."

"Of course."

"It was a year ago yesterday that I learned I was pregnant. Dean and I were so excited. We were happy then. We thought the world looked so good. In no time, life turned to hell."

"I'm so sorry, Diane," he hugged her again. "When did you lose the baby?"

"First week in December. Dean was diagnosed the following week." She shook her head and had a sarcastic little laugh. "I was such a fool. I thought I had everything in the world a person could want, and then I got a lesson. A big one."

"That happens to all of us, you know. I can't honestly tell you that I understand why sometimes things have to be so damned miserable, but I do know that if we can just hang in there, things will get better again."

Diane never looked up but kept her head on his chest, "Matt. I'm afraid to try again. I couldn't take going through all this again. I don't even want to."

"I know. I know," He held her a while and then kissed her cheek. "Tinker, do you think you can rest now or should I call Nora?"

"No, I've been such a bother today already," Diane lay back on her bed. Matt covered her with the afghan.

"I really hate to leave you. I could call Darrell and stay."

"No, you go. I'll be fine, really." She held out her hand and he took it. Then he leaned ahead and gave her a kiss.

"Okay, now I *have* to get out of here," he grinned. "Sleep tight. I'll see you in the morning."

"Okay."

In the kitchen, Matt gave Nora a hug. "Is she resting now?"

"Yes, she is trying to sleep. I can't come back until tomorrow morning, but if you think she needs me, will you call?"

"Of course, Matt, I will." They walked outside, "Matt, I was thinking. Her birthday is next Saturday. We'll celebrate on Sunday at dinner, but I was wondering if you could take her away most of the day on Saturday? I mean, get her out of the house?"

"Sure, but why?"

"We're going to get the piano for her birthday present and the boys can set it up. Then you can bring her here for supper and we can give it to her. Okay?"

"I didn't get a chance to talk to her about it."

"Don't have to, really. I think she is so confused now, that she doesn't know. Besides, this would be a birthday present."

"Nora, did she tell you about the baby?"

Nora frowned, "No, what?'

"She just told me that it was a year ago yesterday that she found out she was pregnant. I think that is part of why she is so bummed. She said she was so happy then, and now her life has fallen apart."

"Thanks for telling me. I'll talk to her. I'm sure it is hard for her. Don't worry, Matt, I will talk to her but I won't let her know that you told me."

Matt kissed her cheek, "Thanks."

❧ 48 ❧

THE NEXT MORNING MATT WAS on the phone before his first cup of coffee. Elton confirmed that Diane had slept throughout the night after taking a sleeping pill that Zach had provided. She was still sleeping, but Nora had checked in on her and she seemed to be resting soundly.

It was a little after nine, when Matt arrived at Schroeders. His Mom and Ian were going to pick up Ruthie and they'd all meet at the church. Grandma Katherine met him at the door with a hug and said, "Have you had any breakfast, young man?"

"A piece of toast," Matt answered.

"That won't keep a bird alive," Coot said and he motioned for him to sit down. "Tinker is getting beautiful, so you have time for a bite."

Nora set down a plate of ham and hash browns in front of him. "Would you like me to fry an egg or two?"

"No, really. This is more than I need."

Lloyd frowned at him, "Did you come to give me my ride?"

"This afternoon, if Zach says it's okay," Matt replied.

"Don't talk to him. You can't trust a tall guy," Lloyd announced. "I can go."

"We'll see, Lloyd," Katherine patted her husband's hand. "You aren't going if the doctor says no. Zach wants to listen to your chest first."

"What does he know? He can listen to your chest."

Diane came into the kitchen, looking very pretty but tired. She wore the peach dress that Matt loved so much and she had a little make up on, so she didn't look quite so pale. She was fidgeting and Nora looked at her.

274

"Calm down, Diane. You're just fine. The only thing they can see is the neck brace," then she grinned, "Folks usually think car accident."

"I can't wait to get this off. I feel like an ostrich!"

Elton chuckled, "And just how is that?"

"You don't get better with age," Carl groaned. "Do you? How many days have I got left here?"

"Way too many," Elton laughed. "Want some coffee before you go, Tinker?"

"No, thank you. I have never drunk so much coffee in my life as I have since I have been here."

"Probably because this is the world's best, huh?" Elton winked.

"It certainly is delicious." Diane checked her handbag and fidgeted with her coat.

"Are you anxious to go?" Matt asked as he quickly ate the last bite of ham. "I'll be right with you."

"Take your time. I think I could miss this week, huh? No one would care, would they?" Diane tried to convince the family.

Nora giggled, "Nice try. You just can't hide out and you have no need to. Remember, most folks are too involved with their own lives to worry about yours."

Matt took his plate to the sink and helped her with her jacket. "Come on before you talk yourself out of it. Thanks for the breakfast Nora. We'll see you soon."

In the car, Diane said, "I feel like such a mooch. I should contribute more to this family. They don't ask a thing, or let me do much."

Matt grinned, "Didn't Elton drag you down to milk cows yet?"

"Not yet, but when Zach said the brace could come off this week, he said he would warn Snowflake. Matt, I don't know how to milk a cow."

"He'll teach you. He always does. Don't worry. Have the ladies had you cooking yet?"

"Yes and so has your Dad. Carl had me stir up his biscuit recipe yesterday," She giggled. "Those folks are busy all the time. I've never been around people like them before. And there are all sorts of people around. Annie, Darlene and Keith, Carl and I all live there! It is unbelievable."

"Does it bother you?"

Diane thought, "No, I'm surprised, but I really enjoy it. I took your advice and asked Kate to show me her beading. Matt, it's fantastic. She is going to show me how to do it next week. I told her I am all thumbs, but she just smiled. I don't think she knows how much of a klutz I am."

"I think you aren't really, just a bag of nerves. You'll get over it. Oh, by the way, do you ride horse?" Matt grinned.

"Horse? Heavens no. I've never been near a horse. Why do you ask?"

"Darrell wants me to get two horses. One for me and one for you so you can go riding with us. What do you think?" Matt asked.

Diane got quiet for a minute, "Maybe not yet. I don't know if I can even ride a horse. And we need to slow down. I mean, a cat, a dog and a horse?"

"And a steady fella?" Matt added. "Don't forget that."

"I'm not so sure this is slow," Diane pointed out. "When I get well and move out on my own, I'll have to rent a farm!"

"Yah, talk to Darrell. I gave him the same speech. See how much good it did me?"

Diane drew a few stares when they entered the church, but tried to pay them no mind. Ruthie motioned to them because they had saved them a place in their pew. It was about half way through the service before Diane calmed down.

She was unable to kneel and Matt just shook his head no when she tried. After the service, Father Vicaro greeted them with a big smile. "I'm glad to see you. Matt, will you let me know about CCD."

Diane interrupted, "We'll be there this week and then let you know. I wouldn't want to leave you in a lurch. I've been irresponsible. You've been a saint."

Father Vicaro chuckled, "Hope you have St. Peter's ear! See you later."

Matt drove them to his cabin after church. Diane questioned why the drove past Schroeder's farm and he said, "Well, I wanted to change clothes. I'm sorry. I just never even thought you might want to go home first. Do you?"

"I guess not. I was just surprised. I'd like to see Lady and Skipper."

"What about Murphy? He is the coolest cat ever! I tell you. He sits on the arm of the sofa and watches Lady. She is so busy running and jumping. He just watches her. I have to laugh. I noticed you told Father Vicaro that we would do CCD. I wasn't certain about that."

"Oh my, I'm sorry I should've talked to you first. I shouldn't have spoken for you." Diane started to get worried.

"It is fine, Tinker. I'm not at all bothered by it. I'm rather glad you said yes. I enjoyed our last class together. Besides, it gives me an excuse to see you."

"Like you need one?"

When they got to the farm, Matt brought Skipper to the house. Diane cracked up when she watched the foot wiping procedure. "Do you honestly think that you can train her to do that?"

"Of course. Why not? You're as bad as Darrell. I have never met so many people who have so little faith. Just like Ian always giving me a bad time about my begonia from the rectory. Just because it looks a little dead. It'll come back. I just know it."

"A little dead?"

"Yah, I can show it to you," as if he was convinced that one look would vindicate him.

"You have it here?"

"Of course. Brought it back from Boston. Let me show you," He went into the laundry room and returned with the pot that contained a few dead twigs. "It is a tuberous begonia. See? It'll come back."

Diane raised one eyebrow, "You really believe that? I tend to think that Ian might be right. It looks totally dead, Matt. And if you want it to grow, maybe you might want to water it and give it some sunlight. Do you think?"

"Ah," Matt studied the plant, "You might have a point. I'll do that. Anyway, I'm going to change my clothes."

Diane was digging in the pot when he came back in the room. "Whatcha doing?"

"I was looking at your plant and pulling off the dead leaves. I decided to loosen the soil. Matt, were you aware there is no bulb in there anymore! It was just the dead leaves sticking up from the soil."

"Hm. How could that be? It was in there. Where would it go?"

"How long has it been dead?"

"It isn't dead. Just dormant," Matt corrected her.

She shook her head, "How long has it been dormant?"

Matt thought, "About a year and half or maybe two."

She gave him a hug, "Honey, it probably rotted away. I think it's done for."

Offended, Matt picked up his plant and carried it back to the laundry room, "You guys just leave my plant alone. It will bloom. I just know it. In the spring."

"Okay," Diane agreed. "You don't teach science, do you?"

"Nope. Well, are you ready to go or do you want to give me a bad time about my begonia some more?" Matt was obviously hurt she didn't appreciate his green thumb.

"What time do we have to be there?"

Matt put his arms around her, "About noon. We have a while yet. Why? Want to neck?"

"No, I'm just concerned about all those folks being there." Diane sat down.

"Want a Coke?" he handed her one and took one himself. "Don't worry about it? Church went okay, didn't it?"

"Yes, but no one had a chance to talk to me. They will now." Diane played with Lady. "And I don't have anything to bring for the big dinner."

"Okay, let's look." He went to the fridge and took out a head of cabbage and an onion. "Know how to make coleslaw? Let's whip some up."

She giggled, "Okay. Got some carrots?"

Within a few minutes, the couple was engrossed in making coleslaw. Skipper thought it was a lot of fun to trip them both as often as possible and make her presence known, but in less than a half an hour, they had a large plastic container of Coleslaw to bring to the dinner. Tinker tasted it and thought it was passable.

"Passable?" Matt chuckled. "I think it is fantastic! This is our first joint culinary effort! Oh, tomorrow night, Father Vicaro is coming for dinner. He sort of invited himself for six-thirty. What would you suggest?"

"May I look through your freezer?" She asked timidly.

"Of course," Matt watched her as she moved the meat around.

"You could make pork chops and baked potatoes. If you got it ready to go and threw it in the oven before chores, it should be done when he arrives. Save a little of this coleslaw for your dinner. You could thaw out this apple pie. It'll be good."

"Could you help me?"

"I would be happy to," Diane smiled. As she put the frozen pork chops in a baking dish and seasoned them, Matt turned on his classical radio station. Fortunately, the second piece was a Chopin etude.

Diane turned around when she heard it, "Oh, I love this. It's one of my favorites."

Matt figured it was a great opportunity and while he was scrubbing the potatoes and wrapping them in foil, he asked. "Do you mean Chopin or this one piece?"

"Both." Diane got very quiet.

"What is it?" Matt asked after he put the potatoes in the fridge for the next night, "Why so quiet?"

"I used to play piano. I loved it. I taught for awhile back in Maine." Diane related. "I even brought my piano out here with me."

"Do you still play?"

"No. Wag hated it. He wouldn't allow that foolishness. He destroyed the piano and all my sheet music. I haven't played in a year. No matter, I probably forgot how," she gave him a weak grin.

"I don't think that you could forget that soon. If you enjoyed it, you should do it."

"Oh maybe someday. I don't have a piano now. Anyway, dinner is all ready. Tomorrow just put it in the oven at 300 and you'll have supper ready when chores are done."

Matt gave her a kiss, "Thank you for showing me how. I suppose we had better get moving now. I'll take Skip down to the barn. Want to walk along?"

"Sure. You should get her a collar and a leash."

They walked down to the barn. Matt told her that when they were a little older, Darrell was going to let the pups run all day. For now, he didn't trust them to not run off and get lost. When they put Skip in her pen with Ranger, Matt asked, "Have you seen the barn?"

"No, I've never been in a barn."

"I'll give you a very quick tour."

They arrived at Schroeder's just minutes after Mo and Ian. Nora was very surprised when Diane presented her coleslaw. "You didn't have to do that."

Matt answered, "We wanted to contribute to the meal like everyone else."

"I hope it's okay," she smiled. "Tuck helped me."

Nora tasted it, "It is great. Thanks, you guys. Come, let's get this on the table."

"Do I have time to change first? I would really like to wear my jeans and tee shirt. This belt and the hose are beginning to hurt my bruises."

"Whatever is more comfortable. We aren't going to eat for about half an hour," Nora said. After Diane left, she asked Matt, "How is she doing?"

"Okay. A little concerned she won't know anyone today, but I told her she will."

"I think she knows almost all of us."

"Nora, I learned a little more about the piano. I think she would like that. I get paid this week. Let me contribute."

"Nope. I have been hitting everyone up as the arrived and we have enough already and some left over. I'll give you the extra and you worry about the sheet music." Nora grinned.

Matt hugged her, "Thanks."

The day went fine and it was relaxing. After Matt took Lloyd for his drive, he went for a walk with Diane before leaving for home.

"What did you think? Was it okay today?"

"Yes, I had fun. You and I have to practice playing whist though. I'm afraid I am a lousy player."

"Me, too. Maybe Darrell and Jeannie will give us lessons. We aren't the most with it couple in the world, are we?" Matt grinned.

"No, we aren't. Matt, I hope you won't be disappointed if things don't work out between us. I'm not much," Diane searched his face.

"I really wish you'd quit saying that. I think you are. A lot of folks do. So, try to get Wag's opinion out of your mind. I know it will take time, but you need to realize, he was a demented man."

Diane nodded. "What if we don't work out?"

Matt crossed his eyes, "Yea gads Girl! You are always telling me to slow down. What are you doing? We are only starting on forever, not half way through it."

She looked at him and frowned, "I don't know if that made sense."

"Probably not, but I enjoyed today. Next week, we can plan ahead to bring something for dinner. I'll pick you up on Saturday and you can spend most of the day with the pets and me. We'll make our treat for dinner Sunday then, so we don't have to hurry after church. Okay? Schroeders invited us for dinner Saturday night." Matt took her hand. "I'd love to plan on that. I can give you the break down on my family. They'll start arriving during the next week. You need a primer."

"Oh, Matt. Are they going to be upset since they just learned about you leaving the priesthood? I don't want to be the other woman!"

"Mom has that all under control. They won't think you are the other woman. Besides, Carl and Ian would knock them silly if they even started. But I have to warn you, they aren't like the Engelmann clan."

"Few people are. Oh, I talked to my Mom yesterday. She is quite anxious to meet you. I didn't tell her any more than we were friends, but

I think she knows me too well. Her only concern is that you are another Waggoner. I assured you that you are not. I told her that she'd like you."

Matt squeezed her hand, "I hope I can live up to that good press. Well, I have to get home. Jeannie and I will pick you up on the way to school."

"Jeannie already said that. I need to start paying back."

"You will, be sure. I'll only give you a little kiss before I go. I don't trust myself and there are too many clanners around."

Diane giggled, "Good for us, huh? Goodnight. I had a wonderful day. Hey, guess what? No tears!"

"Wow! I knew something was missing! See you in the morning."

❦❦❧ **49** ❧❦❦

THE WEEK WENT PRETTY WELL. Diane was very nervous on Monday about returning to school; but by Tuesday, felt much more confident.

Matt worked out things with Clyde and then talked to the whole Calculus class. He told them that it had come to his attention that he didn't explained the last two chapters very well and he was going to do it over. Then he extracted a promise from the students to let him know if they didn't understand something right away. "If you try to struggle through it, we'll just keep moving forward and you will just begin to slowly sink."

Matt's dinner with Father Vicaro was a lot more fun than Matt had anticipated. Frank was a nice man and they were very comfortable talking about all sorts of things. Vicaro thought it was amusing that Matt had such a pile of pets. "You seem very domesticated. You might make a pretty good farmer!"

"I don't know about that. But it does keep my mind occupied."

They visited about his feelings about the changes in his life, including Diane, and Father Vicaro only cautioned him to take it slow. "You both have had a lot of things going on and it isn't good to rush headlong into a serious commitment. Remember you aren't finished with the church for a short while yet. I sent your letter of resignation off. My guess is that your Bishop is as anxious to get you out of his hair as you are to get out of his. I only wish the church wasn't so rigid about not letting you be more involved at St. Johns. I'm worried this Bartholomew is going to be an authoritarian. He is but a whippersnapper. I just know he and I are going to clash. Oh well, it is my cross to bear. Give him a couple years and he'll learn."

When Matt gave Clyde the test again on Tuesday, he passed it with a B. They both felt a lot better.

Wednesday, Matt picked up Diane for CCD. They had a good class and enjoyed working together. It was fun and the kids seemed to get a lot out of it too. Matt was pleased how well their class went.

Thursday afternoon, since Matt didn't have to go to St. Johns, he went to Bismarck. He had talked to Keith and Kevin, so, he had a pretty good idea of what to pieces of sheet music to pick up. Then he went to shopping for groceries. He picked up some things for the cobbler that Tinker wanted to make for Sunday dinner and a few groceries. Then he purchased a coffee pot with a timer, a collar and leash for Skipper.

He wandered around the stores racking his brain about what to get for Diane's birthday. He wanted something special but not over the top. He was at a loss.

He ended up at a bookstore and bought her a book of Robert Frost's poetry. When he was leaving the mall, he passed a store. One glance in the window and he knew what he wanted to get her. Then he decided it was too much, and walked away. He was almost to the car before he turned and went back. He bought her the golden locket that had a single rose engraved on the cover.

The inside was empty, but had a place for two photos. When he got home, he took a couple photos of the pets. He would put a photo of Lady and Murphy rolled together into a ball on one side and Skipper on the other. He decided it was rather dumb, but she could exchange them with some other photos if she wanted.

Friday after he took Lloyd for his ride, he and Diane went for walk.

"What time are you going to pick me up tomorrow?" Diane asked.

"I thought after morning chores. Is that okay?"

"It'll be fine. What are we going to do all day?"

"I don't know. I have to do some school work, what about you?"

"Yes, I have a lot. Should I bring it over?"

"Sure. It's supposed to rain all day. I bought some chocolate chips. I thought cookies sounded like a good idea," Matt grinned.

"I suppose you'll be baking them?" Diane smiled.

Matt frowned, "I could, or I would help. Do you know how?"

She smiled broadly, "Of course, you knucklehead. I'll bake them. And then make the peach cobbler for Sunday. Say, what's going on with Grandpa Lloyd?'

"Why? He seemed fine to me," Matt was surprised.

"Oh, he has been telling me, 'I can't say a word. Nora Girl will wring my neck!' He must have said that a hundred times."

"Who knows? He comes up with the darnedest things sometimes. Say, how did your milking go?"

Diane sighed, "I'm sure Elton thinks I'm a numbskull. This morning was my first time. It must have taken me half an hour to milk poor Snowflake. He should have been a teacher. He is very patient. And so was Snowflake."

"You'll get faster." Matt chuckled. "Practice makes perfect."

"I don't know how much I want to get good at it."

"You will. Believe me."

Matt spent the evening cleaning his house and doing laundry. He changed the kitty litter and wiped out his refrigerator. He could hardly remember a time he had been more anxious about the next day.

The next morning after chores, he changed clothes and checked the house. Assured that everything was in place, he went over to Schroeders. There was a nice steady rain and it looked like it planned on continuing for a while.

He managed to drive in just as Schroeder's were sitting down to eat breakfast. "Would you believe that, Nora? This guy just happened to show up when the first waffle came off the iron!" Elton said as he let him in. "Should we let him join us?"

Matt chuckled, "Don't mind if I do!"

He enjoyed having breakfast with the family again. He was surprised at Lloyd. He sat there like a cat that had swallowed a canary all through breakfast. No wonder Diane wondered what was going on with him.

After a cup of coffee, he said, "Better you two go now. Go. Get her out of here. Tractor guy, don't forget!"

Grandma finally ushered him into the living room and told him to hush up.

On their way to the cabin, Diane asked, "Did you notice Grandpa? He really wanted me out of there. I don't think he likes me living there. I should be looking for a different place. I wouldn't like to upset him."

"Don't worry about him. He just has a wrinkle."

Diane gave him an odd look and then shrugged. "I really have difficulty understanding any of you."

Matt chuckled. "We need to stop at Mom's. She called and asked me to stop. Okay?'

Mo and Ian were having a cup of coffee and invited them to join them. "I have to talk to you about the weddings and your brothers and sisters, Matt! I'm no longer related to any of them!"

"Mom, not me?" Ian chuckled.

"No, you're okay but the rest are whackos! The Saints above us! They're all at each other's throats!" Mo announced.

"Why? I haven't heard a word from them since I called and told them I was leaving the priesthood," Matt frowned as he pulled out a chair for Diane.

"And be thanking the mighty Lord above! They have been yowling at me day and night! I think Colleen should be an Archbishop, the way she carries on. So I told her that and she decided it was because I don't like her Frank and the kids. I explained I liked them fine; it was her I didn't like. So she went into another spiral! Yea gads. She is so holy, you'd think she was Sister Theresa herself!"

Matt poured coffee for them, "I'm sorry Mom. I knew she wouldn't take it well, but you two shouldn't argue about it. Want me to call her?"

"It would only add fuel, so there's no point. Ah, my child, what do you have a family for? It is only to hone your gladiator skills. She no more than got through bawling her head off and Vivian got into her Pope-mobile! I'm ready to slap them both. So, know what I did?"

Matt studied her face and then asked Ian, "Do I want to know?"

"Probably not, but she's our Mom and we're kind of responsible for her," Ian chuckled. "Just wait until you hear!"

"I just got my dander up just a little and I told them, Ruthie had been a nun too. Boy, that revved up the old pistons! It was hilarious. The first time in Colleen's life she couldn't think of a word to sputter! Now they can either get it all out of their system before they get out here or they can stay out there! Then I hung up and cried like a baby. Before I could call it done, I called Egan and bellowed to him. He said he was going to call a family meeting. He'd tell them to shape up. Most of them are fine, it is just those two. He said most of the cops knew about those pedophiles and he was going to get them to spill it to the rest. It is time. So, maybe we won't need such a big wedding cake after all! I know that Rain will be here, even if she has to hitchhike! It'll be okay, but Lordie be, those other two girls are acting like they fell into a vat of communion wine!"

"How are Nana and Pappy?" Matt asked.

"Egan said they never said anything except the whole damned family is destined for hell, so what difference does one more make," Mo giggled. "Tinker, I hope you'll forgive my kin. They hail from Stupidland in eastern Ireland, but someone needed to raise them. I wish I hadn't won that lottery!"

Diane smiled, and then she offered, "Maybe I should stay away from all the wedding festivities. I wouldn't want to get them any more upset."

Mo looked at her, "Oh no you don't. They can put their hair in a knot if they want, but you're a sane one. We need more like you, not less! You're coming to my little Ruthie's wedding and after Mattie walks me down the aisle, I want him to have someone to talk to that isn't suffering from rabies!"

Diane giggled, "Then it is a certainty that I should stay away!"

Ian grinned, "No, you shouldn't. I want you there; even if you don't want to be around my goofy brother. I can certainly understand that! I feel that way myself. Oh, Matt, Ruthie and I need a favor about the wedding."

Matt squinted at his brother, "How can you do that? Insult me one minute and then ask a favor? Unbelievable."

Ian shrugged and said undaunted, "It is, isn't it? Since Catholics cannot have outdoor weddings, we'll be getting married in St. John's in the morning. I need you guys to meet us there at the crack of seven. Father Vicaro is going to do a very simple wedding for us and then we will renew our vows at the evening service outside, in front of everyone."

Matt nodded, "I wondered how you would handle that. Good. Seven?"

Diane cleared her throat, "Us guys? Surely you don't want me there."

Ian chuckled, "I'd prefer having you there to having Matt show up; but I don't think that you'd want to be my best man!"

"Who is going to be there?" Matt asked.

"You and Suzy, just the witnesses and your partners. Mom and Coot. It should be all done by seven-thirty. You'll still make it to work on time. We just want to get it all sorted out now, because we don't want the whole family there. We want to keep it under wraps so everyone doesn't get all bent out of shape they weren't invited to it. Okay? We still want to have the big outdoor wedding be the thing. You know, that will be like our real wedding," Ian tried to explain.

Matt shook his head, "I'll take your word for it. So, who is doing the evening service?"

"Byron, Marv and Father Vicaro. That's what Ruthie had dreamed about. You know she had worked like a maniac since Zach and Suzy's wedding and I want her to be happy with it. As far as I am concerned, the morning service would be sufficient," Ian laughed. "But my Ruthie has never had a big deal for just herself. I want her to have that."

"That's so nice, Ian," Diane smiled. "You're a very kind person."

Matt shook his head, "No, he isn't, Diane. He is always ragging on me!"

Diane smiled sweetly and raised her eyebrow, "And I'm sure you never bug him!"

Ian got up and gave her a kiss on the cheek, "You are the best, Diane!"

Matt made a face, "I don't like either of you."

❦✿ 50 ✿❦

ON THE WAY OVER TO the cabin, Diane became concerned. "Matt, does your family get very—, I mean—, like violent when they get upset? I don't think I could handle that. I love your Mom and Ian, but I don't know the rest. I think I'd rather not meet them if they're upset."

Matt reached over and took her hand, "Listen, Tinker. I'd never knowingly put you in a situation that got physical. They just argue, but they aren't physical, and neither Coot, Mom or anyone else in the family would even allow them to get out of hand verbally. It'll be fine. Besides, they'd never yell at you about any of it. It is me they're upset with. Okay?"

"Maybe it would be better if I just stayed away," Diane withdrew her hand from his. "I'm not too happy about meeting the whole family. I think I should give that a miss."

Matt put his hand back on the steering wheel and never said another word. They drove home in silence. Matt was shattered. He had envisioned this whole wedding week with her being by his side. Suddenly, he realized he may have been unrealistic and it was probably unreasonable for him to expect, but that had been his desire.

He dropped her at the house and took the car to the shop. Then he brought Skipper out of the barn and carried her to the cabin. "Gee Skipper, I guess I got my cart way ahead of my horse. You should have warned me, Skip. Now what do I do?"

Skipper looked up at him and licked his cheek.

"I love you, you crazy pup."

Diane had opened the door to the laundry and let Murphy and Lady out to play. Diane was on the floor playing with them. Skipper went right over to her and licked her cheek while she petted her. After he hung up their jackets, Matt started the logs in the fireplace. Within minutes, it was very cozy in the cabin.

The only thing they said to each other in all that time was when Matt asked if she wanted some tea. After Skip went to take her nap and the cats rolled up in the afghan at the end of the sofa, Diane came into the kitchen and washed her hands. Matt had put their cups and teabags on the counter. His whole countenance was devastation. Tinker knew she had really hurt him.

He leaned against the counter and watched the teapot just beginning to boil on the stove. She very much regretted having ruined his day. She leaned against the counter next to him, "Matt, I'm sorry."

He just shrugged, "No, it was my fault. I should've never taken it for granted that you'd want to meet them all, or be a part of my family. I was going overboard again. I have a hard time finding the lines."

Diane took his hand, "No. You aren't wrong. It makes sense that you'd have your steady date be with you in all these celebrations."

He looked at her, hoping she'd say that meant she'd attend everything. She put her other hand on his cheek, and with tears in her eyes, she said, "Maybe we shouldn't be going steady."

Matt was floored, and felt a little dizzy. He looked at her and around the kitchen. He could hear the water beginning to bubble in the teakettle and the rain on the roof. He looked at his tiny living room with animals all at home in front of a cozy fireplace. He thought he might faint. This was horrible. He had never expected this. His eyes finally came back to her and he just walked out of the kitchen. He went into his room and closed the door. He was sick. He threw himself across his bed and lay there. He didn't cry. He was totally without any sense of anything positive. He was in the abyss.

He heard the teapot start to whistle and Diane make the tea. Then he pulled his pillow over his head so he didn't have to hear anymore. He couldn't have felt anymore desolate.

Then the door opened to his room and Diane came in. She sat on the edge of his bed and put her hand on his back, "Matt, I'm so sorry. Would you like me to call over to Schroeder's and have someone pick me up?"

Matt immediately remembered that she was there because they were setting up her party. He couldn't let that get messed up. He sat up and said, "No. I need to shape up. Okay? Forget I acted like this. Is the tea ready?"

Diane nodded, "If you still want to have tea with me."

"Folks have tea with their acquaintances all the time. I think even I can handle that."

He started to get off the bed and she took his hand. "I am sorry."

"Quit. You don't need to apologize about how you feel. It is perfectly understandable." He squeezed her hand and then dropped it. "If you don't want us to be more than acquaintances, then that's what we'll be. But Diane," he looked directly at her, "Then that's all we'll be. I can't deal with it otherwise. I hope you understand that."

She looked at him as if she didn't really understand, "Do you want to take me home?"

Matt stood up, "No. I don't. Let's have our tea. Then we can figure out what we're going to do today. Just remember, whatever you decide, is what you decide. You can't push me away and then expect me to be there."

She dropped her eyes, "I know. Matt, I don't know what I'm doing. I wanted this to be a fun day. Look what I've done?"

"You made tea and if we don't go drink it, it'll be cold." Matt went to the door and made a motion for her to go out ahead of him. She did.

He put the tea and the cups on the table and motioned for her to sit down, which she did. They drank their tea in silence, avoiding looking at each other. The phone rang and it was Darrell.

"Hi, Matt. Could I ask you to help me? I need to bring that combine back from the north field while I still can or it'll get bogged down in the mud. Jeannie is busy making stuff for the birthday dinner tonight, so I need someone to give me a ride and help."

"Sure, no problem," Matt said, almost relieved to have a break in this situation. "How soon?"

"About fifteen minutes? Is that okay? I know you have company."

"I'll be ready. No problem. Tinker has some school papers to take care of," Matt tried to not let on about their difficulties. Then he said goodbye and hung up.

"You have to leave?" Diane asked.

"Yah. Might be good I get out of your hair for a while, huh?" Matt tried to be positive. "Can you watch the fire and the pets? You can make yourself at home. If you want to use the stove, just help yourself and you can look through all my cupboards to find what you need. Or if you don't want to, that's okay too."

Matt went into his room and put a sweatshirt on. He came back into the kitchen and she was still standing in the same place, unmoved. He looked at her, "Or Diane, if you'd feel more comfortable, you can go up to Jeannie's. I can put Skipper back in the barn. You don't need to babysit."

Diane shook her head no. "Matt?" she took his arm, "Please don't shut me out."

He looked at her, "Diane, you tell me what you want and I'll try to do it. But I beg of you, don't send mixed signals. I'm no good at that."

She started to cry and put her arms around his neck, "I don't know what to do. I'm so afraid."

"Okay. I have an idea. Do you want to hear it?" he said as he took her arms from his neck.

She nodded, "I suppose I do."

"Can we just have a nice day? Can you make up your mind as we go along? I'll not ask or expect you to attend anything with me unless you tell me that you will. But Diane, if you tell me you will, then you have to? You know?"

She nodded, "I know. I'm being very unfair."

Matt smiled at her for the first time, "No, you aren't. I just want this to work so much and I wanted to go too fast. I need to think. So, is it okay for you to stay in the house, while I go help Darrell? Or should I take Skipper to the barn?"

She hugged him, "Skip is just fine here. It's very nice and cozy here and I appreciate you opening your home to me. I wanted to make that cobbler and you got all the ingredients for chocolate chip cookies. I'll be right here. Please don't be upset with me. I couldn't stand that."

He kissed her cheek, "I'll try not to be, but I'm very hurt and confused right now. I see Darrell coming, so I better get my jacket on. Make yourself at home, Diane."

Darrell knocked twice and Matt opened the door. He came in with his big grin, "Hi Guys. Sorry to mess up your quiet day together. I'll try to have him back as soon as we get that combine out of the field."

Diane smiled, "About how long do you think it'll be?"

"If it isn't stuck, about an hour. Otherwise, who knows?"

"Okay," she shrugged. "Good luck."

Diane cried at the window as she watched them walk away. Just what the heck did she want? She wanted to be with him, she was just so afraid.

As it turned out, the men took a lot longer than an hour. They had left about ten and still weren't home at one. Diane had made the cobbler and the cookies. She had a lunch keeping warm in the oven and the table set for lunch. Jeannie had called when she realized the men would be late and asked if she was okay. They visited a little bit. She wanted to talk to Jeannie about what had happened, but never mentioned it. She wouldn't do that to Matt.

Then Diane took Skipper for a walk and even tried to go through the foot wiping procedure with her when they came back in. She was amazed that Skipper really did seem to know what to do. When they came back into the kitchen, she looked around.

She had been so wrong. She did want to be with Matt. She was extremely attracted to him, not only physically, but in many other ways. He couldn't have been any better to her. She loved the fact that he had got her these pets, bought groceries for her cobbler and made the house so welcoming to her. She'd have rocks in her head to not think he was the best. She also knew that if she kept sending mixed messages, he'd say to heck with it. She wouldn't blame him. It was all her own fears. Fear of it all falling apart, fear of people's anger, fear of confrontation, fear of the impending trial, fear she'd never be good enough for him and mostly the fear of her own judgment. She was consumed by it. She needed to really talk to someone about it, but strangely, the only person she'd consider talking to was Matt.

She curled up on the sofa with the book she was reading for her class and covered up with the afghan. The cats promptly curled up on her feet and Skipper fell asleep on the floor in front of the sofa. She soon put the book down and just watched the fire.

When she woke, it was to Matt's voice. He was next to her, "Wake up Sleepy Head. I'm sorry I was gone so long. We had a heck of a time. You look very comfy."

Diane sat up and her book fell to the floor. "Matt, I need to talk to you." She stood up and put her arms around him, "But lunch is ready."

He hugged her quickly and said, "I have to go wash up. Boy, was that a muddy mess. It's still raining like crazy."

He started to walk away and she grabbed his hand. "While you were gone, I did a lot of thinking. I was wrong this morning. I want to be your girl. I really do. I think you're a fantastic guy and I love being with you. I'm just so afraid of everything. Can you forgive me? I don't want to change my mind again. It isn't fair to you. But I'm terrified."

Matt stopped walking and studied her for a minute, then he took her in his arms. "I know you are. I promise to help you with your fears. Diane, I also promise to try to go slow. I've never been in love before and I just want everything. I'm very unrealistic. Will you forgive me?"

Diane kissed his cheek, "Yah. I hope we don't have this conversation again for a long time."

"I vote for never," Matt grinned. "It isn't going to be an easy journey for us, but the destination will be worth it."

Diane put her arms around his neck again and they shared a very emotional kiss. Then Matt backed away, "I need to get washed up. I think I smelled a lunch in the oven?"

"You did," Diane giggled, "I hope you like Tuna Noodle hot dish?"

As Matt headed to the bathroom, he smiled back, "One of my favorites."

Lunch was fun. They talked about how the combine got stuck, Skipper wiping her feet, the cobbler and their pile of work for school they needed to get finished. "Are you going to have time to get it all done before tomorrow?" Diane asked.

"Yah, if I get in gear. I'll help you do dishes after I test out the cookies and then get to work. I only have about an hour and a half. Then I want to help Darrell milk before we go over to Schroeders for supper."

"Do you want me to help milk too?"

"That is up to you. Do you want to?" Matt asked.

"I read *Heidi* several times when I was a girl and she milked goats. I have always wondered what it'd be like."

"Well, then, no time like the present," he grinned, his eyes sparkling. "I'm sure we'd appreciate the help. Jeannie helps some times."

"Think she will today?"

"Don't know. I suppose you could call and ask her."

Diane looked out the window toward Jessup's home, "No, I think I'll just go down with you if that's okay?"

"It is okay. Diane, can I tell you something? Earlier today, I felt like my life was ruined. I never realized how dependent one person could be on another."

"Yah, Matt. It isn't fun and it isn't good. Some folks say you should never give anyone else that power over you, but I don't know how you could ever love someone and not feel that way. Do you?"

"I don't know."

❧ 51 ❧

THEY GOT BUSY AND GOT their schoolwork nearly finished. Then they put the kittens in the laundry room and got ready to go do chores. Diane put on one of Matt jackets so she wouldn't get hers dirty, but the sleeves were too long. By the time they were rolled up, she could hardly move her arms! Matt looked at her, "I think I'll ask Jeannie if she has an old jacket. That'd work better."

He called and she said of course. She would bring it down when they went to the barn. She was very glad that Diane was going to help and said that she was too. A little later, the two couples with their two dogs were off to do chores.

They had a lot of fun. It was the most relaxed Matt had ever seen Diane and she blossomed when she was comfortable. He wished she could be comfortable with just him but the four got along very well.

After chores, they put their dogs in their pen and went back to their houses. Matt was going to shower and change clothes, but Diane was going to change clothes when she got home.

As he was getting dressed, he noticed the two packages he had for her birthday. He had planned to give them to her, but now doubted if he should. He went back and forth a few times before he decided to just give them to her. It would make more sense to give them to her now, than some day when it wasn't her birthday.

When he came out of the bedroom, she was just wrapping up the cobbler to take over to Schroeders. She looked up and smiled, "You look nice."

"Thanks," Matt was still debating about giving her the gifts. He just stood there.

She looked up again and he was still standing there. "What is it Matt?"

"Could you come here a minute?" he asked.

"Give me a second. I'm almost done." When she was finished covering the cobbler, she came around the counter.

"I got you something," he handed her the two gifts.

She gave him a funny look, "What are these for?"

"I believe it's your birthday?"

"How did you know?"

"Is it?"

"Yes."

He handed her the gifts, "Happy Birthday, Diane."

She took the gifts and read the tags. The bigger gift was signed from Matt and the other was signed from the kids. She giggled. "Which should I open first?"

He shrugged. She opened the larger one first. It was the book of poetry by Robert Frost. She got tears in her eyes and said, "That's so nice, Matt. I love it."

Then she sat on the sofa, "What could be in this one?"

Matt was grinning anxiously, "Just open it."

"From the kids? Hm." she read and smiled at him. "You didn't need to do this."

"Open it," he could hardly wait.

When she unwrapped the paper and saw the small box was from a jeweler, she got a worried look on her face but he just kept grinning. "Will you hurry?"

She opened the lid and saw the locket, "Oh Matt. This is too much. You shouldn't have."

He grinned, "I didn't. It's from Skipper, Murphy and Lady. Tell them, not me. Hey, open it."

She opened the locket and started to smile. "It's just precious."

Matt got serious, "You can replace the photos if you want."

"I wouldn't think of it. I love the pictures of our family." She looked at it closely, "It's so nice. I love it. Can you help me put it on?"

He clasped it around her neck and she turned to give him a big kiss. "It's so beautiful."

Before very long, the kiss was getting out of hand. She pulled back, "Okay, stop it. We'll get into trouble."

He looked at her, "We had better get over to Schroeder's before Elton has the whole dinner eaten."

Diane hugged him again, "I'm looking forward to the day when we don't have to stop."

Matt looked deep into her eyes, "Don't say that Diane. You have no idea what that does to me."

"Sorry, let's get moving."

They got everything ready to go and Matt went to get the car. When he came back in the house, she met him at the door with a big hug. "It was the most wonderful day. I'm sorry I almost spoiled the whole thing."

"But we were able to work it out. That's good, right?"

She gave him a kiss on the cheek, "Yes, it is. Matt, I love my presents. Thank you again."

When they drove into the yard, Ellisons were there. Kevin and Carrie were just going in. As they went up the steps, Darrell and Jeannie drove in right behind Mo, Ian and Ruthie. She stopped and looked at Matt. "You never said they'd be here for dinner."

"Oh, I must have forgot," he smiled.

"I'm not so sure," Diane frowned.

The group in the kitchen all yelled, "Happy Birthday Diane!" when they came into the kitchen. Kevin and Carrie joined in as the came in behind them.

Diane started to cry. "You guys! I had no idea you knew." Then she noticed Grandpa Lloyd, grinning away. "Oh, now I get it. Grandpa! You did this, didn't you?"

The old man was so pleased with himself he almost burst. She gave him a kiss.

They had a wonderful dinner and Annie and Pepper had decorated the dining room and the living room. After dinner, Nora brought out the chocolate birthday cake and everyone sang, *Happy Birthday*.

"Is this why Grandpa was so anxious to get rid of me today?" Diane asked.

"Partly, but mostly because of this," Keith said as he and Kevin went over to the huge package on the wall behind Grandpa's chair.

Diane looked at them and then at the package. It was beginning to dawn on her what it was.

"Come over here and open this," Kevin said. "It isn't from just us; it is from the whole clan!"

Diane was shaking when she tore back the paper. When she saw that it was a piano, she cried. Trying to keep herself together, she said, "You crazy people. I cannot possibly accept this. It's way too much."

"No it isn't," Elton stated. "It was from everyone and there are so many strings attached, you will think it's a cob web. Besides it isn't new."

Diane shook her head, "What strings?"

Darlene giggled, "We want piano lessons for all of our kids, for free."

"But I haven't even played for a long time. I don't know if I still can."

Grandpa looked at her, "Well, then you better try."

"I don't even have any sheet music," Diane explained.

"Why don't you look in the seat?" Matt grinned.

She looked at him and then slowly lifted the seat cover. That was when she really cried. "This is just way too much."

Charlie went over to her, "That's okay, Tinker. You don't need to teach me. I don't care, but the girls are goofy to learn."

Diane smiled, "Don't you want to learn?"

Charlie frowned, "I don't think that boys do that. It's girls stuff."

"Charlie," Diane smiled, "Did you know that most of the famous composers are men?"

Charlie raised his eyebrows, "What's a composer?"

"The people who write the music. How about I give you a couple lessons and then you can decide?"

"I guess. You did take a kitty. But if I don't like it, I won't have to do it anymore. Okay?" the little boy asked.

"Okay," Diane smiled.

"Diane, if you feel comfortable, we'd love to have you play something," Nora said.

"I'm pretty rusty," but she looked through the sheet music. "Here is something I used to play a lot. If you forgive my mistakes, I'll try. Okay?"

She played Chopin's *Nocturne Op 27. No.2* flawlessly. When she finished, everyone applauded except Charlie. "I don't think I need to do that."

"How about this one?" Diane giggled. Then she played the theme song to the *Lone Ranger* television series.

Charlie started shaking his head yes, he'd learn that. Grandpa listened for a while and then announced he was going to bed. He hugged Diane good night and said, "Now you won't cry anymore."

She gave him a big hug, "How could I? You're all so wonderful. How could anyone be sad with wonderful friends like you guys?"

Grandpa shook his head in despair, "We're your relatives, not any old friends."

Diane hugged him again, "I love you, Grandpa."

"I knew it," he said. "You better."

She giggled, "Sleep tight, Grandpa Lloyd."

After Grandpa went to bed, Nora said, "Diane, there's one more present here. It is from Elton and me."

Nora handed Diane a square box about a foot square. She frowned and opened it. It was a porcelain teapot very similar to the one that Wag had broken from her grandmother. She cried and hugged Nora and Elton. "I love you guys so much. This is the best birthday in my whole life."

Later that night, after everyone went home, she walked Matt to the mudroom of the old farmhouse. There she gave him a warm kiss. "I cannot even begin to tell you how wonderful you've made my day."

"As much as I'd love to take all the credit, I can't. It was Nora, Kevin and Keith. But I want you to know something, Diane. And you can just store this in your heart. I'm falling in love with you." he kissed her cheek and turned immediately to leave, "Good night. I'll pick you up before nine o'clock Mass in the morning."

❦❧ 52 ❦❧

SUNDAY MORNING, IT FINALLY BEGAN to clear off. It still drizzled a little, but the sun was trying to peek through the fluffy clouds that were now more white than gray. It was a relief. The roads were getting very muddy and filled with ruts. The pups loved it when Darrell and Matt let them play in the barn without being in their pen. They weren't allowed outside because they would have been mud pies, but they had a ball.

They were underfoot and explored everything. The men spent a good share of time picking up things, removing objects from puppy mouths and scooting the little dogs from every conceivable corner. Both pups managed to get stepped on by some goats before the adventure was over, and that taught a very quick lesson. The most important thing they learned was to leave the animals alone during milking.

Back at the house, Matt helped Skipper wipe her feet. Then he announced, "By next week, I expect you to do this on your own. Got it?'

Skipper looked up at him with her big soft eyes and wagged her tail. Matt patted her and gave her a big hug, "Why don't I believe you?"

Inside the house, Matt saw all sorts of things that reminded him of Diane. She had wrapped everything neatly in the refrigerator for him, and left a big piece of cobbler there for his breakfast. On the table were some of her notes on a note pad for a class. The cats were curled up in the afghan that she had taken her nap with.

He thought about the day before. It was rather unsettling. He loved having her there. He wanted to be with her, but they did have a lot of things to face. It wouldn't be a walk in the park.

How could he help her overcome her fears? How much was fear and how much was maybe that she just didn't care for him? He thought she did, but maybe she didn't. He couldn't understand what she wanted. She seemed to want to be close to him, but always seemed to be pushing him away. It was driving him crazy. He didn't know if she was just really afraid, confused or maybe she was playing him. He didn't know. He needed some advice.

Father Vicaro wouldn't be the one to talk to and he didn't want to talk to Darrell because they were friends of hers too. He wouldn't do that. Carl and Ian were busy with the wedding stuff and had their hands full. Who could he talk to?

Then it struck him. Elton. He wouldn't tell anyone and he knew Diane as well as anyone. That was what he would do, he'd talk to Elton. Having decided that made him feel better. He finished his piece of cobbler and jumped in the shower.

Diane woke up from a sound sleep to Pepper's alarm. Before a few minutes, she was standing in the Schroeder kitchen with her coffee cup. She took her place with the rest of the family, staring blankly at the perking pot.

"Nora, how many cups are in that pot anyway?" she finally asked.

"It is a thirty-five cup. We thought about the fifty cup, but it takes so long to perk. This one is done in about fifteen minutes," Nora smiled.

"Matt got one with an automatic timer," Tinker giggled. "You should get one of those automatic things. Then we wouldn't all be standing her like Zombies every morning."

Elton chuckled, "Then when would we take head count?"

Darlene giggled, "These are usually just numb bodies, Dad. No one's head it working for at least a half an hour!"

"I don't know if that is right," Carl said. "I know I wake up alert every day!"

Keith rolled his eyes, "Oh brother, here we go."

"I'm not even acknowledging that with an answer," Elton shook his head. "It is too easy. So, Coot, need me to help you pack your bags? I'd be happy to make time to help you move."

Carl chortled, "You're going to so miss me, Magpie. You just wait. You'll be calling me the first morning. I'll have to take the phone off the hook for my honeymoon!"

Elton covered his ears, "I don't want to hear about you and a honeymoon. The mental picture just makes my mind convulse!"

Nora snapped at them both, "Knock it off, you two. Hey, speaking of weddings, have you and Mo got it figured out where everyone is going to stay?"

"Mo and I sat there with paper and pencil last night and sorted it all out. It is going to be an undertaking. I'll get the paper, okay?" Carl left to get it.

"I would leave, if you need the space," Diane offered.

Keith looked at her, "That is about the dumbest thing I've ever heard. This is your home, right Dad?"

"Yes, Keith is right. This is your home," Elton smiled. "And you're family."

Diane looked at him in surprise, "You guys."

"Yup," Elton grinned, "Us guys are your family; so get used to it."

Carl returned with the paper. Everyone filled their cups and gathered around the kitchen table. Kevin and Carrie came in to join the confusion.

"Here is a list of her kids and their families and here is a list of places they can stay," Carl pointed to the columns. "Now we were trying to figure out who we can put where the most conveniently. I started to have heart palpitations after a couple minutes. Danny and Jenny offered and so did Andersons but Oxenfelters are staying at their place, and Uncle Eddies are staying at Danny's. So we thought this would work. Byron and Marly decided it'd be neat to have the girls that are about the same ages stay with their girls. Guess Katie and Ginger thought of that, although Ginger insists that Miriam wanted them to also. We all know how Ginger controls her vote. Then Charlie almost collapsed at the thought! So we're having him stay with us, because Turk will be with us. Turk wouldn't hear of staying any place but with his Gramps, so they are at our place. I don't know how wise that is, but those guys might get along real well.

"Then Rain wanted to stay with her Uncle Matt. She was most disappointed that he had no room and even offered to sleep on the sofa, but Darrell and Jeannie invited her whole family to stay at their place. So, she and her family will be only a stone's throw away.

"Abby and Carrie are both expecting and so we put Abby and Allen with them. Abby and Allen are easy to get along with and Kevin and Carrie don't have a lot of room.

"Zach and Suzy have taken James and Viv and their four boys, since they have the room. Also, the boys wanted to be near a farm, so they will be just over the fence from here.

"Marv and Glenda are taking Colleen and Frank and their son. Colleen and Viv are the ones that are so torqued out of shape about Matt leaving the priesthood and all that baloney. Marv is prepared to handle that.

"Pappy, Nana, Det. Diaz and his wife, Egan and Van are staying here. Pappy and Nana can have Carl's room because they are older. So are Egan and Van, but they can still handle the stairs. It should work out well." Carl shook her head "I'm so glad I had all that experience working with the State Department!"

"Where are you going to be, Carl?" Kev asked.

"Hiding under my bed," Carl stated. "I never imagined life was such a turmoil in the Petunia patch."

"I could move upstairs," Diane offered. "I really don't need a main floor room anymore since I healed up. The other girls are upstairs, so I'd like that. Then that other couple could stay in the guest room. Do you guys know that I have gone over a week without being hit or getting a bruise? Isn't that something?"

The family looked at each other. What a horrible anniversary to have to celebrate, but Diane was genuinely happy about it. "Don't look at it as a bad thing! I look at it as a good thing!"

Elton gave her a hug, "I think it's wonderful. Just think, some day you will not have any black and blue marks! Do you know what color your skin really is?"

"Dad!" Pepper yowled, "That is mean to say."

Diane giggled, "Not really. I have to say, I have wondered myself. My favorite color is the pale green of a healing bruise! I have a bit of that color now."

Then everyone had a good laugh. They all decided that Monday would be their moving day. They would move Diane upstairs and move Carl's stuff over to Mo's. The guests would start arriving on Tuesday.

Nora said, "Mo and I made a list of that too. We have been trying to get rides for everyone from the airport. It's crazy. I don't know why I had the notion they would all just magically appear at the door! We got it all worked out though."

"What'll be going on all week?" Kevin asked. "I hear that we are having a fishing trip to Lake Sakakawea at Garrison Dam on Sunday afternoon, right? That is a crazy way to spend a honeymoon Carl."

"We're going to do our honeymooning after everyone leaves. It will be too crazy with everyone here," Carl grinned. "I think folks are starting to leave on Tuesday, right?"

"Yah. I know that Mo wanted to get married the following weekend, but since you guys changed it to Saturday the fourth, it works better for everyone who is traveling," Nora asserted.

"And for me. I'll be glad to have them all gone. They're nice, but there is so many of them."

Elton burst out laughing, "That is what folks say about our clan. However, I have to say, I wouldn't want to put up with all of us for a week!"

The milkers headed to the barn and Diane did quite well. "Do you think I'm getting the hang of this, Uncle Elton?"

He came over and checked Snowflake's bag, "Why you surely are. I heard you were milking goats yesterday. You are turning into quite the milk maid."

Then he squatted down near her between the two cows, "I wanted to tell you how much we have enjoyed having you here and are pleased you seem to be doing so well. If you have any problems with anything at all, feel free to talk to me or Nora. Okay?"

She looked at him with tears in her eyes, "I love it here. I'll talk to you guys if anything is wrong."

He patted her hand, "Have I got your word?"

She smiled, "You do."

He patted her shoulder, "Good." Then he stood up and went off to do the separating.

She was milking when it dawned on her. She should talk to Nora about yesterday. She had felt very conflicted about it. She loved being with Matt and he was so nice to her. Better than she deserved. She knew she couldn't keep doing that to him. Why couldn't she just relax and accept his kindness? She had a very difficult time believing that he cared about her. She easily believed that he was conning her when she found out he was a priest. That was simple. But to believe he was good, that was almost impossible. She needed advice. She didn't want to tell Jeannie since they were so close to Matt. She would talk to Nora.

❦❧ 53 ❦❧

MATT ARRIVED AT SCHROEDER'S AT eight-thirty on the button that sunny Sunday morning. Carl was waiting for Harrington to pick him up for Mass. "You can ride with me," Matt offered.

"In my own car? Nice of you?" Carl chuckled. "No thanks, I want to ride with my lady. Mattie, I'm not sure I'm liking all this."

Matt gave him a quick hug, "You'll do fine, Dad. I admire you. Not many men could handle it half as well as you. I'm sorry that Ian and I've been such a burden. Maybe we will grow up,"

"I've been almost grateful for your dilemma," Carl confessed. "Keeps the heat off me! Yea gads, Colleen and Vivian are losing their marbles over it. Why do they care if you're a priest or not?"

Matt shrugged, "I think they blew it up in their minds to be something that it wasn't. They think it reflects on them. I'm sorry I let them down, but I am glad that decision is made."

Elton looked up from his coffee, "You should tell them they should do it if they think it's so dandy."

"I would love to, but that wouldn't be fair. I think Vivian wanted one of her kids to be a priest."

Elton chuckled, "I'll just be glad to keep mine out of the penitentiary!"

Carl laughed, "I think you are safe with your crew, but Charlie? Who knows?"

"Charlie is a good kid," Matt disagreed. "I like him. And what is with you having both Turk and Charlie at your house? I think you have lost all sense of reason! Man, it's a brand new house! I am expecting at least two fires and a flood before the week is over!"

Carl's eyes got huge, "No, you don't really think so, do you?"

"Remember when Charlie brought the straw to church?" Elton grinned.

Carl shuddered, "Mo will handle it. You guys are just trying to scare me."

On the way to Mass, Matt said, "Diane, I've something to tell you."

She had been very quiet that morning and was withdrawn again, "What is it? I hope it isn't a big crisis thing between us. I'm not up to that today."

"Me either," Matt was a bit offended by her comment, "It is about Kevin's car. He fixed it up for Ruthie. She and Ian are getting a new car tomorrow—,"

"I know, she offered it to me and I told her I couldn't accept it. I can't Matt. I can't afford to pay-."

"Diane, may I finish my sentence? She and Ian want me to have it. I said yes. I'll get it licensed when I get this one licensed that I am buying from Dad."

"Why do you need two?" Diane asked.

"I'm going to leave Kevin's parked at Schroeders. It will be licensed and insured. Then if you need to use it, you can. Okay? You don't have to feel in any way responsible for it. But I want you to be able to have wheels if you need them."

"Matt, that's too much."

He was frustrated, "Look, just leave the damn thing parked at Elton's and give him the keys. If you ever need it, you can use it. Otherwise, forget it."

Her mouth dropped open and her eyes filled with tears. He looked away from her and focused on his driving. They rode in silence for a while and then she said, "Matt, do you know how many times, I mean how much trouble I got into with Wag over his car?"

"No, I don't. You never told me," he didn't look at her.

"Well, it was a lot. I know you're all being nice, but I don't know if I can cope with it."

Matt didn't answer her. He knew he was not being helpful, but he was having a difficult time dealing with his own hurt feelings. They didn't say anymore until they got to the parking lot. As soon as he stopped, she started to open the car door.

"No," Matt was adamant. When she stopped, his voice softened, "Listen to me. I'm not Wag. Neither is Kevin. We're trying to make things easier for you, not harder. It will be there for you, if you need it. Can you just allow us to do that? Diane, I'm having a very difficult time now. I thought I could handle the rejection, but it almost kills me. I'm sorry and I know I'm being selfish."

Diane shook her head, "No, it's me. I don't know what happens to me."

Matt leaned across the seat and gave her a quick kiss on the cheek. "Ready to go in? Let's have a good day."

She took his hand and nodded. "I don't know why we always end up hurting each other."

Matt came around the car and opened the door, "I think it's because we both want everything to be so perfect and are afraid it won't be. Does that sound right?"

She smiled, "About right."

They walked into the church arm in arm.

Dinner was nice and they had a good afternoon at Schroeders. There was a lot of talk about the wedding guests and all the plans. Diane had a couple girls interested in piano lessons, but they all decided that wouldn't start until after the weddings. Katie was first, Becky Oxenfelter, Maddie Lynn, Ginger and of course, Miriam. Clark and Charlie wanted lessons but only to learn fun stuff. A few of the older girls, Carrie and Jenny, were interested but needed to work out their schedules. Diane was rather jazzed about that.

That afternoon, Matt and Elton found an occasion to talk a couple minutes alone. Matt asked, "Elton, I need to find some time to talk to you soon. I'm going crazy."

Elton put his hand on his arm, "I noticed. Whenever. Want me to come over to your place?"

"That would be great," Matt sighed. "I really need to talk to you."

"Tonight after chores."

After chores, Matt put his coffee pot on. Skipper and the cats were playing on the floor and the fireplace was radiating the room with warmth and comfort. How he could feel so uneasy was unbelievable. He was relieved that Elton said he'd come over.

He and Diane had played cards together, but barely spoke to each other. It was like that horrible week and a half when he had honored her request to stay away.

Elton came into the cabin and smiled, "Looking pretty homey, Matt. Are you all settled?"

Matt nodded, "It is homey, isn't it? Want to sit in the living room or the kitchen table?"

"Makes no difference to me," Elton looked at the kittens curled up on the sofa and Skipper asleep on the floor in front of it. "I think it might make a difference to the critters."

"Yah, they could move," Matt raised his eyebrows. "They're so spoiled."

"Table is fine." Elton pulled out a chair and sat down while Matt served the coffee. "I have to say, Matt, I'm glad you asked to talk to me because I was going to talk to you if you didn't."

"That obvious?"

"Don't know about what others notice, but Nora and I know things are very uneasy between you two. Can I speak openly?"

"Of course. That's what I want. Elton, I don't know what to do. I'm at a loss. I try to promise myself not to get hurt or upset and that's just what I do!"

"Well, I'm not about to tell you things out of school, because I don't do that if I can help it. Although I will, if I think it is necessary. Diane is not reacting any better than you."

Matt shook his head, "That isn't good. I want her to be happy, Elton. I really do."

"I know, Matt. First, if it makes you feel better, she is that way with everyone. One minute she is reaching out and wanting to belong and the next, she is pushing us away and withdrawing. Zach says it's a fear of being rejected. She'd rather do it herself first, than to have someone do it to her, not consciously, but subconsciously. Also she is afraid of triggering an abusive response, so she avoids things. She is terrified of making a mistake or hurting someone. A lot like Miriam, except grownup. She accidentally burnt a batch of cookies, ran out the door and started walking down the road! Nora went after her and told her that if she had left after every batch of burnt cookies she would have ended up in Siberia. She'll start to relax and then some darned thing will happen and she clams right up again. You know who she is the best with?"

Matt shook his head.

"Katie. They talk and do things together. It's fun so see. The girls at the house, Annie, Pepper and Darlene make it a point to include her in almost everything, but it's only about a third time she'll do it. And then if she does, she will start and the minute she gets relaxed, she withdraws." Elton explained. "She seems very reluctant to be around Carrie, Ruthie and Suzy even though they have tried. She is most comfortable with Jeannie."

Matt nodded in agreement, "Jeannie is good with her and of course, they were friends before. Also, Denise Anderson. I know she thinks the world of Nora. Does she open up to her?"

"Only little bits. More than most others and they talk about some deep subjects, but Nora says the conversations often end abruptly. Not unkindly, it is like she just can't do it anymore. So, what have you been seeing?"

"A lot the same. I feel like I'm talking about her behind her back, but I hope you understand I'm really not. Or am I? I don't even know that."

"I guess in a way you are, but you have to keep from going nuts yourself. So, I don't think of it that way. And I'm not telling, so don't worry about it. I may share it with Nora if you say I can."

"That'd probably be good if you told Nora. One time Diane told me to stay away from her. So I did. Then for a week and half, I kept running into her everywhere. I'd just remove myself, politely and inconspicuously, and then I saw the hurt in her eyes. It was like she didn't want me to avoid her. I stuck to my guns, and then when the situation arose that I couldn't, she begged me not to shut her out again. But since then, it happens all the time. Not for as long, but we'll be fine and then suddenly she pulls away. I try to respect that, and then she gets hurt! Elton, I can hardly take it. I try; honestly, I try. But sometimes I'm so frustrated I'd like to scream."

"Have you told her?" Elton asked.

"Yes, I have. I told her I can hardly stand it and then she gets all self-incriminating and says she's sorry. I say I understand, which I kind of do, and tell her not to be sorry. Then we're better again and before too long, we're right back at the same place." He put his head in his hands, "I told her I can't continue this. I can hardly stand it. The other day, I was relieved when Darrell called and needed help moving the combine. I had to get away from her. What should I do? Just stay totally away from her and act like we're nothing. Let her sit with it all by herself? Sometimes when I'm angry, that is the way I feel. Or should I keep putting myself out there and not backing away even when she wants me to? This is such a mess."

"Well, dunno. You do not deserve to be treated that way either. I understand she had a lot of issues, but it isn't fair to hurt you. Are you with me on that?" the older man asked.

"Yes, but—,"

"Matt. You don't want to start this kind of habit in your relationship. Once you get into the habit of doing that, it'll continue. From what you have said, you can't take it. I know I couldn't. So you need to make her appreciate that."

"Am I just being selfish?"

"Hell no. I think that you need to work it out in your head, without her input, how much you can or cannot stand. I know you guys are going slow and that is wise, but it sounds to me like it's stagnated right now."

"That's one word for it. Do you think that it'll be okay when the trial is over?" Matt asked hopefully.

"Nope, not at all. That's a concern and a burden on her, granted," Elton agreed. "But it'd be logical that she would rely on you through it. So, I don't think so. It has nothing to do with your relationship, really."

"The priest thing?"

"Yah, maybe a bit. Once you get the letter, or whatever, that will make her feel better, but she knows you have resigned. So, to some extent, it's done. If I were you, I wouldn't expect a big change."

"What is it then?"

"Nora and I think that it's like this. She was forced to move into Waggoner's home before Dean died. Once he died, she was still there. They never let go of him and turned any feelings that she had for him into a weapon to beat her with. Part of her has to hate him by now. She has never been allowed to mourn in a normal way. When Nora talked to her about losing the baby after you mentioned it to her, she had a heck of a time. Finally, she said she was almost mean about it. Then Diane finally started to tell her how she really felt. She didn't to go the funeral because she was in the hospital. She has never seen her baby's grave. That has been a year. When Nora offered to take her, she started to panic and ran away. They have not talked about it since." Elton continued, "Zach was thinking it'd be helpful for her to go see Dr. Samuels, but she says she can't afford it. When he offered to pay, she walked away."

"She is good at that," Matt nodded. "You know she rarely mentions Dean. I mean she does, but not in a personal way. Like he used to like this or we used to do that. She never does."

"My guess is that Waggoners pretty well destroyed those memories. This morning, Grandpa asked her to play the piano and before long, she was playing beautifully, but she had tears flowing down both cheeks. She has a lot to work through."

"So I'm being selfish?" Matt concluded.

"No, you aren't. She cannot continue to do that to you or any of us. She'll burn too many bridges. I believe she really wants to be involved in life and I know she loves you Matt. I don't care what anyone says, but that's why you'll have to take the brunt. You are the most important to her and she's terrified she won't get it right. I know, she has confided in Nora that she doesn't want to make a mistake with you."

"We have talked about that. What do you think she means? Does she think I'll end up like Wag, or does anyone know how Dean was? I have wondered sometimes."

Elton agreed, "Me too. But the only ones that I think would know are Eddie and Denise or Darrell and Jeannie. I worry that he was his father's son and often that abusive behavior continues. But I've never heard that about him."

Matt shrugged, "Well it's for sure she won't tell us. Maybe I've to just decide to let her do this and not get myself hurt. Maybe I really don't love her?"

"That's the stupidest thing I've ever heard you say! Sure, we all have to accept minor bits of that from those we love, but not a steady diet. This is like abuse too. You can't allow her to do that to you. I think you need to draw your own lines. You need to say, if you do this, this'll happen."

"I did tell her that with these weddings, that if she says she's going to do something with me, she has to do it. Or if she isn't, she needs to tell me and then accept that I won't. It fluctuates so much I'm about nuts. One minute she wants to be my girl at it all and the next, she isn't even going to come to any of it. Is there any way I can let her decide that?"

"Nope. You make it a point to talk to her, like tomorrow is all that is left. Ask her point blank what she wants to do."

"I sort of said that to her, and I said whatever she says she has to stick to. Then she started to cry. Elton, I can't make her do that. I hate to make her cry."

"Do you like her to make you cry?"

Matt was taken back and then he thought, "No, I really don't. So, if you say yes, then you will for certain. If you say no, then I'll expect you don't want to. And then stick to that, even if she feels bad. Is that what you are saying?"

"It sounds mean, but she has to realize that. The other night, Annie and Pepper asked her to go bowling with them. She hemmed and hawed before she finally said she didn't think she should. So they left. She stood at the window for the longest time, and Nora and I both knew that she was wishing she had gone. But she has to begin to make those decisions herself. If not, we all have to keep living our lives. We can understand and be patient by continuing to invite her. You know, normally after a couple times, a person would stop inviting someone; but in this case, we wouldn't. Know what I mean?"

"Yah, I do. If this was a regular girl, I'd have broken up with her long ago," Matt chuckled. "A stupid thing for a priest to say, huh?"

"That's what I love about you! You and your pickle jar! Lloyd is convinced that is where you are going to end up."

"I'm almost convinced myself. I really don't need all this turmoil with my family all here."

Elton laughed, "Ah, Mattie! That's when the Petunia Patch is the most fun! The family gathers and everyone should be on their best behavior but they all go off the reservation, sure as shooting. Yea gads, I have no idea why we all put ourselves through all the commotion!"

"More coffee?" Matt asked.

"One more refill and then I have to head out. I hope that I have helped some, but I can't imagine how," Elton said.

"I don't know if there is a help."

"There's always a help. You can pray for a miracle, but I have noticed that most of this stuff is fixed one stitch at a time. The miracle is usually that we even survive it!"

Matt laughed, "Amen. So, what about the baby? That's just wrong. I think she needs to go see the baby's grave at least."

"Nora does too. We were thinking we would take her soon, but after the weddings."

"Do you think I should go along?" Matt asked.

"Yes, I do. We were going to mention it to you later. Then she can get mad, cry or throw a fit. She needs to deal with that," Elton said.

"You're an amazing man," Matt said quietly.

Elton crinkled his face, "Not so much."

"Yah, you have compassion for people."

Elton chuckled, "It isn't compassion. I just think we are all an iota from falling off the edge. We just have different things pushing us. It usually makes a big mess to fix when someone does go off; so it's a good idea to stop it before hand. So, what about you? Do you have any ideas how to keep both feet on terra firma?"

"Not really. I think that she and I need to talk tomorrow night. Maybe I'll take it a little at a time. Like, do you want to be my girl at dinner or not. Then act accordingly. The hard part is going to be to stick to it when she says no and then I can tell she really wants to. But if I know it'll only be a week, I think I can handle it."

"Good. If you weaken, you know my number. Matt, don't be afraid to call. Okay?"

"Thank you so much."

"No problem."

❖·∽ 54 ∽·❖

MONDAY MORNING WAS VERY SUNNY but chilly. "Fall is really with us," Jeannie giggled as Matt climbed in the car. "Well, this is the week of adventure, huh Matt?"

"Yes, it is. I don't know if I am looking forward to it or not."

"Rain sounds like my kind of girl and the rest of the family seems pretty neat. Which ones are all upset with you?"

"That would be Vivian and Colleen. Hopefully, they will be cooled down before they get here. Either that or I will need to take them for a walk out in the pasture and let them have at it. I can drag my tattered remains back to civilization to heal," he chuckled.

"Sounds like fun. Let me know so I can bring the camera!" Jeannie laughed. "Matt, need any help with Diane?'

He frowned at her, "What do you mean?"

"Darrell and I noticed she is acting like a chameleon most of the time. I think she just needs time, but I don't know how you can handle it. If you need some help, let us know."

He shook his head, "Everything is so difficult for her. I feel so badly, but I have to admit, sometimes I get so frustrated because I don't know what she wants."

Jeannie made the observation, "Matt, neither does she."

Then they turned into the drive at Schroeder's to pick her up.

At school, none of the three ran into each other all day. The ladies were waiting at the car when Matt returned from St. John's.

"How did it go today?" Jeannie asked.

"It went. I got word today that Father Bartholomew will be here at the end of the week and will begin teaching on Monday. Sooner than I expected. I have to admit, it rather threw me."

Jeannie reached over and patted his cheek, "I'm sorry Matt. I really am. If you need to talk, Darrell and I are here for you."

"Thanks," Matt smiled, "You guys are the best. But, I'll be okay. Mr. Palmer has asked me to teach Latin on the last two periods of the day. That will fill in my time! Oh, before I forget, Diane and I have to be some place at seven on Friday, so we won't need a ride in."

Diane was sitting quietly in the backseat through all this, "Oh, Matt. I was going to tell you. I won't be going. So, I'll need a ride."

Matt turned and gave her a firm look, "Are you certain, Diane? You can't change your mind."

"I'm certain."

"Okay, I'll pick you up like usual then, Diane," Jeannie smiled. "I am anxious to see Ian and Ruthie's wedding. Ruthie has made so many plans! It'll be something."

Matt tried to hide his disappointment, "Yes it will be. I just want it to be happy for them."

Jeannie asked, "Are you the best man?"

"I have been sworn to secrecy! Ruthie almost made us sign in blood! She's so funny. I love it when she is excited. She just radiates. All I am allowed to say is that Elton is giving the bride away."

"Well, here we are Tinker," Jeannie grinned. "See you tomorrow."

"I will see you in a bit," Matt added, "I'll change and then come give Lloyd his drive."

"Okay, I will tell him, but you might not see me. I have a lot of homework to do. See you in the morning."

As they drove away, Jeannie shook her head. "I still want to pull hair!"

Matt started to laugh and by the time they got home, they were both laughing like idiots.

Matt changed his clothes and was back at Schroeder's before long. He and Lloyd went for a drive and Lloyd was very happy it had quit raining. When they got back, Charlie was sitting on the steps holding his Chicken Man hat in his hands.

"What's up, Charlie?" Matt asked.

"It's all this Solomon stuff, Matt. I have to do it two times!" Charlie confided. "I'm never ever getting married. I'll just tell my wife to go to the house, but no married stuff!"

"Sounds like a good idea, Charlie." Matt chuckled, as he sat down next to him on the steps. "What gave you the long face? We know you can do it."

"I know, but why can't these guys carry their own rings? They should just tie yarn on their fingers. They wouldn't need ring carriers. It is just stupid."

"I'll make you a deal, okay?"

"What is that?"

"If I get married, I won't ask you to be a ring carrier guy."

Charlie threw both his arms around Matt and hugged him. "You're the mostest best."

"Thanks, Charlie. So, you only have two more times. Okay?"

"Yah, but Pepper said she might want me. Matt, I just don't know. I'd rather run and play. The only good thing is that I get a good spot to see everything."

"At my wedding, you won't have to be solemn and can sit in the very front! Deal?"

"Deal. Okay, I'll do this," the little guy rolled his eyes, "But you and me will know that I don't have to do it for you!" He hugged Matt again, "I better go do my Chicken Man chores."

Matt went in the house, chuckling. "Hello everyone."

Grandma gave him a big hug, "Coffee?"

"Don't mind if I do. How's all the moving?"

"We are all finished. Carl moved this morning and Harrington moved his stuff this afternoon. Ruthie moved hers to their house and we got Marly's room set up for the girl guests. We're getting there. We had most of Diane's moved upstairs before she got home today. Nora and I have Carl's room all ready for Nana and Pappy. Quite confusing."

"Oh Matt," Nora smiled as she came in, "Could you help Diane move the dresser in her room? We put the desk in there so she had a place for her school work and the desk needs to go on the other wall so she can open the closet door."

"Certainly," Matt got up and went upstairs. There he heard some noise down the hall so he easily found her room. He went in and saw her taking the drawers out. "I hear you need some muscles."

Her look gave it away that she might have needed muscles, but not his. He tried not to let it phase him and asked what she wanted moved. She lamely pointed to a large dresser and mirror.

"Okay, where to?"

Within a few minutes, it was in place as was the desk. "Need anymore help?"

"No thank you," she said sweetly but dismissively.

"Okay," he said and went downstairs to have coffee with the ladies. After a cup, he went on home to help Darrell milk.

After chores, he ate a quick sandwich and went back to Schroeders. He needed to talk to her, but this time he did have a bit of a plan in his head. When he got to the house, the family except the grandparents and Diane were relaxing on the patio. He asked if Diane was busy and Nora said she was doing her homework. Nora made a suggestion, "I think that you should go get her. I would, but I think it might be better for you to go."

Matt nodded, realizing that Diane probably said she didn't want to be bothered. So, he went up to her room. He felt a little awkward, but had to talk to her. He knocked on her door, and she answered, "Yes, what is it?"

"It's me, Diane. May I speak to you for a minute?"

"Matt, I really have a lot to do. Not tonight, okay?"

He opened the door, "I won't take no for an answer tonight. I really need to talk to you."

She pursed her lips and said, "Then why did you ask?"

"Formality."

"Formally, when someone says no, you honor that."

"I know," he said coming in, "I'd like us to go for a walk to that big rock in the pasture I told you about."

"I don't have time."

"It's important, Diane."

She looked at him and threw her pencil down. "Okay. A quick walk, but I really do have work to do."

A few minutes later, they had passed the family and were heading toward the pasture. Not a word was spoken between them. When they got to the creek, she had to take his hand to keep from falling in the water. Then he didn't let go when she tried to squirm out of it.

Calling it a walk would be wrong; it was more like a dragging. But she did go to the rock and they sat down on the boulder. She looked around, "It's a huge rock."

"Isn't it? I love it here. Isn't it a wonderful clear sky?"

"Yes. Well, we need to get back. Thanks for showing me the rock."

Matt took her hand again, "Not yet. I have to talk to you about a few things first. Then I promise. I know you said today that you weren't going Friday morning."

"I can't Matt. I just think we need to give each other space."

"I know. You need to tell Ian and Ruthie however."

"Can't you?"

"Nope, it's your decision. You need to do it. I won't," Matt said firmly. "Now what about tomorrow?"

"What's tomorrow?" Diane sighed.

"Tomorrow is when my two oldest brothers and their families arrive. Also Uncle Egan and his fiancée, Vanessa. Nora is having a big dinner here tomorrow night. She and Mom are cooking up a storm."

Diane gazed off toward the horizon, "I was thinking I should ask Denise if I can stay with her this week. I'd be out of everyone's hair."

Matt frowned, but it was as he had expected. She was pulling as far away as she could. "You're really something, you know."

Diane was stunned, "What do you mean? I just want to be out of everyone's way."

"You tell us all the time how you can never repay everyone's kindness and then we need you, you make sure you're far out of range. Good plan. You're going to make sure you protect yourself. Do it, if that's what you really think is right."

"That is very unkind," Diane started to cry.

"Go ahead and cry. How you figure yourself the martyr in this scenario is beyond me," Matt continued calmly, "But if you can, do it."

"Matt? Why are you doing this to me?"

"Diane, why are you doing this to us? Mom and Nora could use the help. The folks from Boston don't give a rat's ass about your issues because they haven't even met you! You know Ian, Ruthie, Carl and Mom are counting on you. If you want to hurt me, that's your prerogative; but I can't see how you figure you have a right to not be there for everyone else."

By now, Diane was crying inconsolably. He wanted to bring her into his arms and comfort her, but he didn't. She cried for a bit and then he handed her a tissue. "As soon as you pull yourself together, I'll walk you back to the house. You can tell the ladies that you are going to bug out on them. I'm going home. I know where I stand."

He stood up and she cried even harder. Then she stood up, "No, Matt. Please stop. Can we talk about this?"

"Don't know what else there is to say." Matt sat back down and put his head in his hands. "I can't do this. I would love to Diane, but every time you push me away, it hurts worse. I still love you, but don't you realize that it'd be easier for me if you were at Denise's too?"

Diane's mouth fell open, "Oh Matt, I'm so sorry. What the hell am I doing? I'm so messed up."

"So, what do you want to talk about?"

"Okay, I'll stay and behave. You have my word on that."

"At least until tomorrow morning, right?"

"Matt, that isn't fair."

"Isn't it? I just need to know for tomorrow."

"I'll be your girl for this whole week. You have my word. And I'll help Nora and everyone. I love your Mom and Coot. I love Elton and Nora. Matt, I love you. I really do. I just worry I'm messing it all up."

"You're messing it up. Trust me, you are." Then he turned and took her hand, "I promise you that I'll be cool. Okay? I'll stay out of your way as much as possible, but please be there for the rest of them."

She studied him a minute and then threw both her arms around his neck, "Matt, I want to be there for you too."

"I know you do, Tinker. But it'll be hard for you, so you will probably need to have some place to back away from. Let it be me."

"I'll make it. I know I can do it, with your help."

"That's fine, but I might need to lean on someone this week."

"I noticed today what a good report that you and Jeannie have. You two are so relaxed and easy with each other. We aren't like that and we should be."

"Jeannie and I know where we stand and we don't need to pretend. That's why it's easy. Annie and I are too. But I'm in love with you."

"Sounds wrong, doesn't it?" Diane asked.

"I'll only accept that you'll do tomorrow and have your word on that. You can think about Wednesday and let me know tomorrow. I know you'll just change your mind about all week. However, you need to call Ian and Jeannie what you're doing on Friday. That is your business, not mine. If you want to be with me, I'd love it. But if not, that's okay too."

"I will, Matt. I'll be your girl tomorrow." Diane sat back down on the rock, "So, who're the ones coming tomorrow?"

"Aaron is the oldest and his wife Terrie and their three kids. They are staying at Ruthie and Ian's place. The other bunch is James and his wife, Viv and their kids. They are all staying with Zach and Suzy except Linda who'll be staying at Ellisons. Although, maybe not this first night. Uncle Egan and Vanessa will be staying here. He is a character. He was like a father figure to Ian and I after my Dad died."

"I'll try to remember them all. Viv is one that is upset with you?"

"Yes, she is. I'll need to take some time to talk to her tomorrow night."

Diane took his hand, "Matt, will you make me a promise?"

"Sure. What is it?"

"That you won't hate me, I couldn't stand that."

"You silly thing, I don't hate you. I want you to be happy. I just can't take it when you blow hot and cold. I need something to hang on to. But that's my problem, not yours. I just hope it doesn't end up being yours."

"Meaning?"

"If I can't handle it."

"Is that a threat?"

"No, a fact. There's a difference you know."

"Yes, I know. Matt, before we go back, can I give you a kiss?"

Matt grinned, "Anytime."

She initiated a very erotic kiss and he was very aroused. "I want you," she said, "And I know you don't believe me, but I want us to work out. I really do. Now, let's go back before we get into trouble."

Matt held her close to him, "Diane. You are killing me."

"Matt, I appreciate you pointing out to me how selfish I've been. I needed to go to the woodshed. And I also appreciate that you didn't hit me. I deserved it."

"No. Feelings are definitely hard enough to heal, we don't need bruises." Then he chuckled. "Besides, it's a long ways to carry you back to the house."

"I suppose we should head back and I need to get with the program. Right? I need to act like part of this family." She looked at him, "Did you know that Elton and Keith both said I was part of the family, so I should get used to it?"

"No, I didn't know. But isn't that great, Diane?"

"It really is." Then they started to walk, "What if it doesn't last?"

"Will you just enjoy it while it's here? When you do that, you are questioning it, you are assuring it won't last. Do you realize that?"

"No, I didn't, but you're right, huh?'

Back at the patio, Matt and Tinker had a Coke with the family. Diane asked what she could do to help and soon the ladies were chatting away with the plans for the next evening. Elton walked behind Matt at one point and patted his back. Matt knew that Elton understood what had happened.

That night in bed, Matt told Skipper all about it. "Skipper, I think that people girls are very confusing. I like you a lot better."

Skipper licked his face and wagged her tail. "You crazy pup."

⚜ 55 ⚜

TUESDAY WAS ROUTINE, BUT MATT was a basket case. Before he left for St. John's, Matt heard an overhead page for Diane to go see Mr. Palmer. It bothered him all the while he was at St. John's and he could hardly wait until he got to Jeannie's car.

The girls were chatting in the front seat, when he climbed in the back. "So, is everything okay?"

Jeannie waited for Diane to answer and then told him herself. "It was Sheriff Bernard. He stopped by to inform Diane that Wag had pleaded guilty to all charges. There'll be no trial. That is over now, only the sentencing remains."

"That is great, huh Diane?" he said. "I bet you're relieved."

"I am. I guess we'll just have to work out some legal things and then I can put that part of my life behind me. I thought I'd feel better."

"It'll take a while to sink in, I'm sure," Matt encouraged her. "It is really a good thing, Tinker."

"I know."

After they dropped her off at Schroeder's, Matt asked Jeannie, "So, how was she about it?"

"I don't know. She is feeling guilty about the trouble Wag is in! Maybe it would have been cathartic to go through a trial. But I agree; it's fantastic news. That girl couldn't let herself be happy for all the tea in China.

"I know."

Matt had explained to Lloyd he wouldn't be over to give him a ride that afternoon but he didn't care anyway. He was mostly concerned he'd have to wait to eat supper.

He finished the chores, took a shower and headed over to Schroeder's place. When he arrived, he found Diane in a good mood and helping the ladies. He was so relieved. He got busy and helped out.

Half an hour later, the cars drove in. Keith, Zach and Ian each had a car full of Harrington's when they arrived home from town. Matt went out to greet them. There were hugs all around, except from Vivian, who avoided Matt like a case of bubonic plague.

Ellisons, Jeffries and of course, his Mom and Ian were all there. Diane sat next to Matt during dinner, but no one would have ever guessed they were a couple. She hardly said a word to anyone, but was friendly.

Katie made it a special point to visit with Linda and by the time dinner was over, Linda was very content to stay overnight at Ellisons. While every one was visiting on the patio, Matt asked Vivian to go for a walk with him. She ignored his first request, but the second time he asked, James told her to go with him. Reluctantly she did.

They walked along the country road for a ways before Matt said anything. "Isn't this sky beautiful?"

"Yes, it is." Then she turned on him, "Why did you do it? Do you have any idea how devastating it was to my boys? I so wanted some of them to follow in your footsteps. I had built you up as a role model and now what do I say?"

"I'm sorry, Vivian." Matt said, "But I had to leave. I had to request a laicization."

"I know you never even thought of them, did you?"

"Yes, I can honestly say I did. Would you have thought I set a good example to them by turning a blind eye to what was going on with Butteron?"

"Of course not! But you shouldn't have done this. You should have changed it!"

"Honestly I tried. I tried to work within the church. I followed all their rules, but they did nothing. The more I tried, the more they wanted me to be quiet about it. I didn't just willy-nilly walk away from the priesthood. I took my vows seriously and I still do. I've been thinking about this for well over a year! What could I do?"

"Well, I don't know what you should've done, but not this!" It was obvious she had her mind made up.

"Should I have stayed quiet and let this continue as if I condoned it? What would you have thought then, if you knew that I did that?"

"I don't know that either. It's just so embarrassing."

"Do you think that I wasn't embarrassed too? Or did you not think of that?" Matt asked.

"Well, I guess I didn't. I can't believe that you just walked away. The first thing goes wrong and you just up and walk away."

"It wasn't the first time, or even the third time. It was several times. I prayed, I worried and I put a lot of thought into this. I didn't want to let you all down, but I felt it would be letting you all down even more to not take a stand. I hope you can accept my decision, but Vivian, I really didn't do this on a whim. I hope you can find it in your heart to try to understand."

Just like that, she started to cry, "You big dope. I do understand. I just didn't want it to happen. I just didn't. When I heard about it, I was mad at the church. They should have handled Butterton differently. I just didn't like any of it."

He put his arms around her, "Neither did I. Can you at least bury the hatchet with me?"

"Ah, I guess. Uncle Egan really gave me hell and so did James. I guess I will get over it. The entire situation just makes me furious. Makes a person wonder what Butterton has on the Bishop."

"I won't go down that road, Vivian."

"So, what are you going to do with yourself now? Just milk, what is it—goats?"

"Goats and cows, over fifty head. And I teach high school full time. Vivian, I had to give up a lot too. I can no longer serve communion or give a homily. I have to walk away from all that. It isn't easy."

"I don't suppose. What ever happened to once a priest, always a priest? Okay, we can bury the hatchet, but I'm still mad about it. Can you let me be mad?"

"Knock yourself out," Matt chuckled. "Just don't knock me out."

"Would be no point in trying. You're one of those hard-headed Harringtons."

Matt chuckled, "Oh, you know us, huh? Hey, maybe one day you can come and help Darrell and I milk goats?"

"You're insane, I hope you realize that." Vivian shook her head.

They walked in silence for a while, and then she said, "These folks seem nice. I can see why Mo, Ian and you feel so welcome here. It's amazing how many people live here. Who are they all?"

"Carl just moved to Mom's. It used to be me, Mom and Ian here too. I enjoyed living here."

"Confusing to me," Vivian said.

"Have you ever wondered what your family's schedules of meetings and events looks like to other folks?"

"No, I haven't. I'd guess it looks confusing too."

"Yes Ma'am. It really does."

Matt and Vivian rejoined the group, but before long, everyone went home. Matt stayed behind to talk to Diane. They went for a walk toward the pasture, but decided not to go too far.

"Wow! This is only part of your family? How do you ever keep track of everyone?" Diane giggled.

"Notepads."

Diane laughed, "I had fun tonight. I think they're all nice. How did it go with Vivian?"

"We decided she could still be mad, but we buried the hatchet." Matt chuckled, "Sort of an armed truce."

Diane took his hand, "I'm glad. Matt, I'm happy about the Wag deal being settled. I just had to let it sink in. There are still things we have to get sorted out but at least there is no trial to deal with."

"I'm so glad, Diane. That could have been very difficult. Are you happy you decided to be here tonight?"

"Yes, I'm," she giggled, "And I told Jeannie I wouldn't need a ride on Friday. I'll go with you. Scouts honor."

Matt grinned, "How about tomorrow?"

"Who arrives tomorrow?"

"The rest. I guess they're all going to Mom's. Some arrive in the morning and some in the afternoon, while we are at work. Then we have CCD tomorrow night. So, what do you say?"

"How is this to work?"

"All I know is that we are supposed to go to Mom's after CCD. I don't know when we'll eat. I guess whenever we can grab a bite."

"Okay. Will you pick me up?"

"My chariot awaits."

"I'd like that. Matt, I had fun. I want to be here for you." Diane stopped walking, "May I tell you something?"

"What is it?"

"I had a talk with Nora the other night, when Elton went over to Darrell's place. I told her what I was doing and she really talked to me like a Dutch uncle. She told me that I had to quit doing that to you. I always knew it, but it just seems to happen. The very next morning, I could hardly talk to you. I felt like I was being forced or trapped."

"I don't want you to feel like you are forced to be around me, Diane. Ever," Matt was adamant.

"I know I wasn't, it was me. All by myself. Nora would never say that either. I just can't seem to figure out how to feel. Ah, I don't know. It's like if I relax, I'm afraid it will all turn bad. I don't know how to think about being around anybody without having to deny being myself. Most of the time, I don't even know who myself is. I just can't do it."

"Have you thought about seeing Zach's counselor? He has worked with Zach, Ruthie and Miriam and their abuse issues. Tinker, it isn't an easy thing to get over."

"Matt, I can't begin to afford that. Do you think I'm insane?"

Matt raised his eyebrows, "Do you think Zach, Ruthie and Miriam are insane?"

"Oh heavens no," then she looked at him, "See, I just don't quit being wrong, do I? I think you know I don't think that about counselors or their patients. I don't know what's stopping me. I'm just afraid again. Anyway, Nora told me to just pretend. Pretend it's okay and relax for just this week. She told me I can worry and panic next week. She promised that she and Elton will pull me back if I start to get into trouble. So, I'm trying to do that. Also, if it gets too hairy, they'll help me back away."

"You have some very good folks watching out for you. That's great Diane."

"And I have you. I am very fortunate, you know. Matt, I do appreciate you."

"Did you decide about tomorrow night then?"

"Yes, CCD and then dinner at your Mom's to meet the rest of the people." Then she stopped talking and squinted at him, "You know, you're very lucky."

"Why is that?"

"I only have one brother and one mother for you to meet!"

He gave her a kiss and then they walked back to the house. At the steps, they kissed goodnight.

Matt was so relieved that night when he went to bed. The news of the deal with Wag, the situation with Vivian, the family and his Diane were all beginning to work out. It had been a good day.

❧ 56 ❧

MATT WOKE ABRUPTLY WEDNESDAY MORNING, when Skipper stood up on her back legs and barked like a maniac out the window over the bed. Apparently some bird was disturbing her. So, before five, Matt had already had his first cup of coffee and had been outside for a walk. He used the time to do some schoolwork before he went down to do chores.

Mr. Palmer called him to the office and gave him the schedule for the two Latin classes in the afternoon. Genevieve Spann was moving to Indiana to take care of her parents who had been in a car accident. It was a relief to Mr. Palmer that Matt knew Latin and could take over her classes. She had to leave suddenly, so Mr. Palmer just gave Matt the pile of notes and said he'd have to figure out where she was with things.

He spent his lunch hour in his room looking it all over, so he saw no one all day. That afternoon, when he arrived at St. John's, he was told that would be his last day. It seemed overly unceremonious, but in a way Matt was glad. Thursday he was off anyway, and Friday was going to be a busy day with the weddings. However, it did mean that he'd have to hand over a pile of papers to Father Bartholomew, like Miss Spann had done. It seemed silly, when he was going to be in the same town and he could easily talk to the man. But that was more of the punitive arm of his Bishop in Boston.

By the time he got to the car, he was bummed. The girls were being silly and he felt like the Master of Gloom when he got in the car. They asked what was wrong and he told them and they commiserated. He tried to be cheery, but could barely carry it off.

He went home and started on Darrell's chores early. He could only get things set up before he had to get ready to go to CCD. He took his shower and while he was dressing, stared at his bed. He could just take a little nap. No one would ever know. Just a few minutes. He was so tempted and was about to give in when the phone rang. It was Father Vicaro.

"Hi, catch you in the middle of something?" Father Vicaro asked.

"Yah, and just in time! I was thinking about taking a nap. That would have been disastrous. Skipper woke me up at four-thirty this morning. It has been a long day."

"I heard what they did at St. Johns. I'm really sorry about that."

"I was taken by surprise, but no big deal. I knew it was coming. Guess I need to face the retribution."

"Well, Father Bart showed up in all his glory. I sure hope he doesn't get the job as door man at the Pearly Gates, or there'll definitely be a population reduction up there! He has already let me know that I'm being watched because of my liberal attitudes."

"Does that bother you? Are you worried?"

"Not in the least. Those hoity-toities can do whatever they please. I'm at peace with my decisions. Maybe if they watch, they'll learn something!"

"Are you trying to tell yourself that, or do you really believe it?" Matt asked.

"I really believe it. They've been questioning me for years. You know I started out all legalistic, but things change when you finally start to wise up. I remember Ellison and I going around about things years ago. We have both mellowed and I think it has been good for the community in general. I enjoy his company now. But, I called for a reason. Father Bart wants to meet you after CCD tonight. Be prepared for him. Okay?"

"What about Diane?"

"Don't think he plans on bothering her," the older man chuckled. "But if it gets cantankerous, I'll take her for a walk. You heard Earl pleaded guilty, huh? The attorney told me that after sentencing and that business, Gladys and Diane will have to finish up the business mess. Matt, almost all those things that Wag had Diane sign are illegal. She still owns a lot of the roofing business. But that's for another time. Thanks for listening to me and do not take a nap!"

Matt laughed, "Okay. I won't."

The CCD class was just dismissing, when Father Vicaro and Father Bartholomew came into the classroom where Diane and Matt were gathering the papers. Father Bart, as he called himself, what a wiry, sandy haired fellow a bit younger than Matt. He had a smug demeanor and Matt instantly saw why Father Vicaro didn't like him.

"Hello, you guys. I'd like you to meet our new priest, Father Bartholomew."

Diane smiled and shook his hand, "I'm Diane Waggoner."

Matt held out his hand and said, "Matthew Harrington."

Father Bart shook his hand while his eyes pierced Matt, "I'm surprised you still teach CCD. I would've thought since you turned your back on the church, you wouldn't want to do it."

"I didn't turn my back on the church," Matt said firmly.

"Well, I'd be more than delighted to take this class over. I can teach it with Mrs. Waggoner."

Diane snapped, "Well, no you can't."

Father Vicaro and Matt both dropped their jaws.

"I need a ride in from the country and so if Matt doesn't come in, I can't either. However, if you feel you can do it better, you can teach the class by yourself. I'm certain you have the expertise."

Father Vicaro and Matt were staring at each other now, trying to control their astonishment.

Father Bart was oblivious to them and was not happy with Diane standing up to him. "That seems a bit contentious."

"No more contentious than your comment."

"How long have you been Catholic?" the young man countered.

"All my life," Diane stated, "But maybe it's been long enough. Matt. Put these papers down. I think we have Wednesday nights off from now on."

The young priest was very taken back, "I think we got off on the wrong foot. You misunderstood. I didn't mean it that way. Please reconsider."

"I have known people like you all my life, and honestly, you just annoy the hell out of me. I'm out of here." With that, Diane put down the papers that she was holding, took her purse and jacket and walked out of the room.

Matt and Father Vicaro were still standing in disbelief. Father Bart didn't know what to do either. Then Father Vicaro started to laugh. "Well young man, you keep this up, we won't have to add an extra service! We'll be able to hold communion in a coat closet."

Matt was still motionless. Chuckling, Father Vicaro patted his arm, "You better go take Diane home before she walks. I'll talk to you later."

Matt set down the papers, grabbed his jacket without a word and went out to the car. There he found Diane, still angry, leaning against the door. She moved so he could unlock it and she got in. By the time he came around the car, he was chuckling.

He got in and looked at her, "Where did that come from?"

"I've never done anything like that in my whole life! I think I just told someone off! And a priest no less! What got into me?" Diane was now beginning to think about what she had done.

Matt laughed, "I'm very glad you didn't have audience with the Pope tonight!"

She was thinking about being offended at his laughter, but instead burst out laughing herself. "That felt good, Matt. It really did! It was downright exhilarating!" Then she got quiet, "Do you think I was out of line? Do I need to apologize?"

Matt grinned at her, "Not unless you want to, but give yourself a day or so. Bart should be apologizing to you. Father Vicaro and I don't need it. It isn't wrong to let people know when they have crossed the line. I was proud of you, but shocked as hell, I have to say! I never expected that in a million years!"

"I didn't like his attitude. He was so self righteous and smug. Did you notice? He didn't even have smile wrinkles, just big frown lines. You can tell a lot about a person that way! I can tell you already that you're a much better teacher than he could ever be. So, let him do it. Imagine, he just presumed I'd teach with him! Who does he think he is?"

"Down girl."

"Matt, something inside me just snapped tonight. I guess I missed not being in a boxing match for a while, huh? I won't always be like this, will I?"

"I hope not! It's good, Diane. I'm so proud of you. Let's get out of here," Matt started the car.

Diane said thoughtfully, "It was Nora's fault you know."

"Why is that?"

"She told me that I have as much right to state my opinion as anyone else. But I really should've been more subdued, huh? It was his demeanor. He is arrogant."

"Well, I wouldn't want you to go around telling everyone what you think all the time, but he was arrogant. I rather liked having my girl stand up for me. I never expected that."

"It probably was a once in a lifetime thing. I don't think we should mention it to you family, huh? Let's not say anything until they're gone. Matt, did I quit the church tonight?"

"No, you didn't. You were just letting him know to not to tread on you. Father Vicaro thought it was hysterical. Bart has been bugging him since he arrived. You did Father Vicaro a service. They'd both be glad to have you come back to Mass whenever you feel like it. You were just angry."

"Want to go to a movie next Wednesday night? Just you and me?" Diane asked. "Like a real date?"

"I'd love to." Matt smiled, "Do you realize you just asked me out?"

"Yes, I did, didn't I?" Diane giggled. "Must be my wild side, huh?"

"Okay, you pick out the movie, alright? I would like that."

They parked in Coot's yard and Matt stole a quick kiss before they walked to the house. Inside was pandemonium. The kitchen door no more than opened when a young girl flung herself into Matt's arms! "Uncle Matt, I just couldn't wait to see you! I'm so happy to be here!"

Matt returned her hug and then introduced her to Diane. "Diane, I'd like you to meet my niece, Lorraine Harrington. We call her Rain and we call Diane, Tinker."

Rain looked at Matt and then at Diane. Her face spread into a broad grin and Matt knew she had it all figured out. She gave Diane a big hug and said, "I think my Uncle Matt is my favorite guy in the whole world! What about you? What were you guys doing tonight?"

"We were teaching CCD. Class was just over," Diane explained and she and Rain went into the dining room.

Mo jumped up, "Everyone, this is our friend, Diane Waggoner. She and Matt just got back from teaching CCD. Diane is teacher with Jeannie at the high school. She lives at Schroeder's too. She is part of our family. And here is Matt."

There was a flurry of greetings and introductions. Colleen never moved from her spot. Then Mo told the kids to sit down and she would heat up some of the roast beef dinner for them. Colleen was still glaring at Matt.

"Little Matthew," the older sister finally said, "You've always gotten away with everything, haven't you? Guess that figures because you're the baby of the family."

Frank took his wife's hand, "Not now, Colleen."

"He's my brother. I can talk to him whenever I want," Colleen had obviously been storing up for this. Frank got up from the table.

Coot invited the others all out to the patio that they had set up. "Let's let them get it out of the way and we can have a good time. We'll come back in later to mop up the remains."

Mo stayed and so did Pastor Byron. Colleen was undaunted, but did wait until everyone else was gone. Mo set down the plates for Diane and Matt. They both said a quick grace and then Matt turned his attention to his sister. "I know you have a lot on your mind. What do you want to say?"

Then she opened up both barrels. "What the hell possessed you to just walk away like that? You've never had any backbone! You just crawled away without standing up for your beliefs. I'm ashamed to say I know you, let alone related to you."

Diane and Byron both watched Matt for his reaction. He just looked up and said, "I'm sorry you feel that way, Colleen."

"Oh don't come off so Mr. Calm Goody-Goody! Why didn't you just get rid of that bad priest and stay where you belonged? Didn't your vows mean a damned thing to you?"

Diane opened her mouth to respond and Byron caught her eye and shook his head no. She looked down at her plate.

"Colleen, I did my level best to get the church to remove Butterton. They would not do it. The first time was well over a year ago. I tried to go by their rules. All I accomplished is getting into trouble. So did another priest. He has also resigned because of it. Colleen, I didn't make any of these decisions lightly or quickly. I know you don't understand and I don't expect you to. But please think. I don't tell you how to handle your vows; don't tell me."

"So, are we supposed to think you are a hero or feel sorry for you? Just what do you want from us?"

Matt shook his head, "Just to be treated like any of the rest of you. I just want to be a regular person."

"But you aren't," Colleen said. "You never have been. You've always been our special brother."

Matt asked, "Did I ask for that?"

"Well, no. But you were the only one that didn't want to be a cop. What were we to do with you?"

Matt frowned, "Maybe I should go knock someone silly. Then would I be okay?"

Byron cleared his throat, "I think that is a bit over the top. Maybe you could just actually really get to know each other? How would that be?"

Colleen almost snarled, "I already know him. He was always the good guy while the rest of us were just ordinary."

"Well," Diane smiled, "So now he isn't. Isn't that a relief? He is ordinary too."

Colleen kind of frowned and then smiled. "I guess you're right. Just ordinary. Now I can treat you like everyone else."

"I think I'd like that," Matt smiled.

"You just have no idea, Matthew. Ordinary isn't easy. Okay, if that's what you want, that's what you got. Let's just forget this. I always thought you made a lousy priest anyway."

Matt chuckled, "And I never thought you would make a good nun."

"Speaking of nuns," Colleen was on mission, "I hear Ruthie was a nun and she dumped that too. Is that why they are having a non-Catholic wedding? What's the story? Is this a refuge for folks who can't keep their vows?"

Byron couldn't abide that, "Sometimes Colleen, it isn't wise to make a comment like that unless you really understand the situation. Ruthie is a fine person. I can make a fair wager that she had to deal with more trauma in her life than most. She loves your brother and he loves her. That's all you need to care about. Don't you think? And they are having a Catholic wedding. The vows will be made in a house of worship. All legit."

Colleen leaned back in her chair, "Matthew, what do you think? You should know that stuff!"

"As a brother or as a priest?"

"Both."

"As both, it's very legitimate. I think they are the best thing that ever happened to each other. May I ask a personal question, Colleen? Have you always followed all your vows to the letter?"

"I beg your pardon!" Colleen retorted.

"Well, so do Ruthie and I. We beg your pardon."

"Okay, that's enough now!" Mo said. "No more talk. Shape up or go out to the pasture and beat each other into submission. You're messing up the air in my new house!"

"You guys will do fine," Pastor Byron suggested, "Just try to be a little careful of each other. This week isn't about you two anyway; it's about the weddings. Try not to mess it up for the rest of the folks. Okay? If you want to talk about it, let me know. I'll be glad to listen."

Colleen blurted out, "You aren't a priest."

"I know, but I still have ears," Byron chuckled.

Colleen realized what she was doing for the first time and flushed with humility, "I'm so sorry Pastor. I was way out of line. Please forgive me."

"No big deal. Hey Colleen, would you like to go for a short walk with me? You could vent away like crazy," Byron grinned in his disarming way. "I specialize in screaming and hollering."

"I guess I would. Would you mind if I take a beer along?"

"Only if I can have one, too."

After they went out of the kitchen, Matt put his head in his hands. Diane patted his shoulder.

Mo sat down next to him and he asked her, "Mom, do all the rest of the kids think that I thought I was something special like Colleen said?"

"Nah you didn't think it, but you were. You are, and so are they. We are all special. Extremely odd and very special. We all knew Colleen was the cauldron of hot temper. She acted like she had the burden of being prosecutor and judge for all her siblings, but my girl never wilted under that formidable task! Not her! She got away with her big mouth more than anyone else, even the boys. She just doesn't realize that. Why if I had washed her mouth out with soap for all the rotten things she said, she'd be doing Tide commercials to this day!"

Diane started to giggle, "You're so funny."

"See Diane, you are the sane one," Mo smiled.

"Mo, you wouldn't have thought so if you had seen me earlier! I mortified both Matt and Father Vicaro. I told off that new priest at St. John's tonight!"

Mo raised her arms to the heavens, "May the Angel's chariots swoop down and gather me to the Saints! Promise you don't tell Colleen or she will organize an exorcism!" Then she leaned down and whispered in her ear, "I'm proud of you Girl and I can't wait to hear all about it! Were you proud, Mattie?"

"I was, very much so. We'll tell you after the wedding stuff is over."

After they ate, they went out to join the rest. On the way, they passed through the playroom. All the little ones and the girls were busy, but in one corner, sitting alone was Turk. In the other, was Charlie. Matt and Diane surveyed the situation and Matt grinned, "I'll take Turk. You get Charlie."

57

MATT SAT DOWN ON THE floor next to Turk, "What's up? Not having fun?"

"Uncle Matt, I thought Gramps would need me to help him, but he doesn't. I was going to be his best buddy."

"He does need you to be his buddy and it is very important to him that you and Charlie get to be friends. You are his favorite guys and nothing would make him happier than to have you two hit it off. You know?"

"I don't think he cares if I am here or not. Look at all these kids. They all call him a nickname that I don't even know," Turk fought back the tears.

"They call him Coot, but guess what? You call him Gramps. That's even more special. He loves all you guys. And I'll tell you a secret. Charlie is really a good guy and he is my friend too. I know him pretty well and he was really looking forward to meeting you. You know what happened to him?"

Turk shrugged, "No. What?"

"He was going to have to stay at his house with all these girls you see here! Can you imagine?"

Turk's eyes got huge, "This is terrible! No guy should have to do that!"

"No, so that is why he is staying here. Carl thought he and you could hang out. Carl figured you would help him out. It'd be better for you guys to stick together, huh?"

"Yah. I couldn't stay in a house with all those *girls*. Yuck!"

Matt grinned, "Look, our friend Diane is bringing Charlie over to meet you. Do you think you could try to be cool to him?"

"Sure Uncle Matt. I never knew he had that problem. I'll be his pal."

Diane came over and held out her hand to Turk, "Hello, my name is Diane. Folks call me Tinker. Did you know that we call your Uncle Matt, Tuck? What do folks call you?"

"Turk."

Charlie frowned, "They just call me Charlie."

"That's because you have a fine name Charlie. Have you met Turk yet?"

Charlie lifted his hand and said, "Hi."

Turk did the same.

Matt said, "I was just telling Turk that you have all those girls sleeping at your house!"

Both boys instantly crossed their eyes. A bond was immediately forged, and it became doubtful the world would survive. Within minutes, they were commiserating with each other about girls. Matt and Diane just looked at each other and smiled.

The rest of the evening was rather fun and much more relaxed. But it was late and everyone was tired. Before long, they all headed to their homes. Diane rode home with Annie and Pepper after giving Matt a quick hug.

Rain was determined to ride home with her Uncle Matt. Once in the car, she reminded him of a dam that burst! "I just knew it! I knew it! I knew it!"

Matt was bewildered, "What did you know?"

"Leaving the priesthood is what you were thinking about when we went for our walk in Boston. The trap you set for yourself, right? Right?"

"Yes, it was."

"And now you got your own main squeeze. I like her Uncle Matt. I won't tell the rest of these Dodo heads. But I can tell. She's great."

Matt looked at her, "Rain."

She got serious, "Uncle Matt, don't insult me by trying to lie. I won't tell. But you and I have always connected, right? I know. Diane is cool. I love her."

"Don't get too carried away. We are just moving from being friends. This may not amount to anything."

She smirked, "Poppycock! It is much more. I know this stuff. Your love is written by the stars! You are kindred spirits whose paths are printed in the cosmos! I know that stuff. I read all about it in a magazine."

Matt chuckled, "Rain, calm down. We care about each other a lot, but we have lots of stuff to work out. Real life isn't that easy."

"It can be, if you want it to be. You know? Nothing is easy if you think it to death. That is why I don't think."

Matt laughed, "Speaking of which, how is school going?"

"Oh, I love that psycho stuff, but I really don't like the rest of it. Can't I be a shrink and not learn to add? I was thinking I should be a psychic fortuneteller. Then I don't have to go to college."

"I don't know, Rain. That might not go over with the family."

"Did you get bashed by Aunt Vivian and Aunt Colleen? Boy, you should've heard them! You'd have thought you shrunk their corsets! I think they are upset because they thought you could get them into heaven. I wouldn't want to have to explain that to St. Peter! Can you imagine?"

"Did I ever tell you I love you?" He laughed.

"All the time. I know it. So, this is your cabin. It is so cool. Can I see it?"

"How about in the morning? You're going to help us milk, right?"

"Can I, really?"

"Yup. Darrell already knows. But Rain, you have to listen to him. I don't want you or any of the animals getting hurt. Promise?"

"I promise. Where are we going now?" She asked as they parked the car.

"I have to get Skipper and take her to the house. She has been in the barn."

"What is Skipper? A goat?"

"No, a dog."

A couple minutes later, Matt, Rain, Ranger and Skipper were headed to Darrell's house. Rain's parents Patrick and Margie and her twin Lonnie, all met them at Jessup's patio.

"Look Dad, Mom! Uncle Matt has a dog and her name is Skipper. And Mr. Jessup has her brother, Ranger. Aren't they cool?"

"Thank you for bringing Ranger to the house, Rain," Jeannie smiled. "I hear you are going to milk in the morning. Want me to wake you up?"

"That'd be nice, Mrs. Jessup."

"Please call me Jeannie. Mrs. Jessup is Darrell's mom."

"Jeannie," Rain giggled. "Good night Uncle Matt. This is way cool."

Pat gave his brother a hug. "You have no idea how excited that girl has been about coming out here. I hope she doesn't drive you all crazy."

"Insanity is our norm," Darrell laughed. "Right Matt?"

"Amen!"

At five-fifteen, Matt's phone rang. He answered and heard Rain bubbling, "Are you up? I am. Can I come see your cabin?"

"I am and you can. See you in a minute."

Matt doubted she had even hung up the phone because she was knocking on his door so fast. "Did you fly down here?"

"No, I think that you and Diane should make it a covered walkway from here to Jessups! Wouldn't that be wonderful?"

Matt chuckled, "We'll think about it. Calm down, you'll wear yourself out. I'd like you to meet Murphy and Lady."

A few minutes later, Darrell was at the door, "Are you and Lightnin' ready yet? That girl is a live wire! Come on Kid! We got milking to do. And your Mom said you would be my hired hand all morning! Think we need to clean the barn, huh Tuck?"

"Yes sir. Fine plan. And grind feed."

Rain narrowed her eyes, "Are these the worst jobs? I bet they are."

"Not the whole worst, but close," Darrell grinned. "If you do good work and calm down, I'll teach you how to drive the tractor. How does that sound?"

"Am I going to like this, Uncle Matt? Is Mr. Jessup okay?"

"He is the best, and I bet you'll love it."

"Lonnie and Dad said they might come along for some of it. I suppose they don't trust me," Rain started to pout.

"Now just why would you be selfish? Don't you want them to have fun too?" Matt asked. "Besides, I thought that was just for the horseback ride. Right Darrell?"

"Annie is organizing that. We're going to use their horses, ours and borrow some from Swensons. I am not familiar with their string, so I'm not very secure with that."

"What is a string, Mr. Jessup?" Rain asked.

"Call me Darrell. That is what they call a ranchers collection of riding horses."

With that, Darrell and Rain were deep into conversation.

When Jeannie pulled the car up to the cabin, Matt got in and they both laughed. "I never realized my husband had so much charisma!"

"Rain will never be the same. Oh, by the way, Ian is picking me up at the school at two, so I won't be riding home tonight. Okay?"

Ian picked up Matt to try on the tuxedos. Marly's house was filled with flowers, lace and sewing needles. Matt could easily see why Charlie wanted out! Byron met them at the door and just shook his head. "Now I understand why Elton says he doesn't like foo-foo stuff."

"Quiet Byron," Marly reprimanded her husband. "You are on a short leash."

Miriam toddled up beside Marly, and told the brothers with great gravity, "Byron no more."

Matt picked her up and gave her a hug, "I'd like to have ten kids like you!"

"Fodder gophers?"

"Better just settle for this one," Ian gave her a hug, "My little Miriam is a good egg."

"Gopher good egg," she patted her chest.

After the fittings, the men went over to Schroeders and took Lloyd for a drive.

"Did you hear about the weddings?" Lloyd asked. "Guess that is why all the strangers are here. One of those guys is a detective and other one talks funny. Don't understand a damned thing he says. I think he is a foreigner."

"Do you mean Detective Diaz? He used to work with Coot at the FBI. His name is Rafael and his wife is named Rosa," Ian explained. "The foreigner is our Uncle Egan. He really isn't foreign, he just talks funny."

Lloyd nodded understandingly, "Never went to school, huh? I won't tell. He must have a lot of cows, uh?"

"Why do you say that Grandpa?" Matt asked.

"Because he has a fine wife. Couldn't have got one without at least three cows!"

Matt and Ian both cracked up. Then Lloyd got serious, "Who is getting married anyway?"

"Ruthie and I," Ian answered.

Lloyd thought for a bit and then asked, "My girl? What's her name again?"

"It is Ruthie, Grandpa."

"Yah, a guy should really remember his girl's name. Damnedest thing, I just don't but she is short like my Katherine."

"Yes, she is Grandpa. She's your special girl."

"I suppose I should go to that wedding, huh? Do I have to wear a tie?"

Matt got home and changed. He went out to join Lonnie, Patrick, Rain and Darrell as they cleaned the barn.

"Glad Lightnin' and I saved this for last. We have tons of help," Darrell grinned. "She has been a pretty good hired hand."

"Uncle Matt, that grinding feed is so itchy! You should have warned me," Rain giggled, "I'll have to grow a new layer of skin for Granny's wedding."

"How was the horseback ride?" Matt asked.

It seemed that everyone had a good time. "Uncle Matt, Darrell said it was like herding cats! Everybody knows you can't herd cats," Rain blabbered.

"I know," Matt laughed. "That is what he meant!"

She stopped and frowned, "I think he is right. I love Annie. She is the coolest, and that Marty. Guess what? Turk and Charlie got into hot water with Granny already."

Matt chuckled, "Not surprised one bit. What did they do?"

Darrell grinned, "Charlie got out of school early today and he and Turk dug a trench, right across the back of the patio! Mo almost broke her neck, so now they are filling it in."

"Is this what it is always like here?" Pat asked.

"Sometimes it's even worse!" Darrell chuckled.

That night, the wedding party assembled at the picnic grounds for the rehearsal of the wedding. It was fun because Father Vicaro, Byron and Marv were all officiating. Father Vicaro was delighted to have shed Father Bart for the evening and the other two were usually clowns. Then they all went to Schroeders for the rehearsal dinner.

There were even too many people for Nora's dining room! It was nice outside, so they could spill over to the patio. After dinner, there was a lot of visiting going on and about an hour after dessert, Matt noticed that Diane was missing. He checked with Nora and she said, "I missed her too a bit ago. I noticed she was very quiet right after dinner. Why don't you go check her room, Matt?"

"Think I should?"

"Yes, I do."

Matt knocked on her door even though there was no light under it. After a minute, it opened a crack. There was Diane with a tear stained face. She dropped her head and opened the door. "I hope there isn't a search party."

"No, just Nora and I. Is there something wrong?"

She shrugged, "Not really. It just suddenly got to me. Everyone was being nice, but suddenly I realized that this isn't my world. I remember being so excited like Ruthie is when Dean and I got married. That sure was a big disaster. I just had to get away. I'm sorry Matt."

Matt went in and closed the door. Taking her hand, he walked over to the bed to sit down. "That's okay. You did really well for a long time. I shouldn't have left you alone for so long."

"No, really that is okay. I'm just a bit tired out. I have been with folks more this last few days than probably in the last year! It's a bit overwhelming."

Matt put his hand on her neck, "I want you to know how much I appreciate all you have done. Sincerely."

They could both feel the electricity in the room. Matt quickly gave her a kiss on the cheek, "Are you coming back out to join us?"

"We have to get up early tomorrow, so I don't think so. Will I offend anyone?"

"No. I'll just tell Nora and if anyone asks, we can say you have to get up early tomorrow. Okay?" then he pulled her into his arms, "Are you okay? Want me to stay?"

"Of course I do, but you can't," then they melted into each other's arms. They nearly lost control and then Matt got up. "I'd better go."

She nodded, "Yes, you better. Good night Matt."

"I love you."

"I love you, too."

·~ 58 ·~

MATT WAS ON SCHROEDER'S STEPS by six-thirty in the morning. The rest of the family was getting ready to go milking. Chris, Pepper's fiancé had arrived from Grand Forks that morning for the gala events, and an air of happy anticipation permeated the place. Diaz and Egan were going to help milk that morning, and Elton was looking forward to that. Pappy was content to sit quietly in the midst of the confusion.

Matt grinned, "I almost feel out of place in a suit!"

"Dressed like a Dandy!" Elton chortled. "I think your lady is almost ready. She was here a bit ago and looked good enough for me. But then, I would just take her to milk cows!"

"Uncle Elton," Diane giggled as she came into the kitchen, "You take all your girlfriends to milk cows. Why is that?"

"Need to get the chores done so I have courting time!" he laughed. "See you guys about when?"

"I'll be home at two-thirty and Diane is coming home with Jeannie, right?"

"Right," she hugged Nora. "See you later."

After the door closed behind the couple, Pappy asked everyone, "Are they going together? Seem awfully friendly."

"Would it be better if they disliked each other?" Elton smiled. "They're very good friends. Matt has a lot of good friends."

Kevin laughed, "I even like him."

Pappy shook his head like they were all a bit wacky and went back to his cinnamon roll.

343

Diane and Matt arrived at St. John's. There they met Zach, Suzy, Maureen and Carl. They went into the sanctuary where they were met by a surly Father Bart. Father Vicaro married them in a short, simple ceremony, accentuated with a few grunts from Bart. Matt was worried that Diane was about to take him on toe to toe, but the ceremony was short enough so they avoided that. Zach and Suzy signed the papers and then said their goodbyes.

Before they went to school, Matt asked Diane, "Would you like to share a caramel roll with me at the Hen House Café?"

Diane giggled, "If I don't, I'll probably die of hunger before noon. That was the shortest wedding service I've ever seen."

"Father Vicaro turned it on high speed to try to keep you and Bart from a show down. You guys sure don't like each other, do you?"

"I don't know how he feels about me, but I sure don't like him. As Ian would say,—that's a blasted fact! He just rankles me." Diane giggled.

Zach and Suzy hailed them from another table, "Want to join us? We are just grabbing a quick bite. Zach has to go to town to do his rounds. If you want to gobble with us, you're sure welcome."

"We'd love to," Diane smiled.

They had a very quick breakfast snack and Zach was chuckling, "Ruthie has this service so top secret, I wonder if she knows who'll show up!"

Suzy laughed, "Oh yes. She has every detail worked out. I think that Marly has the master plan."

"So," Matt asked "I take it Glenda Olson is a maid of honor?"

"She is an attendant. Yes, she and Ruthie became quite good friends while working on some of the things for church. You know, Ruthie is mostly Marv's secretary and Glenda is his wife. So they do a lot together."

"I thought you both worked at Trinity Lutheran," Diane asked.

"I work mostly for Grinchboss, I mean Byron."

Zach shook his head, "You should hear Byron and Suzy go at each other. You'd think they can't stand each other. But Marly and I know that neither of them could survive without the other."

Suzy crossed her eyes, "Don't believe him. He is a compulsive liar. Besides, he and Marly are always talking about going on a date together."

"Out to coffee," Zach grinned. "Marly and Elton are going on the date."

Diane smiled, "You guys are so funny. I would've thought that Marly would have been her attendant. They live together."

"Marly is her personal attendant and like her Mom. Besides she'll have her hands full. Trust me."

"I can't wait to see this," Diane giggled. "Did you and Zach have a big wedding?"

"Yes, did you and Dean?"

Diane's face fell and Suzy could have died. "No, it was actually very small. But it was a lot longer than this morning's ceremony. Well, Matt, we had better get to school before the first bell rings. See you guys later. I can hardly wait for tonight."

In the car, Matt apologized, "I'm sorry that Suzy asked that. I am sure she didn't want to upset you."

"I know. It is a common question. Someday, Matt, I would like us to talk about it. Okay? But let's have fun today. Why am I always a poop?"

"You aren't,—always!" Matt teased.

"You rat, and to think, I was going to dance a smoochy dance with you tonight." She teased, "Too bad for you."

"No smoochy dance. You know what would happen with a smoochy dance. That'd be awful," Matt was almost serious.

"It'd give Nana and Pappy something to think about. You should hear those two. They are so busy trying to figure everyone out! They do have a time. But your Uncle Egan just gives them the business. Grandpa Lloyd is afraid they are all going to live there forever! It is crazy to watch."

"I'm glad it's at your house. I just have Rain being worried about you and me. She said that she knows we are cosmically connected or something."

Diane laughed, "She confided that to me and she told me I could trust her with any secrets. I love that girl. She's so funny. She offered to help me plan our wedding and seemed most disappointed when I said we weren't engaged. Then she giggled and said, 'You will be!'"

Matt laughed, "That's my Rain."

"Oh, Matt," Diane took his hand, "Can I ask you an enormous favor?"

"You can ask. If I can do it, I will."

"Good, since Genevieve left for Indiana, I lost my assistant for the school play. Since you are doing her Latin classes, could you help me with the play?

He furrowed his eyebrows in bewilderment, "Are you doing a play about Julius Caesar?"

"No, why?"

"Why do you need a math and Latin teacher to help with a play?"

She smiled innocently, "I don't, you dumbbell. I need you. Besides, you have Wednesday nights free now."

"You're such a con man," Matt grinned. "Okay. You got me."

Without thinking, she leaned over and kissed his cheek. Just then Jeannie drove up. She was grinning and told them when they got out of the car, "You had better watch it, you two. I think all this wedding stuff is going to your heads."

"I think you're right, I had to promise Charlie that when I got married he wouldn't have to be ring bearer! He was delighted." Matt grinned. "He told me that guys should just tie yarn around their wife's finger and send them to the house! You should hear him!"

Jeannie laughed, "I can about imagine."

That afternoon, all chores were dispatched in record time. The men were all on notice to get to where and when with no hesitation. All had learned the Nora, Marly, Katherine trio were not to be trifled with. And Mo was no slouch, either. Throughout history, men have been committed to fierce combat with less precision.

By ten after seven, the men of the wedding party were gathered behind the cook tent at the park, since the girls had taken over the rest rooms. Ian, Carl and Elton were having their last cigarette. Matt sat down beside them, "It is times like this I wish I smoked."

The smokers all laughed.

"It's times like this, I wish I main-lined!" Carl joked.

Harrington looked at Carl, "Just think, tomorrow night at this time, you'll be married too."

"I try not to think about it," Carl admitted. "I'm scared to death,"

"I was just fine before my wedding," Elton boasted. "I never had any doubts!"

Byron came up behind him and said, "What in the devil are you saying? You were so unglued it was pathetic!"

"Oh, yah," Elton grimaced, "I guess I forgot."

"No you didn't, Magpie. You are such a braggart all the time! I can hardly stand being around you." Coot snarled.

"Ah, you guys love each other and you both know it," Pastor Marv chuckled.

Meanwhile, in the restrooms, Ruthie was like a caged squirrel. Finally Grandma Katherine sat her down, "Look here girl, I'm going to have to smother you if you don't calm down. You've been through so much in your life; I'd think this wedding would be a piece of cake."

"But Grandma, I want it to be perfect," Ruthie started.

"You silly thing! However you and Harrington get married will be perfect. Would you rather have a perfect ceremony or a happy life?" Katherine smiled at her, "Take a deep breath. Marly is out there whipping things into shape. It'll be wonderful."

"Thanks, Grandma."

"Yah, settle down Ruthie. My Ian needs a rock, not a bit of loose gravel! So get your grips about you! It'll be grand, and anything we miss tonight, we'll make up for tomorrow!" Mo laughed.

"You're right, Mo. Are you going to have a heart to heart with Ian?"

"I was going to, but Carl said he thought he should do it. So, I agreed. Besides, I have no idea what men say to each other. My guess tips on how to keep from putting their dirty socks in the hamper!"

"Are you getting nervous?" Ruthie asked.

"For me or you? Lordie girl, my prayer bones are so worn out that if I get down, I'll never get back up again! God has said He doesn't want to hear from me for a full two days! Guess I might have overdone it, just a bit."

"It's time," Nora said as Marly put her head in the door.

Marly took Ruthie aside and said, "Byron and I feel like our oldest daughter is getting married. We love you and we know that you're doing the right thing. Remember, whatever happens, you'll always be our family."

They hugged and the tears already started. Marly kissed her cheek and said, "Elton will be here to walk you down the aisle. Now, don't be alarmed, he'll be crying all the way."

In the men's tent, Elton looked at his watch. "Well, it's time."

He embraced Ian and said, "Good luck, son. You made a great choice."

Then he wiped his tears and before he left, Zach quipped, "I think you should have had a tissue bearer!"

"Watch it Zacharias," Elton grinned. "I made it through your wedding."

Then Carl stepped forward, "I promised your Mom I'd say something to you, but I have no idea what to say. All I can think of is that I'm so very proud of you."

"Thanks Dad," Ian said. Then they hugged and both had to wipe some tears.

The many guests were seated in the tent that was decorated festively with shades of yellow flowers. The music started and Rodney and Doug Anderson lit the candles.

Kevin and Keith seated the grandparents; Nana and Pappy on Ian's side and Katherine and Lloyd on the other. The Grandmothers wore matching dresses of deep gold. The men wore their black tuxedos. Following them, the parents were seated; Mo and Carl on Ian's side and Marly and Nora on the other. All three Moms wore dark green dresses.

The organist played on an organ that Darrell and Danny had moved in earlier that day. While she played, the clergy entered; Father Vicaro, Pastor Byron and Pastor Marvin. Then groom and his attendants appeared at the front of the church wearing black tuxedos with gold flowers in their lapels. They also wore gold cummerbunds. Matt was best man. Zach Jeffries and Ken Ellison were the other attendants.

The music changed and the bridesmaid's filed in. First was Katie Ellison, who looked radiant in her pale yellow dress. The dress had a full skirt and was gathered at the waist. There was a draped neckline and full length, lightly gathered sleeves down to beaded cuffs at the wrist. At the waist was a large tie that ended in a huge bow at the back. As Ruthie had planned, her hair was up inside a golden tiara in a pile of curls. She carried a bouquet of white flowers with dark green fern. She met Ken who looked extremely handsome and they went forward to the altar. She was followed by Glenda Olson, dressed like Katie, who was met by Zach and then the matron of honor, Suzy Jeffries who was met by Matt.

Next were the flower girls and the ring bearer. The flower girls wore dark green dresses of a similar pattern to the bridesmaids. Ginger carried a white basket with yellow flowers. Ginger, Miriam and Charlie came down the aisle. Ginger and Charlie each held one of Miriam's hands so she didn't carry a flower basket. They had to go slow because Miriam couldn't walk very fast, but she did it. Charlie was very "Solomon" and the only emotion he showed was a quick smile to Matt when he got to the front. The others took their place in front, but Miriam went to sit with Marly.

The music changed and everyone stood for the wedding march. Elton took Ruthie down the aisle. She looked simply radiant. Her dress was similar to the bridesmaids, except that her ruffled sleeves ended at the elbow where they turned into an iridescent beaded lace sheath to the wrist. She had an open rounded neckline, filled in with beaded lace and ending in a heavily beaded Mandarin collar. The ties of the huge white bow in the back were down to the floor. Her veil was floor length and had a train of a couple feet. She carried a bouquet of yellow roses and dark green ferns.

When Elton put her hand on Ian's, he whispered, "Bless you both." He took his seat by Nora, tears streaming down his cheeks.

It was a wonderful service and each of the clergy took part. When Byron said a few words, he referred to Ruthie as one of his daughters. Marv said she was the best secretary he had ever had. Father Vicaro repeated the vows and then introduced them as Mr. and Mrs. Ian Harrington. They all marched down the aisle and into the larger area of the tent where the reception and dance was held. It may not have been conventional, but it was wonderful.

There was a wonderful prime rib dinner and then the toasts. Lucy Schroeder and Elsie Oxenfelter had baked and decorated an enormous and beautiful cake. It was decorated with yellow flowers and of course, had a bride and groom on the top.

As dinner ended, Matt gave the first toast, followed by Zach and Ken. Then the bride and groom cut the cake. As dessert ended, the wedding party gathered for the grand march which began the wedding dance. Bill Heinrich and his Boys band played.

Ruthie and Ian shared their first dance to their favorite song, *The First Time Ever I Saw Your Face*. It was very romantic.

Then the bridal party joined in. Ruthie danced the father-daughter dance first with Byron Ellison and then with Elton Schroeder. For a little girl, who had such a tormented childhood, she had been given a wonderful family.

After a few dances with the wedding party, they began inviting others to the dance floor. Before long, the congregated guests were all dancing. Boston Irish and North Dakota German-Scandinavians found they all knew how to celebrate a wedding with vigor. And that they did.

Matt danced with a lot of ladies, Glenda, Katie and Suzy, of course. Then he gave Rain a good run at the polka and then he and Katie showed Rain the Schottische. Before long, he went to find his favorite partner. Diane had been dancing, too. She was having a good time and danced with most of the clan, Darrell's brothers and Matt's brothers. Finally, they got to share a dance.

It was a waltz but after extracting a promise it would not be 'smoochy', they danced closely. Matt whispered in her ear, "Diane, are you having fun tonight?"

She cuddled closer, "The best. Are you?"

"I am too."

The picnic grounds had rules about closing at one o'clock. Bill and his Boys played *Good Night Irene* at quarter to one. Most everyone went straight home because they had another wedding the next night, but Matt and Diane took the very long way home. They stopped on a prairie dirt road and spent a little time in each other's arms, but decided they were playing with fire. They headed back to the farm.

When Matt stopped in front of the Schroeder house, Pepper and Chris were just saying good night. They all four got out of their cars and laughed.

Pepper was hysterical. "Good grief, it used to be Zach and Suzy, now it is you two. Chris, we have to get married soon! We are beginning to feel like homesteaders on the Peyton Place!"

"I thought you were getting married this winter," Matt chuckled.

"We are, when are you?"

"Don't know if we are," Diane said. "But we'll let you know. Would you guys promise to keep quiet about seeing us?"

Chris cracked up, "Your secret is safe. Like what are we going to say anyhow? We were getting after it and who did we see? That conversation will never happen!"

"I'm getting out of here," Matt chuckled.

"Me, too," Chris laughed.

The girls walked to the house together.

❦❧ 59 ❦❧

DOWN AT DARRELL'S BARN THE next morning was the quietest that anyone had seen Rain in days. However, her being quiet was like Kevin being subdued. Neither of them were what anyone would call serene. The wedding had been unbelievable to Rain and she probably only missed two dances all evening. She danced with almost everyone and she loved it.

"Uncle Matt, if you get married, can I be your bridesmaid?" she asked.

"I suppose you could."

"Dad, do I know anyone else that is getting married? Mom says I shouldn't ask to be a bridesmaid, but otherwise no one will ask me right? So, I kind of gotta," Rain pointed out to the men. "Wasn't it just cool, Lonnie?"

"I guess, if you like that stuff," he shrugged.

"Of course, I'll be in your wedding because I'm your twin. So, you need to get a girlfriend," she ordered.

"Good grief, I'm not even interested in any girl right now," Lonnie made a face.

"I'll see if I can find you one," Rain offered.

"I would prefer to do it on my own," Lonnie stated.

Rain gave him an exasperated look, "Be that way, then. Dad, do we know anyone else?"

"Maybe your cousin, Liddy. She has a guy she has been going with for a while," Patrick suggested.

"I doubt it." Rain's eyes got huge as if she was revealing an enormous truth. "Have you ever heard her and her friends scream? It is awful! One says something and they all scream and jump around. I just want to deck them. She likes that kind of stuff. It gives me the heebie-jeebies. I just like the dance part."

"Well, you'll be invited to a lot of dances," Darrell said. "You don't have to be an attendant to go to one. It is a lot easier. I have been an attendant real often. Pepper and I usually end up together. It's funny. I have been to the altar with Pep a hundred times, and with my Jeannie only once!"

"Darrell, do you have any single brothers?" Rain asked bluntly.

He grinned, "Yes, Sammy and Joey are both single. You danced with both of them last night. Why?"

"Maybe if I lived out here, they and me would be attendants. Huh?"

"It could happen," Darrell chuckled, "But if you don't take that milk machine off Blanche, she'll have to kick you."

"Oh, I'm sorry. I'm so flaky."

Matt got back in the house just in time to catch a call on the last ring. It was Father Vicaro. "Hello, I wanted to give you the news. It came yesterday afternoon, but last night was too busy. Oh, by the way, I had a great time at that wedding."

"It was fun. So, what is the news?"

"Heard from our Bishop, who spoke to your Archbishop. Your petition for Laicization was received at the Vatican. They had put it as a Petition of Justice. They are going to ask for dispensation for you to marry. They asked me if I thought you wanted that. I said I thought it would be a logical choice. Your Bishop had asked if you any interest in marriage and my CIA self took over! I did a little bit of finagling. I didn't want the Bishop to think that you might be leaving because of that so he could use it to get himself off the hook. I said I didn't know, but pointed out to him that if you married or got interested in the ladies, you'd be less likely to want to re-enter the clergy. He glommed on that immediately. So, your petition includes a request for dispensation to marry."

"Thanks. I do want that. Can I ask you something, seriously? And I have to say, I have tried not to think about it myself, but why do you think the Boston Bishop is so determined to keep that pedophile under wrap?"

"I agree. I have tried not to think of it either. My guess it is either that he is worried it would reflect on the church or his management skills. Regardless of what it is, we have no control over it."

"That's about what I thought, too." Matt poured some coffee for himself, "Thanks for handling that part about the dispensation to marry for me. You have been a saint to me."

"I know," Father Vicaro chuckled, "And you have no idea how nice it is to have someone to call and whine to about this Bart. If he keeps it up, I'm going to invite you and Diane over some evening. We'll go to the local bar until she knocks him silly. She seemed to have a great time last night. I noticed she was mingling a lot. I even got a dance with her!"

Matt laughed, "Get your own girl! Can you imagine having Father Bart handle your resignation?"

"Heavens no!" Father Vicaro chuckled. "Oh, I guess they are going to try to get the Holy See to deal with the petitions in a month or so. The Bishop said there is the request of yours and another Jeff guy, they want to get expedited. They gave some excuse why they needed it dealt with right away."

"Jeff is that friend of mine who is in New Mexico now. You know, the one that went to that kid's funeral."

"I figured. Well, I have to go talk to Black Bart. See you tonight."

Matt hung up and had a good laugh. He knelt down and rubbed Skipper's ears. "Vicaro is a nice man, isn't he Skipper? Your Daddy really likes him. Yes, he does."

Matt got showered and was ready to go the wedding rehearsal. While he was waiting for Darrell, the phone rang. It was Diane, "Hello Matt. How is your morning?"

"Good, and yours?"

"Nice. I had a great time last night, did you?"

"Yes. Diane, Father Vicaro called this morning. He had some news about my resignation and I'd like to talk to you about it when you have time. Today might not be good."

"Is everything okay? I mean you'll be granted the petition, right?"

"Yes Ma'am. Sounds like it." Matt changed the subject, "So, are you polishing your dancing shoes for tonight?"

"I might just wear bandages! I could hardly walk this morning! I would've felt worse about it, except that Rosa and Van both feel the same way! How is Rain?"

"Gearing up for tonight! Oh, to be eighteen again!"

"Yes, Pep is all recharged for tonight, too. Chris is here, so she is so excited. I guess she and Darrell have been in so many weddings lately that Jeannie and Chris always sit together. She thought it was neat to spend the whole time with Chris!"

"Darrell said almost the same thing."

"I wanted to let you know, I won't be at rehearsal this morning."

Matt instantly got worried, "Is something wrong?"

"Not at all. I'm helping Darlene, Pep and Carrie with the rehearsal luncheon. Okay?"

Matt was audibly relieved. "That's great."

Diane hesitated, "I just realized how nervous I must make you. I'm sorry for that. I need to be more reliable."

"Not to worry. I understand. I'll look forward to seeing you after rehearsal. Thanks for calling, Diane. Oh, you should have seen Skip this morning. She tried to wipe her front feet by herself!"

Diane giggled, "I'm so happy for you and her. And how is the bedraggled begonia."

"I refuse to discuss the begonia with either you or Ian." Matt was firm. "You're both going to be so jealous when it blooms!"

"We are so worried," Diane teased. "Talk to you later."

Matt had never seen so many little kids at a wedding rehearsal in his life! One would have thought the church was running a two-for-one special on baptisms. It was nutty, but then knowing his Mom and Coot, what would anyone expect?

On the way to Schroeder's for lunch afterward, Darrell and Matt chuckled about it. Rain had not been that involved in weddings before and didn't think it unusual, but the guys did.

"I think it's going to be so cool! Just wait 'til you see me in my dress! Have you ever seen me in a dress, Uncle Matt?"

"Not since you were old enough to talk!" he teased. "Yah, I guess I have. At your first communion and your confirmation and there were pictures taken at both events!"

"Darrell, I'm glad you have other friends," Rain said smugly. "This one isn't much good."

Darrell agreed wholeheartedly. Matt grumbled, "Okay, you guys. Knock it off!"

Darrell and Rain shared a wink, "I think we better not hurt his feelings, huh Lightnin?"

The fancy luncheon was all ready when the wedding party returned from the rehearsal. The girls had done a fantastic job decorating and everything was very cheerful. Mo had asked Diane to play some music in the background while the family gathered before they ate. She did a beautiful job.

Then Pastor Byron led the group in grace and everyone sat down. Diane had made it a point to sit by Matt. Matt noticed she was so relaxed. That really pleased him.

Lunch was over by one and after dishes, everyone began to disperse. There was a hot softball game in Schroeder's yard and a couple horseshoe matches going on. The girls had set up the croquet and badminton games. Everyone was doing something.

The ladies made several trips over to Heinrich's barn with food and the younger adults had been over there during rehearsal to decorate.

Matt and Diane had planned to go for a walk, but they never got away. It was a busy afternoon, but the Harrington and Engelmann tribes were melding. It was nice to see.

Before they knew it, it was time to do early chores and get ready for the wedding. On time, Matt stopped by to pick up Annie and Diane to go to the church. In the car, Matt was deluged with a million questions. Annie asked, "We want to know! What are they doing with all those kids? They aren't going to risk that many in a wedding are they? They are both nuts!"

Matt just smiled, "If you think I'm going to tell, you are mightily mistaken! My life wouldn't be worth living if I spilled the beans!"

Annie laughed, "I can believe that, but Tinker and I thought we'd try!"

St. Johns sanctuary was fantastic. The Sanctuary was decorated with candles and deep red and white roses. Mo's older grandsons lit candles at the end of every pew before the boys sat with their parents. The organist was playing some of Mo's favorite background music while the guests were ushered to their seats by Eddie Schroeder, Doug Anderson, Jerald Oxenfelter and Rafael Diaz. The last seated were Pappy and Nana Harrington and Lloyd and Katherine Engelmann on the other side. Both men wore black tuxedos with a red rose in the lapel and a deep red cummerbund. The grandmothers looked lovely in their princess style deep red floor length dresses with short jackets of matching fabric.

Then Father Vicaro and Father Bartholomew entered the sanctuary. When they were in place in the front, the groom and his attendants, Elton, Byron, Zach and Darrell stepped out beside him. The men looked very nice and amazingly, Carl hardly looked nervous. Even though he had confided to the men he was less worried the first time he had to testify against some mob boss in a murder trial.

Everyone was expecting to see the bridesmaids enter next; but surprisingly, the next to enter the sanctuary was the Gophers. Kevin led the group and Allen Adams came behind to bring up the stragglers. The kids did very well, but Carl and Mo were both dying a million deaths.

They held hands, in pairs. They had been given so many lectures about behaving, they all looked terrified. But Coot remembered the fiascos they were capable of and had no desire to repeat one of those adventures!

The little girls all wore short deep red dresses with white tights and matching red ribbons in their hair. The boys wore black suits, white shirts and deep red bowties. The first couple was Ginger Ellison and Junior Oxenfelter, followed by Tammy Harrington and Little Bill Anderson, Maddie Lynn Olson and Tony Harrington, Miriam Jeffries and Clark Olson and they all were followed by Turk Harrington and little Charlie Ellison. The kids took their seats in the very front row all the way across the front. Kevin and Carrie sat on one side to supervise and Allen and Amy took care of the other. Danny and Jenny had taken a seat earlier on one side with Baby Matthew, the littlest Gopher. Keith and Darlene were seated on the far other side.

Carl looked with pride at what he called Rodent Row! They were a cute bunch of kids and all spiffed up. They behaved, but were scared to death to even breathe. Agent Coot had promised them ten to life for any infraction, no matter how minor. No plea bargain or reduced sentence would be considered. Carl only hoped that Father Vicaro not get too windy. He knew those guys and anything over a half an hour, there was a genuine risk of St. Johns remaining habitable.

The first bridesmaid to enter was Rain. She did look beautiful. Her hair was brought back from her face and held by a red rose and then fell gently down her back. She wore a princess style dress in deep red with a boat neck and short capped sleeves. She had long above the elbow white gloves and carried a bouquet of white roses.

Since few had ever seen her dressed up, she drew gasps from the Harrington side of the church. This girl was simple gorgeous and gracious. The congregation wasn't aware of the crash walking lessons she had endured from Annie, Pepper, Jeannie and Diane, just a few hours previously.

When she got to the end of the aisle, Darrell stepped forward and took her arm. She was so glad he was her partner. He made her feel at ease. She decided if you clean barn with someone, you feel like you really know them. He gave her a wink and they both smiled.

Suzy Jeffries had started down the aisle before Rain got to the front. She was met by her husband Zach. She was followed by Marly Ellison who was met by her husband, Byron. And the last but not least, the matron of honor, Nora Schroeder was met by the best man, Elton Schroeder. Even though Carl had a fit that Magpie was in his wedding and Elton groused he had to be there, everyone knew it was the only way it could have been.

For a loner, Carl had some very dear friends to share his wedding. Of course, Magpie and Preacher Man; but also Zach who was like a son to him and Darrell, the best partner any guy could ever have.

Then the music gave the signal and Father Vicaro motioned for the congregation to rise. The bride, on her youngest son's arm, came down the aisle. Maureen was dressed in an ivory cream dress of the same style as the attendants. She carried a huge bouquet of deep red roses. She wore a simple necklace with one stone as did her attendants. The girls all had a pearl drop, but she had a garnet teardrop.

When Matt placed his mother's arm on Carl's he gave Carl a quick hug and said, "Take care of our Mom, Dad."

Then he kissed his mother's cheek, "Be happy Mom."

Then he quickly sat down in the pew next to Nana and Pappy. The service was traditional and very nice. Father Vicaro kept it under an hour and the Gopher's managed not to squirm too much.

Kevin had taken Miriam on his lap before it was over, but only because her hip was starting to ache. The other Gophers were as good as one can expect from a nest of active creatures, but there were no disasters.

When the service was over, the wedding party formed a reception line outside the church. The Gophers didn't have to be there, but they decided themselves to be. After all, it was their wedding! Turk and Charlie especially shook every hand. They even thanked Father Vicaro and Father Bart for coming that evening.

At the barn, Pepper, Chris, Marty and Greta were the hosts and hostesses for the dance. The dinner was like the many wedding buffets which Elsie and Lucy had overseen. They had also done the cake. It had ivory frosting and red roses. On top was a cross, because Carl didn't want 'plastic toys' for his cake top. Little did he know how Lucy and Elsie had searched relentlessly for those little gophers to spread around the cake amongst the candy red petunias.

There were toasts and the grand march. Then the party started. Matt didn't care anymore; he wanted to be with Diane. He sat next to her and they spent the evening together. They did dance and visit with many others, but a person would have had to be blind to think she was not his date.

Father Vicaro came and sat with them for a bit and then Father Bart showed up. He was having a difficult time with the whole thing. He hadn't approved of Ian and Ruthie's outdoor ceremony or having the Gophers in Carl and Mo's. He didn't like it that a Lutheran pastor was an attendant at their wedding. It was the first time he had been to a wedding dance in a barn and now a non-practicing priest who was still awaiting the Holy Sees approval of Petition was obviously on a date with someone. It was almost more than the poor man could take in. Matt and Diane were not at all mushy or anything near that, and they did nothing inappropriate; but Bart was certain there was something amiss. Partly it was because Diane and he had not hit it off, and also he had no use for priests like Matt.

When he came and sat down with Father Vicaro and the couple, Diane did the unthinkable. After a few minutes, the band started to play a good dancing two-step. She took Bart's hand and asked him to dance. Before he could answer, she had drug him out to the dance floor. Sadly, the next song was a Schottische and Diane and Darrell grabbed him to join them. When it was over, he was gasping for air, but had actually smiled!

The dance was a wonderful time. It was well after one-thirty when Bill and the Boys played *Good Night, Irene* and everyone started for home. Matt and Diane danced the last dance and then Matt gave Diane a ride home. Rafael and Rosa Diaz rode home with them, so they weren't tempted to join the Peyton Place crew in Schroeder's yard. Matt did give Diane a kiss on the cheek to say good night.

❖❧ 60 ❧❖

THE CHORES THE NEXT MORNING were grueling. Matt was certain that Darrell should sell most of his livestock, if not all. Even Rain was quiet. Darrell was enjoying her obvious misery. "Well Lightnin', what happened to the bell of the ball?"

"Oh, I just need to sleep. Dad, I really don't need to go to Mass, do I? I can go twice next week. Besides, don't weddings count?"

Pat looked at his daughter, "If I have to go, you have to go and weddings don't count. Where are we having lunch today?"

"We are going to Schroeders," Matt answered. "The clan usually eats there on Sundays after church."

"We have since I was a little kid," Darrell added. "That is just what you do on Sunday. The clan either meets at Schroeder's or in some cases at Ellisons. Now, I guess we'll meet at Coot's because they have room."

"How many are there in the clan?" Patrick asked.

"About fifty, huh, Tuck?" Darrell asked.

"Yes, about that."

Pat shook his head, "Well, it's a fun bunch, I'll say that. I was looking forward to going fishing, but I have to say I'm glad it was put off until tomorrow. Two nights of wedding dances almost killed me. All we would need is an Irish wake, and I would gladly give up the ghost."

"So what's the deal with the fishing?" Matt asked. "I only heard it was going to be Monday, so I couldn't make it. Charlie was most upset, because he has school. He felt better when he found out Jeannie and I'd give him a ride to school. Now he thinks he is something special because

359

he gets to walk in to the school from the teacher's parking lot! He is quite the guy."

"I heard your Mom asked Zach for that psychiatrist's phone number last night," Darrell shared. "I think she is about to string Turk and Charlie from the highest rafters!"

Matt laughed, "It is their own fault. I told them they were asking for trouble."

"It will likely be better that Turk and Charlie won't both be fishing on the same boat, huh?" Pat grinned.

"We won't have one big boat like in Boston. It'll be several smaller boats," Darrell explained.

"Isn't Lake, what is the name of it any way?" the Bostonian asked.

"Sa-kak-ah-we-ah. Sakakawea is named after the Indian lady who guided Lewis and Clark to the west coast. Garrison Dam is the third largest earth filled dam and backs up almost 370,000 acres of water. It is 178 miles long. It is big water and can handle big boats, but we're cheap. So, we tried to gather a bunch of boats from friends and clanners and it won't cost us so much," Darrell chuckled. "Free is our favorite price, although deeply discounted ranks right up there!"

Pat looked at him and shook his head, "You're a crazy person, do you know that?"

Darrell had a good belly laugh, "So I have been told. Anyway, there is some darn fine fresh water fishing in there. Lots of Muskies, Northerns and Walleyes, but other kinds of fish too. I am a Northern Pike person myself, but Jeannie prefers the Walleye Pike."

"It'll be fun. I have rarely fished fresh water. So, who all is going?" Patrick asked.

"Let's see, those that can, pretty much," Darrell said. "There's a bunch, but of course, Rain won't go."

"Whaddyah mean? I'd love to go! It'll be the coolest, right? I can go, huh Uncle Matt?" Rain blustered.

"He is just teasing, Rain," Pat laughed. "We all know you'd go along if you had to tread water next to the boat! But I know something you don't know."

"What's that, Dad?"

"Your Mom is coming along!"

Rain had to digest that! "My very own Mom? Margie Harrington? I didn't think she even knew how to fish! That's really something, huh?"

"She used to fish, before you kids came along."

"Is anyone else?" Lonnie asked. "I mean any of the old ladies!"

Matt, Pat and Darrell all turned to the young man, "Never let them hear you say that or there won't be enough of you left to use for bait!"

"Gee, I just meant—," Lonnie stammered.

"We know." Patrick chuckled, "I guess Nancy, Terrie, Rosa and Van. Too bad Viv and Colleen won't come along. It'd be good for them."

Matt gave Pat and his family a ride to Mass and Diane drove the Catholics that were staying at Schroeder's in Elton's station wagon. Father Vicaro confided to Mo after Mass that he was hoping her family would all move to Merton. "This congregation could use some new blood! You know, throw a few lobsters into the prairie stew!"

Dinner was fun and after the dishes were done, the couples opened their wedding gifts. The living room looked like a department store when they were finished and Elton was trying to figure out what his commission should be.

Everyone was rather worn out by the time chores were done. Matt was looking forward to just going to his little cabin, eating a sandwich, sitting in front of the fire and making it a very early night. Imagine his surprise, when he returned from the barn to find someone in his house.

Diane had come over and made dinner for him. The cats were playing on the floor and the fire was warm and inviting. She had pulled the curtains closed and had dinner waiting in the oven.

He looked around and beamed, "Who let you in?"

"The door wasn't locked. You should be more careful," Diane teased. She put her arms around his neck and gave him a big kiss. "Get washed up, dinner's ready."

"What is my family going to say?"

"I didn't invite them. Jeannie knows and she said they're planning a quiet evening up there. She told me to just pull the curtains closed." Then she panicked, "Did I make a mistake? Did I do the wrong thing? Are you—"

"Sh. No, you didn't make a mistake. This is a wonderful surprise. I want you to know you can come to my house whenever you want. In fact, I'll give you a key to put on the key ring to Kevin's car. This is a wonderful surprise."

While he cleaned up, Diane put their dinner on the table. It was a nice, simple dinner of hamburger steak, mashed potatoes, gravy and corn. It looked delicious. When they sat down, he said grace and they ate. Over dinner, they visited about the weddings and the dances. Then Matt told her about Father Vicaro's call and explained it all to her. "So, I should be free from it all by Christmas, until then I cannot marry."

Diane became thoughtful and quiet. Matt was afraid that the conversation had put a damper on the most relaxing evening they had ever shared. He didn't know if he should say anymore or if he had said already too much.

"Is there a chance the Holy See might not grant the dispensation?" she finally asked softly, nearly fearing the answer.

"Very unlikely. It only happens in extremely rare cases."

Her face filled with tears, "Matt, what would we do then?"

He got up and moved over beside her, "Don't borrow trouble. That's so unlikely that it isn't even worth the worry. Okay?"

"You aren't just telling me that, are you?"

"No. I wouldn't do that. Ever. You have my word," Matt hugged her and kissed her forehead. Then he moved back to his seat.

"I never imagined they could do that. I always assumed if a person left the priesthood, they could get married. I guess I never thought about it."

"Honey, I'll be a priest forever. That is the way it is, but I'll be a priest who has returned to the laity. I will no longer be allowed to give communion and all that. But if the need should ever occur, I'll always be able to give the Last Rites."

"So, what would happen if the Vatican wouldn't give that dispensation? We'd never be able to marry?" Diane was crestfallen.

"If by some obscure chance it would, I'd marry you anyway. Period. I wouldn't want to do that outside the church, but I would. Please believe me."

She was lost in thought, "I thought it'd be more simple, I guess. You know, I tried not to love you. I really did. In many ways it would be so much easier for both of us."

Matt was waiting for her to say she was all done with him. He fully expected it. He had himself almost convinced that honesty wasn't one bit what it was cracked up to be.

Then she gave him a weak smile, "But I do love you. So, there we have it. I guess I'm not one that is supposed to have that happy idyllic marriage everyone talks about, huh? Oh well. If I we're together, I don't care. I want you to know Matt, I'm with you to the end. Even if we have to live in sin or turn Methodist! Okay?"

Matt almost cried with relief. "That is the most wonderful thing anyone has ever said to me in my whole life. I'm so lucky to have met you, convenient or not."

"That's the way I feel. So, we just need to pray that the paperwork comes from the Vatican as soon as possible. Right?" Diane asked mostly to seek encouragement.

"Right. And I hope it doesn't take too long." Matt said. "Father Vicaro said the Bishop seems to want to get rid of both Jeff and me in short order, so he is rushing it. That is a very good thing. We need to work through a lot of stuff anyway, so I think this time might be very good."

"Me too. I guess it will make sure we go slow, huh?" she smiled, "That is probably a good thing. By then, all the mess with Wag should be settled. I have something to talk to you about too. That attorney called yesterday and told me that I was to meet with Gladys and her attorney to work out all of Wag's property stuff. I guess I still have ownership of Dean's share of the business. I don't know what to do about that."

"What is the question?"

"Gladys will need something to live on. My instinct is to just sign it over to her. What do you think?"

"I don't know. You could use the money, but she does need something to live on. When you find out all the particulars, I'd be happy to help you make your decision, if you'd like. Diane, may I ask you something that has concerned me? If you don't want to talk about it, just tell me to butt out. Okay?"

"What is it? I think we're at the point in our relationship where we need to get the cards on the table. So ask me whatever you need to."

"Was Dean ever abusive to you?"

Diane looked at her plate and tears started to flow. "I'd rather not talk about it tonight. Okay? I wanted us to have a nice dinner."

"I'm sorry. It's a wonderful dinner. I loved it to come in and have you here with our little family and the warm fireplace. I'll change the subject."

She wiped her tears and removed their plates. She returned from the kitchen with their dessert. He got up and refreshed their coffee. Then they sat down again and Matt looked at his plate. "Two kinds of wedding cake! Was there a lot left?"

Diane giggled, "Not really, but I think we'll be eating at it for a day or so. And they froze the top layers."

"Why do people do that?"

"To eat on their first anniversary. It is a tradition, supposed to bring good luck."

"And they probably just finished the last of the left-over cake the week before!" Matt chuckled.

The phone rang, and it was Jeannie. "We were going to play cards and wondered it you guys would like to join us. I haven't said anything to the others yet and I won't if you don't want me to. We'd like to play two tables, though and Lonnie and Rain need partners."

Matt asked Tinker and she nodded, "If you want. But not late, okay?'

"We'll be up after dishes. We have to get home early though."

"Thanks. We'll be shutting down early too. See you in a bit."

They finished their cake and started to do dishes. Diane was washing while Matt was drying when she said, "Yes, he was a bit, but nothing like his father. That's why I don't trust my judgment."

Matt kissed her cheek. "I'm sorry. I kind of thought that. It is a learned behavior. My Dad wasn't, if that helps."

She smiled, "From what I know of your Mom, she would have punched him in the aorta."

Matt broke out in laughter, "The aorta? Where did you get that?"

"Don't know. It just came to me." Diane giggled, "I'm going to have to study your Mom. I want to be like her."

"Lordie above, the Angels will swoop you up!" Matt mimicked his Mom. "I think I like you to be Diane."

The group played whist and had a good time. The only good players were Darrell and Jeannie. Pat and Margie had played bridge so they were pretty good too, just not as familiar with whist. The better players divided up with the not-so-good players and it ended up that no one was any good; but they had fun. At nine-thirty they all declared defeat, had some more wedding cake and coffee. Diane and Matt were on their way back to the cabin before ten.

Diane told the kittens and Skipper good night and then Matt walked her to her car. "Thank you for coming over. It was a wonderful surprise. You could do that every night, I think." Matt took her in his arms.

Diane kissed him goodnight, "That'd probably not be the best idea. I certainly would hate to have to confess that to Father Bart!"

Matt started to laugh, "You know what Vicaro called him? Black Bart!"

Matt watched as her car lights disappeared down the road. He really had enjoyed the evening. It was the first time that he felt she was really relaxed around him when they were alone.

❦⸰◦ 61 ◦⸰❦

MONDAY MORNING WAS COOLER BUT the sun was bright and there was little wind. It looked like it'd be a great day for the fisherman. There was going to be dinner at Coot's that evening and the good byes would begin. Rafael and Rosa Diaz, Van and Eagan, and Allen and Amy were on the late flight to Minneapolis to make their connections to Texas, Massachusetts and Baltimore.

While they were feeding the horses, Patrick took the opportunity to speak privately with his youngest brother. Pat was the second oldest in the family and always seemed the most flexible and easy going. He and his wife, Margie seemed to go with the flow on most things and not get too bent about details. Of course, raising children as opposite at Lonnie and Rain, could likely make folks that way.

"Matt, I don't want to interfere, but I feel I need to tell you something."

Matt was shocked and felt his stomach curl into knot. He hadn't imagined getting the 'sinning priest' lecture from him, but then he guessed Pat had as much right as anyone else. Matt turned to him, "What is it?"

"I don't care what anyone else thinks, although I know that Margie agrees with me a hundred percent. You have a fine lady there, Matt. We both really like her and are very happy for you."

"We're not—,"

"Oh crap man, I'm not stupid. Even Lonnie told me he thought you two were in love. Lonnie, of all people! A person just has to see how you look at each other. I know it is a difficult time and I heard she has had a tough time herself, so you kids take it easy. Just being in love doesn't make a marriage work. No matter how you feel about your spouse, some days you'd just like to clobber them. I want the best for you, little brother, and I think she'd be a wonderful choice. Just wanted you to know." Then he looked at Matt, "I know Mom and Ian know. It is easy to tell they think a lot of her too."

"What do you think the rest would say?" Matt asked.

"Well, Viv and Colleen have their roles, you know. Every family needs their pissers and moaners, and they do well with their titles. I think the rest would be just fine. Maybe not Pappy and Nana, but trying to please them would be an overwhelming task. I know Nancy's John told me that he really likes Tinker and James mentioned it too. Terrie and Margie had a lot of fun visiting with her. And of course, Rain," he stopped and grinned. "You know you're her idol."

"I don't think so any more. I think I have been replaced by Darrell." Matt grinned.

"You might be right. He is hell of a guy, huh? And that Jeannie, I tell you if I ever want to replace Margie, Darrell better watch out!"

"Don't think he has to worry. She is very committed to him."

"Yah, probably right," Pat agreed. "Besides, I'm too old for her. Anyway, I just thought I wanted to tell you. I know I'd leave the priesthood for her."

Matt hugged his brother, "Honestly Pat, I didn't leave because of her. I left because of the other stuff. I had made up my mind before we met. Well, actually we met about the same time, but my decision wasn't because of her."

"I believe you and you sure don't have to explain. I am just saying, she would have been enough reason for me. And that Ruthie! I can see why Ian loves her. She is so full of energy and life. It is just nice to see. They adore each other. I'm happy for you both you guys."

"Thanks, I'll tell him. It means a lot to hear that. So what are you going to do with our Rain?" Matt chuckled as they went back to the milking area.

"I was thinking of hiring her out at a profession bridesmaid. Think there'd be much money in it?"

"Doubt it. Those dresses would run you plenty!" Matt laughed.

"Yah, you are right about that." Patrick grinned, "You know, since you were out, she has been helping me with my old car. She does a hell of a job on the body! She sanded and fixed the whole back fender by herself and it looks really good!"

Matt ran in to pick up Charlie for school while Jeannie waited in the car. He and Turk embraced each other as if Charlie was about to meet the executioner. Carl looked at Matt and shook his head. "Words cannot express it," he chuckled.

Diane came out of the old farmhouse and got into the back seat with Charlie. "Good morning, Charlie. Isn't this a grand day?"

He looked at her like she'd lost her mind, and said flatly, "We have to go to school."

"Of course we do. Oh, you guys, you should just hear Grandpa Lloyd. Grandma is about ready to flatten him. He keeps say to the guests, "Nice of you to come visit, but don't you have to get to the airport?" Or "Come again anytime. We don't mind you hanging around all the time." She giggled, "This morning, he almost got killed when he told Diaz, "Elton would be happy to give you a ride the airport. I'm sure there are planes to take you back home.""

"Was Diaz upset?" Jeannie asked.

"No, they all know it's just him and think it is funny. When Diaz told him he was leaving late tonight, Lloyd looked at the clock and said, 'It's a long ways, Elton will take you now so you don't miss the plane.' So Pappy gives him a dirty look and says, 'Well I'll be—,' and Lloyd says, "Yup, you'll be late. Nora will help you pack.' I was giggling so much, I almost got the hiccoughs."

"Think he will miss them when they are gone?" Matt asked.

"Not in the least," Diane giggled.

"I'll miss Turk," Charlie said sadly. "We are going to do so many things together and ran out of time. But we did talk Coot into planting a big tree with good arms so that we can climb up it. Won't that be cool? Turk's folks said they are coming back out to visit and he can sleep over again. Maybe we won't have to do the wedding junk, so we can climb trees. Turk says it is almost as good as digging. Is it, Tuck?"

"It is a fine thing to do, for certain Charlie."

Charlie proudly walked in to the school from the teacher's parking lot. He was correct; many of his classmates did think that it was worthy of respect. The teachers thought he overdid it when he shook hands with each of them and thanked them for the ride. They looked at each other, "I think that receiving line did something frightful to his mind!" Jeannie giggled. "Wait until I tell Darrell."

"Yea gads, one minute I think he'll be a convicted felon and the next a politician!" Matt laughed.

Jeannie agreed, "The same with Ginger. I really wonder what they are doing to Miriam? I shudder to think what she will turn out like!"

The day went by quickly and Matt enjoyed meeting his Latin classes. His students seemed very astute and he knew he'd have to work to keep ahead of them. By the time they all climbed back in the car to head home, Matt was beat. Charlie however, had gathered a small entourage of at least eight kids to witness his actually climbing into a car with three teachers.

When they left the parking lot, Matt asked, "Did you sell tickets, Charlie?"

"No, do you think I could?" the little guy perked up.

"No," Jeannie said, "Matt was just causing trouble."

Charlie looked at Matt with compassion, "I know how that is. It happens to me all the time. Tinker, I'll let you help me do Chicken Man chores tonight, so you won't feel left out. Okay?"

"That is very nice of you Charlie," Diane grinned. "You're a pretty good kid, you know that?"

"Yes I do," Charlie agreed. "But Kenny says we shouldn't brag on ourselves!"

Dinner that night was a lot of fun, but Matt had to admit he was beginning to feel a lot like Grandpa Lloyd. He was glad the company would all be gone soon, even though he would miss them.

The boasting that evening about the fishing was almost impossible to cope with. Mo, Nora and Marly with the help of the other ladies all worked furiously to fry the catch. It was a good end to a fun trip. Flash bulbs were going off all over and photos commemorating the occasion were plentiful. There were almost seventy folks there that night and they all felt comfortable at Coot and Mo's Petunia Patch.

About ten, Matt had to say good night. He was beat and had to teach the next day. After he said his goodnights, he headed to his car. Diane came out behind him, "Could I get a ride home with you?"

"Sure. I'd have asked, but you seemed to be having a nice time."

"I was, but I have to get some sleep. I'm among the walking dead, I have to admit," she said as she slid in the car.

After they turned out onto the gravel road, she scooted over beside him, "This was fun, but I don't know if I could take it all the time. How did your Mom do it all these years?

"Or Nora and Elton?" Matt shook his head. "I have no idea. I guess it just sort of creeps up on you when you have a big family."

"Have you ever thought if you would like to have a big family?" Diane asked.

"No, never did. I was going to be single all my life, remember?"

"Well, what do you think?"

He grinned broadly, "It is like this Diane, if we had one Charlie that would be enough. Otherwise, a bunch would be good."

She nodded and thought, "How are we going to know if we have a Charlie?"

Matt shrugged, "Wait three years after each kid to see how they are!"

She giggled, "Of course, Byron and Marly quit after Charlie, but they already had three."

"They probably should have been very cautious after Ginger. From what I heard, she was another Charlie before the burns." He stopped the car in front of Schroeder's and gave her a kiss. "A sweet little Diane Junior would be nice."

She returned his kiss passionately, "Or someone like your sister, Colleen! I bet she was born yelling, huh?"

"Most likely." Matt stopped kissing her, "Hey, are we still on for our date Wednesday night?"

"Only if I get some sleep tomorrow night!"

"I agree. I doubt I could stay awake through a movie. Well, I'd better get out of here. I love you, my little Tinker."

"I love you Matt. Good night."

62

TUESDAY MORNING, THERE WERE A lot more goodbyes before the group arrived at the school. Matt felt good that both Vivian and Colleen had hugged him goodbye. Vivian seemed to have put the whole thing behind her, but Colleen was transitioning into the martyr role of having to suffer the burden of a renegade brother. At least, she was good at it.

That afternoon, Nora met them at the door when they dropped off Tinker and Charlie. "No need to give Lloyd a ride today."

"Is he okay? This week has been hard on him." Matt commented.

"He is fine," she giggled, "He is so happy that everyone is gone. He was just awful! He told everyone to come back again in a few years or so. After they left, Elton asked him why he said that and he announced he figured he would be dead by then! Grandma assured him he would be sooner than that if he didn't knock it off! So, he is napping now."

Although few felt as extreme about it as Lloyd, there was definitely a sigh of relief when all the guests were gone. Matt wondered just how much food had been consumed. The ladies had put out huge banquets of food almost three times a day! He was glad he wasn't a girl. He could hardly handle a ham sandwich with ease.

Diane had really blossomed. Once she made up her mind to help the gals, she seemed to come out of her shell and relaxed more. Matt noticed that she had spent time with almost all the clan girls and was developing a good relationship with them. He was so thankful. He felt confident that she was now making some true progress in putting the Wag stuff behind her.

After chores, he was glad to start his fireplace and have time to get his homework done. He was almost finished when the phone rang. It was Diane.

"Hello Tink, how are you tonight?"

"I'm fine. Did you get a lot of schoolwork done tonight?"

"Yes, only math papers to correct and I'm done. How 'bout you?"

"Yes. I was looking at the schedule for the school play and we need to figure out what play we are going to do, so I can get the scripts and stuff ordered."

"When is the play?"

"Mid-March."

"Seems like an early start, doesn't it?"

"Everything takes forever. If you don't want to help, I could probably find someone else."

"I want to help. Really. It'll be fun," Matt said. "When do you start your piano lessons?"

"Next week. Ginger, Katie and Miriam and the Olson kids will start then because they have pianos to practice on. Oxenfelter's and Danny Schroeder are renting pianos this week so Becky and Jenny can practice."

"What about Charlie?"

"He and I are having a meeting next week about it. He watched Bill Heinrich play his accordion at the wedding dances, so he thinks that might be up his alley." Diane got quiet, "I miss you tonight, Tuck. I wish we could just cuddle up in front of the fireplace."

"That would be nice. Very nice." He stopped before he let his mind wander too far. "Best we change the subject."

"Okay, next week I have to meet with this attorney, Mr. Wolf, about some of this Waggoner stuff. Could I ask you to come with me? You don't have to if you would rather not."

"I'll be there for you, Diane, for whatever you need. I'm your guy, right?"

"I haven't forgotten. Well, I better get to bed. I love you, Matt."

"I love you too, Diane. Sleep tight."

63

MATT KNEW THERE WERE MANY things that still needed to be worked out between he and Diane, but he felt secure in their devotion to each other. That made all the difference. He took Skipper for a walk. Murphy and Lady had graduated so they no longer had to be kept in the laundry at night. They spent the night at the foot of his bed, while Skipper, of course, had staked out the other pillow. Matt looked at his bed before he crawled in and wondered when they got married where Diane would sleep.

Ian and Ruthie got to spend their first night alone together. Their wedding had been the dream that Ruthie had planned and that made Ian happy. He was glad that his life was the way it turned out. It wasn't like he would've ever imagined it ten months earlier, but it was a lot happier than he believed possible.

He was delighted with his new home and career. It was more fulfilling than he had thought it could be. Ruthie was doing very well at Trinity and had developed so much self-confidence. She was no longer the scared little lady he had first met. But she still had her warm heart, fun sense of humor and an effervescence unparalleled by most. His friendship with Zach was growing and he had become closer to his brother Matt then ever before. He loved all the Schroeders and was especially happy with his new step-dad, Carl. He was the best.

The joy that he and Ruthie both felt over Miriam's recovery was unbelievable and they were both encouraged to start a family soon. If there was anyone that he would want to be the mother to his children, it would be his Ruthie.

He knew their life was not about to be a smooth road, but he also was confidant that they would make it. He got out of bed and looked out their bedroom window. To the east, he could see the Darrell's yard light and the light from Matt's cabin. To the south, he could see the lights from his Mom and Carl's home. Carl's Petunia Patch.

Those crazy people and their Gophers. Ian grinned, thinking of Carl's Rodent Row at the wedding! He knew when he and Ruthie had children, they would be Gophers also. For some crazy reason, it was comforting.

He looked at his beautiful wife, sleeping. He crawled in his side of the bed and put his arm around her. She woke a little and he kissed her cheek. "I love you," he whispered. Then they tenderly made love again.

Carl had gone outside to check the garage door. On his way back to the house, he looked south of his house. It reminded him to talk to Darrell about breaking up the sod in a strip from the ditch to the house. That is where he was going to plant his petunias in the spring. He would have the biggest petunia patch in the world and his yard would be more magnificent than Magpies. Then he grinned.

It had been the most amazing last year. His entire life had changed and he was glad about it. It was a far cry from that Louisiana hospital room. Little did he know then, that between Magpie, Preacher Man and a little lady that called him Coot, how things would change! He was happier now than he had ever been, even though it required getting used to not knowing what was going to happen from minute to minute.

Now he had a family. He was stepfather to eight kids and all their families. Ian and Matt were some of the best stepsons any man could ask for and he was very close to both of them. He had a partner, Darrell that had to be the best guy in the world and a passel of friends that really liked him; and he actually liked them too! They were a confusing lot though. There was always a tragedy, disease, catastrophe or challenge somewhere. There was always something that made a person proud, joyful or stark raving mad. That crazy mob laughed, argued, cried, sympathized and cajoled each other every day.

He was aware he had become such a petunia. It was the very thing that he had spent his life ridiculing. Even Diaz had commented how he would have never imagined him being happy in this life, but thought he was living it better than most. That meant a lot to Carl Kincaid, the loner who needed no one.

He had three people to blame or thank for it all. First, one was a very tall, skinny doctor who was the supreme Petunia. Zach Jeffries didn't just sign the papers to be responsible for him while he was in the hospital. He became truly responsible for him. He became a son, confidant and a better friend than anyone could have. He never went away or gave up. No matter how Carl tried to drive him away, he wouldn't go. Now he thanked God he didn't.

Then there was a little abused girl who was terrified of everyone. He had saved Miriam; but in reality, she had saved him. Someone had told him that if you saved someone's life, you were responsible for that person. That meant he was responsible for that little girl. Carl knew nothing about children, but he never shied away from his responsibilities. When the times were tough and he wanted out, which was frequently; Miriam was what held him there. He owed it to her. The best part is, she seemed to love him. Not because he felt responsible, just because she did.

The third person was a grumpy old man. Bert Ellison was the most obnoxious, ornery person Carl had ever met in his life. And what was worse—he was his roommate! They argued and grumped at each other constantly, but it was that old badger that extracted a promise from him to stay in the Petunia patch. He told him straight out he didn't care whether he was happy there or liked petunias, he wanted him to be there. And the old goat kept it up until he got him to concede he would stay.

Carl shook his head. How ever did it happen? He would probably never understand how he ended up with this life. He was happy and he was now knee deep in a Petunia Patch. He was wise enough to understand it was not going to be a slam dunk and that surviving in the Patch required effort. But he also knew the rewards, and they were worth it.